The Space Tracers Organitron U.F.O

A tongue in cheek and humorous deviation from Charles Darwin's theory of evolution! "The True Origin of Species!"

A universe constantly changing, Earths metamorphic evolutionary range, Mankind changing Earths dynamics daily. It wasn't always this way! The Space Races Organitron, their universe decimated by "The Big Bang!" Moulded the newly formed Earth into a living breathing Leviathan against all odds! This is the story of their past and their legacy left to Mankind!

The Space Tracers Organitron U.F.O "The New Veginnings!"

Emmesville H.E. Diggan

ISBN: Softcover 978-1-4990-8868-7
eBook 978-1-4990-8869-4

This book was printed in the United States of America.

Rev. date: 10/09/2014

To order additional copies of this book, contact:
Xlibris LLC
0-800-056-3182
www.xlibrispublishing.co.uk
Orders@xlibrispublishing.co.uk
659256

CONTENTS

CHAPTER ONE—Brief encounters of the evolutionary kind 11

CHAPTER TWO—Where there be Fasterfoids, there be trouble! 29

CHAPTER THREE—Garlicazure or a trap set to lure? 42

CHAPTER FOUR—Club Cappuccino / A stranger pops on-board, but, not for coffee! 56

CHAPTER FIVE—Garlicazure or bust, where Veggie-angels fear to tread. 63

CHAPTER SIX—Now there is a whole lot of cooking going on........ 86

Part one—Milnedew, messenger or misfit?................................ 86

Part two—Jump for Soupaura dejour.. 91

Part three—Fasterfoids are go-go 100

Part four—Captain Carrot just loves it when a plan comes together!... 105

CHAPTER SEVEN—To Fight, the unbeatable force 122

Part one—The preparations for Garlicazure 122

Part two (1)—Earthanon starts to lose its patience / a real pea souper!... 133

Part two (2)—A real Pea souper! 135

Part three—The liberation of Garlicazure................................ 139

Part four—With Garlicazure secure, Earthanon calls.............. 170

CHAPTER EIGHT—A turn for the worse? 188
Part one—O.S.S.S Earthanon saves the day. 188
Part two—Volcadis doom and gloom. 202

CHAPTER NINE—An Organiman's home is his castle, his memories, in its dungeons he keeps. 229

CHAPTER TEN—Better late than never! 241
Part one—All aboard for the O.S.S Satsumuroo 241
Part two—Oh what an Atmosphere! 264

CHAPTER ELEVEN—For the good of all kind! 279
Part one—The beginning of the end! 279
Part two—To reach the point of no return. 294
Part three—If the mountain won't come to Marrachinello! 306

CHAPTER TWELVE—The olive branch and the brave 325

CHAPTER THIRTEEN—Coupe de Gra`ce The finishing strokes! 338

CHAPTER FOURTEEN—Ugh? 409

EPILOGUE 423

Glossary of Terms

Bubbleonion Squeak Vegitalis	=	Solar System
Vegitalis Plexus	=	Tuber Vegetables
Fruitalia quadrant	=	Fruits
Herbaflowturu	=	Herbs and Flowers
Fruitanutes plexus	=	Fruits and nuts
Vegitalis Legume	=	Root vegetables

Weapons

Gunge Guns	=	Ketchup Lasers
Blazer Guns	=	Gravy Lasers
Blazer Tractor Beam (BTB)	=	Fires Gravy Beam
Oudag Capsules	=	Organitron Uni-Vegimatter De-Acidulating Gellogas
Cluster Bugs	=	Candy floss Mine belt, Sprout Gas Protective Energy field

Organitron Natural Enemies

Faster fritters	=	Chipped Potatoes
Crinkleozones	=	Crinkle Cut Chips
Burgerites	=	Hamburgers
Chickonaldirs	=	Chicken burgers

Star Fleet Terminology

O.S.S	=	Organitron Sun Ship
O.S.S.S	=	Organitron Sun- fleet Space Station
UFO	=	United Foliage of Organitron
S.F.A	=	Sun-Fleet Admiral
Aqua Asteroids	=	Ice Asteroids
Sodium Star belt	=	Salt Gas Pockets

Void well	=	Black Hole
Slither void	=	Worm Hole
Starhectoid		Hour
Starlectoid		Day
Starwektoid		Week
Startechtoid		Year
Stardechtoid		Decade

Adapted from the original story written 20/09/93
Written by Emmett Hedigan

Alias

Emmesville H.E. Diggan.

Titled "The Space Tracers Organitron U.F.O." "The New Veginnings!"

"Based upon a series of short stories called; once upon a time, but not so very far away."

By Emmesville H.E. Diggan.

DEDICATION TO MY DAUGHTER

Jade Martin-Hedigan.
To my inspiration, my one salvation!

To John and Joan "The Butts" Hedigan.
To whom my gratitude holds no boundaries!

To all those who have invested in this book, my gratitude is abundant and I hope the Journey you are about to take, leaves you thinking about life, our planet, the environment, and a healthy diet! Long-live the "Human Race!"

Thank you Book Reviewer: Miss Jessica Aldous

Snapshot Reviews:
The Space Tracers Organitron UFO- The New Veginnings

Alice meets the Star-ship Enterprise in an innovative approach, with Captain Gillespie J. Carrot and the Organitron leading the way on their heroic adventures across the Bubbleonion Squeak Vegitalis. Prepare to fall down the wormhole and enjoy the trouble they get into and the Fasterfoids who live to make their jobs difficult.

Thank you book reviewer: Mr Jay Henley

The Space Tracers Organitron U.F.O "The New Veginnings!"

This is a novel that is, witty, full of slapstick, but also has its deeper earthier or "Earthanonier" side! A fine mix between "A bugs life" and "Farscape" It sends you venturing through the universe on a journey through time and space collectively! In Captain Carrot and his crew we find a stoic leader with humility and a bunch of die hard Organimen and Organiwomen willing to follow him to the brink, because he is one of them yet above them or is he? I can't quite figure him out! I suspect Diggan is pulling his punches for a later date! More to come I am sure, an Organiman's man with no doubt! Honestly ladies and gentlemen in my humble opinion, I like to think outside of the box! Going by Diggan's new masterpiece "The New Veginnings!" We are definitely going to need a bigger box! Infinite in fact! And with an ending like that, please tell me there is more to come! Don't push me I'm on the edge of a cliff!

Thank you Book reviewer: Mr Ted Phillips

The Space Tracers Organitron U.F.O "The New Veginnings!"

Prepare to be taken on what is initially a fantasy journey through the ages, meeting some wonderful characters along the way and let your imagination run wild with them. But reflect on finishing this gripping and thought-provoking book that you, the reader are part of it, and it is your responsibility to assist Captain Gillespie J Carrot and his chums in ensuring that peace is always the route to a more fruitful future and that it is our responsibility to put in place the building blocks for future generations to prosper on this wonderful planet that we inhabit.

Thank you book reviewer: Mr David Heenan

A Snapshot review.
The Space Tracers Organitron U.F.O "The New Veginnings!"

Getting started on The Space Tracers Organitron U.F.O - "The New Veginnings!" by Emmesville H.E Diggan wasn't easy. In some ways the same can be said for Asimov, Tanaka or even Lynda Williams. Once past the first ten pages the book flows, is well written and not as bad as I imagined it would be. Captain Carrot isn't boldly going where no veg have been before, but he is having plenty of action and never hesitates to admonish himself if anything goes awry. There are no hidden agendas, there are no unnecessary deaths and there are no attempts to place a product for consumer consumption like so many books and movies these days – though thoughts of a nice soup for tea were often in my mind. "The New Veginnings!" Is uniquely placed; with a humorous and intelligent story interlaced with factual information. A pleasant read!

CHAPTER ONE

Brief encounters of the evolutionary kind

The Space Nations of Organitron ended their first inhabitation of Earthanon on **Sundate 2.000, 000,003/ 067 Biltechtoids**. The evacuation order, given then by the head of the Premier Consul Seed Council, the Bright Honourable, High Admiral Capilliar Brocclekight, came in response to the gradual cooling of the Earthanon surface and its atmosphere, leading to a rapidly accelerated big freeze, known in latter Organitron history books as, "The Great ice age of Earthanon." This ice age was to last a period spanning over four hundred and seventy two million of your Earth years.

When the inhabitation of Earthanon ceased, nearly one quarter of the land surface had been open cast mined and vital minerals excavated. Minerals that were essential in enabling the construction of the artificial home Planets. Geographical surveys of the time confirmed that Earthanons water surface had increased from twelve percent, to eighteen percent. This was a result of a combination of factors; increased moisture in the atmosphere created by the foliage Plantations forming rain filled cloud cycles in conjunction with the natural springs, which had been tapped and directed to service the ecosystem farming programme's irrigation grid.

At the time of the evacuation, all the water sources of Earthanon were pure drinking water, sustaining no substantial life forms, apart from micro organisms such as algae and plankton. As the Space Nations of Organitron moved all priority farming programmes and personnel to the newly constructed Organitron Planets of Crushtonutes, Fruitalia Salaard, Minestrone Soupoura, Mixed Vegaris, and Casserule, they could only hope that the change in the atmospheric conditions of their much valued Earthanon would be a short interlude in the on-going chapters of The Space Nations of Organitron. Unfortunately, as it transpired this was not to be. Strict guidelines were to be placed in such terms as, energy conservation, habitat facilities and rationing, while family enlargement applications were vetted rigorously. By the time an answer was found to speed up the great thaw, all military, science and clerical personnel, were relocated and centralised. They had been relocated to the newly constructed internal accommodation, along with their families in the under surface caverns of the Silicone Sphere; a place you on Earth will know as the Moon.

Scientists of the time had formed a plan to artificially warm the Earthanon surface. This would be achieved by tapping into Earthanons core through specially constructed strategically placed heat generators. Although an answer to artificially warming the surface of Earthanon had been found, it was in no way a quick solution and would use a great deal of valuable energy resources in the process. Failure would have meant an uncertain, but certainly uncomfortable future, for many of those Earthanon Organitron placed precariously on the edge of their home galaxy.

Professor Plintho Vocado, the head of the science body of the Earthanon consul, is the Organiman accredited with the plan, and work it did. Slowly, but surely, the surface warmed and the great thaw was in full flow. The heat generators were formed by drilling through the specially constructed mountains using high acidulation ionisation laser beams. It took one hundred of your Earth years for the Earthanon surface to fully thaw. A further twenty five years elapsed, until the surface was sufficiently dried out to re-inhabit Earthanon.

It was the year, Sundate **2.472, 000,600/ 154 Biltechtoids**, when the Earthanon re-inhabitation was completed by the Organitron. Though it took some fifty years, to reconstruct the Ecosystem Farming Programme to a point of self sufficiency. The heat generators were proving to be, as ever, volatile, sometimes erratic, and occasionally deadly in their velocity and always requiring close observation and strict management. We know them as the Vocado heat generators, but you will know them as Volcanoes, an unfortunate but necessary legacy of the Space Nations of Organitron to the beautiful Planet of Earthanon.

There was one vital evolutionary change that the Planet Earthanon had undergone during this chilling period. After the great thaw, the Earthanon proportion of the water surface area had increased from eighteen percent, to forty three percent. Where open cast mines were once situated, great fresh water lakes had formed. The mines were, on the whole, depleted of valuable minerals, so drainage seemed both pointless and time consuming, meaning therefore, that it seemed sensible to establish new mining settlements and irrigation grid systems.

Utilising the natural water stocks made sense in more than terms of irrigation. It had become more than just a source of water for the farming programme. One day leading a lake charting expedition inspecting the old mining district settlements, a famed scientist, Whalon WD Seedweed discovered that it had become an unexpected breeding ground for new life forms. These waters had become a domain ruled by large, intelligent and friendly mammals, which we had come to know and trust as Whalons the name sake given by their discoverer. You will now know them as whales.

The Whalons a new nation of friends, gentle giants in the truest sense of the word lived together in harmony with the Organitron. Linking cultures for the benefit of all, communicating and working together for a common cause, survival. Within the great new lakes of Earthanon, the mammals helped to manage the new kelp farms established by Whalon W D Seedweed, by tending the crops and transporting them to the shores for Organitron consumption.

The Whalons too, enjoyed the rich nutritious food that they helped to grow, but in return the Organitron developed for them a generic fishy matter food source. These fishy matters grew to such abundance, in a variety of forms, that the Organitron began to vary their own diets with this rich and plentiful food supplement. And so begun a new and magical world of inhabitation for a new life form, enriching the already filled to the brim chapters of Earthanons history books.

Eventually, as would often happen in the natural tides of change, the new life forms mutated and grew in the deeper, murkier waters of the great lakes. These life forms were discovered by the renowned irrigation Engineer, Rasputin P Pau-Paw. They too were named by their discoverer, and had become known as the friendly, wise and intelligent race called, the Paupawses. Later in your history, to be known as Porpoise or Dolphins.

Paupawses were very agile and much smaller than their giant counterparts, the Whalon. Whilst the Whalons managed the kelp farms, the Paupawses charted the lake beds for the Organitron. All races lived together in complete co-operation and happiness for many of your Earth years. This existence was shattered by a fresh discovery, one which changed the course tranquillity and peace for ever.

It was a cool start to the normal working day, the sun rising over the palm tree surroundings of a small island known as the Banamas. Here, where an outpost Organifarm were working and experimenting with Kelp grown in a Sodium chloride lake, or salt as is more commonly phrased, the tides of change were to reach a much more ominous new chapter in history.

The infamous chief scientist Organigirl, Sharkalia V Baananda, was working on the trial farm with her dear friend and close companion Porpetula. A Paupawse of great character, known for her sense of humour and love of music, and was constantly at the side of Sharkalia whenever she was in the water. This day however, would be the last day that the sun would warm the smooth back of Porpetula.

Porpetula worked alongside Sharkalia as usual collecting cuttings, singing away as happy as could be, or as a fish in water as the saying became known. She and Sharkalia talked merrily as they started to play tag amongst the great columns of kelp reaching up towards the water's surface dancing in the currents of the sea.

"Ahhh …ha, got you Sharkalia you are it, catch me if you can?" Shrilled Porpetula.

"Is that so Porpetula." Laughed Sharkalia chasing her dear friend through the kelp farm with little success. "This really isn't fair, you glide through the farm like a water winged angel, twisting and turning with the ease of a corkscrew, your too quick much too fast, to catch you I'm not able. So I will sit this one out and watch you cause compared to a fish I am feeble." Said Sharkalia coming to rest on the seabed as Porpetula flew into the kelp and got into a terrible tangle.

"Oh help. Sharkalia who turned out the lights I do believe I am stuck, what a predicament to find oneself in!" She said embarrassed as Sharkalia came to her rescue.

"Don't worry Porpetula; we will soon have you out of there." Laughed Sharkalia tugging at Porpetula's tail fins. With one final mighty pull she tugged and they both went hurtling backwards and rolled along the seabed stirring up the silt laughing loudly.

"One of the drawbacks to being a fish." said Porpetula as she started to cough.

"What, over grown Gardens?" Chuckled Sharkalia.

"No. Ha... Ha... ha... Hatchooo! All this house dust." sneezed Porpetula loudly as the silt began to settle slowly. Sharkalia watched as Porpetula lay on the seabed stroking her tummy with a contented smile on her face.

"If you could change anything about yourself Porpetula, anything at all what would it be? What would you be if you had the choice to be someone other than a fish? Asked Sharkalia softly.

Porpetula lay quietly as she pondered the question. She looked around at the various life forms that shared her world as they also gathered to hear her answer. Porpetula swam in a circle and began to sing while the Scallops, prawns, sea horses, Lobsters and crabs backed her song with vocals and percussion.

"The wonders of waters so blue."
You ask what I would be if I weren't fish,
I'll tell you right now I wouldn't know what to wish,
I honestly don't have a clue; it's hard to imagine what else I could do,
Much easier to explain my regrets just a few,
Of missing the world you describe up above, with the wonderful views.
For I know in my heart in my thoughts I would croon,
For the wonders, for the wonders, for the wonders of the waters so blue.

You see we are the lucky few,
All of this space not a great deal to do,
Yes it's true we can't fly through the sky and view the world from a high.
We can't feel the breeze or swing through the trees,
Feel the soft scented grass underfoot.
Feel the wind in our hair; flap our wings in the air,
Kick up high, raise our arms walk around,
Ride the waves, skim the surf, I would love to experience that surge.

You ask what I would be if I weren't fish,
I'll tell you right now I wouldn't know what to wish,
I honestly don't have a clue; it's hard to imagine what else I could do,
Much easier to explain my regrets just a few,
Of missing the world you describe up above, with the wonderful views.
For I know in my heart in my thoughts I would croon,
For the wonders, for the wonders, for the wonders of the waters so blue.

I'd love to walk and to run I'm sure that would be fun,
Just to lye back in the breeze and soak up the sun.
I think it would be, exciting crazy and new,
But I know in my heart I would get in a stew,
I would yearn for, pine for, wish for its true,
For the exhilarating wonders of the waters so blue.

All the little fishes swim around the sea,
While the molluscs and the shell fish bask there happily,
The Whalons and the Paupawses live in perfect harmony,
And our friends the Organitron keep us perfect company.
So you see this place is our ship we are just one big happy crew,
Look around at the smiling faces; you'll see it's absolutely true.
We all grow together in this fun loving wondrous lagoon,
That's the wonder of this water so blue.

So you ask what I would be if I weren't fish,
I'll tell you right now I wouldn't know what to wish,
I honestly don't have a clue; it's hard to imagine what else I could do,
Much easier to explain my regrets just a few,
Of missing the world you describe up above, with the wonderful views.
For I know in my heart in my thoughts I would croon,
For the wonders, for the wonders, for the wonders of the waters so blue.

Together they danced and sang then fell around playfully with the other life forms that shared in the joy of the music. Suddenly the shell fish and prawns, along with the lobsters and crabs scuttled off in fright as great a shadow overcast them from above, an image that was to stay with Sharkalia for the rest of her life. At first, it circled the pair as they finished collecting their samples, the circle ever decreasing until it become very clear indeed.

Its eyes cold, black and lifeless burning a hole in Sharkalia with its mean penetrating stare. Suddenly its mouth gaped open revealing a mass of sharp uninviting jaws lined with triangular teeth. All Sharkalia can remember of those last few precious moments with her devoted friend of the deep, is Porpetula grabbing Sharkalia's hand in her mouth as the thing gave chase, whisking her away as quick as she could. They stopped in shallow water and Porpetula let Sharkalia go ordering her out of the water.

"Run; Sharkalia; Run; Get out of these waters! Jump! I'll draw its attention. Run my friend and don't look back. Whatever happens, stay out of these waters until I come back!" cried Porpetula hurriedly.

"But Porpetula you can't..." shouted Sharkalia as Porpetula interrupted her.

"No buts my sweet friend, when all is said and done, this is my water world and in it there is a newcomer, I have to learn how to deal with it, we have to know what we are up against?" Then Porpetula turned and swam towards the large fin coming towards Sharkalia at great speed. Sharkalia ran backwards out of the water falling onto the soft silicone bed beneath her feet. Looking up, she saw the two fins following each other in circles, the larger of the two, speeding frantically from the rear. Then Porpetula rose up out of the water being dragged against her will crying out in pain.

"I am going to have to leave you Sharkalia; you will have to protect yourself from this evil. Remember me Shark... glugerglug!"

With those last words, Porpetula was gone and the shark was born. Broken forever was the easy existence of the Organitron and their friends from the deep. Evolution delivered many more such fearful creatures, but also many more friends.

This existence was to take place for the rest of the inhabitation period. The Organitron's were hoping that all of Earthanons future evolutionary change could be managed and met with peaceful, cross-integration. The lessons of the great lakes had never been far from the thoughts of those Organitron best placed to understand the principles of the evolutionary chain. The Scientists, and the elite body of wisdom known as the premier consul of the seed council, had pondered this scenario in order to make precautionary evacuation plans. These plans would hopefully never be enacted, the fears never be realised.

The home Planets, within the Bubbleonion Squeak Solar System, had now become within easy travelling distance of Earthanon. Technological advances were increasing rapidly with every stardechtoid, new minerals and metallurgic discoveries from within Earthanons crust, began to provide materials and compounds only dreamt of in the minds of the scientists and engineers. New generations of Sun-Fleet space ships began stretching the boundaries of space exploration enabling the Space Nations of Organitron, or the Space Tracers Organitron to continue and complete their missions with renewed vigour and determination. The old, antiquated space fleet of Foliage Vanguard space stations had been replaced with the new mother ships, Organitron Sun-Fleet Space Stations. Ten times the size of the old class of space station, the new generation root class Sun Ships, had replaced the old Tuber travel class cruisers. Star Fighter ships, warrior class, became the Organitron first defence arm. Thus, accelerating the de-commissioning of the trusted Trojan Asteroid slayers of meteor class. The Bubbleonion squeak Star system could be reached from the Earthanon sector in as little as forty Starlectoids that is forty of your Earth days. New Slithervoids or Wormholes had been discovered as the advances of exploration broke new ground in previously uncharted galaxies. Speeding an otherwise long drawn and dangerous journey, reaching new levels of space travel, Califoric K speeds replacing the previous highs of warp speed. Calorific proton reactors rendering the old vitamin fusion reactors defunct.

Sundate 2.475, 000,725/ 101 Biltechtoids.

The Dindivar, Splutterbun and Rugerplotts, the only space races other than the Organitron, indicative to the Bubbleonion Squeak Vegitalis Solar System. Their Planet found floating in the darkest space corridor heading uncontrollably towards the Bapmacdo Aurora, and the Fasterfoid home lands until they were saved by the Space Tracers of Organitron, and managed to re-establish themselves on Earthanon with relative ease. Certain animal races had evolved from the cross breeding of the Soya, Meater matters bred by these animal races as a food source. There were also animal specimens establishing themselves that were not derivatives of any of these breeds. Birdsirs, Snakeroos, Monkietos, Horsechesters and Ellefennels began to roam the plains of Earthanon. Again they were intelligent and friendly with endearing personalities that worked in unison with the cultures of the Organitron.

These changes in themselves were a comforting security, a safety net to the uncertain future of the Planet Earthanon against the harboured concern about the need to evacuate the Planet which, although buried deep and well covered, was always present, and as it turns out dauntingly realistic and well founded. Towards the end of the current Startechtoid, without warning disturbing events overtook the natural course of life on Earthanon. Events which were to lead to yet another evacuation, three million Startechtoids later.

Sundate 2.478, 001,536/ 361 Biltechtoids

Commander Dino B Saurkraut, Commander of the Organicus Space Station had taken a party of twelve crew members on shore leave, to the high mountain district of the Europetriennes. They were there to log and monitor the plantation growing capabilities of the high altitudes, and to collect atmosphere samples to establish the possibility of creating high ground defence stations. The Fasterfoids had once again become active in their provocative feud on the Organitron Space Tracers. Night time sky battles were now common place in the lives of the inhabitants of Earthanon.

Commander Dino B Saurkraut had been leading a party of four from the base camp, to collect samples from the second highest peak in the mountain range. ComCaptain Miala Fusiala snagged her foot in a crevice at the last approach to the summit. She was in considerable pain so Dr Thervo Grapevard treated her injury and she was ordered to remain where she was until their return in two starhectoids. Approaching the summit a rock fall sent them scurrying under ledges for protection.

"Stay close to the rock face, team," shouted Commander Saurkraut, tucking himself into the ledge. "One blow from a rock and you're compost!" He continued. Dr Grapevard edged to his right as the portion of ledge above him started to give way. Every time he moved the crack above him seemed to move with him, covering him with dust as he repeatedly brushed himself off.

"For Helios sake," he said starting to lose his patience, "I think I must have been a rock in my former life and really upset this one! All right, all right, I've got the message, you great lump of granite misfit." He muttered, spluttering mouthfuls of dust into the face of Privado Coconeuter.

"Be caah... caah... careful Dr Grapevard," choked Privado Coconeuter, "I have heard tell," he whispered, "that walls have ears, you don't want to stir the mountains wrath, do you?"

"Walls have ears indeed," grimaced Dr Grapevard. "May I remind you, Privado Coconeuter, I am a man of Science and intellect; arguably the most respected Organitron in my field. So, you can take my word for it when I tell you, that walls do not have ears, eyes, brains or any of the other useful accessories which accompany a worthwhile life form!" Dr Grapevard paused momentarily looking at the rock, then back at Privado Coconeuter. "May I field a question at this juncture Privado Coconeuter?" Asked Dr Grapevard.

"Yes Sir of course." Confirmed a pensive Privado Coconeuter.

"You seem to posses all the visible accessories, but judging by the recent statements coming from that Voidwell you call a mouth, I have to wonder whether your brain is somehow distantly related, perhaps even directly descended from this, this benign mountain of rubble."

"Please Dr Grapevard, not so loud, you may be wrong and it might be listening to every word?" Shivered the fearful Privado Coconeuter.

Dr Grapevard looked Privado Coconeuter up and down in disgust, shaking his head fervently.

"Might be listening to every word eh? To think that Sun-Fleet spends millions of credits creating a stringent IQ test so that its ranks are filled with the maximum of intelligence, and you still slipped through the safety net I ask you, I, Thervo Grapevard, wrong?" He shouted, disturbing yet more loose rock dust on top of him.

"Pipe down you two." Whispered Commander Saurkraut. "What are you trying to do, bring this mountain down around our ears? Tell me Dr Grapevard," he continued. "Being a man of Science and intellect you would have heard of avalanches, wouldn't you?"

"Yes Captain, of course. Forgive me I am sorry." Apologised Dr Grapevard quietly.

Commander Saurkraut turned to ComCaptain Leekarbour.

"ComCaptain Leekarbour we had better link ourselves, in case one of us falls?" He said, passing his guide rope.

Privado Coconeuter, still chuckling under his breath, suddenly became aware that Dr Grapevard's gaze was burning a hole in him.

"Give me your guide rope, buffoon," said Dr Grapevard holding out his hand. "I'll tell you what we are going to do, Privado Coconeuter. We grown-ups are going to do some serious work. You, my childish moronic friend, will be in charge of finding this walls ears, and when you do? I will box them, personally." At that moment, the ledge beneath Dr Grapevard gave way. "Aaaaahhhhh!" He screamed as he began descending some thirty feet before finding a minute ledge to hold on to. Privado Coconeuter threw a rope down to the dangling Dr Grapevard, a rope that was sadly not long enough to reach the good Doctor who was staring down into an abyss able to do nothing to better the situation, apart from hanging on for dear life that is.

Suddenly, from the ledge above them, the hugest Birdsir ever seen flew off, obviously startled by the panicked screams of Dr Grapevard. It was an unusual specimen it appeared to have no pretty markings or feathers: quite ugly in fact. Commander Saurkraut stretched his hand out to grab Dr Grapevard after moving some way down the ledge, but could not reach. He quickly tied two ropes together. Even the two guide ropes joined together were not long enough to reach where Dr Grapevard had fallen. The big Birdsir swooped and turned hovering as if to observe the activity of the intruders.

"I can't hold on commander, I'm slipping." Panicked Dr Grapevard. Then the giant Birdsir screamed a loud shrill and within seconds, was joined by three further Birdsirs. Up until that moment, Dr Grapevard was blissfully unaware of this new presence. As his eyes set upon them he broke into a sweat, his grip, loosing strength with every passing second. The ledge that the rest of the crew were standing on gave way, all four of the team began what they thought was the perilous journey to certain death. Between them and the ground was nothing but fourteen thousand feet of fresh air.

ComCaptain Fusiala heard the screams, but could not see as the team had moved out of sight. Trying to contact them on the mobile comcon, she struggled on foot moving round to reach a better viewpoint.

"ComCaptain Fusiala to Commander Saurkraut come in please." she called growing desperately anxious as time went on without further communications. But there was nothing but silence in return! The four Birdsirs swooped down after the team, grabbing them gently in their talons just before they hit the ground. Then climbing to the dizzy heights of the mountain peaks in full view of an amazed ComCaptain Fusiala. Hurriedly she contacted her ship to raise the alarm of the trouble that the team had found themselves in and to organise six Star Fighter backup response units. Meanwhile, as the team were carried by the Birdsirs into what looked like an un-activated Vocado heat generator, they could spot in the dim light of the massive cavern, a huge citadel of vast beings, not just Birdsirs, but also other indescribable life forms. Suddenly, they found themselves gently dropped into the centre of a circle of these creatures. For what Commander Saurkraut hoped and indeed wished for was for purposes of purely observational reasons.

The team of explorers still shocked by their near death experience quietly examined their captors, who were obviously doing the same to them, unless of course, this was the calm before the storm.

"Pinch me. Am I dreaming? I really thought we were goners, didn't you commander?" Dr Grapevard whispered slowly.

"We still may be?" Said the Commander wisely. "Make no sudden movements, any of you; let's establish what we are up against before we make any rash decisions or actions." he continued. Commander Dino B Saurkraut stepped forward, slowly clearing his throat. Stolidly seated in front of him was what appeared to be the leader of the pack the largest of all the creatures, flanked by the next two largest specimens of race?

"Aaah... hum. I am Commander Dino B Saurkraut of the O.S.S.S Organicus, I; that is we represent the Space Nations of Organitron. We come in peace and we thank you for saving us from a fate of certain death. The giant Birdsir stood behind the largest of the specimen races, seeming to communicate in his ear.

"I don't know if you understand me?" He continued. "But we would very much like to communicate with you."

Suddenly the specimen races fell around with raucous laughter, as whispering was spread rife around the acoustic auditorium. Commander Dino B Saurkraut turned and shrugged his shoulders at the rest of the team. Then the leader's voice boomed out over their heads. "Apparently, we are the ears of this mountain and one of your group wishes to box us. Step forward Man of science and intellect, let us see if you also posses, bravery." Privado Coconeuter shook in his boots turning to Dr Grapevard.

"You see, I told you, but will you listen? Oh no, not you. Not the great Dr Grapevard, arguably the most respected big mouth of all Organitron."

Dr Grapevard cowered as he stepped forward, saluting the leader as he eyed him from head to tail, swallowing profusely.

"Gulp, ah... Gulp, I, I' err... I am Dr Thervo Grapevard. "Pray tell, to whom do I have the pleasure of addressing?" He asked nervously.

"I am Rexan," roared the leader, so powerfully that it nearly knocked Dr Grapevard off his feet. "King Tyrannosaurus Rexan," he continued. "King of the Sauruses, allow me to introduce my fellow colony members and subjects. You have already bumped into the Pterandon, this is Petra their leader. Rato, the leader of the Triceratops, Ruthour, the leader of the Struthiomimus, Achiron, the leader of the Brachiosaurus, Toska leader of the Brontosaurus and Stegar leader of the stegosaurus. That is who we are but, as for what we are? We are still in the process of finding out. We were rather hoping that you," he laughed pointing towards Dr Grapevard menacingly. "Could help us reach that conclusion. If you wish? First we will fight, then afterwards, one of us will rise as victor and rule supreme, I wonder which one of us it will be, umm." Said King Rexan, as the giggling continued to spiral around the great hall.

Commander Saurkraut stood in front of Dr Grapevard, shielding him from the long probing tongue of Rexan that now waved in his face. "King Rexan, if you will or must fight any one, then it must be me. Please understand that I will fight, but with heavy heart. We are the Space Tracers of Organitron, seeking only peace as our search for the lost Planets of our Solar System continues."

"You are a brave warrior Commander Saurkraut, I think, maybe, our worlds can live together in harmony, after all if we are honest, we need your help and we will do whatever we can to help you in your cause." smiled King Rexan, dropping the hard face of the captor, replacing it instead, with a warm and familiar face of an ally. After much discussion, the collective name for the Sauruses was agreed and they were called the Dinosaurs, named by Commander Dino B Saurkraut himself. For three million years they worked together, farming the lands and lakes in return for supplies of Soya, Meaty, Fishy and Vegimatters.

Then, one day, the Tyrannosaurus changed the rules under yet another new leader, known as King Rextraitor. He believed the Tyrannosaurus Rex should rule "Supreme!" above all living creatures and promptly waged war on them all, fellow Dinosaurs and Organitron alike. The Dinosaurs had mutated into other specimens, such as the Ichthyosaurs and the plesiosaurus that ruled the lakes growing partial to dining on Organitron subjects.

As did the Tyrannosaurus Rex on land, leaving the Organitron no choice but to evacuate yet again from the Planet Earthanon.

The evacuation was **Sundate 2.481, 002,540/ 350. Biltechtoids**

They did however continue the farming programmes of the lands, making frequent but heavily defended visitations to the Earthanon surface. Those visitations were dangerous, but vital to the survival of the space nations of Organitron. Both on the new Planets and the home Planets of the Bubbleonion Squeak Solar System, the population was not severe, however, without correct management, could send them hurtling towards the hard days of the first Evacuation's consequences.

The Organitron's Vanity was still at a premium. All races remained firmly of the opinion that in some way they were supreme. Because of the rationing situation in the days of the first the evacuation of Earthanon, Cross-Vegimatter consumption was general policy. No longer did they insist on consuming only those Vegimatters, moulded and grown in the design of miniature versions of themselves.

They had balanced their diets with measured amounts of Soya, Fishy and Meater matters. One could say that they had grown to actually enjoy it. Each Organitron Nation was no longer permitted to design their ships in their own form only, this was deemed racially unacceptable. It was the thinking of the present Sun-Fleet Admiralty that sat on the Premier Consul of the Seed Council. That greater integration was imperative to ensure a harmonious existence among the Organitron. After all, it was bad enough having to fight off the constant attacks of their Painstakingly annoying enemies, the incredibly persistent Fasterfoids without the space nations' vanity alerting the enemy, as to the technological capability and nation's make up they were up against, before any contact whatever.

The Dinosaurs ruled the Earthanon for a hundred and sixty million years or so, their reign being brought to an abrupt end by the famed bombardment of meteors from space. It was these meteors, huge in size and red hot on impact, peppering the Earthanon surface indiscriminately, that forced the surface temperature of Earthanon to increase to such high levels, that once again, the Science Foliage Ecosystem farming programme was completely destroyed.

The Rugerplotts, Dindivar and Splutterbun races were moved to the specially constructed Planet of Casserule. Along with many of the life forms that had formed on Earthanon, all except the Dinosaur races had been rescued and given safe haven wherever possible. All those life forms requiring water for survival were caught and placed in the great lakes of Casserule. Unfortunately the sharks were among them. In the rush to save the Whalons and Paupawses from certain destruction, sharks had managed to go unnoticed in the transportation tanks and were set free in the lakes of Casserule. A Science Foliage Ecosystem farming programme was already under way on Casserule, dampening the effects of the certain Earthanon losses. Stockpiles of Soya, Meater, Fishy and Vegimatters were vast.

The Organitron were comfortable with the fact that their economic and nutritional futures were reasonably secure. For as long as they maintained sensible Planet management, and continued to steer the cultural integration of the Organitron with those of the new life forms. It was important to the Organitron that natural resources, lifestyles and life forms should co-exist hand in hand, until such time as Earthanons surface was cooled down sufficiently enough for them to re-inhabit it. It was to be a further eighty-two million years until this was possible. The order to re-inhabit Earthanon was given by the then head of the premier consul of the Seed Council, the Bright Honourable, and High Admiral Marshmallot Bangpottatio.

It was **Sundate 2.723, 004,590/ 113 Biltechtoids.** The long trek towards re-establishing the Science Foliage Ecosystem farming programmes, and re-integrating the various life forms to their natural habitats took some thousands of your Earth years. The cooling of Earthanon was a dangerous and complex process. It was neither instantaneous, nor at the same constant rate all around the globe. Science had pushed forward all the boundaries of the Organitron past on **Sundate 2.867, 126,106/ 311 Biltechtoids.** Chief Carridionaries Science Officer, Professor Vegbetto Artichokule, discovered the method of Matter Anti-Matter transferral, which he named Vegitamisation. Increasing the savings in the precious fuel elements, not to mention the time element saved in transportation terms.

For a further one hundred and thirty-two million years, the Organitron, were happy in the new in-habitation era. Then the next testing chapter of the Organitron history books began. Organitron's Life span had increased from one hundred and seventy-five years, to two hundred and fifty years. This was due to advancing technology in space travel, and a much researched and improved nutritional intake and balanced diet.

This story begins on **Sundate 2,999,999,999/ 321 Biltechtoids,** in the autumn of the celebration year of the new millennium. The missions of the Space Nations of Organitron remain the same, as does their cultural beliefs. The original Bubbleonion Squeak Solar System comprised of one hundred and twelve home Planets. As well as a space collective known as the Farinaree, who lived isolated on five planets in the Farinaree quad. Then, when the Star cluster explosion spread the Planets across several galaxies, the Seed Council of Organitron based on the Planet Carridionaries formed a pact. They would no longer consider themselves, "The Space Nations of Organitron." Not until all of their fellow Planets were found and repatriated with the new Bubbleonion Squeak Solar System, or, until they had found conclusive proof of those Planets disintegration or destruction. Until the Planetary Solar System was complete, they would search the galaxies venturing into even the potentially fatal uncharted space sectors.

Forever aiming at that day of completion, they would be the Space Nations of Organitron secondly, but primarily they are and will be, forever riding under the banner of, "The Space Tracers of Organitron." Of the original home Planets, after the explosion, forty-seven of the one hundred and twelve Space Nations were blown relatively close together within sight of each other at least. Six other Planets were within transmitter range; and gradually, the long task of reforming the Solar System was under way. The Farinaree planets remained in the spatial area dotted amongst the surviving home planets. A further nineteen Planets had been found and repatriated; some of them, suffering millions of Startechtoids or years of physical, mental and emotional torture, as they struggled with the uncertainty of their futures, and under the constant threat of starvation, disease and potential attack from as yet unknown Space Races.

The Bubbleonion Squeak Solar System now consists of seventy-two Planets. Eleven Planets have been found totally uninhabited, with no living survivors of their race in existence. Those Planets have been moved to the planetary graveyard of Valveggarnova, ready for re-inhabitation by their rightful space race. And so lays the second mission of the Space Tracers of Organitron, to seek and find the Asteroid Plato of Templevegarial, the Temple of the Seed Vault Covenant. It is the covenant of seeds that holds in its vaults, the capacity to reactivate the lost Nations of Organitron.

It is within these vaults that the founder Organiseed's are kept in a deep carbon dried state, alongside the, "Thermo Proton Germinisation Chamber," which cannot be recreated by artificial intelligence. Its power source is a rare gem unseen or found anywhere else. A gem called the "Fusion" or the stone of Helios. Capable of harnessing incredible energy output by simply being placed at the correct angle to the sun. The Vault Guardian Elect is or was the wise prophet Widdup of the Farinaree Space race. No-one knows whether the prophet Widdup or Templevegarial has survived, but if he has, then in his hands Templevegarial is best protected.

Widdup, who is said to be blessed with immortality, for as long as he feels worthy of the position Guardian Elect possessed many strange and powerful capabilities, not least of which the ability to shape shift and manifest himself into any form imaginable.

Preying on the worst fears and nightmares of all potential invaders, whatever their greatest fear was, he would appear as that vision of inner enemy or element. The Asteroid in itself is one of a kind. It is bright orange in colour and emits a strange and power full magnetic field. Yet it has still managed to evade detection from the Organitron, given that it is the last hope of the lost races. Because of this, the search will continue. For whilst there is hope, there is reason to exist and expand, and while there is reason to exist and expand, there is a determination to be the best collection of races they can be. Individually for sure, but, collectively for certain.

CHAPTER TWO

Where there be Fasterfoids, there be trouble!

Earthanon Arcticus region 11.45 starhectoids, Sundate 2. 999,999,999/ 321.

The sun was shining high in the sky warming the Arcticus region with a blanket of comfort that the Organitron had grown to love and respect. Ground Commodore Cu-Cumbala, the head of Earthanon ground force personnel had ordered a national vegeday break, due to the exceeded targets of the mining workforce.

Commander Marrachinello, the Squadron leader of the ground force Star Fighter's defence arm, also known as, "Red Sector Leader Fighter Command," lounged with his wife Pipmeena and their children Blossey and Pipette the, two girls, and Stoner the oldest child, and only son. They had decided to venture into the woods of the Arcticus region with a mass picnic party of the Engineers division. "Ahh, breakfast under the sun don't you know?" Said a snooty lord of the manor styled Commander Marrachinello, tucking into a huge slice of watermelon. Pipmeena and the children laughed as he turned towards them covered in pips and juice, his handlebar moustache drooping with saturation.

"What? What? Haven't you ever seen me eat watermelon before?" Stoner handed his father Pipmeena's mirror which she had passed him, to light the fire under the skillet. As he looked into the mirror a smile reached from ear to ear.

"Oh dear," mused the Commander, "that is not a pretty sight is it? Why; I look like a monster, yes, a monster from the woods. Coming, to cuddle my children and slop vast quantities of melon juice all over them, Aaaahaaa! With that, he started to chase them around the picnic blanket until he caught Blossey, the youngest, blowing raspberries on her belly button, sending the whole family into a fit of the giggles.

"Stop it, Dadski, it tickles," Blossey cried uncontrollably. "No, stop it, you're all sticky. Ahh... Ahh... Ha... ha... ha. Your moustache is all fuzzy. Stop it, Dadski. Oooh... Oooh." The Marrachinello family were not aware that they had been joined by FO Twizzlepasta, the First Officer of the O.S.S.S Milkymarrow way, and FO Yamura, the First Officer of the O.S.S.S Junipitaris.

"Ahhum," coughed FO Twizzlepasta trying to alert them as to their presence.

"Aahum... Hum..." She interrupted again, but louder this time.

Commander Marrachinello stood covered from head to foot in melon juice and grass. Not a befitting appearance for the most respected squadron leader of the fighter command, the Warrior of the skies.

"Excuse me Commander Marrachinello, but your presence is requested on board the O.S.S.S Milkymarrow way immediately Sir. We are sorry to interrupt your leisure time, Commanderette Marrachinello; children. It is very important. Please forgive us."

Commander Marrachinello jumped to his feet and brushed himself down as best he could.

"I don't suppose I will have time to change before meeting with Captain Beetrouly, am I right, Umm, eh what?"

"Unfortunately not Sir. It is a matter of extreme urgency!" Reasoned FO Yamura.

"Very well FO Yamura, we had better Vegitamise now." Then he turned to his family and they all had a group hug.

"Got to go my loved ones, duty calls and all that jiggery pokery don't you know? You enjoy your day now, you hear me? If Daddy can make it back in time, he will, but if not, save me a slice of that spiffing Banana Flapjack, will you?"

"Yes my love," whispered Pipmeena lovingly. "The biggest one we have got. Say good-bye to Daddy children. Come along quickly." Blossey and Pipette gave him a kiss on each cheek and Stoner had put his hand out to shake his father's hand. Obviously believing that at the ripe old age of fifteen Startechtoids, he was too mature to give his father a hug in front of witnesses.

"What's this? No hug for your old Father, eh what?" Enquired the stiff upper lipped Commander Marrachinello.

"Daddy, can I come with you please? Why in one Startechtoids time I'll be enrolled at the Spaceark Academy. Take me with you, please?"

"No my boy, your time will come. Besides, you need not run from your youth so freely. Trust me, when you get to my age you spend the rest of your life trying to recapture your youth, it is both a long and impossible task."

"All right Daddy, for now I will stay at home, but one day we will travel the constellations together; you and me, side by side."

"And I look forward to it my son, but for now a hug would protect me on my way. Do you think you could manage that old bean umm?" He said holding out his arms.

Stoner smiled and ran into his father's arms squeezing him tightly.

"Go well father, may Helios be with you."

"Thank you son and remember, even when you grow to be strong and wise it is always good to hug another with genuine affection."

"Are you ready now Sir?" Asked FO Twizzlepasta.

Commander Marrachinello stood in between the two officers and signalled his readiness, giving his son Stoner the Organitron salute.

"FO Twizzlepasta to O.S.S.S Milkymarrow way come in Ensign Chilleater, over."

"This is Ensign Chilleater, come in FO Twizzlepasta, over."

"We have located Commander Marrachinello and we are now ready to be Vegitamised on-board."

"Ensign Chilleater acknowledged and understood; fixing co-ordinates logged and computerised, Vegitamising now."

Suddenly the party of three were gone as they disappeared in blue beams of light. Pipmeena looked on warmly as her gaze from her husband's eyes was broken.

"Come along now children, let us dance and sing a song, before you know it Daddy will be back amongst us." Said Commander Marrachinello's wife trying to cover up the disappointment of the children at their father's withdrawal. Up above the Arcticus region of Earthanon, the Milkymarrow way and the Junipitaris space stations were positioned, monitoring all Earthanons shipping transportation's, mining excavations and atmospheric movements.

On the bridge, Captain Rouly Beetrouly was seated at the helm with SO Sweetpea at the Nav com, and Viceroy Cornettle seated at the steering column. Ensign Tommitower stood at the communication's com with Viceroy Dilltip, operating the ship's analyser and Grid Finder security station in the absence of FO Twizzlepasta. Standing on guard at the elevation chamber were Ensigns Appleorn and Pearbelle.

"Excuse me Captain Beetrouly; I have received a courier communication from Admiralette Xion Ru Roser of the Carridionaries SFA Seed Council. Shall I put it on screen Captain?" Asked Ensign Tommitower.

"Yes Ensign Tommitower and have Commander Marrachinello shown to the Strategy room as soon as he Vegitamises on board will you?" Said Captain Beetrouly making him-self comfortable at the Command com.

"Aye Sir, they are in transportation as we speak. Visaid on playback now Captain." Confirmed Ensign Tommitower.

On screen appeared the bold shape of the fiery femme fatale Admiralette Xion Ru Roser, her Red thorny hair shooting off in all sorts of directions. As she spoke there was certain nervousness in her voice.

"Greetings Captain Beetrouly, this is Admiralette Xion Ru Roser of the Carridionaries SFA Seed Council, Sundate **2,999,999,999/ 281.** I have had this message brought to you via courier envoy Ensign Pilot Starfruitier of the travel cruiser SFA Bavois Creme. When I tell you the information, you will understand my not wanting to risk transmission interception. As you know, the O.S.S.S Earthanon has been undergoing her refit at the Spaceark academy resource centre. You will be pleased to hear that she will be in the Earthanon sector of the Solar System, ETA **Sundate 3,000,000,000/ 065 Biltechtoids.** She is currently undergoing space trials in the uncharted space sector G17, in the Soupaura dejour quasar. This should guarantee that the yellow neck Fasterfoids do not spy on her activities too closely.

Your ship will be the next in line for refit. You will be expected to leave Earthanon at **Sundate 3.000, 000,000/ 130 Biltechtoids**, after the changing of the guard handover ceremony to Captain Gillespie Jethro Carrot of the O.S.S.S Earthanon. This will give you sixty five Starlectoids to close down your security and Shore based operations. I would appreciate it if you hand over control of the Earthanon operation to Captain Carrot when he arrives, then you can concentrate on the hand over timetable that must be met! Your arrival at the Spaceark Academy resource centre is expected on **Sundate 3.000, 000,000/ 170 Biltechtoids.**

I look forward to seeing you on your return to the Bubbleonion Squeak Solar System. I must admit, it is a little difficult to find a chess player of your cunning and tenacity, try as I have, the Vegitalis plexus is very short of any real competition. Until then my friend, may Helios be with you. This is Admiralette Xion Ru Roser, SFA, and UFO over and out."

Captain Beetrouly was relieved to hear the news of the refit. This had been a long and eventful five Startechtoids stint in the Earthanon Solar System, with little or no time for relaxation with the recent upturn in the Fasterfoids futile behaviour. He and his family were looking forward to going home to the Bubbleonion Squeak Vegitalis Solar System. In particular to visit his parents, who still resided on the Planet Beetrojanous, the home Planet of his space race the "Beetragia Organitron space race." Then the realisation that he would again have to face the Admiralette Xion Ru Roser, in competition across the chess table. She wasn't secretly referred to as the, "SFFFA." For nothing, oh no. She was called this, which is short for Sun-Fleet Femme Fatale Admiralette, because she was incredibly competitive in everything she did. A so, called friendly game of chess was no exception with the SFFFA. The last time the Organitron held the space race finals she was one of the finalists, and the other was Captain Peabazzare of the O.S.S Satsumuroo

He was the other by default. Not because of his superior playing strategy, but because all personnel with any flair for the game, were collectively sent on a wild goose chase mission the week before hand. They were sent to a sector that made it impossible to return for the tournament. Their mission; to investigate a rumoured report of a possible Templevegarial sighting. This left practically no competition to speak of, and a sure fired victory for the scheming, budding floweret of supposed innocence. "In fact," thought the Captain. "The only person never to be beaten by the SFFFA is the undisputed chess champion, "Captain Gillespie J Carrot of the O.S.S.S Earthanon."

It was his ship that was ordered to head the spear force on the bogus mission, "Unfortunate really," laughed Captain Beetrouly to himself. As he was the defending champion, she won by default taking his title without so much as touching the board, indeed, she has made it impossible for them to meet for a rematch ever since. Then a shiver rushed down the spine of Captain Beetrouly. The one and only time he had beaten the SFFFA, he was given very sudden departure orders from the Planet Carridionaries. The very next day, he was posted to the Bapmacdo Aurora sector on an undercover reconnaissance mission, the Fasterfoids Home Lands Sector of the Solar System. "No," he smiled, "that will not happen again. I would rather take a dive every time and loose, than be sent there again." he thought.

Mushroid Fungenius, the ships mobile Mechanoid, emerged from the service elevation chamber and approached Captain Beetrouly.

"Excuse me Sir," interrupted the Mushroid, "but here is the information you required for your meeting. All sightings have been confirmed by the various Robopods on active duty in those sectors." Reported the Mushroid hurriedly whizzing around the bridge.

"Thank you, Mushroid Fungenius. Let us hope that these activities are not about to erupt into something more, sinister?" Said the concerned Captain Beetrouly, Frowning.

Mushroid Fungenius whizzed back into the service elevation chamber and re-energised the doors disappearing into the lower holds of the O.S.S.S Milkymarrow way, the last bastion of hiding for all the ships Mechanoids. The ship's Municipal Mechanoid team had reached the finals of the war games against the Science and technology team, of whom Mushroid Fungenius was the Captain. He would never again be able to hold his head up high if they were to lose the war game's finals to a bunch of, "rusty old domestic wastepaper bins."

Captain Beetrouly stood and moved towards the elevation chamber, signing the Captain's log that was handed to him by Viceroy Dilltip.

"SO Sweetpea you have Command com. Have Ensign Cauliflowet report to the bridge and service the Nav com."

"Aye, aye Sir," she said, activating her personal channel. "This is SO Sweatpea to Ensign Cauliflowet. Please report for Nav com duty on the bridge. On the double if you will Ensign."

"Ensign Cauliflowet to SO Sweatpea, A OK and on my way Sir." He confirmed.

Captain Beetrouly de-energised the elevation chamber doors and stepped inside as Ensign Pearbelle piped him off the bridge, whilst Ensign Appleorn announced his departure. Then the doors closed and Captain Beetrouly disappeared from sight.

"Captain off the bridge." shouted Ensign Appleorn.

"Stand easy on the bridge." Ordered SO Sweatpea, as she sat at the command com.

Meanwhile, far across the galaxy, a flotilla of Fasterfoid ships had gathered in sector F9 of the uncharted Bervedo quadrant, masked by an Asteroid belt; or so they thought. Little did they know the Sun-Fleet Robopods were on their case? The flotilla was headed by the new Mayo class Star station, the FF Shallow Fryer, along with three flash cruisers, the FF Hotbox, the FF Fatpan and the FF Lardlip. Inside this curtain of protection lay another ship, quite unlike any other ship in the Fasterfoid Fleet.

On-board the Mayo class Star station the FF Shallow Fryer, it's Commanding Officer, Major General Icky Chicky Fattyspot, and his second in command, General Ghi Chickydigit, both Fasterfoids born to the space race Chickonaldir, chaired a meeting of the Flash Cruiser ship's Commanding Officers. General Greasy Pattie and his second in command, Principle Officer Griscillian Burgerbuns of the FF Hotbox, formed the Burgerite section of the Fleet. General Breasto Chirpychick and his second in command, Principle Officer Burgirty Chickwings. These were both born to the space race Chickonaldir in control of the FF Fatpan. Also present at the meeting, were General Satu Pomline, a straight-cut chip born to the space race FasterFritter, and his second in command, Principle Officer Corrigate de Digeridoo, born to the space race Crinkleozone, both of the FF Lardlip.

The meeting was being held in the Major Generals, private command bunker room; stiflingly hot and arid in atmosphere with stark surrounding decor, just as the Fasterfoids like their climatic conditions.

"Generals, Principle Officers of the Fasterfoids. The reasons for the tests that we have been running are about to be fully explained. They are complete and we believe that they have been successful. Now is the time to press ahead with our ingenious plan.

The ship that you have been assisting in the working trials and have been unable to monitor or keep track of, is the latest technology to be unmasked by the great scientists of the Fasterfoid combined mission, to oust the Organitron from their pitiful self imposed pedestal supreme." He said, thumping the table, his annoyance showing obvious distaste for who, in his opinion, were the healthy, nutritionally superior do-gooders of the space galaxies. Then he pressed the button on the panel at his side, dropping the heat shield in front of the plasma steel observation window.

"Ladyfryers and Gentlegrills, I give you the newest innovation of space travel, the very latest in the superior technology stakes of the Fasterfoids, verses the insignificantly inferior Organitron. I give you the FF Francaisfry, a new class of Flash cruiser, one capable of something more valuable than all the Oilio plasma, and starch oil reserves in all the galaxies combined."

As the ship lit up, its frame was in their opinion, more beautiful than anything they had seen before. A ship with triple saucers in the form of a Burgerite, a Chickonaldir and a Sauteudez, placed and held high on great towers of Sausagia replicas. These were attached to a latticed body in the form of the Fasterfoids known as the Waffleoid, with three boosters at the rear in the form of a Crinkleozone, a FasterFritter and a Croquetteoily Fasterfoid. Larger than the usual flash cruisers and certainly more intricate in design, but nowhere near the size of the Mayo class Star station on which they were based for the meeting. On the screen appeared a well-known Fasterfoid, who went by the name of General Satuese. The only Fasterfoid to command a ship that has never sustained damage by way of attack. An unmatched record by any other serving officer of the Fasterfoid Star fleet. As they turned towards the Screen, General Satuese addressed them quickly.

"Major General Fattyspot, General Chickydigit, Ladyfryers and Gentlegrills. Quite something isn't she, eh?" Said the smug, proud and elitist General Satuese. "Or is she?" he continued

They turned again to admire the ship, but the ship was gone, disappeared into thin air without a sound or trace. General Breasto Chirpychick laughed loudly, as did all the others joining in with him nervously.

"So, you have cracked the silent running mode propulsion system, now we'll show them." He laughed as he jumped in the air singing with excitement. "We're on our way to victory, we'll show them just how mean we can be, Just watch us and you will see. We are on our way to victory."

"Yes," said General Satuese smugly. "We have cured the teething problems in the silent running mode propulsion system, but I'm afraid Ladyfryers and Gentlegrills the general and more important idea, is to show them nothing at all!" continued the General.

"Are you mad General Satuese," Cried General Breasto Chirpychick. "Listen, we have been testing something that we had not even seen up until today, let alone heard, that must mean its speed ratios are phenomenal, making it undetectable by the Fasterfoid eye. Therefore, I think that one can safely assume that it would also be undetectable to the Organitron eye. You seriously expect us to stand here and except that we will not unleash this magnificent breakthrough on our mortal enemies? Its madness, utter madness!" shouted the now steaming General Chirpychick.

"I said," interrupted General Satuese "you great tub of blubbering lard, that we will not, repeat not, show them anything, but do not be mistaken, we will unleash this incredible step forward on those vitamin freaks the Organitron. They just won't see it coming; or going for that matter. Here, my Fasterfoid friends, is why?"

As the General briefed the Fasterfoid collective of the cunning daring mission ahead, the resonance of laughter and excitement sent shock waves across the Galaxies of the universe.

Captain Beetrouly entered the strategy room of the O.S.S.S Milkymarrow way where FO Twizzlepasta, FO Yamura and Commander Marrachinello were seated with Captain Sunfleur of the O.S.S.S Junipitaris. He was flanked by the Earthanon Security chief FO Pumpkinallian, and the chief science officer of the O.S.S.S Milkymarrow way, FO Pommegranza. They all stood as Captain Beetrouly took his place at the head of the table, opening the report book in front of him.

As he sat, the shock waves from the Fasterfoids seemed to run up his spine, chilling the atmosphere around him. He did not know its exact cause but in the pit of his stomach, he had the sneaking suspicion that the Fasterfoids were somehow the cause of the uncomfortable air that surrounded him.

"Thank you for coming at such short notice," said Captain Beetrouly shaking off the eerie feeling dwelling in his mind. "But I fear it is necessary that we discuss certain movements in the Fasterfoid ranks as soon as possible. One can never be too careful or cautious where the Fasterfoids are concerned. My particular apologies for dragging you from your family Commander Marrachinello. National holidays seem to be the only time we get to spend quality time with our loved ones. So, on that note, this meeting, I hope, will be brief and is now in session. It has been brought to my attention by routine Robopod relays in the Bervedo quadrant that the Fasterfoids appear to be assembling some kind of task force in the Asteroid belt sector of that quadrant. As you are aware the Robopods are not programmed to deal with Asteroid belt terrain negotiations. Though the report relays are highly detailed, it is not unreasonable to assume that they may not be entirely complete." He said passing around the table, the copies of the report, and activating his Computron.

"Captain Beetrouly to Ensign Chilleater, respond please." Said Captain Beetrouly urgently.

"Ensign Chilleater responding and ready Sir." She confirmed.

"Ensign Chilleater," continued Captain Beetrouly. "I am fully aware that the O.S.S.S Earthanon is to remain outside of Transmission contact until its trial period is over, but tell me how long will it take for a Star fighter to courier a copy of this Robopod report to Captain Carrot of the O.S.S.S Earthanon?" He enquired.

"Approximately six Starlectoids if we activate the Slithervoid Sir, but if the Fasterfoids are monitoring us, then we may just lead them straight to the O.S.S.S. Earthanon Captain! However, if we take a tactical zigzag route, it could take up to thirty Starlectoids Sir; even then, there is no guarantee that we will avoid being tracked; one might argue, that we would improve their chances of detecting us by giving them six times as long to follow us Sir." She reasoned.

Captain Beetrouly remained quite deep in concentration. It was a possibility that the O.S.S.S Earthanon was already the focus of the

Fasterfoids attention. The O.S.S.S Earthanon may not be able to track the quadrant, because of the Asteroid belt interference, and it was well out of range of the Bervedo quadrant to enable it to carry out a Robopod reconnaissance surveillance of its own.

"Any suggestions?" Said Captain Beetrouly simply.

"If I may interject Captain Beetrouly?" Asked Science officer Pommegranza, an Organigirl Organitron, born to the space race Pommegrantis from the space race home Planet of Pommegralia, which is located in the Fruitalia Quadrant of the Bubbleonion Squeak Vegitalis Solar System.

"Certainly, let it be known, FO Pommegranza, all contributions are gratefully accepted."

FO Pommegranza initialised the Computron and punched in the scenario data. In the middle of the table appeared a hologram sequence of the Soupaura dejour sector Slithervoid.

"May I suggest Sir," continued FO Pommegranza, "that we send through Seven Robopods at intermittent intervals of five seconds between the first and fifth Robopods, and fifteen seconds between the sixth and seventh Robopod, Just after the sixth Robopod, launch the Star fighter, programming the last Robopod to explode in the Star Fighter slipstream."

Captain Beetrouly interrupted her scenario with an observation of concern.

"Excuse me FO Pommegranza, but if they are monitoring the Slithervoid, won't they pick up the calorific proton emissions from the Star Fighter?"

"It is possible, but I don't think so Sir," replied FO Pommegranza, "you see, if they are monitoring the Slithervoid, they will almost certainly assume because of the Robopod probes course and direction into the uncharted quadrant, that we are simply sending Robopod probes out to reconnaissance the area. They would have no reason to assume, that we have ships in the uncharted sector or that we are sending a ship out there. Because of the Robopods presence, I think if they have any ships in or around that sector, they will move well out of monitoring range for fear of being discovered within the Robopods Grid Finder range. However Captain, I have considered and I believe pre-empted your concerns where calorific emission detection is a possible factor. I understand this is accrediting the Fasterfoids with too much intelligence, so therefore, I propose a counter measure as an insurance policy. We set the sixth

Robopod to explode within six seconds of expulsion from the Slithervoid, then, we set course for the Star Fighter to take an adjacent course of forty five blimits on immediate expulsion from the Slithervoid. At that point, the Star Fighter will jump into Califoric K propulsion from standby. On the detonation of the second more powerful explosion of the seventh Robopod, it will initialise the K Factor. The fall-out and shockwaves from the two Robopods will flood any Grid Finder with proton emissions masking any calorific emissions from the Star Fighter, which will almost immediately follow a zigzag pre set course." With that, FO Pommegranza sat in silence awaiting some kind of response, a little embarrassed by the silence. "Of course, it is only a suggestion off the top of my head. I would quite understand if you found it a little ambitious?" She said trying to draw some reaction.

Captain Beetrouly sat in silence at the depth and precision of the plan, as did the rest of the group assembled in the strategy room.

"FO Pommegranza," stated Captain Beetrouly suddenly, "if that is the best you can come up with off the top of your head, then-well," he paused menacingly. "Then I think we could safely say that we would love to see what you would come up with given two minutes notice. Yes, I for one like the plan. As for ambitious, I would be disappointed if you didn't include a little ambitiousness in all that you seek to conquer. If conquer you must, then conquer in style. Well done FO Pommegranza. Any objections anyone?" Captain Beetrouly looked around the strategy room as their heads remained still. "Good," he continued as no-one raised any objections. "Then we will go with the plan. Now Captain Sunfleur, will you please brief the congregation on the Science party's visit to the Europetriennes as you have all the details from the SFA! FO Pommegranza, you are dismissed to prepare the Robopods for the mission. Commander Marrachinello, would you do me the honour of courier envoy to Captain Carrot of the O.S.S.S Earthanon?"

"Absolutely, old bean. Hey what, tell me, when will you be ready for my departure FO Pommegranza, umm?" Said the commander, twanging his handlebar Moustache.

"Four starhectoids should do it Sir." She confirmed.

"Then would you permit me to leave Captain Beetrouly? Perhaps I might spend a few precious starhectoids in the bosom of my loved ones before my departure?"

"Certainly Commander Marrachinello, report to the bridge before you depart will you please?"

"Will do Sir," he said standing up and walking towards the exit de-energising the doors in front of him. "Until then T.T.F.N Chap's, Chapess's." Then he gave the Organitron salute and left, with FO Pommegranza.

Captain Sunfleur stood and lowered the map on the wall in front of him which had the Europetriennes highlighted in several areas.

"What you see before you are, the areas of interest to the visiting science party of the Planet Macadamia. They have detected various core sample readings that indicate properties similar, if not exact, to that of the lost Asteroid Plato of the Templevegarial; We have agreed to supply transportation and protection for the Macadamian delegation for their period of inhabitation on Earthanon. FO Pumpkinallian, as you are in charge of the overall security services of the Mother ships and Earthanon, I would appreciate it if you would hand pick the Sun-Fleet Organitron carefully. Only the most sound of men if you please. During bad weather cycles the Sun-Fleet Organitron may be cooped up with them for days. This close quarter co-habitation with the Bubbleonion squeak Vegitalis Solar Systems Loony platoon, could send even the strongest of us over the edge, so, regular changes of personnel will be essential and have councillors standing by for the returning security team members. Any questions?" FO Pumpkinallian coughed to gain the attention of the Captain, who was busy flag marking the map indicating the Core excavation sites.

"Ha... Ha, excuse me Captain Sunfleur, but would it not be advantageous to issue them with an army of Mushroids to protect them? Not even the loony platoon of Macadamian jeepers' creepers could affect those metallic motherboard viruses' breeding grounds. Not to mention saving the valuable personnel with whom we have invested millions of credits in the training programme from certain insanity." They all laughed at this point and began to draw up a hit list of those officers, who needed reprimanding for various breeches of Organitron Dignity. The Mad Macadamians had the un-canniest knack of cracking the most respected of Organimen until they were nothing more than a proverbial moussky or mousse as you will know them. Therefore no-one too important can be sacrificed, in theory ha... Ha... Ha.

CHAPTER THREE

Garlicazure or a trap set to lure?

TIME: 13.50 starhectoids Sundate 2.999, 999,999/ 321 Biltechtoids.

Across the galaxies, millions of starmillo's away in sector G17 of the uncharted territories of the Soupaura dejour quasar, the O.S.S.S. Earthanon and her crew were undergoing the final stages of their Space trials. Accompanying the ship, keeping a protective eye on the surrounding space activities, the O.S.S.S Earthanon was flanked by the O.S.S Satsumuroo, Captained by the fearless Captain Banier Dillo Peabazzare, and the O.S.S Ommelettra, Captained by the incredible Captain Pipleerer Tubain Macoronite, also the O.S.S Capsicumby, Captained by the slightly extrovert Captain Venusio de Fleetrap.

As the elevation chamber arrived at the bridge and the doors de-energised, out of the chamber came Captain Gillespie J. Carrot, a tall, slight but stern Organitron born of the Space race Carroteenardune. The most respected race of all the Organitron's, who originate from the Planet Carridionaries, located at the centre of the Vegitalis Legume quadrant within the heart of Bubbleonion Squeak Vegitalis Solar System.

On the bridge, was First Officer Benzo Marrowlar at the Command com, Ensign Tilda Strawballis at the communications com and Ensign Cairo Viola at the Navigation com. Seated at the steering column was Viceroy Zilot Rhubarblatt, busily running through the various tactical battle manoeuvres while Second Officer Sara Tulipina was standing at the ship's systems analyser watching for various signs of malfunction. Standing guard at the elevation chamber were Ensigns Vigon Rasperillo and Rixtan Melonture.

"Captain on the bridge." said Ensign Rasperillo as Ensign Melonture piped him on board with the ships whistle. "Pheweeeeee... phewoooooh," bringing the bridge crew to attention.

FO Marrowlar stood bold and upright, rather like somebody had applied too much starch to his tunic, as he handed over the command com to the Captain.

"You have Command Com Captain." He said briskly.

"Thank you FO Marrowlar. Stand easy on the bridge. "Captain Carrot looked on as FO Marrowlar walked stiffly towards the security com. "FO Marrowlar," said the amused Captain. "That's another way of saying relax umm."

"Yes Sir, I will relax immediately." answered FO Marrowlar unsure of what exactly the Captain was getting at, but, he dropped his shoulders an inch anyway just to be on the safe side.

"Status report Ensign Strawballis?" Enquired the Captain, as he took his pride of place at the Command com.

"Well Sir, the Calorific Converters have passed all SFA inspection criteria's FO Potatree insists that they are ready to be placed on line and calibrated to link with the Calorific Proton reactors Sir." Confirmed a very nervous Ensign Strawballis.

"The last time he assured us that they were ready for Calibration Linking," noted the Captain, observing the tension in the bridge crew's manner. "He nearly cooked the entire ship's compliment. Ensign Strawballis, ask him if he is absolutely sure this time? I would hate to end my days as the galaxy's largest floating soufflé, which would not go down well with the top brass at Carridionaries SFA, with the exception of Admiralette Xion Ru Roser." chuckled Captain Carrot.

"Why Captain, would the Admiralette Xion Ru Roser not be disturbed by the demise of a legend of the Fleet such as you?" Enquired a confused SO Tulipina.

"Ah of course, SO Tulipina, you were in the Gamma quadrant, Asteroid sweeping Flotilla at the time. Let me see now. What was it? Oh yes," said the Captain as he remembered the incredibly bad looser in the chess arena. "Not to mention," he thought, but then, remembering his position and status, felt it unwise to tempt retribution from the Admiralette Xion Ru Roser, should she find out his indiscretion at boasting victory over a superior Sun-Fleet Premier Consul. "No, out of respect, I really shouldn't' couldn't tell you."

"No Sir," croaked FO Marrowlar. "Out of respect to the Admiralette, it would not be good for you to be seen to gloat, but I, Captain," FO Marrowlar smiled like a child let loose at play time. "I, on the other hand, I could without fear of retribution convey the story for you, could I not?"

Captain Carrot Laughed, I could consider that as an act of, shall we say, Insubordination FO Marrowlar, but you could tell the bridge crew and I could be engrossed in my log book and, miss it, if you wish." Reasoned Captain Carrot. FO Marrowlar handed the Captain the log book from SO Tulipina.

"Thank you Captain, if you could inspect the entries please Sir?" Requested FO Marrowlar.

"Certainly FO Marrowlar." He said burying his head into the log book.

"The annual war games convention," announced FO Marrowlar. "Where Admiralette Xion Ru Roser rigged the board to blow up all the enemy ships before it was her turn to face battle, artificially wiping out all other life forms with a pre-loaded doomsday scenario, in which nobody could possibly win, unless of course they were in possession of the Matrix security code to disable the countdown sequence. Captain Gillespie J Carrot was not the flavour of the month when he managed to escape death and go on to win the game by Vegitamising the Admiralette's team on board the fictional O.S.S.S Earthanon and Vegitamising his team into the secret bunker that she had housed herself in, prior to the explosion Sequence countdown."

"She was so angry." remembered the smiling Captain Carrot, as his second in command conveyed the rest of the story. "She forgot momentarily," said the jolly FO Marrowlar. "That it was a fictional scenario, and demanded his court martial on the grounds of extreme cowardice. Then, her anger turned to Vocado heat generation proportions when the rest of the seed council fell off the Judge's bench with girdle splitting uncontrollable fits of side cramping hysteria.

"What, pray tell, do you find so funny?" she wailed in frustration and despair. "This Organiman is a blaggard and a coward, a disgrace to the uniform, a cad, no, a charlatan and a cheat. I demand satisfaction at once, nothing but the immediate court-martial of this Mutinous Traitor will suffice." She demanded.

"But Admiralette Xion Ru Roser," they said. "We can't, don't you see? In the attempt to rule supreme, you have killed us all with your greed and, might I mention at this point," shouted the head judge. "You too, are in the very unfortunate position of being very dead therefore, not exactly in the position to demand anything!" They laughed. "Admiralette Xion Ru Roser, stormed out of the auditorium, smashing her way through several rows of spectators, whom by this stage were also struggling to contain their deep sense of admiration for the victorious Captain Carrot.

"Get out of my way! Get out of my way now I say!" "She hurled across the room as she de-energised the main doors. She suddenly turned to face the judge's panel, "Captain Carrot," she bellowed. "You will report to my office first thing next tour of duty, and before you get any smart ideas," she yelled. "That is an order from Admiralette Xion Ru Roser, the living one, not the dead!"

The bridge crew were appreciating the fable of the past when suddenly, the ship came to a shuddering halt, as if they had struck something, throwing several of the crew to the ground. The alarm bell sounded and Captain Carrot leaped into action, activating his personal com.

"FO Potatree, engineering. Damage report?" Enquired the Captain, fearing another failure with the calorific reactor Calibration process.

"To be sure Captain," answered the puzzled Chief Engineer. "No damage sustained here. What in the blazes was that? I can't be sure from down here in the engine room Sir, but it felt like we hit something."

"Okay, FO Potatree. Carrot out. FO Marrowlar, damage report?"

"Ship's system analyser indicates minimal damage Sir. There is damage to the port phaser housing Captain, but the shield deflected the bulk of the impact. Other than that, the ship would appear to be un-compromised." He confirmed.

"Grid Finder readings, Ensign Viola?" Ordered the thoughtful Captain Carrot, Ensign Viola turned to the Grid Finder particle scanner. As he looked into the gyroscope module his facial expression seemed to indicate an element of surprise, then he transferred the information readings to the ship's analyser, initialising the computer data banks search sequence.

"Computer," said the bemused Ensign Viola. "Initialise computer data banks search sequence." Then he turned to Captain Carrot, unsure as to the approach with which to deliver the news. "Captain Carrot." he said. "It would appear that the O.S.S.S Earthanon has been struck by an ancient probe of some kind. My scanner readings indicate that it certainly belongs to an intelligent life form, and it appears to be orbiting our ship, issuing some kind of communication. I am running type and language diagnostic through the computer now."

"Are you picking up any signs of alien or known life form Spaceships in the immediate vicinity?" Asked the Captain, now pondering several questions of his own. Such as, "where the probe had originated from? Who had sent it, and why?" As Ensign Viola collated the computer information, the ship began to twist and turn in its flight path throwing the entire ship's crew violently into turmoil. Ensign Viola found himself on the floor. Gradually, pulling himself up against the Grid Finder, he began to access the new development analysis that appeared to halt the O.S.S.S Earthanon in its tracks.

As Viceroy Rhubarblatt fought with the controls at the steering column, he shouted towards the Captain, the state of the ship's power and steering systems.

"Captain Carrot I am receiving minimal power output from the drive momentum conduits. It is getting very heavy Sir. I'm fighting it, but it seems we are being pulled to a power source far greater than our engines at present, can counter- act... moving all available power resources to the main proton reactor, but it just isn't enough." panicked Viceroy Rhubarblatt.

"Captain." interrupted SO Tulipina. "The Ship's integral structure is encountering extreme pressure; now at six thousand blimits per square inch above normal, and increasing Sir. Captain, we are approaching the danger crumple zone fast. If we exceed ten thousand blimits above normal levels, we run the severe risk of imploding." Said SO Tulipina at the ships systems analyser.

"SO Tulipina," exclaimed the Captain, now thinking quickly on his feet, "give me full power increase to the deflector shields, divert the auxiliary power systems to the frontal power shields,"

"Aye, aye Sir," confirmed SO Tulipina. "Power convergence initialising now."

"Captain Carrot," interrupted Ensign Viola. "Bearing, Two, six, seven point five blimits. I am picking up an incredible power source, at best Sir, possibly an uncharted vortex, at worst, an unprecedented Voidwell of magnanimous proportions."

"Ensign Strawballis," said Captain Carrot, "convey these co-ordinates to the O.S.S Flotilla. Have them hold their positions and steer clear of this area. There is no sense in all of us going down the pan. Tell them under no circumstances should they enter this zone!" Insisted Captain Carrot fighting to protect even the crew members of the other Sun-Fleet Crew in the sector.

"Aye, aye Captain, Ensign Strawballis, on all points' communication. All ships hold positions until further notice, please acknowledge..."

Captain Carrot opened his personal channel.

"Captain Carrot to FO Potatree. Come in, over," he snapped as the pressure began to mount, his options beginning to run out. One thing was for sure, the only thing that could pluck them from the grasp of this, as yet, unknown power source was a power source to match.

"FO Potatree here, Captain. What in Bubbleonion is going on? We are being tossed around like pancakes in the galley." shouted FO Potatree.

FO Potatree," interrupted Captain Carrot, "we need you to link the calorific converters to the calorific proton reactors, do you understand me FO Potatree? I need the Califoric K Factor, now! Acknowledge please."

"Captain Carrot, Sir," shrieked a very worried FO Potatree. "I'll need to run the Calibration ratios through the computer first. It would be madness to connect them straight up without running the synchronisation sequences. It could shatter the momentum drive shaft and kill us all." Pleaded FO Potatree.

"We don't have time, FO Potatree, believe me, we either risk the link up untested or disappear into a Voidwell." Reasoned Captain Carrot.

"A Voidwell did you say?" panicked the now very distressed FO Potatree. "A Voidwell, well why didn't you say so Captain? I'll have to take a guess at the syncro speed output Captain, but... But I'm blowed if I'm buying a one way ticket to a Voidwell!"

"I have every faith in you FO Potatree; grow with the flow my friend. Confirm how long it will take?" Ordered the Captain.

"Give me three minutes Captain, just three minutes." confirmed FO Potatree.

"You have two minutes FO Potatree, or we're crushed nuts, acknowledged!"

"Aye, aye Sir, two minutes it is. FO Potatree out." As FO Potatree signed off Captain Carrot launched himself across the bridge towards Ensign Strawballis.

"On Visaid Ensign Strawballis," ordered the pensive Captain turning toward the screen.

"Aye Sir, Visaid on line now." Said Ensign Strawballis.

"Let's see what we are up against?" As the Visaid came on line, instead of conjuring up a vision of comforting assurance, on screen was a frightening void of absolute nothingness. Captain Carrot looked to the screen as he fired a rally of orders to the bridge crew.

"Ominously invisible for an incredible power source. Most disconcerting. I usually like to see the whites of their eyes before I come out fighting." He thought.

"Magnification enhancement, Strawballis. Viceroy Rhubarblatt, transverse pivotal thrusters and take your mark from FO Potatree for full thrusters engine inversion, as soon as he links in the calorific converters, jump into K factor," Captain Carrot paused briefly. "If they pulled away too quickly," he thought, "they ran the risk of ripping the O.S.S.S Earthanon apart with G force displacement. Precision was of the highest importance, demise due to failed escape was unthinkable and not the way of Organitron honour." "Viceroy Rhubarblatt, set hyperspace jump to K factor three, increase by one K at five second intervals." Said Captain Carrot as he sat at the command com strapping him-self in.

"Captain Carrot," said FO Marrowlar. "I am picking up a power surge from the Vortex epicentre. Sir, it is increasing by two point four Kilohertz per nano second, current status is one million, seven hundred fifty thousand kilohertz." FO Marrowlar punched in the data completing the computer scenario programme.

"Computer has sufficient input, Compositing data now." Confirmed the computer.

"Captain Carrot," shouted SO Tulipina. "Look at the Visaid Sir, whatever it is, it's growing!"

Captain Carrot looked up at the screen. The bridge crew looked in amazement as the Vortex started to glow with a bright white Aura. Then a mighty explosion rocked the ship again. From the centre of the explosion came an object, shooting toward them on a direct collision course, the bright white glow disappearing into the distance.

""Great Helios, Viceroy Rhubarblatt. Evasive action!" Ordered Captain Carrot, captivated by the wondrous yet frightening sight.

"I'm sorry Sir, but the steering column is, to all intensive purposes, running its own show. Frankly I'm just along for the ride." Admitted the struggling Viceroy Rhubarblatt.

"Impact in twenty seconds Captain." Confirmed FO Marrowlar, tracking the object.

"Computer simulation complete," announced the computer to the bridge of the O.S.S.S Earthanon. "Objects identified," it continued. "Trojan space probes from a previously lost race. Language traced to the lost space race Nation of Garlicazure. Objects are not loaded with any form of explosive material, Conclusion. Mayday device or warning shot from friendly partisans. Subject matter; cause of suction tract, analytical process concludes, previously uncharted Voidwell. Estimated mass spectrum of twenty six thousand starmillo's in circumference. Computer analysis complete."

Captain Carrot activated his personal channel. "Captain Carrot to FO Potatree. Where is that K factor?" shouted Captain Carrot, growing ever impatient with every second."

"Ten seconds until impact Captain." Confirmed FO Marrowlar.

"She's hooked up and on line now Sir. Use her when you will, on my mark!" said FO Potatree.

"Make ready, Viceroy Rhubarblatt." Said Captain Carrot. "Sound general alarm, Ensign Strawballis and put me on ship's com!"

"Aye Sir, on com now." Confirmed Ensign Strawballis.

"Ship's company, ship's company, brace for K factor jump." Shouted the Captain.

"Five seconds until impact Captain." Confirmed FO Marrowlar.

"Three, two, one, and on line, engage Viceroy Rhubarblatt." shouted FO Potatree.

"Three, two." Confirmed FO Marrowlar.

"Engaged." Said Viceroy Rhubarblatt. As if by magic, the O.S.S.S Earthanon jumped into hyperspace. The Trojan probe brushing the ships energy shield as she pulled herself from the Voidwell's deadly grip.

"K factor three and holding." said Viceroy Rhubarblatt.

"Nav com reads course setting free, clear and confirmed. O.S.S.S Earthanon is riding high and K Factor is aligned and fully functional, Sir."

"K Factor four, all systems on line." Confirmed Viceroy Rhubarblatt.

"Security systems confirm no damage sustained from Trojan probe Captain." Said FO Marrowlar, scanning the ship's security com.

"K factor five and clear of the Voidwell tract Captain Carrot, Sir." Said Viceroy Rhubarblatt regaining full control of the steering column.

"Ship's systems analyser confirms all systems are clear and on line, Captain."

Assured SO Tulipina, as she completed the ship's scanner.

"One quarter pulsate, Viceroy Rhubarblatt," said the Captain. "Hold position for Voidwell observation." ordered Captain Carrot, relieved at the successful conclusion of a very unsatisfactory predicament.

"Aye, aye Sir, engines one quarter pulsate, position held." confirmed Viceroy Rhubarblatt.

"Very good Viceroy Rhubarblatt, keep your eyes peeled for further probes!"

Smiled a now, relaxed Captain Carrot. "SO Tulipina full energy shields if you will, maintain until further notice.

Captain Carrot to FO Potatree." He said, falling back into his chair with a thump. "Kill the alarm please, Ensign Strawballis, down grade ship's company to blue alert." Now! Said the Captain, mopping his brow slowly.

"Aye, aye Sir. Phew!" answered Ensign Strawballis, breathing a sigh of relief.

"FO Potatree here, Captain Carrot." Followed FO Potatree's flustered response.

"Well done FO Potatree. It was a close shave, but you pulled it off."

"Pleasure Captain Carrot Sir. Just one more thing Captain." Said FO Potatree with a smug, even cocky, tone to his voice.

"Yes FO Potatree. What is it? Just name it and it will be yours."

"Next time Captain," sniggered FO Potatree. "Could you not give me a little more time to save the universe as we know it?"

"You didn't save the universe, FO Potatree, just the ship and all that sail in her." Remarked Captain Carrot, begrudgingly awaiting his response. If there was one thing that he hated, it was being in debt to the egotistical FO Potatree.

"You owe me one anyway Captain, just remember that when it comes to pay day!" Laughed FO Potatree.

"How short the memory of some can be, FO Potatree. What I will remember, come pay day, is that when I asked you to link the calorific converters, you, my fiery friend, belly-ached about the dangers of doing so. Indeed, if my mind serves me correctly, you were preparing to have me committed. Madness is the term you used, I recall. So, as I see the situation, where the Calorific Conversion link up is concerned, I had to force you to do so! Maybe I should transfer some of your pay to mine, given that I had to delegate the life saving order?" Said the Captain as the bridge crew chuckled loudly.

"N... N.. No Captain that won't be necessary, of course I was only joking Captain, as usual, I think we can all share the credit for this latest solution." Said FO Potatree nervously.

"We'll call it even then, shall we FO Potatree?" Enquired Captain Carrot.

"Oh no Captain," creeped FO Potatree. "Perhaps we should say that I am forever in your debt. Yes, for allowing me to serve under the most respected Organitron in Sun-Fleet." Continued the Chief Engineer, now crawling beyond the call of duty.

"Enough FO Potatree, I don't think I can take any more! Your pay is safe, Okay?" Cried the Captain, at pains with the infernal wittering of his good, but extremely big headed friend.

"Message received and understood, your Holy Vegmolyness, FO Potatree over and out." Quipped FO Potatree, anxious not to push the Captain towards a complete breakdown and end up being thrown in the brig house for diminished responsibilities, another terminology for fired. Captain Carrot signed the ships analyser log report book, handed to him by SO Tulipina.

"FO Marrowlar." said Captain Carrot, turning his attention towards the recent scenario put forward by the ship's computer. "Is it possible that these warning probes are actually from the lost Planet of Garlicazure, or just some dastardly plan of the Fasterfoids to spy on the O.S.S.S Earthanon? It wouldn't be the first time they had gone to such lengths to capture Sun-Fleet flagships, although it would have been the first time that they have very nearly succeeded." he continued.

"I don't think so, Captain. There is a vast amount of energy stored in the vortex of a kind as yet unseen before. No Sir, I believe there may be some relevance behind the computer's scenario. Whatever the reasoning for the probes, surely Captain, we must investigate it?" reasoned FO Marrowlar.

"Indeed we must, FO Marrowlar." Captain Carrot stopped and weighed up his options. The possibilities of discovering part of the Garlicazure culture was indeed exciting. Little did Captain Carrot and the crew of the O.S.S.S Earthanon realise, the depth of importance that lies behind the recent re-acquaintance with the alleged Space race from the past.

"Ensign Strawballis." ordered the Captain. "Get me Captains Venusio de Fleetrap of the O.S.S Capsicumby, and Pipleerer Tubain Macoronite of the O.S.S Ommelettra please. Secure channel if you will Ensign Strawballis."

"Aye Sir," confirmed Ensign Strawballis. "Ensign Strawballis to Captains de Fleetrap and Macoronite. Come in, over." Captain Carrot waited with baited breath as the O.S.S Captains returned communication transmissions with Ensign Strawballis through her communications com headset. "Captain Carrot," said Ensign Strawballis, turning towards the command com. "I have the Captains on response Sir, splitting the Visaid now. Captain Carrot, you are on line. Please proceed at will." confirmed Ensign Strawballis, scrambling the channel frequencies.

On the Visaid, appeared the Captains Macoronite and de Fleetrap. Silence prevailed awaiting the contents of the communication from Captain Carrot.

"Venusio, Pipleerer, I trust you have been monitoring the situation from your tactical positions?" Enquired the Captain.

"Yes Captain." They answered together. "You will excuse my observations Captain Carrot, but that whole situation looked a little too close for comfort!" Stated a deeply concerned Captain Macoronite. "According to our data, you have received little or no damage, please confirm Captain. Help is at hand should you require it, of course." said Captain Macoronite, an old friend of Captain Carrot.

"Thank you Pipleerer my good friend, but that will not be necessary." Captain Carrot stopped and thought of his plan and its implications to the flotilla and its protection capabilities. "Captain de Fleetrap," said Captain Carrot. "I want you to track down the second probe and capture it. When you have done so, I would like it brought back to the O.S.S.S Earthanon for carbon dating and close quarter scrutiny by Dr Goosegorgon. This could be a very important discovery. We believe they are probes sent from the lost space race of Garlicallia, from the Planet of Garlicazure. Approach with caution. There is every possibility that this is a trap." Said the Captain with a tone of respectable disbelief. He cared not to remember the false hopes offered and lost from previous discoveries of the past. "Captain Macoronite," continued Captain Carrot. "I want you to track down the first probe, but do not engage until further instructions. Let us take this opportunity to observe from a distance any rendezvous or pick up attempts from, as yet unknown life forms in this uncharted sector. You will both initiate tactical zigzag manoeuvres and place all personnel on Green alert," Captain Carrot thought deeply as the situation entered a new phase of complexity.

If it were true; if these were Mayday devices from the lost Planet of Garlicazure, and the inhabitants of the Planet were still in existence, then they could have changed their cultural make-up beyond recognition. He had to ask himself and his colleagues, two fundamental questions. "Captain's de Fleetrap, Macoronite," he commented after a brief interlude. "Great care must be taken in approaching the probes. When you do eventually bring them aboard, house the probes in isolated hangers. Better still, hold them in Gravitational chambers. Ours will be prepared and placed on standby. There is every possibility that they are not cries for help, but warning shots to stay away; they might even be Graviton activated incendiary devices. One more thing Captains," added the sceptical Captain Carrot. "At all times remember these two points. Point one; if they can expel probes from the vortex, how and why is it that they have not sent a manned shuttle to contact us. Point two," continued Captain Carrot. If it is a Mayday device for help, then is the vortex simply a larger kind of Voidwell than ever seen before? Or, is it a complicated, as yet un-encountered defence shield, made to take on the characteristics of a Voidwell? If so, then if they are holding any or all members surviving from the space race Garlicallia, we must assume that they are aware of the probe launch and may well be rallying their defence forces as we speak. This too, could explain the lacking of a manned shuttle, who knows? Whatever the reason, we must find out, and we must find out fast; if these are our long lost space relations then I'm sure I need not explain the importance, and I am sure you will agree that we must make every effort to free them from their captor or captors, whether it be elemental or unfriendly life forms. Captain Fleetrap, as soon as you have recovered the probe make your course directly back to the O.S.S.S Earthanon. Captain Peabazzare, and the crew of the O.S.S Satsumuroo, will be alerted and on standby to escort and defend your safe return. Once you have breached the O.S.S.S Earthanons defence system's range."

Captain Carrot stood up and offered the two Captains the UFO salute. "That is all, Captain's de Fleetrap, Macoronite. Go safely and return triumphant. Until then this is Captain Carrot on the bridge of the O.S.S.S Earthanon, UFO and out, ending transmission." Captain Carrot looked on as the two Captains returned the salute and disappeared from the screen. "UFO and out Captain Carrot," they said in unison, "End transmission." Captain Carrot took his place at the command com once again, with the added comfort of knowing that the top ranks of Sun-Fleet Fighter S.S Command were on the case and would leave no stone unturned to find the probes and return them to the O.S.S.S Earthanon. He knew that, short of his own, there was no better hands that the situation could be in.

"Ensign Strawballis," chirped Captain Carrot. "Get me Captain Peabazzare of the O.S.S Satsumuroo on the communications com Visaid, if you will. Then ask Professor Goosegorgon and Science Officer FO Cornelius to meet me in the anti- gravitational chamber in fifteen minutes," Captain Carrot shuddered as he thought of the next request he had to make. It wasn't that he didn't like FO Potatree. On the contrary, in fact FO Potatree was his dearest friend. It was just that Captain Carrot found himself forever in a race to beat FO Potatree in all situations that they had embarked on, purely because FO Potatree was an antagonistic, egotistical renegade of the highest order. He had been offered a Captaincy commission of an O.S.S class on many occasions, but had declined, his reason being that Engineering was where his heart lies. Both a gallant and wise decision, if that is how FO Potatree felt deep in his heart. Though personally, Captain Carrot felt FO Potatree stayed within his service to keep him on his toes, and or drive him completely insane. One thing was for sure however, FO Potatree was the best Engineer in Sun-Fleet, not to mention his uncanny knack of achieving the impossible on a regular basis. Yes, there were many occasions where FO Potatree had saved the proverbial bacon of the O.S.S.S Earthanon and her crew.

In terms of hidden weaponry arsenals, when FO Potatree's back was against the wall, his volatile fiery temper was more than a match for your average Fasterfoid Star station. "Instruct chief Engineer FO Potatree," continued Captain Carrot, "to rendezvous with us there in twenty minutes. Have him bring Ensign Broccleman with him, and Mushroid Fungola. Me thinks, my friend," said Captain Carrot turning to FO Marrowlar, "it's time to analyse the facts, weigh up our options and act swiftly, decisively and with vigour. FO Marrowlar, you will join me below decks, SO Tulipina, you have command com." Said the Captain, signing over the ship's analytical log to her.

"Captain Carrot," interrupted Ensign Strawballis, "I have Captain Peabazzare on line, will you talk to him on your personal channel?"

"No, patch him through to the Visaid; you will inform him of our plans SO Tulipina."

"Aye, aye Captain Sir, thank you." She said taking her place at the Command com module.

The bridge crew stood to attention as the Captain and FO Marrowlar de- energised the elevation chamber doors and stepped inside.

"Captain off the bridge." Announced Ensign Melonture.

"Pheweeeeee- phewoooooh." piped Ensign Rasperillo.

"Computer elevation descent level 5 section B 11."

"The gravitational chamber Sir?" enquired FO Marrowlar.

"Yes FO Marrowlar, but first, we will pay a little visit to the Widdup database sanctuary. Let's see if we can't find some sort of answer to our very large Voidwell vortex friend?"

"Well Sir," said FO Marrowlar boldly. "I do have one suggestion Sir, Perhaps we could send FO Potatree to talk to it. With respect Captain, his technical analysis on the calorific conveyance molecule could quite possibly bore it to death." Laughed FO Marrowlar. Captain Carrot smiled, and then thought of a better reason for sending FO Potatree to the Vortex epicentre.

"I don't know about that, FO Marrowlar," said Captain Carrot. "They do say, to fight fire with fire reaps logical rewards. So surely the Voidwell being a black hole of magnanimous proportions, would possibly blow itself away when being confronted with a hole the size of FO Potatree's mouth," laughed Captain Carrot. "Not to mention one of his five starmin lectures filling it with all that hot air. Holy Vegmoley FO Marrowlar, he could blow it clear away and us with it! No, seriously Benzo, we need all the help we can get. Who knows, just maybe what we need, is in the heart of the Widdup archives.

CHAPTER FOUR

Club Cappuccino / A stranger pops on-board, but, not for coffee!

In the leisure deck complex on deck 12, Viceroy Councillor Au Paw-Paw sat in the Cafe` Cappuccino lounge, enjoying a well-earned rest from the rigours of crew psycho-analysis. For some reason, the crew members were undergoing some very strange mood swings. Explaining it was beyond her, there was no particular recent reason or event that could possibly be held responsible for these strange cases of character displacement. The only unusual event that did coincide with the situation was the emergency docking of the Carrier class shuttle ship of the popular singing band, "Yam." They were hiding in the uncharted sector practising their new album release, when suddenly their ship suffered a major fault in its propulsion system. They were lucky that the Sun-Fleet Flotilla was in the sector. Otherwise they could have been stuck there forever, although they didn't feel very lucky after Captain Carrot had torn a strip off of them for being in a restricted zone without authorisation. Though she couldn't explain the current spate of personality changes, there was something in the air, but for now it had evaded her detection. She had just undergone a tedious session of therapy on the very disturbed Dr Kiwitranus, Dr Goosegorgon's assistant better known as the Goosegorgon doormat. "A very sad case," thought Viceroy Councillor Au Paw-Paw as the cafe garcon brought her a frothy chocky topped Organichinno. In her opinion, Dr Kiwitranus was undergoing extreme bouts of anxiety and paranoiac tendencies. He was convinced that Professor Goosegorgon was losing his marbles. This morning, he found Professor Goosegorgon running around the laboratory in a Macadamian straight jacket, trying to escape from its grasp.

A Macadamian straight jacket consisted of a nut shell with five holes, two for the arms, two for the legs and one for the head, sealed with a combination mind lock. Apparently, by the time Dr Kiwitranus had arrived for duty, Professor Goosegorgon had already spent some four and a half starhectoids in the jacket, and contrary to Dr Goosegorgon's reading of the situation, was no closer to escaping than when he first started. Macadamian mind locks can only be operated by a Telekinetic Macadamian, except for a few instances.

Dallying with the mad Macadamian mind, was a dangerous area of research, practised by only the strongest of minds, even then for short periods of time only. Professor Goosegorgon it seems, had mastered the art of mind transferral for locking the straight jacket, the result of which left his mind drained of any capacity or strength to reverse the process. "All was not lost!" exclaimed the weary professor. "I hav'a written the coded power translator deactivation frequency on a piece of paper." "Where is the piece of paper?" enquired Dr Kiwitranus, looking on the work surfaces. It was at this point Professor Goosegorgon's marbles appear to go awry, or, "Into another galaxy." to coin a phrase supplied by Dr Kiwitranus.

"Well," muttered a tearful Professor Goosegorgon. "It'sa in'a my blasted pocket." Which of course was denied access on two counts? The first being, that on locking the straight jacket, it constricts itself to the exact shape of the prisoners complete body surface, except for the hands, feet and head; allowing expansion and retraction only to the prisoner's respiratory wall. All bar this section hardens like steel. Secondly, the straight jacket could only be cut open with a high density diamond headed crystalline plasma jet.

The plasma jet was kept in the weapons security locker, the key to which was also in the Professor's pocket. Though there was a spare plasma jet held in the engineering's mining resource supplies department. Professor Goosegorgon pleaded with him to find another way round the problem of the plasma jet requisition. He really couldn't bare the certain indignation of FO Potatree's jibes; not at the expense of himself and his precious science organisation. Dr Kiwitranus felt however, that he had no choice, and that he and the Science department, would manage to hold their heads high through the entourage of ribbing and Mickey taking. Besides, there was a certain appeal to seeing the Organitron with the biggest head in the Solar System, deflated to a point of absolute zero.

Viceroy Councillor Au Paw-Paw jumped, as the MC startled her with the microphone on stage. MC Ramputin is a small Organitron descended from the space race Ramputainus, who lived on the Planet Rampurial, in the Fruitanutes plexus of the Bubbleonion Squeak Vegitalis before it was lost after the great explosion. MC Ramputin bellowed across the lounge with his deep tenor voice, his operatic training shining through whenever he spoke.

"Hello Organigirls and boys. Have I got some exciting news for you? Yes, I have. Due to the unfortunate failure of their momentum drive chamber in the Proton reactor, several weeks ago my special guests had to dock here, for emergency repairs before they can continue their journey to Earthanon, for a special concert to the Mining district's personnel. They are never happier than when they are on stage, and have asked if they could deliver their new number, which, they tell me is of a special significance to this cafe` which lies behind its inspiration. So much so, that they are not entirely convinced that Helios and fate, aren't working hand in hand, to ensure that Cafe` Cappuccino is the place of its first live rendition. Organigirls and boys, the visitors you will know as "Yam," the song is aptly called, "Club Cappuccino!"

Friends, please, please, please, give a huge welcome to our intergalactic masters of sound, singing for their supper the one, the only, "Yam!"

The crowd leapt into the air. Excitement spread throughout the ship as the news of their performance became common knowledge. No sooner had Viceroy Councillor Au Paw-Paw looked up from her table, and then she found the previously sparsely populated Cafe` had become a hive of activity, packed to the seams with younger generations of Organitron, anxious to hear the new sound of the popular "Yam."

Suddenly the lights dimmed, and on stage two spotlights beamed onto the two Organi legends of rock and pop. An amazing backdrop of laser beams shot across the cafeteria turning the crowd Technicolor.

"Thank you Organigirls and boys, we hope that you enjoy this, after all, it was because of this place that it was born. It was all of you that gave it meaning and substance. So loosen your tunics and let down your hair as we give you the one and only "Club Cappuccino." A one, a two, a one, two, three, and hit it!"

(Club Cappuccino)

**Let me shake you in the place where membership's a smiling face,
Rub shoulders with the stars.
Where strangers take you by the cup, percolate and fill you up,
From beneath the Planet Mars.**

**Club Cappuccino grinds your beans,
Fun sun, Froth time there's enough for everyone.
Whoo all that's missing is the cream,
But don't worry you can Latte' eh, eh.**

**Laughter waves and lovers meet, then kiss in the cup of dreams,
Watch the stars shine over head.
Oh, close your eyes, see the blue lagoon,
Boogie on down to the summer tune.
Dream you're on a holiday.**

**Club Cappuccino grinds your beans,
Fun sun, froth time, there's enough for everyone.
Whoo all that's missing is the cream,
But don't worry you can Latte' eh, eh.**

**Club Cappuccino grinds your beans,
Fun sun, froth time, there's enough for everyone.
Whoo all that's missing is the cream,
But don't worry you can Latte' eh, eh.**

**Pack your bags, gonna leave tonight,
Gotta take your time.
We wanna brew you through the mists of life.
Pack your bags, we grinding out tonight,
Gotta take your time, gonna brew you through the mists of life.**

**Club Cappuccino grinds your beans,
Fun sun, froth time, there's enough for everyone.
Whoo all that's missing is the cream,
But don't worry you can Latte' eh, eh.**

Coffeeeeeeeh... Coffeeeeeeeh... Coffeeeeeeeh.

As the music played, the massive group gathered, in the Cafe` Cappuccino, danced and swayed to the music of the hour. Viceroy Councillor Au Paw-Paw, found herself jumping onto her table and strutting her funky stuff to the irresistible beat that had hijacked her feet. She hadn't realised it, but, this was just the kind of therapy she needed. Not that she was running away from reality, just taking a break from the hum drum pressures of the needs of many, striving to fulfil and pacify the needs of the one.

This was a break in her hectic schedule that she could ill afford, but found impossible to resist. After the band had finished, Viceroy Councillor Au Paw-Paw's personal com activated.

"Ensign Broccleman to Viceroy Councillor Au Paw-Paw, come in please."

"Viceroy Councillor Au Paw-Paw here. Yes Ensign Broccleman, what can I do for you?"

"Excuse me Viceroy councillor Au Paw-Paw, but we have a little bit of a mystery down here in the Vegitamisation room, I think you ought to come and take a look!" Answered Ensign Broccleman sheepishly.

"Well, don't leave me just hanging there Ensign Broccleman, what sort of a mystery is it?"

"Surely if I could explain that Viceroy Councillor Au Paw-Paw, I would have! All I can tell you is, that an Organi being Vegitamised onto the ship two starmins ago, and by the looks of him, he is none too healthy. Dr Kiwitranus is here giving him a thorough examination. Councillor, he was conscious when he arrived but all he said before he passed out was." Ensign Broccleman paused, ensuring that he got the message straight. "If there is anyone that can help me," he continued. "Viceroy Councillor Au Paw-Paw will see to it. One more thing Viceroy Councillor Au Paw-Paw, he is wearing shackles, Macadamian shackles." added Ensign Broccleman.

"I am on my way, you will be transferring him to the Medilab I assume?" She enquired, flummoxed as to who the strange visitor could be.

"Indeed Viceroy Councillor Au Paw-Paw, Dr Kiwitranus is standing by to receive him." He said.

"Viceroy Councillor Au Paw-Paw out." she said.

"Ensign Broccleman out." he confirmed.

Entering the Medilab some minutes later, the look on her face showed a mixture of several emotions pity, affection and dislike, but at least she knew who it was.

"My Helios what are you doing here you silly Organiman? And who has done this to you?" Then holding his hand she turned to Dr Kiwitranus. "What do you make of him Dr Kiwitranus, what's his condition?" She said looking closely at the new passenger's body markings.

"What I know about him judging by the look on your face, is not as much as you would appear to know. If that is the case, then I will allow you to fill me in on his personal details. As for his condition, well, let's just say he is very lucky to have made it here alive. He is suffering almost zero levels of Photo synthesis traces indicating a prolonged withdrawal of rejuvenation. The shackles would indicate that he was held against his will. Due to the nature of Macadamian shackles it has caused abrasions of the skin and secondary Vegimatter contusions. He was conscious but inaudible really, we are not even sure the message was correct." concluded Dr Kiwitranus.

"Will he be Okay Dr Kiwitranus?" asked Viceroy Councillor Au Paw-Paw.

Dr Kiwitranus walked around the table and scanned his vital signs. "To be absolutely honest with you Viceroy Councillor Au Paw-Paw, I don't know. It would appear that this is not the first time that our friend here has endured rejuvenation withdrawal, there is a lot of scar tissue here. I can't even tell you if he is young enough to be strong enough to pull through this. The only thing I can confirm at this stage, is that unless he gets stronger he will never make it through the rejuvenation process. All I can do at this stage, is induce plasma photosynthesina and monitor him closely." Dr Kiwitranus looked sad as he passed on the news. Viceroy Councillor Au Paw- Paw, was obviously fond of him, who-ever he was, but he could not provide any certain hope and he disliked that, very much.

"Can you tell me anything about him councillor? It might help" asked the Doctor.

"He is an old," Viceroy Councillor Au Paw-Paw paused at odds with her own opinion. "Patient. He is forty-seven Startechtoids old and goes by the name of Pirate Milnedew. But his real name is Kenthal Marrowmilne. Ex co-pilot of the cargo ship CS Mickymustard." she answered slowly.

"A Pirate, I had better alert security?" said a jumpy Dr Kiwitranus.

"Yes, but not because he in himself is dangerous, you see he is a self exiled Pirate. He has had a rough time already, and it looks like it got rougher. But a pirate he wishes to be and we should respect that. Captain

Carrot would extend him the rights of a Pirate, if he so wished." Viceroy Councillor Au Paw-Paw moved to leave the Medilab and shortly before de-energising the doors turned and faced Dr Kiwitranus.

"Oh Dr Kiwitranus, you will let me know if anything changes, and don't let anyone talk to him, for his own sake, do you understand?" she asked politely.

Dr Kiwitranus agreed and began mixing a solution for the inducer tract. "As soon as there is any change Viceroy Councillor Au Paw-Paw, you can be sure I will inform you straight away." he reassured her.

"Thank you Dr Kiwitranus. Oh, and Doctor." she remembered something that Dr Kiwitranus ought to know. "Remember please, that although he is a technical criminal, it is only punishment of himself by himself. Please make sure that security is tucked around the corner and discreet, and kept to a bare minimum. Oh, and one more thing." she continued. "If he does come round and you consider feeding him, whatever you do, he must consume nothing from the Planets of Macadamia and Garlicazure cultures in any form or fashion!"

Dr Kiwitranus acknowledged her request with a smile and said.

"You really care about him don't you?"

"Only by way of profession Doctor, nothing more and nothing less, let's just say, that particular Organiman needs all the friends that he can get." she confirmed.

"And the Vegimatter food allergies, are they life threatening or not." enquired Dr Kiwitranus.

"Not to him, you had better remember that. I'll explain properly later. Then she was gone, leaving a very confused and slightly worried Dr Kiwitranus behind her. However, to her, a very confused and slightly worried Dr Kiwitranus was quite usual. "Alas, bless his little cottons." she whispered on her way.

CHAPTER FIVE

Garlicazure or bust, where Veggie-angels fear to tread.

Captain Carrot and FO Marrowlar stopped outside a large crystal cut door. It had the appearance and markings of a large opaque nutshell. "Quiet a rare sight in a naturally formed crystal," thought FO Marrowlar as they entered the cosmic passage that scanned them walking through its safety net sensors. The only person that can activate the Widdup database Sanctuary, is the Captain of each ship; a Mother ship that is and that Captain must seek permission for others to enter. FO Marrowlar stood watching in awe of the door as Captain Carrot placed his hand in the crystal cocoon. It scanned his fingerprints using a gas configuration scent detector, the hardest DNA detection lock that was ever naturally formed. Formed, believe the Organitron, from a cross-breed consisting of what you will know as a Venus fly trap, and Oyster Vegimatters, giving birth to a device able to detect a person by their odour and pulse configuration.

As the cocoon tested the operators scent it bound itself around their wrist, ready to pierce the skin with its internal, tiny, sharp hair-like teeth, laced with a noxious substance. If the operator's dual signature analysis was successful, then the third and final signature specimen would be required. Failure in any of the three tests activated the Widdup defence mechanism, rendering death instantaneously, supposedly, though no-body had ever seen fit to find out. If the last thing you remembered was the voice recognition test then, well, you didn't make it.

"Speak to me and you will see, if to my chamber, you may enter." said the voice of the Sanctuary Guardian to Captain Carrot

Captain Carrot spoke slowly as he recited the entry sequence.

"Captain Carrot to Widdup the wise. Let me into the sanctuary mind. With me there is but one, Officer Status; a Sun-Fleet son."

Only Captains and top tier Officers were allowed access to the Widdup chronicles stored in the heart of the Widdup, the archive seed of knowledge. Their contents were filled with history and facts pertaining to the Organitron existence from the earliest possible dates. These were stored in the form of a crystal dialysis consul in which pictorial libraries are stored and housed for independent crisis consultations. Suddenly, Captain Carrot and FO Marrowlar were beamed into the sanctuary, which was filled with a mist, billowing from the floor to the ceiling. In its centre, appeared the image of the wise Prophet Widdup, seated upon an orange throne carved from the rare Templevegarial Asteroid Plato. The wise Prophet started addressing his inquisitors.

"You have activated the Widdup chronicles, assume one must, that you are faced with a problem of extreme complexity. Before you, are the crystals of knowledge. In them you may find the answers to your quandary, but, be prepared to accept receipt of no answers at all. I can only guide with honesty and integrity. Facts of a certain nature set by a previous precedent or occurrence, I can convey. But inventive reasoning is neither prudent, nor wise, and could only lead to false hopes or conclusion. Tell me I prey," he said almost thoughtfully. "What be the nature of your quest?" asked Widdup still staring at the floor, his face half hidden by the hood which draped over his head.

"We seek information of a strange power source, the likes of which we have never seen before. We believe we have encountered its characteristics on previous occasions. The subject matter is one of a Voidwell; a black hole of incredible proportions. It is possible that within its grasp, is the lost Planet of Garlicazure." Captain Carrot looked at FO Marrowlar as Widdup remained silent.

"Could it be that he's fallen asleep Captain?" Asked a confused FO Marrowlar.

"I hardly think that a hologram programme has the need for such luxuries as sleep FO Marrowlar." Whispered Captain Carrot.

Widdup's head lifted without warning, his eyes burning with a bright turquoise and yellow inferno, like a dancing flame on a spring bed of magnesium.

FO Marrowlar felt the capability of breath, denied from his usual bodily functions as the splendour of the Sanctuary, left him gasping with anticipation. He had never seen, or been inside the Widdup Sanctuary. He wasn't sure whether he was frightened or amazed at the spectacle before him.

"Look to the crystal of lost souls," hailed Widdup, eagerly pointing to the ceiling. "There you may find guidance in your quest? Remember, look not too deep and you will struggle, look too hard and you are blind!"

Captain Carrot looked around the chamber. Thousands of crystals surrounded them. None of them marked, all of them similar, many of them out of reach. Widdup the wise, now staring right through them, remained silent. Widdup was born to the space race Farinaree, on the Planet Cannelona, from the cluster of Planets known as the Farinaree quad, of the Vegitalis plexus. This consisted of five Planets. Pasta dejour, Eggolarus, Lasagnitro, Noodledaddoo and Cannelona. A collection of races known for their wisdom, their telekinetic vulnerability and their broken, spoken speech, their nickname being the Riddler's.

"Where might I find the crystal of lost souls?" Enquired Captain Carrot.

The Prophet Widdup closed his eyes and placed his forefingers on his temples.

"Hold out your hand and look to your heart. Close your eyes as your mind you start then the crystal you will find. Place it in the consul and you will see, all of its secrets now think with me." Droned the Widdup Wise, deep in concentration. FO Marrowlar became nervous as the chamber sank into complete darkness, his knees knocking gently under the strain of his nervous bulky frame. On the ceiling above their heads, a crystal started to pulsate with a yellow and red intermittent beam. Captain Carrot, held out his hand whilst his mind linked with the hologram, Widdup. The crystal began to float through the air and headed straight for the hand of the entranced Captain. It hovered momentarily over his palm sending a soothing, warming sensation through his arm. Silently it came to rest in his grasp. Captain Carrot opened his eyes as the Prophet Widdup began to fade into nothingness.

"Remember," said the Prophet. "The answers that you seek may not be held within the crystals, but in your mind. I have taken the details of the scenario that you now face. Your answers will be documented at a later stage, however it resolves? Those who will enquire in the future, will have the benefit of your experiences, and unlike you, need not work in the dark or suffer the hardships of the blind. Good luck, and may Helios guide you to the path of success, for if success is the path that you enter, then you will truly have found light in your destiny."

With that Widdup the Wise was gone, and the chamber returned to a low, comforting, incandescent glow. Out from the floor, came a column of orange rock with one tube outlet prominent in its singularity. Captain Carrot placed the crystal in the tube outlet. Silence fell on them as they waited patiently. In front of them, a three dimensional vision appeared in the form of a brain.

"Who seeks consultation with the crystal of lost souls?" Said a voice emanating from nowhere.

"Captain Gillespie J. Carrot of the O.S.S.S Earthanon. I have come to you seeking information on all previous encounters of unexplained power sources, Power sources in the nature of a Voidwell."

"You are not alone?" said the voice inquisitively.

"No," said Captain Carrot pensively. "I have with me, my First Officer FO Benzo Marrowlar..." he continued but, before he could speak any further, a crack of thunder drowned his voice and with that thunder came a vision of an ancient Sun-Fleet Ship accompanied by a monologue statement.

"In the Veralis minor, sector 27 **Sundate 2.329,417,731/ 125 Biltechtoids.** Captain Thadius Watercreisure of the O.S.S Sorbet Verbena, came under the grip of an unexplained power source. His ship and its entire crew were consumed by the power source, disappearing without a trace. Here are the last transcript communications from Captain Thadius Watercreisure and his gallant crew." Captain Carrot and FO Marrowlar's heads were hung low as the voice of the ill- fated vessel's Captain delivered his last known monologue.

"This is Captain Thadius Watercreisure of the O.S.S Sorbet Verbena. **Sundate 2.329,417,731/ 125 Biltechtoids, time 21.50 starhectoids.** Captain's log, entry 14795. 043. I expect this to be the last entry of the Captain's log for the Organitron Sun Ship Sorbet Verbena. We are still in the grip of the, as yet unknown, power source that is gradually pulling us into the epicentre of its massive expanse. All attempts have failed to pull clear of the suction tract. My Chief Engineer, Zachary Banaldos, has just informed me that the Vitamin reactor is approaching dangerous levels of radiation fatigue.

The ship is starting to creek as we approach, what can only be assumed the final leg of our journey. We have tried every known solution within our power to defeat this, this, unknown entity from the dark side. Molecular dispensation, nuclear explosive charges, even as a last straw, gas pocket mines laced with a deadly cocktail of chemicals, but, to no avail. No matter what we throw at it; it seems to take with no damage to its formation. On the contrary; it expands and tightens its grip with every attempt.

We are minutes away from death, and, I only hope this probe reaches you intact." The figure in the vision stopped; gathering strength and delivered his last Sun-Fleet duty to his race with pride. Passing into the new and uncertain journey with tenacity and honour, but with a fair compliment of regret at the passing and hope that they would be going to a better place, known in Organitron history books as "Composture" or, "Helios's half way house," until such time that they are rejuvenated through the wisdom of the Templevegarial, and the Seed Vault Covenant.

"I hope that nobody ever bears witness to this untameable phenomenon again. The more one tries to flee its deadly grip, the more certain our future seems to be." Captain Watercreisure began coughing as the bridge was overcome with smoke.

"We are.. Ahh.. Ahhh... Ahhh., we are shaking violently now. The ship cannot take much more of this, so, I will end this transmission to ensure that the probe has a chance to make it safely. This is Captain Thadius Watercreisure and the gallant crew of the O.S.S Sorbet Verbena, UFO and out. May Helios be with you. "Our love and thoughts to all our loved ones. End transmission."

Captain Carrot and FO Marrowlar stood in a cold and uncomfortable silence. The feeling of helplessness sending shivers of frustration down the spines of the two Officers, quite used to facing demise on a regular basis.

"What did they go through in those final desperate stages?" whispered FO Marrowlar, the lump in his throat swelling beyond reasonable proportions as he fought back the tears.

"I cannot pretend to know, Benzo," answered Captain Carrot slowly. "It would take a better, but less fortunate man to know! He said thoughtfully. "But we must.." he continued, as he wiped his eyes. "We must thank and salute them for their bravery in sending this information back to our race. In here lies a clue of what we are up against. I mean truly up, Benzo, I.. I. feel it in my bones, more importantly, a clue on how to beat this incredible force." Said Captain Carrot, pacing back and forth.

"I am sorry Captain Carrot, but were we both watching the same thing? Captain, Sir, don't get me wrong, I saw bravery and I do thank them, but unless I fell asleep during some point of the play back, I'm afraid I missed any element of clues capable of helping us through this predicament!" admitted a vague FO Marrowlar, his mind visibly trying to re-run the hologram, but, to no avail.

"With all due respect FO Marrowlar, your mind is being blanked by the pain of the crew of the O.S.S Sorbet Verbena. If and when you accept your own commission as Captain of a Sun-Fleet ship, you must learn to harness the powers of a sixth sense. Let's run it again and take a transcript copy. Captain Thadius Watercreisure didn't know it, but, he may just have stumbled on the solution to our problem." Said Captain Carrot, excited by the thought that crossed his mind.

"Whatever you say Captain. I only wish I could see where you are coming from?" observed FO Marrowlar.

"You will FO Marrowlar. All will be revealed my friend, all will be revealed!" he said, a wry smile crossing the face of the now somehow, fearless but not complacent Captain Carrot. "Remember Benzo, "Look too deep and you are blind." Said Captain Carrot as he played back the transcript in his mind.

FO Cornelius sat in the Gravitational anti-chamber room. As he gazed through the plasma steel wall into the hanger that was to house the recovered probe, the doors behind him de-energised and in bounced Professor Goosegorgon.

"Yo, FO Cornelius, what is 'a the situation, do we hav'a the probe yet?" he said splatting to rest at FO Cornelius's feet.

"Hatchooo," sneezed FO Cornelius. "High... ah... aha." he murmured, as his knee flew in the air. "No Professor Goosegorgon, the O.S.S Ommelettra has picked up the probe and is returning as we speak, ETA four starmins."

"Boy, this is 'a exciting no?" screamed Professor Goosegorgon. "Just imagine, the lost space race of 'a Garlicazure are 'a back in'a the fold of their loved ones..." he continued.

"Professor Goosegorgon," interrupted FO Cornelius. "Your excitement is understandable, but, I implore you, contain it within its correct perimeter. For all we know the probe is a trap. Maybe it was sent in a vain hope thousands, millions of years ago. Please, don't store too much hope in it; at least until we know for sure what or who we are dealing with." he continued.

At that point, Captain Carrot and FO Marrowlar entered the gravitational suite suited up for space walk conditions.

"FO Cornelius, Professor Goosegorgon," said Captain Carrot. "I would like you to join us in the Gravitational chamber. You will find suits in the space lockers. FO Potatree will operate the mechanical arm from this bay consul. If anything goes wrong, he will seal this bay and take command of the ship. Any questions?" he asked looking around the Gravitational suite, double checking that everything was as it should be. Silence prevailed as Captain Carrot's personal channel came on line.

"Ensign Broccleman to Captain Carrot. Come in please."

"Carrot to Broccleman. Yes Ensign Broccleman, what is it?"

"The O.S.S Ommelettra is making her final approach Captain. ETA two starmins Sir, I am on my way to the Gravitational chamber with Mushroid Fungola now Captain." confirmed Ensign Broccleman.

"Ensign Broccleman there has been a change of plan. I want you to take Mushroid Fungola to the Vegimatter room, via the bridge to collect a transcript document from SO Tulipina. She is expecting you. When you have it, I want you to run it through the Vegimatter room Computer. Run a full frame-by-frame diagnostic and voice clarification enhancer sequence. Once those are completed, run the finished transcript analysis into Mushroid Fungola's data banks. I want to see if the ship's battle tactician expert can come up with a plausible plan to beat this Voidwell, and rescue the Planet Garlicazure from its deadly grip." ordered Captain Carrot.

"Aye, aye Captain. I'm on my way." confirmed Ensign Broccleman.

"Carrot out."

FO Potatree came into the gravitational suite with his usual fervour, abound with a sense of urgency immediately taking his place at the bay consul.

"All right, the most important man is here, Ahh.., Captains excluded." he said noting the Captain's presence. "You may begin Organimen." he continued. "Weight station chamber room at normal gravity; pressure lock released."

A small room in between the plasma steel wall and the Gravitational chamber, lit up and the door opened. Captain Carrot and his team stepped into the room as FO Potatree sealed the pressure lock behind them.

"Dropping Gravitational chamber to nil pounds per square inch," he announced through their headsets. "Communications check please Captain?"

Captain Carrot tapped his space helmet. "Carrot to Potatree." "Check." said FO Potatree.

"Marrowlar to Potatree?" Said FO Marrowlar.

"Check."

"Goosegorgon to Potato brain." laughed Professor Goosegorgon.

"Check, you great green lump of acidulous bitter twist." quipped FO Potatree.

"Cornelius to Potatree." Sniggered FO Cornelius. "Hatchooo.. Ah.. Hatchooo."

"Check, mind you don't blow your brains out now, FO Cornelius, not that it would make too much mess if you did!" said FO Potatree.

"Viceroy Rhubarblatt to FO Potatree, come in; over." said Viceroy Rhubarblatt, operating the steering column on the bridge.

"FO Potatree here Viceroy Rhubarblatt, acknowledge."

"Chief Potatree, the O.S.S Ommelettra is slowing to one quarter pulsate. ETA, one starmin." confirmed Viceroy Rhubarblatt.

"Very good. Viceroy Rhubarblatt, bring us about starboard, seventeen blimits and hard flank to her approach."

"Seventeen blimits and holding chief. Handing over docking sequence to Ensign Viola. This is Viceroy Rhubarblatt, UFO and out."

"Ensign Viola to Chief Potatree, docking sequence on the mark at forty five starsecs." said the Ensign, monitoring the O.S.S Ommelettra's approach on the tractor beam radar.

"Are you following the transmissions Captain Carrot?" asked FO Potatree.

"Yes, carry on FO Potatree. You seem to have everything under control. We are ready for de-gravitization." confirmed Captain Carrot.

"Initialising Vacuum chamber to the anti-suite now." confirmed FO Potatree.

"Hold on to your heads chap's. Anything bearing a great weight on your mind, is about to be lifted." laughed Captain Carrot, as they started to float in the air.

"Hatchooo, here we go." Sniffled FO Cornelius nervously.

"Dis is 'a my favourite part of working in space, weightlessness it mak'sa my whole body tingle with excitement, no Capatano, Oooh.. Ooh." Screamed Professor Goosegorgon with excitement bouncing off the walls. "Wheeeeeee..."

"Personally, I find the whole experience of working in the Gravity chamber rather disturbing, nauseating even. If Organiman were meant to fly through the air, Helios would have deemed it fit to give us wings." **"Bang."** "Ow! See what I mean?"

"This is Captain Pipleerer Tubain Macoronite of the O.S.S Ommelettra to FO Potatree of the O.S.S.S Earthanon, come in please."

"This is FO Potatree of the O.S.S.S Earthanon to Captain Macoronite of the O.S.S Ommelettra, reading you loud and clear." confirmed FO Potatree.

"FO Potatree, we are in positional tract of our final approach and requesting permission and directions to land the probe." enquired Captain Macoronite.

"Captain Macoronite, your delivery position lies dead ahead. Opening the bay doors now. Observe, Starboard section, lower aft Gravitational chamber. Please confirm sighting and compliance?"

"Observed and compliance acknowledged." said Captain Macoronite.

"I will intercept your laser tract at zero feet with the Mechanical arm Captain. Have you experienced any form of electrical or plasma emissions from the probe?" said FO Potatree as the great doors opened before them.

The bridge crew of the O.S.S Ommelettra could be seen clearly, and as the probe was just emerging from her Gravitational hanger. FO Potatree moved the mechanical arm into position and awaited the arrival of the mysterious probe.

"No FO Potatree, we have been scanning the probe since it came out of the Vortex. There have been no forms of power emissions at all, except of course for the original vitamin fuel specifications detected earlier." established Captain Macoronite, punching in the information requirements from his ship's systems analyser.

"Thank you Captain Macoronite, Interception in fifteen seconds," acknowledged FO Potatree. "Captain Carrot. As soon as the probe is in the Gravitational hanger, I will run a ship's scanner programme on her Diamatrixalisation construction for explosive elements and bacterial traces. Ten seconds to interception." he confirmed interrupting his flow. "Then I will bring her in and release the partitional net so that you may make a closer examination, Sir."

"Excellent FO Potatree, and remember, steady as she goes. If she is packed with any little surprises, the slightest knock could trigger her mechanisms. Organimen, synchronise scanners, on no account touch the probe until we are sure of its implications to the safety of this ship!"

"Aye, aye Captain." they retorted collectively.

"Five seconds to interception, three, two, one." Confirmed FO Potatree, as he manoeuvred the mechanical hand onto one of the probe's astral antenna. "Control affirmative, Captain Macoronite. Release laser tract now!" Said FO Potatree.

The incandescent blue beam that held the probe in harness, retracted back towards the O.S.S Ommelettra, then, disappeared without a trace.

"FO Potatree you have control. Permission to vacate immediate defence range?" asked Captain Macoronite, eager to free his ship from the potential catastrophe that was now in the possession of the O.S.S.S Earthanon.

"Affirmative Captain Macoronite, you are cleared for departure. One quarter pulsate if you will. No sense in rocking the boat at this stage of the game."

"This is Captain Pipleerer Tubain Macoronite of the O.S.S Ommelettra, signing off. Good luck Captain Carrot, FO Potatree."

"This is Captain Carrot. Thank you for your assistance Captain Macoronite, we can take it from here."

"Pleasure Captain Carrot. You will keep me posted as to what you find won't you?" asked Captain Macoronite.

"You bet Pipleerer. If you see a bright light shooting past at anytime now, prey that it's a shooting star or a comet, and not some part of the O.S.S.S Earthanon." Laughed Captain Carrot signing off. "This is Captain Carrot UFO and out, end transmission."

"Captain Pipleerer Tubain Macoronite, UFO and out, transmission end."

FO Potatree, pulled back the probe into the centre of the Gravitational chamber, as the O.S.S Ommelettra pulled away from the O.S.S.S Earthanon.

"Closing bay doors now Captain Carrot." Slowly, the thick pressurised doors sealed the probe into the chamber, as the bay consul sounded the all clear for the Captain and his team to enter. "Releasing the safety net partition now!" Said FO Potatree, as the door in front of the team opened into the Gravitational chamber.

"Well," said FO Marrowlar. "There is no going back now, it's simply do or die." he continued.

"Hatchooo... Hatchooo. Please FO Marrowlar, could you not find a little less dramatic way of expressing yourself?" questioned FO Cornelius as he floated into the main chamber.

"That was my less dramatic way of self expression FO Cornelius. No point in making a pretty picture out of a "Black hole," that would not be logical." Observed FO Marrowlar, chuckling away to himself...

"There you go again, Hatchooo. Black hole, why did you have to mention the "Black hole?" Screamed FO Cornelius, fighting off his nervous affliction. "Ha-ha.. Ahh.. Hatchooo." again filling the inside of his space helmet with a fine spray of mist. Captain Carrot approached slowly and moved toward the control panel at the top of the spherical probe. Scanning it carefully, he called FO Potatree on his personal Channel.

"Carrot to Potatree." he said.

"Potatree to Captain Carrot. Yes Sir, what is it?" he enquired whispering at an almost inaudible level.

"Run Visaid surveillance and record all communication transcripts. If anything goes wrong, you will have it all on the Compulog!"

"Tis already running Sir, rest assured." said FO Potatree, his voice sinking lower.

"Thank you FO Potatree; but why are you whispering? It is difficult enough trying to understand you at the best of times." giggled Captain Carrot.

"I'm sorry Captain, tis just nervous tension I guess." he said with embarrassment drowning his voice.

"All scanners are clear of any molecular disturbances Captain," confirmed FO Marrowlar.

"Do you have any visible signs of bacterial presence known, or, unknown Professor Goosegorgon?" asked Captain Carrot.

Professor Goosegorgon continued sweeping the probe for bacterial traces, but, there did not appear to be anything on the outside of the probe. On the inside however, there was a different story to be told.

"She, is 'a clean an 'a clear on the outside Capatano, but," Professor Goosegorgon stopped as if he had been stunned by a blazer gun.

"But what Professor?" asked Captain Carrot tentatively.

"W.. W.. Well Capatano," he stammered, "is 'a not living; but is 'a not dead." said a mystified Professor Goosegorgon. "I am picking up signs of a micro molecule in the form of an anti-Vegimatter substance." he continued. "Capatano, I believe what we have here, is 'a the very early stages of a Garlicallian seedling. In some kind of, Bio-generic Cryogenic halted state of growth!" Said Professor Goosegorgon, agog at the conclusion in his head.

"Great compost Professor; if your suspicions are correct, then we really could be on the brink of discovering our lost ancestors of Garlicazure!"

"Captain Carrot, Sir, the computer has matched the probe to an endeavour class of probe, from Trojan descent, the kind specifically used by Garlicazure Sun-Fleet generation Warrior class fighters." Confirmed FO Marrowlar.

"Here is the activation point of entry Captain." Interrupted FO Cornelius.

"This first Syncro switch activates the onboard communications depot storage house. A sort of data processing bank of information. The second Syncro switch operates the pre-set course logging device. The third I believe, operates the internal chamber capsule." Confirmed FO Cornelius.

"That's all very well, but how do we open her up, FO Cornelius? There are no control buttons or switches, just the strange hieroglyphics you call Syncro switches, the likes of which I have never seen before. How do you open them?" asked Captain Carrot, at a loss for any logical suggestions.

"I don't know Captain Carrot, I have never seen one before either. It too, is a mystery to me." Admitted FO Cornelius.

"I think I have the answer," said FO Potatree. "My uncle used to tell me stories of Garlicazure and its space race. When I was a child."

"Not so long ago then FO Potatree," sniggered the Professor. "Stories eh, fables will supply us with 'a the answers only science can understand." laughed Professor Goosegorgon, interrupting FO Potatree.

"Professor Goosegorgon," snapped Captain Carrot. "If, as you say, science can only understand this problem with which we are faced, then why have you not reached any conclusions of your own. Sometimes, it can be argued, that we look too deeply into problematical situations. Perhaps, creating complexity to service our need for scientific reasoning. If the answer does lie simply in a fable, then so be it. Carry on FO Potatree, we are all ears." Reasoned Captain Carrot, leaving Professor Goosegorgon's ears, somewhat smarting from the Captain's verbal dressing down.

"Well Sir, as I say, they were only stories, but, if it might help. While there is a chance then, well, what have we got to lose? As you know, all Organitron space races have, in the past, suffered at the hands of their own vanity, but none more so, than the Garlicallian race themselves. Vanity was the largest downfall of the Planet Garlicazure. As we all know from our space race friends the Garlicallian, they are rather proud of their somewhat pungent odour. Thankfully however, rules and regulations of Sun-Fleet, have curtailed the odour output, due to the situation of shared space and cross cohabitation. Many Biltechtoids ago, when internal wars were common place amongst the space races of Organitron, the Planet Garlicazure's atmosphere was so dense with the artificial perfume, that nobody could bare to live there. This meant a great deal to them. They didn't have to share with anybody, and even less were they concerned with the possibilities of invasion. After all, no-one with all their faculties about them would even dream of moving towards its airspace, let alone the Planet itself.

Therefore, the only threat to their Nation was from the Fasterfoids, or, the mad Macadamian space race." laughed FO Potatree, as a vision of the Macadamian hermit race landing on the notoriously whiffy Planet alongside the equally irritating Fasterfoids, brought only pictures of chaos and doom to his mind. "The story goes like this." he continued. "Are you all floating comfortably? Good then I shall begin. Once upon a time, the leader of the Garlicallian space race, before the United Foliage of

Organitron was formed, known as King Pongo P Garlicphewy, decided in his ultimate wisdom, that the Bubbleonion Squeak Solar System should be entirely ruled, by the Garlicazure Council. They formed a devious plan, to gradually extend the boundaries of their atmosphere, by launching the newly designed endeavour probes by their thousands. Then surrounding all the other Organitron Planets, by leaving the probes hovering above their atmospheres. As the Garlicallians expected, each Planet sent up Warrior class Star Fighters to intercept the probes, with orders to monitor them until the Premier Seed Consul had decided what course of action to take. Quite rightly, in their ultimate wisdom, they decide to bring them back to the planetary surfaces for closer examination, under vacuum held conditions, for fear of bacterial contamination, you see.

At the time, these probes had never been seen before. The general consensus of opinion was, that they were possibly probes from an, as yet, unknown life form, trying to make contact through these strange new devices. The first Planet to bring home the probes did so, because the Organitron races in general, could not gain access to the probe due to the strange Syncro switches. The theory was of course, that they were somehow operated by mind transferral locking systems. This made it a natural assumption on the part of the, then quite reasonable Macadamian race, that they should be the first to crack the codes of the strange new probes.

Little did they know what lay in store for them, or, how it would affect their minds. Turning them into a nation of paranoid schizophrenics, untrusting forever more, of their previously friendly allies. Allies with whom they had forged great friendships, choosing to adopt a reclusive lifestyle that would remain a situation never changed to this date."

"Hyaaaaaa... Hahaa..." yawned the Professor. "Dis is 'a all very interesting FO Potatree, but tell me, does this, fable, have an ending?"

"Ahh but professor, the fable continues," said FO Potatree waving his finger determined not to be thrown off his track. Never changed to the Macadamians' that is. Not for the lack of our trying to heal the rift. However, I digress. The Macadamians brought the probes back under zero gravity conditions. Fearful of dangerous bacterial contamination, they tried for many Starlectoids to operate the Syncro switches by using their tried and tested methods of mind over matter, with no results. Eventually they gave up, deciding that the probes presented no bacterial dangers to the inhabitants of Macadamia.

The decision was made to de-activate the Gravitational chambers and destroy the probe by way of an Ionised laser. As soon as the chamber reached normal planetary gravity levels, the probe started to activate. The third Syncro switch, began turning in an anti-clockwise direction, then, a core lifted itself from the probe and began circling the chamber. Finally, it just hung in the middle of the chamber, emitting, some kind of strange sequence of lights mixed with an ensemble of, high pitched acoustic blips. The Macadamians decided to bring all four of the retrieved probes into a normal gravitational environment, mistakenly thinking that they had somehow made contact with the still, supposedly friendly life form.

As they had expected, the remaining three probes activated in exactly the same way. Whilst the Macadamians set to the task of breaking the thought-coded language sequence, the four core elements had a different agenda to follow. Several hours after their initial release, the cores began exuding the pungent perfume of Garlicazure, as did the internal chamber capsules that were housed in the probes themselves." FO Potatree began laughing so loudly, that he found it difficult to contain himself. Within seconds he became a blubbering, gibbering and uncontrollable wreck on the floor of the bay control room.

Though the others were not in complete ownership of the facts, they understood only too well the affects of the Garlicazure atmosphere on a well balanced Organitron, let alone the now nutty, eccentric race of the Macadamian Nation. They too found it hard not to snigger at the egotistical mind-bending hermit's downfall. Pulling himself together, FO Potatree finished the fable leaving the final decision to Captain Carrot. "Well Captain, the perfume drove them nuts. They couldn't wait to get out of there.

Apparently, the contents of just four probes, contaminated a little under one third of the Planet. Why; they couldn't even step on the ground that was contaminated for over two hundred Startechtoids. So, you can understand I suppose, why they no longer trust anyone, least of all a visiting Garlicallian, whom to this day are banned from even the outer perimeters of Macadamian airspace. Yes indeed, long is their memory; and whenever Garlicazure raises its ugly head in conversation, I'm afraid, short is their fuse. In fact Captain," said FO Potatree thinking of another little story. "If you want to see the Solar System's largest group of angry recluses come out of the woodwork at once, all you have to do is what Captain Knotty T Crabbeapple of the ill-fated Cargo ship, the Mickymustard did."

"What was that?" asked FO Cornelius, now intrigued with FO Potatree's surprisingly logical and humorous delivery of the Macadamian fable.

"Ten startechtoids ago," continued FO Potatree. "An Asteroid cluster blocked the sun from the Planet Macadamia for nearly a half of its crop cycle. This meant that the majority of its crops failed. UFO decided to send a package of aid to the Planet Macadamia, in the form of surplus Vegimatter. Captain Crabbeapple had been commissioned to scout the Solar System, shuttling contributions to the desperate Planet in his ship, the CS Mickymustard.

Unfortunately, nobody had told Captain Crabbeapple, about the facts surrounding the Macadamia's severe distaste of any form of contact with Garlicazure, and the Garlicallian Space Race. Whilst the planet Garlicazure is still lost out there in space, the Space Race still exists in smaller numbers and so do their Vegimatters. Which as it turned out, was very unfortunate for Captain Crabbeapple and the CS Mickymustard? Almost his entire first shipment consisted of raw Garlicallian Vegimatter and Garlicallian oil for fuel. On discovering the contents of the ship's hold, the Macadamians dragged poor Captain Crabbeapple and his co-pilot, Kenthal Marrowmilne, from the ship, and blew it to smithereens. Not content with this severe form of punishment, they placed a mind bending curse on both Captain Crabbeapple and co-pilot Marrowmilne.

Captain Crabbeapple never flew again. If you visit the growing fields of Crushtonutes, then you can find him holed up in a small dwelling, raising tea bushes and living in fear of Macadamia nuts, very similar to the fear the Macadamians have of Garlicallian Vegimatter. In fact, Garlicallian Vegimatter has been known to send the once fearless Captain Crabbeapple, completely out of his tree. Co-pilot Marrowmilne, also lost control of his senses completely. His illness manifested itself in a very strange way. He somehow blamed himself for the madness now resident in the mind of his good friend, and respected colleague Captain Crabbeapple. So much so in fact, that when Co-pilot Marrowmilne tried to speak to his old friend

Captain Crabbeapple. The deeply disturbed Captain ran like thunder at the mere sight of him, threatening to jump off the nearest ravine if he didn't leave him alone forever, making him vow never to return. Co-pilot Marrowmilne did so, vowing never to return under any circumstances and left, thinking that he as good as killed his best, most respected friend. Leaving the Planet Crushtonutes in his newly acquired Root class cargo hunter, he began his travels of the constellations in self enforced exile. As if he had actually killed another Organitron, for which the punishment is exile. And so, he is known as Pirate Milnedew, not a bad pirate, just a sad and lonely Organiman, riding the skies in search of his soul.

Because of his self-imposed exile, he does not have the capability of full regeneration and so, suffers spasmodically with a skin-blight known as mildew. If ever you ever meet him, you will see the scars of continual regeneration malnutrition." "Though, nobody has reported sightings of him for some time now," thought FO Potatree aloud. "The general opinion is, that he has gone for good." FO Potatree stood in silence, as he could do nothing but feel sorry for the two Organitron unfortunate enough to have crossed swords with the mad Macadamian race.

"So," said Captain Carrot, "by way of the fable, the answer would appear to lie in re-pressurising the Gravitational chamber to the ships level?" stated the Captain, positive there would be no danger of Garlicazure trying to rule the Solar System once more.

"Aye Sir, that's about the size of it." Confirmed FO Potatree.

"Hatchooo... Hatchooo." Sneezed FO Cornelius.

"I take it that means you agree?" laughed FO Marrowlar. "As I see it Captain, it would appear to be the most sensible course of action to take." he reasoned, seeking agreement from the dithering Professor Goosegorgon, who was finding difficulty in remaining the right way up. "Would you agree Professor Goosegorgon? Professor? I said do you..?"

"I heard you FO Marrowlar, is 'a this blessed suit. I never could get on with these things. Yes, now that's more like it, much 'a more sensible. Now, where was I?" As professor Goosegorgon corrected his position, he turned the wrong pressure activator and flew around the chamber at great speed, rather like a balloon releasing its air in a sudden rush. Eventually, he came to rest in the arms of Captain Carrot. "Ye.. Yea.. y. y. yes Capatano, I think it is 'a the most sensible solution." Agreed the rather flustered Professor, who would do anything to get out of the pressurised suit, particularly as he had spent the best part of the morning in the confines of the Macadamian straight jacket.

"Very well, FO Potatree, bring our gravitational levels in line with the ship's equaliser, place the ship's company on alert and cross your fingers. We are possibly about to enter the place where even Vegi-angels fear to tread."

"Aye, aye Sir. FO Potatree to Ensign Strawballis come-in, over." confirmed FO Potatree, activating the Computron.

"Ensign Strawballis here Sir." Answered Ensign Strawballis from the ship's main communications consul on the bridge.

"Captain Carrot is going to attempt to open the recovered probe. Alert all ship's personnel to report anything strange in their relative departments, no matter how small or inconsequential it might seem at the time. Alert SO Tulipina to be particularly vigilant with fluctuations in the ship's systems analyser." said FO Potatree, keying the pressurisation dimensions of the Gravitational chamber, into the bay consul.

"Affirmative FO Potatree, Ensign Strawballis out." As Ensign Strawballis signed off, FO Potatree began the countdown for pressurisation.

"Initialising pressurisation now Captain, if you are ready?" asked FO Potatree, with his fingers perched on the gravity booster.

"As you will FO Potatree. Are you ready team?" asked Captain Carrot. They all nodded, signalling their readiness. "Okay team. FO Potatree, it looks like it's going to be Garlicazure or bust. Bring us down."

Captain Carrot and the team floated in the Gravitational chamber as the pressure levelled off to normal. Gradually, they were lowered to the floor as FO Potatree gave the countdown sequence to them.

"Twenty-five percent and increasing Captain. Counteracting pressurised suits on automatic relay. Fifty percent and all systems are clear. Scanning for probe activity, as yet, all systems are negative. Seventy-five percent Captain, your air supply is at normal levels, now; voice check please?" asked FO Potatree, as he checked the team were not suffering from the condition known as, "The space giggletwists" or, "The Bends as you would know it"

"Carrot. Ay'Ok." confirmed Captain Carrot.

"Marrowlar. Ay'Ok." Confirmed FO Marrowlar.

"Respiratory functions are affirmative." confirmed FO Cornelius.

"Goosegorgon. Ay'Ok." replied the Professor, relieved to be back on his own two feet.

"One hundred percent, all medical checks confirmed Ay'Ok. Final scanning complete and negative readings on all fronts. You may remove your suits." confirmed FO Potatree. As the team did so, the three Syncro switches activated, and just as FO Potatree described in the children's fable, the third Syncro switch released a core element that floated into the air. In it was a small screen, below that, a button flashed on and off. Captain Carrot stepped forward to observe the core.

"Well, here goes. You had better stand behind the plasma steel screen!" Ordered Captain Carrot as he prepared to press the button. Crouching behind the screen FO Marrowlar noticed a constant vibration and knocking noise.

"Captain, wait," he said, as he traced the noise to Professor Goosegorgon's knees.

"What is it Benzo?" asked Captain Carrot, who always called him by his first name whenever there was a possibility of a final parting.

"Professor Goosegorgon, could you please control your knees? Honestly, you are supposed to be a grown Organiman." Snapped the irritable FO Marrowlar, conscious of his own knees knocking in the Widdup Sanctuary. However, he was not willing to admit that.

"Hatchooo.. Ahh... Ah... Haaatchoo," sneezed FO Cornelius down the neck of FO Marrowlar. "Oh, do excuse me FO Marrowlar." Said FO Cornelius, wiping down the back of his superior officer.

"Can't you do something about that hideous habit of yours?" enquired FO Marrowlar, "It's costing me a fortune down at the laundry module. Credits don't grow on trees you know. I'm sorry Captain," continued FO Marrowlar. "It was just a couple of minor bugs in the environment."

"Well my friend, let us hope that when I have activated this, they are the only bugs we need concern ourselves with?" With that, Captain Carrot pressed the button and dived behind the screen, as the core shot out what at first, appeared to be a laser. As he got back on his feet, they became aware that it was nothing more than a transmitting pre-recorded Visaid. On the wall of the chamber, appeared a young Garlicallian Organiwoman.

As she spoke they could not believe that they were the first Organitron to lay eyes on a naturally born Garlicallian, presumably from the still intact Planet of Garlicazure. "But then," thought Captain Carrot. "She, and their habitat may no longer exist, Helios knows how long this probe has been searching the galaxies."

"Great compost." murmured FO Marrowlar, as his eyes were drawn to the unusually young representative of a notoriously long-living space race. "Maybe they have discovered the secret of eternal youth." he wondered wiping his chin in disbelief.

"Hatchooo... Ah. Ah.. Hatchooo." Sneezed FO Cornelius. "She is very young Captain, I would estimate no more than twenty five, thirty startechtoids at the most; a mere Organichild." He whispered.

"Something tells me when you are 'a stuck on a lost Planet for millions of startechtoids, on your own, away from 'a your loved ones and familiar space race companions, you hav'a no choice but 'a to grow up 'a very quickly!" said Professor Goosegorgon in awe of the vision set before him.

"Greetings," said the little trite voice of the Garlicallian Organigirl. "My name, is Oilyio Perfumo Garlialla, Queen elect of the space race Garlicallian from the Planet Garlicazure. **Sundate 2.999,999,999/ 320. Biltechtoids 17.30 starhectoids**." The team looked at each other with lumps in their throats. FO Potatree jumped for joy shouting. "Yesterday; they are still alive! The probe was sent yesterday." Then, his face disappeared into his handkerchief as the excitement became almost too much for him to bear.

"This is an SOS" continued Queen Garlialla. "We have been trapped inside a power source for it seems, longer than time itself. We have tried everything within our powers to escape its incredible grip, but alas, to no avail. Ever since we have been trapped here, we have been forced to take refuge under the surface of our once, luscious green Planetary surface. The fact that you are watching this transmission, means that you have activated the probe. We only hope that you can help to free us from this turmoil; this natural and indiscriminate, oppressive regime.

There are no other life forms in this power source. To the best of our knowledge, we are the only space race trapped as a result of a cataclysmic explosion in the times of our distant ancestors. We stem from a Solar System we assume was destroyed by the explosion. A Solar System known as, "the Bubbleonion Squeak Vegitalis Plexus Solar System." Home to the once collective Nations of Organitron. Some of our people believe we may be the only space race to survive, if that is the case, and this truly is survival? Then we would much rather have perished with the rest of our Organitron ancestors.

Our elders seem to lose their will to live at some fifty startechtoids. Habitation underground does not agree with our regeneration requirements. We are able to produce relatively primitive Vegimatters, so food stocks are sufficient. However, should you manage to free us from this place we call "Blottmeager," we can neither offer you a sumptuous banquet, nor riches beyond your wildest dreams. Just our eternal gratitude. We cannot even inform you of our course and position. You see, we truly are lost souls. In the internal chamber capsule from where this core has activated, you will find a detailed list of the inhabitants of Garlicazure. If you cannot help us, then please get this list and declaration to one of our collective Space Races of the Organitron, if any of them have survived. If it is within your capabilities to help us, then within the second Syncro switch you will find a pre-set course logging device, which will indicate the point at which the probe escaped the grip of Blottmeager, giving you the necessary co-ordinates plotting our position.

I must warn you, that this place is a great source of danger to all who come into contact with it." Queen Garlialla stopped momentarily appearing to collect a modicum of courage. "We have, on occasions," she continued, "been aware of ships from space races unknown to us that have been caught in the grips of this fiendish place, only to meet their doom. We know not whether they were trying to rescue us due to previous probes sent. We don't even know if these probes are escaping the power source. For this purpose, in the internal chamber you will find two non-related seedlings, held in Bio-Cryogenic time continuum. If nothing else, these life forms can be re-activated and hopefully our Space Race will live on, somewhere, sometime, in some strange and far away galaxy.

For reasons of the well being of my people, we choose to believe the probes are escaping and the ships were trying to help us. I feel it is only fair to tell you of all the dangers. The choice my unknown friends, is yours. After all, you could end up a prisoner of this place too. To be very frank, I wouldn't wish that on anyone. Because of this feeling that I have, you must be in possession of all the facts.

If you feel our cause is worthy, but doesn't outweigh the dangers, then feel not bad. In my heart I understand; but please, somehow, get the declaration to our fellow Organitron. I must go now in order to send the probe. We think we can only execute a successful launch when the power source reaches a phase of power surge. This is Queen Oilyio Perfumo Garlialla, may Helios be with you, over and out, ending transmission."

The viscid disappeared, leaving the Captain and his team filled with a mixture of pride, jubilation and trepidation. Whatever is sure in life, Captain Carrot knew that helping the people on the captive Planet of Garlicazure, had now moved to the top of the list of priorities.

"Professor Goosegorgon, I want you to take control of our newest crew members from Garlicazure. FO Potatree, can you seal off this area and keep the news of this discovery between the five of us? FO Cornelius, come with me to my strategy room and listen to the Widdup transcripts. There, I think I may have discovered the answer to beating this dreaded Voidwell into submission. FO Potatree, you will join me there please, I think I'm going to need all the imagination you can muster." Captain Carrot left his space suit in the anti-chamber, turned to the other members who were very silent, delivering them a warm smile and a salute. "Back to your assigned duties Organimen, and remember, for the sake of Garlicazure, we must keep our heads. "Aye, aye Sir." they said collectively, then FO Cornelius and FO Potatree accompanied him to the strategy room.

"Viceroy Councillor Au Paw-Paw to Captain Carrot, come in please." activated Captain Carrot's personal channel.

"Carrot to Viceroy Au Paw-Paw, acknowledged. Yes councillor, what can I do for you?" said Captain Carrot with a spring in his step.

"I would like you to meet me in the Medilab at your earliest convenience, Captain." she replied giving no indication as to the reason why.

"Is it important Viceroy Councillor Au Paw-Paw? I am just about to hold a strategy meeting!" He enquired, de-energising the elevation chamber doors.

"We have a visitor Sir. The Pirate Milnedew has Vegitamised aboard from an unknown origin. He has been hurt very badly Captain. I fear he may not live long." she confirmed.

"Hurt badly, who by Viceroy Councillor?" Asked Captain Carrot, amazed that just as they were discussing the Mickymustard Fable, one of its principle characters should suddenly appear.

"I can't say for sure Captain, but he is wearing Macadamian shackles." retorted Viceroy Au Paw-Paw, unsure of the Captain's reaction to Pirate Milnedew's arrival.

"I will be with you right away Councillor. If he has suffered at the hands of the mad Macadamians, then they have broken a long established treaty of trust. For their sakes, I hope that your suspicions are wrong, Carrot out." said the Captain, stepping into the elevation Chamber.

"Viceroy Councillor Au Paw-Paw out." she said now knowing that Captain Carrot, understood and possibly, even respected Pirate Milnedew, despite his self- imposed exile. The elevation doors closed on the party and they were gone, but not for long.

CHAPTER SIX

Now there is a whole lot of cooking going on

Part one

Milnedew, messenger or misfit?

Captain Carrot entered the Medilab, where Dr Kiwitranus was mounted on top of the Vegewell in which the notorious Pirate Milnedew, was harnessed ready for a rejuvenation blast. As he stepped closer to Dr Kiwitranus he spotted out of the corner of his eye that Viceroy Councillor Au Paw-Paw was busy connecting up emergency resuscitation equipment. Captain Carrot had come alone leaving the rest of the team on the Garlicazure project to make preparations for the way forward and to view the copied transcripts of the Widdup chronicles. Giving them seven starlectoids to form their proposals, he hoped that they might reach the same conclusion that he had, in terms of how to deal with this amazing power source that they found themselves narrowly escaping the grip of; only barely breaking free with their lives. He also noticed a sense of urgency in the actions of those in the Medilab, including, Viceroy Councillor Au Paw-Paw.

We're losing him Viceroy Councillor." said Dr Kiwitranus desperately. "He's jumping into spasmodic phibliarisation. I'm sorry Viceroy Councillor, but the only chance to save our outward bound friend, is to shock his system directly with oxygenated plasma, and raw glucose vitiminal protein. I warn you though," he continued. "At this early stage of recovery it could send him into a complete coma at best, at worst," he paused. "It could take him out completely, and well, we could just loose him all together. The choice is yours Viceroy Councillor." Just then Dr Kiwitranus noticed that Captain Carrot had entered the Medilab suite.

"I am sorry Captain, I was not aware of your presence. The situation is this..! Commented Dr Kiwitranus, who was interrupted by the concerned Captain Carrot.

"Dr Kiwitranus. You and the Viceroy Councillor here, are better trained to deal with this sort of situation than I. All I can tell you is, that by rights the choice of procedure is Milnedew's himself, but he is unable to speak for himself. I know he chooses to live in exile, but he came here for a reason, and we don't know from whence he came. That tells me, he has a reason for living, and that in turn tells me that if we do not try and help now, then his reason for living would have been wasted. Nobody's reason for living should ever be wasted, good or bad, because you see, destiny is your only path to life, it is up to the individual to choose that path for whatever reason. Until such time that the situation indicates differently, then this is another worthy life form and as such we will treat it. Now, if you don't mind I will observe and be on hand if you need my assistance, but the decisions I'm afraid are yours and quite rightly so. Most importantly, for reasons that I do not wish to enter into. What we have here, is viewed, for whatever reason, a misfit. I am not convinced of such reasoning. I will go further," said the Captain. "I believe that Pirate Milnedew holds within him valuable information, so, messenger or misfit, we must make moves to ensure his survival."

Viceroy Councillor Au Paw-Paw turned to Dr Kiwitranus and nodded to indicate her agreement with pressing ahead with the only life-preserving act open to them.

"Let's do it Dr Kiwitranus, it's his only chance and deep down, I too know that he came here for a reason and it was not to pass on in familiar surroundings!"

"I agree" said Dr Kiwitranus, "Nursette Scallios, Please prepare thirty celigrades of oxygenated plasma, twenty celigrades of raw glucose vitiminal protein, and stand by with ten celigrades of Carrotendal oparen and five celigrades of rufagious liquid protein, hurry now, we don't have much time!" said Dr Kiwitranus winching Milnedew from the Vegewell onto a nearby table.

"Yes Dr Kiwitranus, right away." Said the nurse, running for the medicine cabinet as Dr Kiwitranus did what he could to level off the life support triabulator. "Come on Milnedew," whispered Dr Kiwitranus. "You have come this far, I am not giving up on you now, stay with me do you hear me Organiman? Stay with me." Viceroy Councillor Au Paw-Paw monitored the tribulation data readout panel with anticipation. Whilst waiting for the serum to be prepared she noticed the critical signs, indicating serious problems for the health and safety of Pirate Milnedew.

"Photosynthesis levels are down to fourteen parts to the million Dr Kiwitranus, and falling fast," shouted Viceroy Councillor Au Paw-Paw hurriedly giving the information to Dr Kiwitranus as he endeavoured to stabilise his situation via the rejuvenation chambers DNA equaliser. "Pulse weak," she continued. "Almost negligible at thirty seven point two to the starmin. Oxygen levels holding at twenty five parts per million." Then the triabulator started to bleep, sending the sense of urgency to new heights of panic, albeit still a controlled one. "Dr Kiwitranus." Observed Viceroy Councillor Au Paw-Paw, "Milnedew's heart is beginning to show the strain of white cell depletion to the blood system. At present indicated at five-hundred over six-thousand and falling, Dr Kiwitranus," shouted the trembling Viceroy Councillor. "We are losing him."

Dr Kiwitranus looked up at Captain Carrot. Nursette Scallios ran round from behind the Captain clutching a tray containing the hopeful antidote in an Organi laser injectionary hand cylinder. Captain Carrot stood forward and held the hand of Pirate Milnedew knowing that if he were in the same situation there would be somebody standing there by his side. Pirate Milnedew had nobody. Captain Carrot felt useless as Dr Kiwitranus, Nursette Scallios and the Viceroy Councillor, rushed to secure the future of the patient, which had arrived under strange and mysterious circumstances. It wasn't much in his book to simply hold a hand, but if thought transferral was any medicine at all, then Pirate Milnedew was going to make it.

"At last, thank you Nursette Scallios," acknowledged a relieved Dr Kiwitranus. Captain, Councillor. Could you hold the patient's shoulders please? It is possible that he may suffer spasmodic muscular fits, we don't want him to do himself any damage!" As Captain Carrot and Viceroy

Councillor Au Paw-Paw came to grips with the patient, Dr Kiwitranus administered the serum watching closely the Triabulator read-out, then shouting out the affects of the medicine application.

"Photosynthesis, rapid increase thirty-five parts to the million, forty-nine p.t.m, sixty-seven p.t.m, eighty-four p.t.m, ninety p.t.m and levelling. Oxygen," he continued mopping Pirate Milnedew's brow. "Twenty-nine parts per million, thirty-seven p.t.m, forty-four p.t.m, fifty-five p.t.m, sixty p.t.m, seventy p.t.m, seventy-five p.t.m, eighty p.t.m and holding.

Pulse running at fifty-one point six over one starmin, fifty-five, fifty-eight, sixty, sixty-five, seventy and seventy-five. We are stabilised at pulse, seventy- five to the starmin.

Captain Carrot felt the sense of urgency begin to tail off as he looked around the room, then Pirate Milnedew began to shake; slowly at first, then rapidly with greater force.

"Hold him," shouted Dr Kiwitranus, "this is the point where we will have to pray." continued the Doctor, enhancing the triabulator instruments. As Pirate Milnedew shook there was no visible sign of pain in his well-weathered face.

"What is it Dr Kiwitranus? Is he reacting adversely to the serum?" asked the concerned Captain Carrot.

"No Captain. The body of this particular Organiman has not had life readings of this magnitude for quite some startechtoids. It has to adjust its natural chemical imbalance to enable the body's own chemical production to compensate for the sudden introduction of external synthetic medicines." Dr Kiwitranus halted to examine the triabulator. "As yet Captain," he continued, "we have completed the easy bit. As you can see photosynthesis, oxygen, and pulse are running at two thirds the normal level, but it would appear to be falling fractionally. These are levels higher than this young Organiman has enjoyed for many startechtoids. We are now entering the critical phase of white cell rejuvenation. The question is, whether the combined improvements in the standard life functions are sufficient to bolster, stabilise and rejuvenate those cells in question." Dr Kiwitranus looked back at the triabulator. There was still no alteration to the downward trend, the count now standing at four, five, nine over six thousand. Pirate Milnedew's fit, began to show signs of curtailing. Captain Carrot looked anxiously at Viceroy Councillor Au Paw-Paw, she too shared his concern.

"Wait a minute," shouted Dr Kiwitranus. "We have turned the corner, he has turned the corner. White cells back to five hundred over six thousand, five, five, four o.s.t, five, nine, seven o.s.t, six, three, nine o.s.t, six, nine, two o.s.t, seven, four, six o.s.t, and levelling at eight-hundred over six thousand." Dr Kiwitranus smiled as he checked on the data readout from the triabulator. "Yes," he cried. "Triabulationary confirmation of all vitals are positive." said Dr Kiwitranus excitedly.

"Is he going to make it Dr Kiwitranus?" enquired a much relieved Viceroy Councillor Au Paw-Paw. As Captain Carrot also eagerly awaited Dr Kiwitranus's opinion. He couldn't quite put his finger on it, but Milnedew had a reason for being here, Somehow, Captain Carrot needed, was determined-to know what it was. Dr Kiwitranus shuffled around Pirate Milnedew, scanning for all significant data. Turning to Captain Carrot and Viceroy Councillor Au Paw-Paw he smiled and said. "Don't get me wrong, but it is a miracle that he has made it this far. All the signs tell me that he has a very good chance of pulling through. We will know for sure in the next twenty-four starhectoids, until then it is touch and go. His body could reject the synthetic plasmas. Something tells me however, this young Organiman is going to pull through. The only thing is he is the only one who knows why?" Dr Kiwitranus signed the patient's chart and handed it back to Nursette Scallios. "Excellent work Nursette Scallios, you did well. Thank you."

"All in a starlectoids work Dr Kiwitranus, all in a starlectoids work." she said disappearing into the Medilab anti-room.

"Well done Dr Kiwitranus, I have to go and attend a strategy meeting now, you will inform me directly if Pirate Milnedew comes round won't you? I can't emphasise too strongly, the importance of why he is hear. Helios knows he would not come here unless it was truly life threatening not to do so." said the Captain de-energising the Medilab doors.

"Of course Captain, I will inform you at once." replied Dr Kiwitranus.

"If I didn't know better Captain, I would say you had a sneaking respect for our dissident friend from the outskirts?" observed Councillor Au Paw-Paw shrewdly.

"Viceroy Councillor Au Paw-Paw." snapped the Captain, uneasy that Viceroy Councillor Au Paw-Paw was knocking on the doors of his mind. "Councillor," he continued. "The first thing you are taught at the Spaceark Academy, is to respect the motives of all, regardless of whether you agree with them or not. An individual's principles often give important clues as to their future actions. Whatever Pirate Milnedew thinks that he has done, he has more than paid the price of his own bounty." With that Captain Carrot left the Medilab, giving both Viceroy Au Paw-Paw and Dr Kiwitranus a great deal to think about, and little time to ponder.

Part two

Jump for Soupaura dejour

Sundate 2.999,999,999/ 321 22.30 starhectoids.

Back on the Star Fighter launch pad of the O.S.S.SS Milkymarrow way, FO Pommegranza awaited the arrival of the suited warrior of the skies Commander Marrachinello. Tight in her grasp, she held a visaid communication from Captain Beetrouly to Captain Carrot of the O.S.S.S Earthanon, and the motherboard consul for the onboard in flight computer of Commander Marrachinello's Star Fighter. It was a hush-hush mission so even the bay ranks were excluded from the immediate zone as a matter of security. Commander Marrachinello emerged from the hanger room donned in his finest battle regalia, his handlebar moustache gelled to perfection and his very lucky mascot for this trip tucked under his arm; a generous portion of banana flapjack. He had two portions in actual fact. However, one had been packed safely away by Commanderette Marrachinello for Captain Carrot and his family. The other was guaranteed not to make the Soupaura Dejour system complete, if at all in fact. "Yes indeed," thought Commander Marrachinello. "It will take all of his strength to fight off the pangs of temptation, not to devour Captain Carrot's little home-baked surprise."

"Ahh... good." said FO Pommegranza, carrying out the final check list of the star fighter's weaponry systems. "We are ready for your departure Commander, all the final checks are complete, the launching mechanism is in place and here is the motherboard for your onboard in-flight computer. All you will have to do is sit there and let the plane take the strain." She said laughing.

"I say old bean, can't I carry out the manoeuvre myself? I am the most experienced Star Fighter Command in Sun-Fleet don't you know?" complained Commander Marrachinello as FO Pommegranza scanned him for the final security check.

"Nobody is doubting your capability Commander, only a fool would be silly enough to do so! There are two reasons why the onboard computer will activate the jump to K factor. Point one, the Mother ship's computer has the exact co-ordinates of the O.S.S.S Earthanon. We don't want to risk any interception of the computer terminal transmissions in pilot space station communications. If the Fasterfoids see even the merest sign of a scrambler frequency channel being used then they may jump to the right conclusions and track you more closely." She said keying in the instruction module matrix code clearance.

"Absolutely," jeered Commander Marrachinello. "No sense in leading the blighters straight to them hey what? Besides, don't know what I am complaining about really, could do with the rest don't you know.. Umm!" he chuckled climbing into the cockpit. "The second point FO Pommegranza?" enquired Commander Marrachinello strapping himself in.

"I'm sorry Commander what did you say?" Said FO Pommegranza unhooking the nose cone coupling.

"Yes old bean, you said there were two reasons why the trip will be on automatic!" Said Commander Marrachinello, feeling that he had got the better of his colleague.

"Oh yes, how silly of me, I nearly forgot." She said chuckling away to herself. "The second reason is," she continued. "That by the time it comes to initiate the K factor jump you probably will have your hands full and your vision impaired quite considerably." She said, sliding the Star Fighter canopy over his head. Quickly he stopped the canopy with his hand and asked her to clarify her statement.

"Beg your pardon hey what? Is there something you're not telling me FO Pommegranza? If there is I shall come back and haunt you if anything goes wrong!" he exclaimed. "Now is your last chance to explain old girl, umm hey what."

"Oh it's quite simple really," retorted FO Pommegranza, the tone of smug mischievousness resonating in her voice. "I'll bet you ten credits that by the time you make the K Factor jump your face; will be buried into that great slab of banana flapjack you're hiding in your tunic." FO Pommegranza held her hand out to shake for the bet, only to be given ten credits by the Commander.

"Here you go, take the money now. I know when I've been rumbled. Resist my dear wife's banana flapjacks? Impossible old bean. Right then, close her up and chocks away Chapess's." Said the Commander pulling the canopy shut and offering the thumbs up.

Inside the Star Fighter, Commander Marrachinello accessed the main computer and inserted the motherboard for the mission instructions. Outside the Star Fighter FO Pommegranza cleared the main flight deck and manoeuvred Commander Marrachinello's Star Fighter into the exit catapult launcher. As it entered the catapult, the servo magnetic barriers activated, lighting the tubular enclosed runway as far as the eye could see. With the plasma steel doors fastening behind him, Commander Marrachinello donned his headset and awaited the countdown for takeoff. He was about to spend the next six starlectoids in his own company, out of radio contact. "A tall order for most people." thought Commander Marrachinello, as he enjoyed the familiar voice of his old colleague FO Pommegranza, hopefully the last voice that he would hear until he made his rendezvous with the O.S.S.S Earthanon. "The Star Fighter is programmed to take me right to them." he thought. "Good job I brought all my medals and lots of polish, else I might just get a tad bored." he chuckled.

"Clear launch bay four. Repeat, all personnel clear launch bay four. Star Fighter take off, V minus thirty seconds and counting." announced FO Pommegranza as the flight deck crew scuttled away to safety. "Voice check please Commander Marrachinello that is provided you have not got your mouth full already?" Quipped FO Pommegranza.

"This is Star Fighter Command, Red Sector Leader, Commander empty mouth Marrachinello reading you loud and clear, hey what?" responded the ready, willing and able, Commander Marrachinello.

"Running computer sequence pre-set course check, all systems clear and on line, calorific momentum charger at one hundred percent. Please check and acknowledge Commander." Said FO Pommegranza, initiating the servo magnetic Catapult power output.

"CMC at one hundred, check, twenty seconds to V minus take off. Take-off mechanism, contact and running." Replied Commander Marrachinello.

"Opening defence shield window for catapult expulsion, V minus fifteen seconds to take off. Launching Probe one, exit, l.p.two and exit, l.p.three and exit, l.p.four and exit, l.p.five and exit, l.p.six and exit. V minus six seconds to take off Commander Marrachinello, good luck. Activating Slithervoid now. Four, three, two, one and Star Fighter go."

"T.T.F.N and tally ho!" shouted Commander Marrachinello as his Star Fighter shot down the expulsion tube and out into the vast, open space.

"Launching probe seven and exit." said FO Pommegranza monitoring the probes heading for the Slithervoid. "FO Pommegranza to Captain Beetrouly, come in please." she responded activating her personal channel.

"Beetrouly here FO Pommegranza." Replied Captain Beetrouly from the bridge.

"Probes entering Slithervoid in V minus ten seconds Captain. Transferring monitor enhancement to visaid now." On screen, as Captain Beetrouly sat at the Command com, the probes could be seen on tract towards the mouth of the Slithervoid. A great swirling mist, filled with thunder like flashes and changing colours with every blinding clash. Truly a magnificent sight, a passageway to another place in the Solar System by way of a power source far superior to anything that Sun-Fleet had to power their ships. Captain Beetrouly watched tensely as FO Pommegranza marked the probe entries.

"Probe one, entered, two, entered, three, entered, four, entered, five, entered, six, entered, five, four, three, two, one. Commander Marrachinello entering the Slithervoid now." She confirmed as the tension grew on the bridge.

"Probe seven, entered." she announced as the last probe disappeared out of sight and all that was left to do was wait for their appearance on the other side.

Inside the Star Fighter, Commander Marrachinello was pinned to his seat as the G-force of the Slithervoid travel made a jelly out of his face, rippling it uncontrollably, his moustache fuzzing beyond recognition. Inside the Slithervoid it was just like travelling down a techno-coloured scarf on a washing line that was filled with fire flies and fireworks.

Back on board the O.S.S.S Milkymarrow way, FO Pommegranza confirmed that the probes were about to complete their journey through the all powerful Slithervoid.

"Probe one, exit," she said. "probe two, exit, probe three, exit, probe four, exit, probe five, exit, probe six, exit. Five, four, three, two, one Star Fighter expulsion now. Can confirm, probe six explosion on mark. Probe seven, exit. De-activating Slithervoid now. Five, four, three, two, one, probe seven explosion on mark, Star Fighter course change of forty-five blimits complete. Zigzag course on mark and confirmed. Manoeuvre complete, Captain Beetrouly. Complete success Sir." Confirmed FO Pommegranza awaiting further instructions.

"Excellent FO Pommegranza." Said Captain Beetrouly. "Sweep the Solar System for Fasterfoid activity. Let me know if they manage to track and lock on to his course trajectory. Good work FO Pommegranza. Let's hope it works the way we hope. Let's not forget, he is on his own out there. Place the Star Fighters on standby. We may have to bail him out in a hurry." answered Captain Beetrouly.

"Aye, aye Sir." confirmed FO Pommegranza.

"Captain Beetrouly over and out." said the Captain signing off.

"FO Pommegranza out." replied the very pleased FO Pommegranza, her brainchild was a success to date, but as yet, not concluded. "No time to rest on their laurels, not just yet." she thought.

As Commander Marrachinello emerged from the Slithervoid, the explosion from the sixth probe lit up the surrounding space with five second interval incendiary proton nuclear explosions. Then, immediately behind him came the seventh probe, which slowed down sufficiently to allow Commander Marrachinello's Star Fighter to clear the coming fall-out boundary a matter of a split second. Commander Marrachinello monitored his onboard computer and initiated the stand-by K factor sequence upon command of the calorific momentum Syncro computer.

Bang, Pitchoow, resonated across the skies as the seventh probe exploded. Instantly Commander Marrachinello's Star Fighter veered course, initiating the K factor jump and taking up a zigzag formation. Commander Marrachinello sat back and placed the Star Fighter cabin in the mobile regeneration mode falling asleep with the comforting vision of his dear wife and family, and only the stars for company.

Far away across the Galaxy on an out-station just staryards from the breach point of the "No Fry Zone, General Pattiebabes Burgerbilge was chairing a disciplinary meeting on the bridge of the reconnaissance vessel the FF Deep-Freeder. Any closer to the "No Fry Zone" and the ship would have been in violation of the Organitron-Fasterfoid treaty. In front of him stood the accused, Privado Tubain Croquettio who was flanked by his immediate superior Officer, Principal Officer Wavygrain Crinklecrunch.

"Privado Croquettio," said the General. "You stand here accused of some very serious breaches of Fasterfoid etiquette. Three counts that have been brought to my attention in fact. Namely, the wilful dereliction of duty in the form of falling asleep at your post, insubordination towards a superior Officer and last but not least, possession of illegal substances in the form of Carrot juice. Treason to be precise." General Burgerbilge looked upon the Privado with extreme distaste. "Now, as I see it," he continued. "You did fall asleep, you did insult Principle Crinklecrunch and remains of carrot juice were found in your breakfast cup in the crew eating area. However I am a fair Gentlegrill, how do you plead Privado Croquettio?" Asked General Burgerbilge with an air of superiority.

"Well Sir, not guilty on all counts" explained Privado Croquettio jumping to attention. "I really don't think that I can be blamed for falling asleep on duty because I had been at the Communications station for over sixteen starhectoids without a break, not even for rejuvenation. When I shouted at Principle Officer Crinklecrunch calling him a corrugated spud thug, it was because he woke me by violently shaking me. As he was already violently shaking me in my dream, it took a few moments for me to realise I had fallen asleep at my post and was no longer dreaming. As for the Carrot juice, well Sir, I can only say that it was a plant!" he said knowing that all but the third excuse were true and he did have some smuggled Carridionaries contraband on board, but he wasn't willing to admit that it was a substance and flavour that he was rather partial to.

"I know that Carrot juice comes from a plant you moron." snapped the General.

"No Sir, with respect General Burgerbilge, you misunderstand me. What I meant by the word plant is that somebody put it there to implicate me in order to secure my disciplinary action.

"Oh I see," said the General. "And who might that be? He enquired.

"I have no idea Sir. All that I am willing to say is that communications is a much coveted post and somebody must want it pretty badly." confirmed Privado Croquettio. General Burgerbilge sat deep in thought at the revelations coming from the direction of his communications trustee.

"Principle Crinklecrunch. Why was this man double roistered on the communications module? Sixteen starhectoids is a long time to go without a rejuvenation break?" asked General Burgerbilge.

"It was as a punishment for falling asleep on his first shift of duty General." smiled Principle Officer Crinklecrunch. "Apparently he didn't sleep very well because of a recurring nightmare." continued the Principle.

"I see. So Privado Croquettio, you try to pull the wool over my eyes. Well it won't wash do you understand me?" he shouted. "For wilful dereliction of duty I find you guilty. As for insubordination, I can understand your reaction to being woken violently if you were tucked up snugly in your bunk, but you were not, you were in your uniform and at your post. Therefore I find you guilty of insubordination. As for the possession of an illegal substance or treason!" said the General. "There is no proof that it was your doing, so I will give you the benefit of the doubt. Not guilty, but there will be a full investigation as to the origin of the said substance and if I find you are lying Privado Croquettio, then you are in really big trouble." Remarked the General as he stood and circled the Privado who was shaking in his boots. Then from behind him he bellowed into the Privado's ear. "You have let me down Privado Croquettio and if there is one thing I do not like, it is being let down. Do it again, and that position which you so rightly describe as the much coveted position of communications, will become vacant. Then I will submerge you in gravy and fill your lungs with sprout gas is that clear?" Shouted the General but no reply came forward. "Is that clear Privado Croquettio?" repeated the General.

"Oh yes thank you your great fattiest. You are too kind yo.. Yo... your great greasiest!"

"Don't creep Croquettio! You are in enough trouble as it is without adding false gratification to the list." Suddenly Privado Croquettio felt a cold chill streaming down his back but put it down to nerves.

"Oh don't thank me yet, you don't know your punishment. No I think if you are having problems with your sleep patterns then we should address the problem. How does a starwektoid off sound umm?" smiled General Burgerbilge.

"Really General that will not be necessary." said Privado Croquettio.

"Then let us lighten up the atmosphere and give you the time off anyway. Yes let us all have some fun on the house!" Laughed the General.

Privado Croquettio found himself surrounded by a force field emanating from the ceiling of the bridge right the way down to the floor. Then General Burgerbilge withdrew his specially designed Gunge gun which had a gas capacitor fitted.

"Oh General," said the Privado. "Surely we can talk about this like sensible Gentlegrills. You're not going to do anything you might regret later are you General?"

"No of course not Privado Croquettio! But, you are going to regret it very much."

Privado Croquettio's eyes widened as he realised the extent of his fate.

"Please General, not the Gellogas! Anything but the Gellogas." He shouted but it was too late. General Burgerbilge had begun filling the force field with the innocuous Gellogas (Laughing Gas) as Privado Croquettio lay on the floor to escape the effects. Suddenly he felt the gas penetrate his throat and lungs and began to giggle like a small child who had hidden a sweetie from his big brother and wouldn't tell him where to find it. As the gas bellowed around Privado Croquettio he boomed with laughter.

"Oh no stop it my tummy is starting to hurt. Ahh.. Ahh.. Ha.. Ha. Ha... Oooh.. Oohwee.. Ow.. Ow... He.. He. He. Haaaa oh no, no, st.. St.. St.. Stop it please," shrilled the Privado doubled up on the floor grasping his stomach and tears starting to roll down his cheeks.

Then as General Burgerbilge looked on him with a satisfied glow, as very happy Principle Crinklecrunch whispered in his ear.

"Excuse me, General." He said. "But we are picking up strange movements on the particle scanner." He continued.

"Oh stop it I can't take anymore. My ribs, my ribs are going to explode. Ha... Ha... Haaaa, he wheezed. Oh dear, oh dear, oooh nooo, stop it, aaaahhhh." cried Privado Croquettio.

"General Burgerbilge withdrew his gunge gun and placed it back in his holster. Then de-activating the force field turned to Privado Hotdogear.

"Privado Hotdogear take this lily livered buffoon to the sick bay and leave him there. He should sleep for a starwektoid if his rib cage will let him."

"Aye, fry Sir." said Privado Hotdogear as he picked up the very sore torsoed Privado Croquettio and carried him off the bridge.

Sitting back at the helm, General Burgerbilge turned his attentions to the new development of the day.

"What is the situation with the particle scanner Vice-Principle Wafflebong?" he enquired.

"We are picking up calorific proton emissions from the O.S.S.S Milkymarrow way Sir. Three expulsions and counting, scanners indicate that their defence shields are down. Confirmed Vice-Principle Wafflebong

"What kind of craft are they launching?" Asked the General.

"Judging by the size of the emissions which are all variable but not to any significant degree, I would say they were standard Robopods. They have activated the Slithervoid Sir." Reasoned Vice-Principle Wafflebong examining the scanner module. "Four expulsions," he continued. "Five expulsions, six expulsions, seven expulsions increased proton emissions, eight expulsions. O.S.S.S Milkymarrow way is closing her launch catapult and has re-engaged her defence shields General." Confirmed Vice-Principle Wafflebong.

"Can you track them through the Slithervoid and confirm the course heading of the probes?" asked the General.

"Already on it General, locking on now Sir." acknowledged Vice-Principle Wafflebong.

"Vice-Principle Wafflebong why were there increased emissions from the seventh probe?" enquired the suspicious General Burgerbilge.

"I'm sorry General, but it could be a build-up of protons around the expulsion tubes of the O.S.S.S Milkymarrow way exacerbated by the Slithervoid activation. Particle scanner frequency clarity at a minimum, General. Boosting output to counteract static, General. The Slithervoid activation is scrambling our frequencies but I am sure I can over-run the static interference," confirmed Vice-Principle Wafflebong.

"Good work Vice-Principle Wafflebong. Keep on it.

"Aye fry Sir. They are coming out of the Slithervoid now, General. One expulsion, two expulsion, three expulsion, four expulsion. Course setting dead ahead, heading for sector F2 General, and no change in calorific proton emissions." he confirmed. "Five expulsions and no change in proton emissions scans. Six expulsions. General, scanner indicates the sixth probe has exploded. Seventh expulsion, eighth expulsion. General, they too have exploded. I have lost track of probe six Sir. The last explosion was approximately twice the size of the first explosion Sir. Scanning the area for rogue activity." he said shaking his head. "Nothing General. Calorific emissions are flooding the proton counter. I think they lost the last three probes, Sir." confirmed Vice- Principle Wafflebong.

"Ha.. Ha... ha, not only are they looking in the opposite direction! But, they are losing their hardware hand over fist. Let them get on with it. They are of no consequence to us. Steady as she goes Gentlegrills-Gentlefrills. It's like taking a holiday watching this bunch of Vege-plebes!"

Part three

Fasterfoids are go-go

Sundate 2.999.999.999/ 327. 17.25 starhectoids

Across the galaxies, far away in the uncharted sector F9 of the Bervedo quadrant. Major General Ickychick Fattyspot, and his second in command, General Ghi Chickydigit stood on the flight deck of the Flotilla force Mayo-class star station, the glorious flagship FF Shallow Fryer. Assembled together were General Greasy Pattie and his second in command Principle Officer Griscillian Burgerbuns of the FF Hotbox, General Breasto Chirpychick and principle Officer Burgirty Chickwings of the FF Fatpan, and General Satu Pomline with his second in command, Principle Officer Corrigate de Digeridoo, of the FF Lardlip.

Whilst they were standing on the flight deck, a shuttle craft that had moments before landed, opened its side doors. Stepping out from the small ship, meeting the whole congregation of the Fasterfoids task force top tier ranking officers in person, for the first time; (Since the hush-hush mission went underway that is). Was the eye patch clad General Faturno Satuese and his second in command, Principle Officer Renderfat Gammachip of the new ship, the FF Francaisfry, met for the final mission meeting.

"Ickychick Fattyspot you old buzzard. How are you my old friend?" said General Satuese shaking hands with a formidable squelch. "Well, exciting times ahead of us Gentlegrills. I do believe we are going to enjoy this! I believe you already know my second in command Principle Officer Renderfat Gammachip?" he said pointing at a waist paper bin. "Oh my mistake it's so dark in here." he laughed re-directing his sticky, dripping, little finger. "Yes Of course we remember you Principle Gammachip." they said collectively, falling about with fits of the giggles. "Tell me Principle Gammachip." asked General Chirpychick. "Is it true that when you were first assigned to the FF Francaisfry, you were in secret dock in Waffleroo, and General Satuese fined you fifty credits for losing the ship whilst it was in your command?" said General Breasto Chirpychick. "And an.. A... and you looked everywhere for it for two Starlectoids, everywhere that is except where it was originally?" Tittered the smug General Breasto Chirpychick as the others wailed with uncontrollable sniggering. Principle

Officer Gammachip nodded silently at first, then becoming infuriated at the continuing frolicking at his reputation's expense, he jumped up and down on the spot like a child who had lost his lollipop.

"You may find the whole thing funny Gentlegrills, but I rather stupidly thought that I would be entrusted with all the information of the ship's capabilities. How am I to know the ship had a stationary visual enhancement disguiser device if no-one deems fit to tell me!" shrugged the Principle Officer as the hairs on his neck began to stand on end. General Satuese tried to halt the joviality from denting Principle Gammachip's pride forever.

"Gentlegrills. Me thinks we treat Principle Officer Gammachip unjustly. After all he did use his head and find the ship in the end." Smiled General Satuese.

"That's right," shouted General Greasy Pattie. "He plum walked straight into it and knocked himself out for a whole Starwektoid. My, that was what I call really using your head!" he shrieked.

"That is it General Satuese, I am not standing for this Kangaroo court any longer." shouted the angry Principle Gammachip.

"Well why let old habits die? As I recall, you weren't standing for very long then were you?" cried Principle Officer Chickwings rolling around the floor.

"Well at least I am standing now! And you may rest assured that is how the situation is going to stay." Then he stepped forward to hand General Satuese the battle plans, in doing so finding the only spot of olio plasma on the deck floor and slipping over flat on his back. As he slid across the flight deck floor, the rest of the gathering could not help themselves but to laugh helplessly, without giving a moment's thought to the feelings of the now inch sized ego of Principle Gammachip. General Satuese helped him off the floor and moved towards the mission board that was covered with a veil. Pinning the star charts in front of him he looked up and ordered the area cleared for a privy meeting of the Fasterfoid Command over the tannoy system.

"Now clear the flight deck. I repeat, clear the flight deck. All unauthorised personnel will vacate the area at once. Privado Wafflaid report to the flight hanger deck doors and allow nobody entry."

Once everybody had cleared the area, General Satuese cleared his throat and begin to deliver the ethos behind the mission.

"Gentlegrills, it is now time to avenge the lost souls of Sausagia, our dearly departed ancestors of the lost space race of the Fasterfoids. We still believe to this day that the star cluster explosion that ripped through our galaxy was as a result of naive scientific experiments carried out by the Organitron that went drastically wrong. Causing millions of startechtoids in which our thriving communities suffered such hardship and losses of our nearest and dearest. Not, to mention the vital riches beneath the surface crust of Sausagia that was lost to our scientific programme. Yes, they were sacrificed." said General Satuese thumping the table. We believe Sausagia," he continued. "Was used as a shield for the experiments and was obliterated in the callous and selfish acts that shortly followed in order to achieve space supremacy. It is also a theory of the time that Sausagia was not destroyed, but captured and taken to a secret hide-out in an uncharted sector in order to excavate the precious minerals that lie within her vast bulk. However that is history, today is the beginning of history in the making. In revenge, we are going to get vital minerals from those who thrived on our heartache. Before I show you the plans Gentlegrills, I want you to join me in "The Fasterfoids verse of victory." To mark this stupendous occasion. General Satuese to Privado Roasteasy." said General Satuese calling the ship's communication com. "ship's open communication if you will." He requested.

"Aye fry Sir, you are on general ship's com." Confirmed Privado Roasteasy.

"Now hear this, Gentlegrills and Gentlefrills of the Fasterfoids. We are about to embark on the mission of our lives. The ultimate revenge on those vitamin stuffed health freaks, the Organitron. So, I would like it if you would join with us in the "Fasterfoids verse of victory" to mark the future success of this dare-devil mission and send us on our way with triumph in our hearts."

(Fasterfoids are go-go)

Prepare for battle, we're gonna stir up a storm.
You had best get out of the frying pan if you don't like the warm,
Watch out Organitrons we're coming to town,
There's no taking prisoners with the Fasterfoids around.

We're rough and we're tough we know what we want,
So we want you to know, that what we want is the lot.
It's a sorry old day, and all we can say,
Is when the Fasterfoids are Go-Go, the Organitrons are no a no.
We're gonna wipe the smiles off their faces some day.

(Chorus)
Fasterfoids are Go-Go, we are setting our sights.
Gonna hit em with ketchup with all of our might,
Gonna pack them off screaming into the night,
When the Fasterfoids are Go-Go they will run with a fright.
Cause when we Go-Go in, they will Go-Go out for the count,
Watch out you Organitrons, Fasterfoids are coming about.

Fasterfoids are Go-Go, Fasterfoids are Go-Go.
When the Fasterfoids are Go-Go, the Organitrons blown out.
Come on Fasterfoids let's rally the troops,
Time to make those Organitron jump through the hoops.
We'll out fly em, out fight em, run circles round em loop the loop,
They will remember the day the Fasterfoids flew the coop,
They will remember the way; we made them into vegetable soup.
(Chorus)

Go to your stations and make all final checks,
Time to rid ourselves of those pains in the necks.
Go crank up your engines, zero hour approaches,
It's time to set sail and crunch those Cockroaches.
So watch out you veg blighters, we're steaming we're mad.
Helios can't help you we're big mean and bad,
You won't know what's hit your healthy freak race,
Because we're gonna drive you into deep outer space.
And finally you'll remember the superior Fasterfoid Go-Go race.
(Chorus)

"Privado Roasteasy, close general ships com, General Satuese, out."

"Aye fry Sir. Privado Roasteasy out."

As they settled themselves in front of the battle plan board after the jolly musical interlude from the rigours of the Fasterfoid superiority race. Major General Ickychick Fattyspot, joined General Satuese on the rostrum and prepared to deliver the cunning battle plan for the glorious revenge on the Organitron Space Races. As Major General Ickychick Fattyspot stood ready to unveil the battle criteria, General Satuese addressed the assembled Officers.

"Gentlegrills, in ten starlectoids we will be departing from this sector to embark on our journey to our target mission and that target my friends, is Earthanon!"

"Ahh... Earthanon." said the surprised Officers who had speculated for some time that the Bubbleonion Squeak Vegitalis Solar System would be the object of their revenge.

"But, before we depart for Earthanon, we will be heading on a bearing of twenty one point five blimits from our current position. Eventually, we will find a small Asteroid Plato that is rich with Silicone powder for the purposes of a dummy run of the battle strategy that will soon be revealed. Our journey to this Asteroid Plato will take two starlectoids.

We will carry out our manoeuvres for seven starlectoids until our manoeuvres are precision perfect. Then we will depart for Earthanon. We have calculated the journey to Earthanon will take twenty-seven point-eight starlectoids. **Sundate 2.999,999,999/ 364. 65 Biltechtoids** to be precise. This will be the very day that the new millennium celebrations will be underway, and the Organitron guard will be lowered. As you know, the ship that you have accompanied in the trials has a cloaking capability. Due to other developments from our science programme we have discovered that currently the two Mother ships guarding the Earthanon Atmosphere are the O.S.S.S Milkymarrow way and the O.S.S.S Junipitaris. The O.S.S.S Earthanon, Captained by the so-called Sun-Fleet legend, Captain Gillespie J. Carrot, is undergoing a refit at their Spaceark academy and is not expected to arrive in Earthanon air space until **Sundate 3.000,000,000/ 065 Biltechtoids**. So unfortunately that little myth of a legend will have to wait for a very large helping of Fasterfoid supremacy. A pity really, I was rather looking forward to bruising his ego. Thus our mission will be strikingly easy." General Satuese looked on the impatient group in front of him who were anxious to be told the full details of the battle plans." And so Gentlegrills," continued the General. "This brings me to the moment that you have all been waiting for! Major General Fattyspot, if you would do the honours please." With that, the Major General unveiled the battle plans, much to the relief of the flotilla force command.

"What you see before you," said the General, allowing several moments for them to study the plan. "Is a step by step account of my plan? Allow me to enlighten you as to how we will implement this stroke of genius on those vain eccentrics, the Organitron.

Part four

Captain Carrot just loves it when a plan comes together!

Sundate 2,999,999,999/ 330 Biltechtoids. Time 19.00 starhectoids.

Captain Carrot, stood at the Command com pondering the importance of the strategy meeting that was shortly to take place. At the last strategy meeting Captain Carrot had given all the respective team members full transcripts of the Widdup chronicle data and the Garlicazure probe data, along with the complete spectral analysis of the Voidwell to date. This was in order that they might go away and come up with some ideas as to how they could rescue the stricken Planet from its deadly grip with some chance of emerging from the scenario alive, giving them seven starlectoids to come up with their respective conclusions. He was hoping that the Pirate Milnedew, would have re-gained consciousness by this time and would prove to be in possession of some important knowledge pertaining to the Voidwell. One starwektoid had passed and no solutions had been placed on the table that were viable. Two starlectoids ago yet another probe was launched from the Voidwell but failed to make it out in one piece. Somehow the Voidwell seemed to be increasing in power output velocity when it expelled the objects. They were now into their tenth starlectoid since encountering the Voidwell. The one thing that he felt deep down was that the mad Macadamians would not have dared to alienate Sun-Fleet over such an old principle of honour. "Captain Crabbeapple and Co-pilot Marrowmilne have more than paid their debt to that society." thought Captain Carrot. Although Pirate Milnedew had stirred, he had not come round which meant, as far as the Captain was concerned, they were still fighting against the odds. Then, his sub-conscious was pulled back to the general order of things as FO Marrowlar alerted him to a presence approaching the O.S.S.S Earthanon's defence range from the port side.

"Captain I am receiving a binary coded approach clearance from a ship that claims to be Commander Marrachinello's Star Fighter. Call sign confirms Red Sector Leader! Distance one hundred thousand starmillo's. ETA, four starmins, no visible readings of activated weaponry systems." said FO Marrowlar scanning the approaching vessel from the security com.

"Really?" said Captain Carrot. "I'm not sure I like the sound of that. Ensign Strawballis, patch me a scrambled frequency to Commander

Marrachinello, on visaid if you please. FO Marrowlar lock on phasers" said Captain Carrot taking his seat.

"Aye, aye Sir. Said Ensign Strawballis. "O.S.S.S Earthanon to unidentified approaching ship, please make yourself known! I repeat. Please make yourself known."

"Phasers locked and tracking Captain." confirmed FO Marrowlar.

As the visaid came on line Commander Marrachinello appeared with a face full of banana flapjack.

"Commander Marrachinello," laughed Captain Carrot. "You are looking rather full of yourself."

"What-ho Captain Carrot old bean, just thought I would look you up as I was in the area hey what.. Wha.. Wha.. Ha.. Hox." replied the jolly Commander Marrachinello hurriedly swallowing the last of the contents of his mouth.

"Permission to come aboard Captain Carrot? Top secret delivery of banana flapjack from the little Commanderette back home don't you know." he said smiling.

"Well, as you have brought something more useful than your old carcass how could I possibly refuse!" replied Captain Carrot wondering what Commander Marrachinello was really doing in the uncharted sector. "You are clear for landing."

"Righty-ho. ETA, three starmins, until then chocks away Chaps and Chapess's. Red Sector Leader out."

"Viceroy Rhubarblatt will bring you in Commander, Carrot out."

"Aye, aye Sir. Commander Marrachinello this is Viceroy Rhubarblatt. Reduce speed to one quarter pulsate and prepare to dock at flight deck 3, dead ahead on the port side. Please acknowledge observation and compliance?" said Viceroy Rhubarblatt activating the landing track beacon.

"Viceroy Rhubarblatt. This is Red Sector Leader, observation and compliance acknowledged. You have me in your grasp so whatever happens just be gentle with me.

"Captain Carrot to Ensign Broccleman."

"Aye Captain. Ensign Broccleman here."

"Ensign Broccleman, Commander Marrachinello is coming aboard. ETA flight deck 3 in two point-five starmins. Meet him there and bring him along to the strategy room as soon as you can please. Captain Carrot out."

"Aye, aye Sir, Ensign Broccleman over and out."

"Professor Goosegorgon to Capatano Carrot,"

"Captain Carrot here. Yes Professor Goosegorgon."

"Capatano" said the chirpy Professor. "I am on my way to the strategy suite. Dr Kiwitranus is in the Medilab with Pirate Milnedew. Capatano, he is conscious, weak but audible." he confirmed.

"Excellent news Professor. Tell the doctor I will be right there!"

"Shall I join you there Capatano?" Asked the Professor.

"No, you continue with your plans. If my hunch is right I won't be long at all. Professor, will you inform Viceroy Councillor Au Paw-Paw?"

"No point Capatano, Viceroy Councillor Au Paw-Paw is already there!"

"Thank you Professor. Captain Carrot out."

"Professor Goosegorgon out."

"SO Tulipina. FO Marrowlar and I will be attending a strategy meeting via the Medilab notify them of our delay and take over the Command com will you." he ordered signing the Captains log.

"Aye, aye Sir." she said, taking her place at the helm, as Captain Carrot de-energised the doors and stepped into the elevation chamber.

"Captain off the bridge." shouted Ensign Rasperillo, as the bridge crew stood to attention.

"Pheweeeeee... phewoooooh." Piped Ensign Melonture.

The elevation doors re-energised and Captain Carrot and FO Marrowlar were gone.

In the Medilab, Pirate Milnedew was lying in a semi-traumatised state, his hand being held by Viceroy Au Paw-Paw as Dr Kiwitranus ran diagnostics on his condition.

"You're a very lucky young Organiman, Pirate Milnedew, I hope you realise that!" said Viceroy Au Paw-Paw softly.

"You don't know the half of it councillor." he whispered. "Where are my shackles?" he continued looking nervously around the room.

"We had to cut them off, they were killing you." Said Dr Kiwitranus.

"At least the Macadamians have got some uses." he laughed painfully, grasping his chest and trying to sit up.

"Whoooo, stay down. Helios knows what damage you could do!" snapped Dr Kiwitranus.

Captain Carrot and FO Marrowlar stepped into the Medilab and rushed to the side of the conscious Pirate Milnedew in case he was to relapse into a subconscious state again.

"Ahh.. Captain Carrot, long time no see." He smiled.

"And happy I am that you can see me again you old sky-flyer you." He retorted. "Pirate Milnedew, time is of the essence so for now I must be brief.

This is my second in Command FO Benzo Marrowlar. I must know from where you came and how you got on board the OS.S.S Earthanon." said the Captain hurriedly. Then it all came flooding back to Pirate Milnedew as he began to panic.

"Great Helios Organiman! Is it still out there? Do you know about it?" he cried grasping the Captain's arm.

"The Voidwell?" asked Captain Carrot as Pirate Milnedew nodded. "Yes, it is still out there, but we don't know as much about it as we would like. Did you come from in there?" asked the Captain placing his hands on the Pirate Milnedew's shoulders. Pirate Milnedew closed his eyes and began talking.

"It was a little over three startechtoids ago, I think? To be honest I lost count, that place can send you mad. I was out-running a Fasterfoid Flash cruiser and hid in an Asteroid mine-belt to escape detection. I jettisoned my Hunter class auxiliary reactor with some calorific trace particles and exploded them with a delayed proton detonation device. I had hoped that they might reach the conclusion I had collided with an Asteroid and perished. Unfortunately the Reactor struck an Asteroid close to the ship and blew me into a collision with another Asteroid. I managed to crash land on the Asteroid, but it took all my spare fuel and cunning to survive in the hope that somebody would come along to help. The Fasterfoids thought they had seen I and my ship smashed to smithereens, and they just left, fortunately. My cargo was an illegal shipment of Vegimatters destined for the "No-fry zone". The Fasterfoids tastes have changed in a big way, but not enough for them to exchange good credits for an honest transaction. They were going to steal my cargo and cast me off into space. Only they hadn't reckoned on my being the proud owner of an anti-Vegitamisation force field. I designed it myself. It's crude, but it works, well, at least it used to work. Anyway, eventually the Asteroid belt was dragged into that infernal Voidwell and that was the last anyone saw of me. Until now that is. Outside, you are lucky if you can see in it. I think it possible to pass it without noticing any significant changes within the surrounding space. Inside, now that's a different story. You cannot miss it. It surrounds you with a stifling power; constant and always on the prowl. It is so filled with energy that you can't see further than ten staryards in front of the ship." Then Pirate Milnedew's eyes appeared to glaze as he swallowed to gain composure. "And lonely, oh so lonely." he continued as his face fell to a bleak and unhappy shade of grey. "Then ten starlectoids ago like a bolt of thunder it hit me. I worked out how to convert the anti-Vegimatter force field to a crude Vegitamisation chamber." All at once Pirate Milnedew's tempo and humour seemed to bring a spark of light back into his eyes. "Ha.. Ha... ha... the next bit is just too comical to be true!" He laughed. "The answer was lying right under my nose all the time. The one relic I have held onto from my dim and distant past, along with a strange finding on the Asteroid Plato that I be-grudgingly come to know as home, were to be my salvation."

"What finding, Pirate Milnedew?" asked a curious Captain Carrot.

"About a startechtoid ago or a little under I think?" said Pirate Milnedew correcting himself. "As I said, maintaining time realisation in that thing is very difficult. There is no night, no day just a constant, brilliant, bright blue static haze, with a background noise of humming ever present. Anyway," he said shaking his head. "I digress. Now where was I?" said Pirate Milnedew losing his track momentarily. Oh yes he continued. "My hunter class ship comprised of four compartments. The rear being the main fuel storage battery banks along with the proton reactors and the momentum drive shaft, which by the way was damaged beyond repair in the crash landing. So, escape with the aid of my vessel was never on the cards, and anyway, with most of my fuel being almost depleted, the object was to conserve energy, not waste it on futile attempts to escape. The two amidships compartments were full to the brim with all kinds of preserved Organimatters and the forward compartment comprised of the living module and the flight deck." Pirate Milnedew closed his eyes and began to recount the strange turn of events that followed. "One night cycle, as I was sleeping in the living module, I was awoken by an almighty shaking. At first I was a little drowsy and thought it a bad dream, then I was thrown off my bunk to the floor and realised it was a reality. My initial suspicion was that the ship, and the Asteroid on which I was stranded, had been struck by another Asteroid. Suddenly the control consul on the flight deck illuminated like an explosion in a fireworks factory. All Helios had broken loose. Whatever it was had breached the hull a mid-ships applying incredible stress factors to the ship's integral structure. After managing to seal of the damaged area, which by the way was confined only to the third quarter section, losing all of the cargo from within and fracturing the oxygenation system and the surplus tanks, this left me with two problems. After sealing all the bulkheads with relative success any emergency problems with the ship's systems meant a short but dangerous space walk to the fourth quarter section of the craft. You see, the on-board computer systems tracking module's link had been irreparably severed in the collision unfortunately depleting any rejuvenation power. I had designed my own primitive system which was linked to the same power conduits channel and brained by the functions of the on-board tracking modules back-up system. The second problem being one of a survival quandary. I had still got more than sufficient Vegimatters to survive a life time, but the recent collision having taken out over half my emergency oxygen tanks and depriving me of the ability to recycle my used oxygen, left me dangerously close to eventual suffocation. My estimates were that I had enough oxygen for approximately one to one and a half startechtoids if I closed down the life support systems to all but the front living module section, which I had moved into the flight deck and sealed from the rest of the ship to conserve the supply. After taking a space-walk to examine the damage to the ship fully, I discovered that the object that had struck the ship was at least a quarter section of some kind of Robopod, or an antiquated probe. There wasn't enough of it to be sure of its origins as the section that had made a home embedded in my hull was almost destroyed, except for a chamber housing section which contained a Syncro switch still intact with a pre-course setting device from what laughingly reminds me of a Garlicallian story I must tell you some day." Pirate Milnedew giggled again nervously even though the word Garlicallian word made his spine chill. "Ha.. He... he... hee! This is where the real irony is, the real twist in the tail." he chortled as FO Marrowlar interrupted him.

"Twist, tail, irony, anyone would think you were writing a novel, Pirate Milnedew." Smiled FO Marrowlar.

"When this is all over I may well do just that because that Syncro switch gave me the final piece of hardware to create my avenue of escape. It didn't strike me straight away but when it did, it was certainly a relief. About forty starlectoids ago it hit me in my dreams. I built an encapsulated room from plasma steel, directed the oxygen into it and donned my famous Macadamian heirloom, the shackles. As you know, they can only be telekinetically operated. With practise I had managed to master the art of locking and unlocking them with mind transferral techniques I picked up when I was a prisoner on the Planet Macadamia. The oxygen was set to be manually operated so that I could adjust the flow accordingly; you see the shackles can be used to lower the respiratory requirements of the primitive bodily functions, needing less oxygen. Therefore, this stretched my oxygen supply from about forty starlectoids to about sixty starlectoids worth of rations. If you hadn't come along I was dead and there's no mistaking that."

Pirate Milnedew coughed and took a drink of grape juice then carried on with his epic tale. "Then I took the Macadamian shackles, hooked them into the static frequency Proton booster and cross configurated the reconditioned Syncro switch pre-set course device, into its housing matrix mechanism and connected it all into the main ship's anti-Vegitamisation defence system. So I had encapsulated myself in the cocoon that I had built, closed down all but the ship's back up power systems to maintain the defence system, taken in enough Vegimatter to last sixty starlectoids, then, made the rest of the ship into a vacuum chamber and lay in wait for my rescue after activating the shackles so that my oxygen requirement was minimised." Then all I had to do was lay in waiting to test my theory of escape."

"Don't get me wrong Pirate Milnedew this is all very interesting, but, how did you escape? I don't understand." interrupted FO Marrowlar

Pirate Milnedew sat up and gathered his strength while Dr Kiwitranus moved the Triabulator from the bed side.

"Picture this." said Pirate Milnedew. "I am lying inside the cocoon with supplies, oxygen, Macadamian shackles which are connected to a static frequency proton booster, and the reconditioned Syncro switch. All three were hooked up to the anti-Vegitamisation chamber that I had reversed the polarity field changing it effectively from a defence receiver to a crude transmitter. As soon as it picked up a proton output increase from either a Phaser firing or a Defence shield, a connection was made, I would die for a split second as non-functional Vegitamisation is relatively simple to achieve. Coming to life through the Vegitamisation process which in itself is a short blast form of intense re-divination, the shackles allowed me to stay alive at the lowest mental and respiratory levels possible, while the Syncro switch acted as the trigger mechanism for the proton frequency link. When that happened the anti- Vegitamisation force field transported me to whatever ship was passing. The rest is here for you to see."

"Brilliant, Pirate Milnedew! Absolutely brilliant. But you are wrong about one thing." croaked the Captain, dreading how he would take the news that his not so distant neighbours for the last three years, where none-other than the Garlicallians themselves.

"There is someone.. Something else in the Voidwell that must be released from its grip!" he said.

"Then trust me Captain," said a surprised Pirate Milnedew. "If we leave them at the mercy of that thing we are as good as murderers. How do you know that they are alive? The chances of survival once the ship has been sucked in is very slim.

"Dr Kiwitranus can Pirate Milnedew be moved?" asked Captain Carrot.

"Well Captain, he appears to be strong enough to re-live his trauma, as long as you push him around in the hover chair I see no reason why he shouldn't take a well earned rest from his bed sores." he confirmed.

"Dr Kiwitranus, Councillor, Pirate Milnedew. I would like you all to come with us." ordered Captain Carrot.

"Where are we going?" asked Pirate Milnedew as Captain Carrot and Dr Kiwitranus placed him in the chair.

"I'll let you know, as soon as we know. Trust me, all will be revealed." said Captain Carrot, again grasping Pirate Milnedew's shoulder.

In the strategy room Professor Goosegorgon had informed FO Potatree, FO Cornelius, FO Melonicord and Mushroid Fungola of Captain Carrot's delay due to the improvement of the condition of the unexpected guest in the Medilab.

"Why is there such concern over a Pirate?" said a miffed FO Cornelius.

"A mad Pirate at that!" snarled FO Melonicord.

"Blind," said FO Potatree. "Small minded, self opinionated group of busy-bodies. He continued. "Don't you people listen to a word I say? Were your ears full of cotton wool back in the Gravitation suite? It was his choice to exile himself. He couldn't cope with the pressures of group existence. I wouldn't wish what that Organiman has been through on any one of us. But, if that is what it would take to get it through your thick skulls then, well, maybe it wouldn't be such a bad thing for any of you to experience!" shouted the Chief Engineer being very protective of the individual concerned.

"Excus'a me FO Potatree, but 'a you are very, shall we say, paternal of this young Organiman, why?" asked the Professor.

FO Potatree clutched his hands in embarrassment. Shows of emotion were not common place in this Organiman's make-up. "Pirate Milnedew's father," he said slowly. "Trained with me at the Spaceark Academy. What I am about to tell you will go no further than these four walls. If it does, then I shall come, a knocking on your door is that clear?" The assembled group stood in silence and nodded in agreement. "Not many people," continued FO Potatree. "Know that Pirate Milnedew's Father is stationed on the O.S.S.S Junipitaris. He was the Chief Engineer, FO Marrowmilne.

Because of the shame his son had supposedly brought on the family name, he resigned his FO status and now serves as an ordinary Ensign rating going under the name of Ensign Marrowmin. At least, that is what he would have us all believe. The real reason is that he sent his son into space, disowning him. "The reason?" I hear you ask, his son's supposed stupidity or negligence in delivering the Garlicallian cargo to Macadamia in the first place. You see, Kenaldoe Marrowmilne is an Organitron of the old school; very proud, very vain and very stubborn. I am sure that to this day he feels guilty about turning his son away when his son needed him most. The real reason he gave up his FO status in my opinion, was that he felt he was not Organiman enough to wear the uniform of a high ranking position of responsibility if he couldn't even face the tough lesson of life within the family unit." reasoned FO Potatree turning to face the observation plasma steel window and staring into the star studded surrounds of space.

"Well, as his friend, you must have talked to him about it, FO Potatree? What did he say?" Asked Mushroid Fungola.

"You can lead a Horsechester to water but you cannot make him drink it!" muttered FO Potatree. "It was as his friend I broke the news of what had occurred on Macadamia to him. That day his son was lying in sick bay with severe mental damage. It was also that day without even going to see his son, that he banished Kenthal Marrowmilne from their family unit. We haven't spoken since." said FO Potatree with regret. "One's flesh and blood is a part of one-self. Cast that part away into the outer depths of limbo and you cast part of yourself away. The day he did that, he cast away the part of him that I had respected and love for." He continued sitting in his seat.

As FO Potatree sat down, the doors to the strategy room de-energised and in strolled Captain Carrot pushing Pirate Milnedew in the hover-chair. They were flanked by the Viceroy Councillor, the good Doctor and FO Marrowlar, closely followed by Commander Marrachinello and Ensign Broccleman.

"Ensign Broccleman." said Captain Carrot closing the strategy room doors. "As the brains behind the Vegimatter room I would like you to stay. Commander Marrachinello welcome aboard." he said offering the Commander the Organitron UFO salute.

"Aye Sir." said Ensign Broccleman.

"Jolly glad to be here old chap. Here is that little package I promised you. Don't go scoffing it all at once now, eh what! I would have been here a bit sooner only I ran into gas pocket storm, had to override the motherboard on the ship's computer blessed thing was going to run me right into it. Thought it best to skirt around her, don't you know? Still what's an extra four starlectoids to see an old friend umm?" he chuckled, twanging his handlebar moustache.

"Commander Marrachinello will you please stay for the meeting?" said the Captain.

"Of course old bean, if you think I can be of some use then I would be honoured, Captain Carrot."

The others took their seats as Captain Carrot took his place at the table, and began to speak.

"Organimen, Organigirls; Many of you will know the facts of the previous meeting, others of you will be unaware of the complex situation. Please allow me to introduce to you Pirate Milnedew who recently mysteriously Vegitamised aboard the O.S.S.S Earthanon. Pirate Milnedew, FO Marrowlar, Viceroy Councillor Au Paw-Paw and Dr Kiwitranus you already know. This is FO Melonicord our transportation Co-ordinator. Professor Goosegorgon our science and technology advisor. FO Cornelius our science and technology chief. FO Pot..."

"Atree, yes we already know each other how are you Chief?" interrupted Pirate Milnedew.

"I'm fine son, tis good to see you are still around my boy." Smiled FO Potatree.

"I see." Said Captain Carrot. "Well this is Comma.."

"Oh we've crossed swords many a time Captain Carrot, blessed fine pilot the elusive Pirate Milnedew, yes indeedy." Chortled Commander Marrachinello.

"Yes, well then, that just leaves Ensign Broccleman who was flummoxed by your appearance in the Vegimatter room, and Mushroid Fungola our ship's strategist Mechanoid. For those unfamiliar with the scenario we find ourselves confronted by, I would briefly like to summarise the facts to date." Captain Carrot stood and began encircling the room. "Eight starlectoids ago," he continued. "We became caught in the suction tract of the Voidwell which is positioned some thirty thousand starmillo's away at twenty-even blimits off our starboard side. Its energy force nearly over-powering our Calorific K factor, but, thanks to FO Potatree, not quite. As we were pulling away, we were struck by a foreign object at the time unknown causing minimal damage, and, we have established no threat intended. Very quickly a second foreign object was observed coming from the epicentre of the Voidwell, exactly the same as the first."

"What were these foreign objects Captain?" asked Pirate Milnedew.

"All in good time Pirate Milnedew." continued the Captain. "Yesterday the Voidwell surged again and yet another foreign object emerged from the epicentre, so we think we have established a starwektoid pattern! Every seven starlectoids the power surge occurs." Captain Carrot looked at Pirate Milnedew who was deep in thought. "If this is the case," Captain Carrot continued. "We would have picked up the power surges long before, but why didn't we?"

"Captain Carrot." said Pirate Milnedew. "I was in the Voidwell for a little over three startechtoids, believe me when I tell you that the inside is one constant power entity. At the end of roughly every startechtoid, there has been four sub-conversion energy displacements of a shattering enormity. Each time I thought my number was up; each time I survived. Once there were two in quick succession. The last of the four is always the most powerful, that is if it plays by the rules. Your next," paused Pirate Milnedew "will be your last until next the startechtoid. One more thing Captain" paused Pirate Milnedew. "The last two power surges are always four starlectoids apart." he continued. Captain Carrot stood in silence gazing around the table almost unnerved by the sudden shocking benefits of the inside information.

"So" said the Captain. "The third power surge took place at **09.27 starhectoids,** that's **two starlectoids** ago, the time is now **19.30 starhectoids**. That gives us by my reckoning **thirty-eight starhectoids**, agreed?" said the Captain as they synchronised their watches.

"That doesn't leave us much time Captain." Said FO Marrowlar slowly.

"Hatchooo.. Hatchooo. Thud." Sneezed FO Cornelius.

"Well that knocks my plan on the head." Said FO Potatree.

"Whatever your plans are to get that ship out of there, you had better get to it fast." stated Pirate Milnedew.

Captain Carrot returned to his seat at the table and caressed his temples, gently giving thought to the plan that still lay unveiled in his head.

"Pirate Milnedew," said Captain Carrot. "It is not a ship stuck in the Voidwell but, but a Planet, a lost space race from the old Bubbleonion Squeak Solar System. A Planet with a fraction of its original population, one hundred and seventy thousand to be precise. The foreign objects we referred to earlier, were probes sent as an SOS from that Planet, and that Planet was Garlicazure!"

Pirate Milnedew's mouth dropped faster than a speeding meteor.

"You mean, for all this time I have been within spitting distance of those, those smelly, in-consequential, vanity-riddled, egotistical megalomaniacs, why didn't anyone tell me?"

"Excuse me." said Mushroid Fungola. "Captain Carrot just did. It's not like you needed to know as soon as you woke up, you weren't strong enough." he reasoned passing Pirate Milnedew a glass of grape juice in order to calm him down.

"That's right Pirate Milnedew," said Captain Carrot. "And it's not as though they didn't save your life; albeit unwittingly! The people you have a feud against the Garlicallians of the past are long since out of existence, until now that is. They are not the same race that the Macadamians distrusted. They have been through much I have no doubt, and like everyone, I believe they deserve a second chance, and by hook or by crook we are going to give them that chance." said the determined Captain.

"But how, Captain?" enquired FO Marrowlar. "We have been searching our souls for an answer to rescue them but to no avail." said FO Marrowlar. "It's just too big, too powerful." Reasoned FO Marrowlar.

This is how, FO Marrowlar!" said the Captain. "Dr Kiwitranus, do we have enough substances to make a sleeping draught that will lower the respiratory cycles of everyone on Garlicazure?"

"I can make up a large batch of Photocynthime Hallomathalate capsules. Once taken," continued Dr Kiwitranus. "The respiratory cycle will be near halted for approximately four starhectoids. Any longer than that and we risk brain trauma in the recipients." said Dr Kiwitranus.

"How long will it take to prepare Doctor?"

"Six starhectoids Captain." confirmed Dr Kiwitranus.

"You have nine starhectoids Dr Kiwitranus. Make two hundred thousand capsules. You are dismissed." ordered Captain Carrot.

"Aye, aye Captain." said Dr Kiwitranus running from the strategy room.

"Professor Goosegorgon, can you rig me up a mobile satellite phaser output unit to fire on the Voidwell at ship's command? And I mean a powerful one Professor."

"I could 'a convert the Vocado ionisation acidulation stabiliser phaser Capatano, bulk it 'a out and increase voltage output with an old 'a network of vitamin reactors for prolonged firing. I have been saving the old 'a reactors." said Professor Goosegorgon smugly. "But I amma gonna need all 'a help I can get 'a with its 'a construction from Engineering, say, six men and you can have it in'a working order in nine starhectoids." confirmed Professor Goosegorgon.

"You've got em me old darlin!" agreed FO Potatree.

"Thank you FO Potatree. Professor Goosegorgon, you are dismissed." said the Captain.

"Aye, aye Capatano." said the Professor bouncing out of the room. **Boing, Boing Boink!**

"FO Melonicord." continued Captain Carrot. "I want you to Contact the O.S.S Capsicumby and the Ommelettra, the last known records show that Garlicazure has a mass spectrum in the diameter of five thousand starmillo's. We will assume it's the same. Ask them to set out a combined energy field, a reverse catapult electron dragnet, seven thousand starmillo's wide by six thousand starmillo's high. Have them set the probes in a cross net configuration one hundred starmillo's apart; by my reckoning that means we will require four thousand two hundred Roboprobes correct?" asked the Captain.

FO Melonicord tapped into the Computron.

"Your maths are correct Sir, but, between the three of us we only have four thousand serviceable Roboprobes, I can requisition two hundred from the O.S.S Satsumuroo?" She confirmed.

"Do it, when we have them I want them loaded with an anti-gravity magnetic proton booster! We will need it to stay linked for at least six starmins, so the two ships will have to run with it. They must maintain the energy output link. Now go, I want them ready to lay the net in nine starhectoids and I want the net laid and established in twelve starhectoids, ten thousand starmillo's from the expulsion point of the Voidwell. Dead centre alignment, FO Melonicord, tell them to allow as much slack for themselves as they can. We will run an established link test at **07.30 starhectoids** tomorrow." Said Captain Carrot rubbing his hands.

"Aye, aye Sir." acknowledged FO Melonicord, running from the room.

"Captain. What exactly are you planning on doing?" Asked Pirate Milnedew.

"When that Voidwell ejects that Planet it will be at a considerable speed. We will need to slow it down to a halt; but gradually, so I am setting out an Electron Dragnet, a kind of Magnetic force-field trampoline, only this one won't bounce it back!" said the Captain thinking quick on his feet.

"What makes you so sure that the Voidwell will reject the Planet?" enquired Pirate Milnedew.

"All will be revealed Pirate Milnedew. FO Cornelius, FO Potatree. Attached to the good Professor's phaser housing, I want an Electronic force-field Radion ring that will give us as much power output as you can muster. Attached to that, I want a sonic perambulator detonation module, mined with ten Anti-Matter Acidulated Califoric Proton Torpedoes set with a thirty second detonation delay, is that clear?"

"Aye, aye Sir, but when that baby blows we had better be more than a million starmillo's from here, or we are grilled Tomatron's Captain." quipped FO Potatree.

"Hatchooo.. Hatchooo.. Thud.. Thud.. Ooh.. Ow. Holy Helios I knew it was a good starlectoid to stay in bed. Said FO Cornelius.

"We'll have her ready in four starhectoids Captain!" confirmed FO Potatree.

"Take your time, you have nine."

FO Marrowlar suddenly smiled as if the penny had dropped and the Captains plan was coming to the forefront of his vision.

"You like it FO Marrowlar; em?" smiled Captain Carrot."

"Energy!" said FO Marrowlar triumphantly as the credit had finally dropped. "You're going to feed it then burp it like a big old baby!" laughed FO Marrowlar. Then his laughter ceased as he looked at Pirate Milnedew and the respiratory sleeping capsules came galloping into his mind. "Captain Carrot." said FO Marrowlar. "How are you going to get the capsules to the Garlicallians in the Voidwell, let alone eject the Planet Garlicazure?" he continued.

"Well my friend, it sort of goes like this," smiled Captain Carrot nervously. "Ensign Broccleman. You and FO Marrowlar will de-activate the CO^2 capsules in an Oudag Missile and replace it with a scent detection resonance finder homing device. Pre-loaded with a sample of DNA from our new Garlicallian crew members. Load it with dual acidulation tanks to hold open the entry channel and then," Captain Carrot stopped in his tracks. "Then my friend comes the difficult bit. Then Ensign Broccleman, as soon as the Oudag Capsule enters the Voidwell, you will Vegitamise me along with the Respiratory minimisation draft, down the root of the Oudag Capsule with a ten second delay. Programming into the Vegimatter room Computer the acid trail chemical balance in order for the Vegitamisation beam to follow it. Of course we will send two Oudag Capsules, the first to be sent at **07.30** starhectoids tomorrow when we run a full systems check." Captain Carrot sat in silence as the truth hit home in a major way. FO Marrowlar jumped on his feet and protested very loudly.

"Captain, this is madness you can't guarantee that the acid channel won't disperse before you have a chance to complete the journey. Why, you can't even guarantee that the Oudag capsule will even find the Planet in that size of energy field. It's madness Sir. Even if you did land on the Planet, you may land thousands of starmillo's from the inhabitation area. We can't let you do it. You could be killed, and for nothing." shouted FO Marrowlar.

"If I know my Garlicallian history, they are all living together under the ground frightened and lonely, desperately needing our help. Don't you see FO Marrowlar! The only guarantee that comes with any of this plan is that if we don't do it, then the "Space Tracers of Organitron" will be all but dead, nothing more than a dream, a lie." Captain Carrot looked at his old friend FO Potatree who sat very stern faced and quiet. "Chief you understand surely, don't you?" asked the Captain quietly. "That thing feeds on energy," he continued. "If we can get to the Garlicallians, put them to sleep, turn off all but the barest of life support systems, the Voidwell will expel it to make way for the strange new power source in front of it that it will think is just as big. Besides the homing device in the dummy run Oudag Capsule will serve as a secondary precaution." Captain Carrot awaited his response.

"Aye, the Captain is right Benzo, it has to be done. All the while there is a chance we have to take it. Commander Marrachinello here knows all about taking chances and you ask him. If the odds are against him, does he run the opposite way? But you won't ask him because deep down you already know the answer!"

"Then I will go with you Captain." said FO Marrowlar. Concerned with the knowledge of his friend and Mentor going alone into the vast unknown.

"No Benzo, I will be asking for one volunteer but it will not be you my friend. Somebody will need to take charge of the O.S.S.S Earthanon if I don't come back. As it is, if a volunteer doesn't step forward, I will go alone, fully understanding why no-one could see their way to taking the risk. The ship will be safe in the best hands I know, yours!" Captain Carrot turned to Mushroid Fungola. "Mushroid Fungola you have all the facts and figures to my little plan, now I want you to go away and work out the odds as to the mission's success. I want all the facts, no matter how bad, before I recruit my volunteer. It would seem only fair they be aware of them too."

"Captain Carrot," interrupted FO Potatree. "Garlicazure runs an artificial sub gravity field which in itself has a massive energy output.

I'm not sure we could beat that, but if I were to go along with.. If I were to go along too, I could switch the polarity field for a few minutes at the right time to convince that thing, that the Planet is dead. It is a very old system and I'm probably the only one who could do it. The tools won't take up too much room in the Vegitamisation chamber and, and I have no family to speak of." He said slowly passing a glance in the direction of Pirate Milnedew.

"Are you sure you want to do this FO Potatree? There are as I say no guarantees." said Captain Carrot.

"No, but there will be if I come along, agreed?" Said FO Potatree smiling.

"Agreed Chief." acknowledged the Captain.

"Right then," said FO Potatree, walking towards the strategy room doors. "Oh and Captain Carrot." he said turning back and facing them while de-activating the doors. "Just one small demand before I go for a long walk?"

"Anything you want FO Potatree; and I guarantee it will be yours!"

"Anything Captain?" said the chief wryly.

"Anything chief, you have my word."

"In that case Gillespie J. Carrot, you will not mind if I say, pick my own volunteer to take your place on this mission? There are many brave Organimen and Organiwomen with the power to make a choice that have no family. And like you, if I can't find one I will understand and go alone."

"But..." interrupted Captain Carrot.

"No buts Captain, to me" counter argued FO Potatree. "The most important thing in this universe is your word, and I expect you to honour the faith that I have in it. FO Marrowlar, I will expect you in fifteen Starmins in the Engineering chamber if that is all right with you Captain?" Captain Carrot nodded, then FO Potatree walked out of the room closing the doors behind him.

"I say chaps, what a jolly humdinger of an Organiman, hey what!" said Commander Marrachinello with a lump in his throat. "Always have liked him."

Pirate Milnedew sat in silence as he felt proud of the only Organiman who ever tried to be his father after his own had rejected him. And now regretted not applying more trust in FO Potatree.

"Captain Carrot." said Pirate Milnedew. "Would you mind if I went back to the Medilab? I'm feeling a little tired and I think I'm going to need all my strength." he continued.

"No of course not. Ensign Broccleman, will you escort Pirate Milnedew back to his Medilab quarters please." asked the Captain.

"Aye, aye Sir." he agreed.

"Captain Carrot," said Pirate Milnedew. "It is an incredible plan, and you have a very special crew from what I have seen, you must be very proud?"

"The proudest, the very proudest!" he answered. "And the plan, well I just love it when a plan comes together!"

Then both Pirate Milnedew and Ensign Broccleman left leaving, FO Marrowlar alone with Captain Carrot and Commander Marrachinello to discuss the problems of the Fasterfoid's Flotilla force gathering in the uncharted sector F9 of the Bervedo quadrant. It was time to face the music and view Captain Beetrouly's vidiscript of his concerns of the flotilla force and its possible implications to the Planet Earthanon 'and' 'or' the O.S.S.S Earthanon.

CHAPTER SEVEN

To Fight, the unbeatable force

Part one

The preparations for Garlicazure

Sundate 2,999,999,999/ 331 Biltechtoids. Time 07.20 starhectoids

Twelve thousand starmillo's away from the position of the Voidwell, the O.S.S Capsicumby and the O.S.S Ommelettra were awaiting final orders to proceed as the extrovert Captain de Fleetrap strolled around the bridge of the O.S.S Capsicumby. He began muttering to himself in a quite undignified way, much to the concern of the bridge crew around him. In an earlier Visaid transmission he had been party to the plans of Captain Carrot's theoretical rescue attempt of the Planet Garlicazure, that plan was about to be tested in reality.

"It's.. It's brilliant, absolutely brilliant." he shouted to himself. "Of course it's absolute madness but a pure stroke of genius." he continued. "Yes it could just work at that. If not it would not be for the lack of trying." Then Captain de Fleetrap muttered in the sudden realisation of danger. "Of course one could also call it suicide, for if it were to fail that is surely what it will be for us. Curtains! The grand exit, the final stage." Realising that the whole of the bridge crew was watching him, he attempted to jolly up the proceedings with a comparative gesture.

"Rather like a game of Planetary tennis don't you think Ensign Ramputinder?" chirped the highly charged Captain de Fleetrap. "Only the object of this game being to aim the ball into the net instead of over It." he continued. "Yes, good sport indeed. Let us just hope that the service is easily returnable, nothing worse than an "out" call when you're playing for your life, umm?" he laughed as he awaited a reply from the fretful Ensign Ramputinder who was based at the Communications com.

"If I might be so bold Captain?" said the Ensign in reply. "One finds it difficult to feel ecstatic about what I would call a game of planetary marbles. Particularly, I mm. mm. might! Add," he stuttered. "Particularly as the opposition's marble is," he paused, "some-what bigger than ours. No, Sir, if you want my honest opinion. I think it is suicide, absolute suicide Captain de Fleetrap and that's no mistake." Captain de Fleetrap looked on the Ensign with a glowing feeling inside. A mixture of butterflies and roller-coaster all served with a generous portion of apprehension towards the unknown.

"Ha Ensign." said Captain de Fleetrap stalking his prey like a cat to the mouse. "My dear Ensign Ramputinder, it's the race, the cut to the chase, the thrill of the encounter. "Space and Organikind," at one with each other, mano-a-mano. What you have to remember Ensign Ramputinder is that it is not the size of your marble, merely the quality of the angled shot and its delivery, Ahh..." Then Ensign Ramputinder received a message from the O.S.S.S Earthanon as did Ensign Pepperailin, the Communication's Officer of the O.S.S Ommelettra.

"Captain de Fleetrap," said Ensign Ramputinder, thankful for the interruption from an Organiman obviously on a different Planet. Ensign Ramputinder liked and respected the Captain, but one day, sooner or later his theatrical bent would deliver its last performance. Ensign Ramputinder fancied it later rather than sooner that was all. "Excuse me Captain de Fleetrap," said Ensign Ramputinder. "O.S.S.S Earthanon confirms Dragnet link test ready at exactly 07.30 starhectoids on Captain Carrots mark. A ten second duration power output only; no-longer; no-shorter. Also, recommend securing Garlicallian Probe in the vacuum chamber, Sir." said the Ensign.

"Signal confirmation and compliance, R. C. E. D test at **07.30 starhectoids**," confirmed Captain de Fleetrap. "Also inform the O.S.S.S Earthanon that the probe is already secure."

"Aye, aye Sir." agreed Ensign Ramputinder.

On the bridge of the O.S.S.S Earthanon, Captain Carrot was seated at the Command com awaiting the hour of the final checks.

"Captain Carrot," said Ensign Strawballis. "The O.S.S Capsicumby and the O.S.S Ommelettra have confirmed compliance, Sir." confirmed Ensign Strawballis.

"Good, we must make sure when the time comes they don't stop that Planet until it is at least one point two million starmillo's from this point." said the Captain activating his personal channel as commander Marrachinello stepped out of the elevation chamber.

"Aye, aye Sir." said Ensign Strawballis.

"Captain Carrot to FO Potatree and Cornelius, come in please."

"Aye! Aye! Captain FO Potatree here." he replied as, "Hatchooo Hatchooo.. Thud!" could be heard in the background.

No need to ask where FO Cornelius is. Are you ready and in position with the Radion ring and mined Sonic Perambulator?" asked the Captain.

"Aye, aye Sir. She's out of our face and out there in space. Set at an angle of forty five blimits into the epicentre, three and a half thousand starmillo's above the central alignment. When the Planet comes out she'll pass right under it! Oh, and professor Goosegorgon's phaser housing," remembered FO Cornelius aloud. "They are hooked up together so we will run all the tests simultaneously." confirmed Cornelius to FO Potatree. "Well," said FO Potatree. "I think you just heard we are on line and ready to "Rock and Roll" Captain." he continued.

"Good work Organimen. Test at **07.30 starhectoids**; a ten second burst no-more no-less. Then if there are no problems get some rest, you may need it. Carrot out."

"Aye, aye Sir." said FO Potatree.

"Captain Carrot to FO Marrowlar and Ensign Broccleman, come in please."

"FO Marrowlar here Captain. Sir, the "Oudag!" has been tested and placed in the torpedo tube, Dr Kiwitranus is here with the sleeping draught capsules and FO Potatree's tools are ready for Vegitamisation." said FO Marrowlar.

"Good work Organimen, stand by for test observations at 07.30 starhectoids. Captain Carrot out."

"Aye, aye Captain, FO Marrowlar out." said FO Marrowlar signing off.

Time 07.25 starhectoids

FO Potatree was in his quarters lying down when Viceroy Au Paw-Paw activated his organ pad entry code. **"Bioooeeeeioooo."**

FO Potatree raised himself from the secure comfort of his Vegewell and straightened his tunic.

"Entry cleared." he said to the computer who de-activated the doors. As it did so, Viceroy Councillor Au Paw-Paw appeared alongside Pirate Milnedew who was looking much healthier than he previously had appeared.

"Viceroy Councillor Au Paw-Paw, Kenthal, to what do I owe the pleasure? Not that I am unhappy to see such a rapid recovery."

Councillor Au Paw-Paw turned to leave the private gathering as she was already aware of Pirate Milnedew's intentions.

"If you do not mind Organimen I will leave you to talk." she said slowly.

"No." they said together doing the Organimanly thing.

"I would, for my part, like you to stay Viceroy Councillor Au Paw-Paw," said pirate Milnedew reassured of her firm shoulder to fall back on should things not go as planned.

"Very well Kenthal; unless of course FO Potatree you really don't mind?" enquired the Councillor.

"Why mind? Why would I mind? Is it bad news or something? It's not like I couldn't use the distraction." he laughed half heartedly. "You wouldn't believe what has been going through my mind in these last few starhectoids."

Then FO Potatree remembered from where Pirate Milnedew came and felt idiotic at once.

"By Helios, what am I talking about? Of course you would have an idea; about three startechtoids worth. Forgive me Kenthal, it is purely selfish thought; nothing personal meant." Reasoned FO Potatree.

"I know exactly what is running through your mind, FO Potatree and believe me you are entitled to your fears. They are not misplaced and not without good reason." replied Pirate Milnedew with an apprehensive smile.

"It's just that I don't know what to think. So much rides on the outcome of my success, and I have doubts whether I am worthy of rising to the challenge." whimpered FO Potatree with a great deal of uncertainty in his voice.

"Relax my friend." said Pirate Milnedew, grasping FO Potatree's shoulder. "You will succeed and with good reason." he continued. "Your heart is strong and beats for the cause. Your mind reasons with the odds and your respect for other life forms is so strong that you would give your last breath; your last heartbeat, for a fighting chance of their survival. No chief; your concerns are justified, but your reasons; your reasons are unselfish and without reproach. Nobody could ask more and you could not offer less." said the Pirate Milnedew looking into FO Potatree's eyes. "Believe me, you are more worthy of the trust that is placed on you, than anyone I have ever known."

"Thank you Kenthal, but you are too kind really." laughed the chief some-what embarrassed by the display of affection in front of another Officer.

"Tell me FO Potatree," said Kenthal. "Do you really want to thank me?" asked Pirate Milnedew.

"I don't understand Kenthal. What do you mean?" he enquired.

"Have you found a volunteer to accompany you to the surface of Garlicazure?" he said brashly.

"Yes.. No.. I mean I have decided that no-one should go in there on a possible mission of folly. Don't get me wrong." said the Chief firmly, bowing his head fearful of what he suspected was about to follow.

"Take me with you FO Potatree?" said Pirate Milnedew slowly.

"Oh now Kenthal," said Chief Potatree fighting back the emotion. "Don't you think you have been through quite enough where that blessed Voidwell is concerned, umm?" answered FO Potatree.

"FO Potatree," said Pirate Milnedew. "I never thought I would say this about the Garlicallians," he continued. "But they have gained my respect for surviving this long. If it weren't for them I would still be stuck in there and the thought of that could send me insane. Whether I like it or not, the two Space Races I hate most got me out of that hell hole; the Macadamians and the Garlicallians. Believe me, I more than anyone hate to admit it but they did. Had they the choice they may not have, but, they didn't! No FO Potatree, they don't know it but save my life they did! And now it is my turn to help them. Please let me do this with you? I beg of you." pleaded Pirate Milnedew.

FO Potatree hugged Pirate Milnedew and whispered in his ear.

"Your Father; if only he could see you now my boy."

"I am not doing this for my Father FO Potatree. I'm doing it for me. Me and the Garlicallians, and for you, the nearest person to a father I have had in a long time. Will you say yes-please Chief?" Said Pirate Milnedew searching FO Potatree's soul.

"Yes my sonny boy, if the Captain agrees then yes, and thank you." said FO Potatree with tears in his eyes.

"Thank me when we get back, just after you have bought me the universes biggest fruitshake." he said. "Deal?"

"Deal." agreed FO Potatree.

"Now wait a minute you two; you pull this thing off and the fruitshakes are on me you hear." Smiled Viceroy Au Paw-Paw.

Time 07.27 starhectoids.

On the bridge of the O.S.S.S Earthanon all was tense as the Countdown sequence was in full flow and FO Potatree stepped onto the bridge with Pirate Milnedew to break the news.

"Ahh FO Potatree, Pirate Milnedew. I am glad I bumped into you Chief. A small matter of a programmed dysfunctional Mushroid ring any bells does it?" quipped the Captain.

"Yes actually, it does," said the Chief. "Funny things those Mushroids!" he continued. "Terrible memory chips some of them. A tendency to have too much of an imagination programme wouldn't you agree Sir?" laughed FO Potatree.

Captain Carrot smiled at the pair as they giggled away. "I couldn't fall out with FO Potatree," thought Captain Carrot. "Not for using his brain with the Mushroid Fungola. Not now, considering he was going to risk his life for the good of the Organitrons and their noble cause. It would be childish not to see the funny side." So the Captain laughed with them. Commander Marrachinello joined in the laughter as Pirate Milnedew suddenly stopped and prodded FO Potatree.

"I think that now is as good a time as any Chief!" He whispered.

"What? Oh yes indeed Kenthal." said FO Potatree. "Captain Carrot, FO Marrowlar as soon as the tests are complete and confirm all systems on line and operational, I would like your permission to make preparation for my departure."

"Of course FO Potatree. Tell me have you chosen a volunteer to accompany you on this Helios forsaken mission?" asked the Captain.

"That's what I wanted to talk to you about Captain." said the sly Chief Engineer. "I had decided not to give anyone the chance of joining me on this trip.." "No." came Captain Carrot's response interrupting the Chief sharply. "It is bad enough that you choose to go at all my friend but I cannot; I will not let you go alone." Captain Carrot thought momentarily. "At least you will take a Mushroid with you.. Won't you?" enquired the Captain.

"It had crossed my mind Captain." said the Chief. "Then something quite amazing happened that made it impossible to refuse the offer of help from an unusual source! He continued.

"And just who is this unusual source FO Potatree?" said the Captain looking hopefully at Pirate Milnedew. "Though I'll bet you I'm looking at him already.. Am I right?" smiled Captain Carrot.

Pirate Milnedew nodded as FO Potatree awaited fireworks for involving a classified enemy of the Organitrons into the planned rescue attempt. "Y. Yo.. You don't mind Captain Carrot?" asked FO Potatree.

"It is not an ideal situation I grant you, and I have no doubt I will receive some flak from the SFA, but, taking all that into account, it is the best possible scenario and, a wonderful testament to the real person trapped inside the notable figure of the mythical Pirate Milnedew. You have my permission, my gratitude and my respect Pirate Milnedew.

"All stations standing by for test sequence Captain Carrot." said Ensign Strawballis.

"Thank you Ensign Strawballis. FO Marrowlar. Time stat please?" enquired the Captain.

"**Time 07.29 starhectoids** and **V minus sixty starsecs** for test sequence... Now." confirmed FO Marrowlar.

"Captain Carrot to Captains de Fleetrap and Macoronite on secured frequency. Come in please." asked the Captain activating his personal channel

"Yes Captain we are standing by." they confirmed together.

"Activate the R.E.C.D on my mark. Professor Goosegorgon, stand-by to monitor the electron output capacity of the Vitamin proton reactors. If there is any strain in the system it must be spotted and put right!"

"Hockey-dockey Capatano, Professor Goosegorgon standing by." he confirmed.

"Captain Carrot to FO Cornelius, prepare to activate Radion Ring and Satellite phaser housing on my mark."

"Hatchooo.. Hatchooo. Thud, thud. FO Cornelius standing by Captain."

"V minus thirty starsecs Captain." marked FO Marrowlar.

"Captain Carrot to Ensign Broccleman,"

"Aye, aye Sir. Ensign Broccleman here."

"Prepare launch and tracking device for the dummy Oudag Capsule on my mark." said the Captain.

"Aye, aye Captain, resting on your mark." confirmed Ensign Broccleman.

Captain Carrot sat back and awaited the ticking clock marking the point of activation.

"Well, this is it old bean, hey-what, umm? No going back now Chaps; Chapess's! Do or die time. Best of luck Organitrons. Make it stick Captain." said a nervous Commander Marrachinello.

"V minus ten starsecs Captain." confirmed FO Marrowlar.

"SO Tulipina, I want you to monitor that Voidwell like it was you own child! The slightest hiccup and I want it registered." ordered the Captain moving to the edge of his seat.

"Aye, aye Sir." she confirmed.

"Ensign Viola." said Captain Carrot. "I want you to pin-point the position of the Voidwell expulsion point any increase energy emissions I want pin-pointed and logged. Viceroy Rhubarblatt.." continued the Captain as FO Marrowlar interrupted again.

"V minus five starsecs Captain." he said.

"Viceroy Rhubarblatt, make ready the calorific proton reactors for Califoric K factor three propulsion. FO Marrowlar you centralise ship's systems, monitor and control." Said the Captain as FO Marrowlar counted down."

"Three, two, and one. Zero hour."

"Activate R.E.C.D." said the Captain. "Lock on satellite phasers and prepare for firing. Stand by Radion ring alignment and initiate Oudag expulsion on my mark." he continued.

Between the O.S.S Capsicumby and the Ommelettra, the probes activated the huge dragnet that lit up the skies like a vast, luminous crossword puzzle. A spider's web of energy gradually linking together awaiting to catch its prey. Incredibly visible; Even ten thousand starmillo's away from the bridge of the O.S.S.S Earthanon they could all see its powerful but deadly beauty.

"Captain Carrot, O.S.S Capsicumby and O.S.S Ommelettra confirmed full proton link established." Said FO Marrowlar.

"FO Cornelius. Fire satellite phaser housing now!" said the Captain.

"Firing now Sir. Hatchooo." said FO Cornelius. Suddenly a constant beam of energy shot into the Voidwell, seemingly stirring some kind of reaction within the Voidwell itself.

"Follow on Radion ring link." ordered the Captain.

"Aye Sir, Radion on line." confirmed FO Cornelius as the satellite phaser housing seemed encapsulated by a bright effervescence looking from an angle remarkably like Saturn and its rings.

"Ten seconds, no more FO Cornelius, FO Marrowlar, from mark."

FO Marrowlar began counting, as Viceroy Rhubarblatt conveyed progress.

"Captain." he said. "We are experiencing a slight intermittent pull on our natural tract. Almost like, like the Voidwell is searching for something." he reasoned.

"Eight, seven.." continued FO Marrowlar.

"The Voidwell is opening up Captain." confirmed Ensign Viola. "Cross scanning for emission expulsion point position now Sir." she continued.

"Five, Four.." said FO Marrowlar.

"Launch Oudag Ensign Broccleman." said the Captain

"Oudag fired now Sir." confirmed Ensign Broccleman.

The Oudag could be seen entering the Voidwell creating an infusion of colours eventually blending into a bright yellow. Then came a spectacular tangerine coloured explosion, rocking the ship slightly.

Two and one Captain; De-activate R.E.C.D." said FO Marrowlar. "Off-line Satellite Phaser and Radion Ring."

As the rocking subsided, the Captain turned to SO Tulipina.

"Damage report SO Tulipina." he ordered slowly.

"All systems indicate no damage, but, and this is interesting Captain," she said working the ship's Particle scanner. "The Voidwell subsided as soon as the power input feeding it was removed, almost, almost as though it was an intelligent life form." she said with dismay.

"That's because that is exactly what it is!" stated Captain Carrot, as the last piece of the jigsaw fell into place. "All previous encounters that we know of, one of them we know to be the Captain of the-ill fated ship the O.S.S Sorbet Verbena. An Organiman whose information made it back to Carridionaries and the Widdup archives. Captain Watercreisure as was his name, confirmed in his last known Captain's log entry said," continued the Captain. "That no matter we they throw at it, it expanded and tightened its grip." In my opinion the thing seemed almost attracted to it, liked it even! Pirate Milnedew here is the first and only living testament to what lies within the Voidwell." Captain Carrot stopped and paced the bridge, his actions resembling something along the lines of what would normally be associated with Professor Goosegorgon. He was muttering under his breath, rubbing his hands. He even reprimanded himself for his own stupidity. "Of course it's intelligent. Living now as we speak, food you fool," he cried now even more confident of the plan on which they had embarked. "sapped energy of the old causing loss of appetite in exchange for external sources of new energy, that much I was already certain but of course-of course, it has a choice making capability." he exacerbated in frustration as the others looked on amazed by the Captain's public self flogging. "Call yourself a Captain? You should have looked deeper, harder without reserve and no stone unturned. Why, if this were not your best and most expensive tunic I would rip off your emblem as we speak." Then he turned toward the assembled crew just in time to catch Commander Marrachinello indicating with his finger that Captain Carrot was cuckoo and had flipped it altogether. "Indeed Commander!" laughed Captain Carrot. "I do believe you are right. I must have been mad not to spot it sooner." said the Captain shaking his head. "The Voidwell eats energy," he continued. "Consumes everything in its path, or, does it? We.. I, believe that we have neglected to look at it with open minds and assumed that a natural phenomenon cannot or does not exist with intelligence. It took in an entire Planet, and yet it did not destroy it. No I'm afraid within that kind of turbulent atmosphere the Planet would have been crushed. I believe it managed to maintain a sensible orbital signature, controlled its axis and just fed from it, leaving its inhabitants enough of everything to exist. It left the Planet with an existence of some sort it's true otherwise they would no longer be there? But, kind or cunning that is the question? To feel for the trapped inhabitants and save their lives, unable to expel it from its own grasp. Or, as I believe, to benefit its own dietary needs by maintaining an energy producing life form. It took a ship that fired untold energy to defend it 'self. That energy was that ship's fatal attraction." Captain Carrot looked at Pirate Milnedew. "Then that brings me to Pirate Milnedew." he said grasping his arm. "Pirate Milnedew had the foresight to build himself, with some help from his universe's worst enemy the Garlicallians, a transportation system activated by energy. Only reversing the affects of intake to expulsion through a channel in the form of energy path finding. But he was in such poor condition that he was dead when he was beamed aboard. I believe he was dead and the energy in the Vegitamisation beam was the only tonic for recovery he needed, supplied only by our phasers and energy shields; don't you see that... that thing, was making a choice. It expelled what was useless to him and discarded it like an unpleasant taste, what was nutritionally no longer of any service to its digestive system. So it chose no longer to consume his power source for a greater consumption." Reasoned Captain Carrot as he sat at the seat he had loved for so long and yet at this time, he half-heartedly felt he didn't deserve it.

"But," said FO Marrowlar thoughtfully. "Pirate Milnedew's energy pathfinder was only in operation for forty starlectoids why wasn't his ship crushed when it entered the Voidwell three startechtoids ago.?" He reasoned as the rest of the bridge crew found themselves nodding in agreement.

"Ahh.." said Captain Carrot wisely. "The energy output from the Anti-Vegitamisation force field, combined with the reasonable sized Asteroid on which his ship was marooned, probably convinced the Voidwell that it had in its belly a star, a star ready to explode. Therefore it would provide an explosive meal at some later date, so it preserved It." explained a proud Captain Carrot.

Then Commander Marrachinello started to clap as did the rest of the crew. Captain Carrot looked on, proud but not jubilant.

"By golly old chap. If it's true, it's incredible but if you are to be taken seriously and I believe you must, it all sounds, quite.. Quite feasible old chap. Absolute corker of a story."

Captain Carrot smiled and raised his hand to stop, what he felt, was a premature yet understandable show of excitement.

"Excuse me, Sir. What makes you so sure that it will expel the Planet and not just suck the artificial power source in? Namely us." said FO Marrowlar. Captain Carrot smiled with an air of uncertainty. "It is my hunch," he said. "That as old as it is, it is unwise and in its greed lies the extent of its immaturity. It can't resist what it can't have and will lose interest in anything it does not want, rather like an Organichild with a new toy at their seedling birthday celebration.

"You mean this is like stealing Organicandy from a child?" said Ensign Strawballis.

"Like I said, that is just a hunch, but I believe you summed it up beautifully." said the Captain. "Only this particular candy is a very dangerous sweetie indeed and we steal it for the benefit and protection of the children concerned. That makes it an acceptable crime."

Part two (1)

Earthanon starts to lose its patience / a real pea souper!

Sundate 2.999,999,999/ 330 Biltechtoids. Time 14.30 starhectoids.

The sun was starting to set in the Arcticus region of Earthanon's main mining district. Arcticus City was an unusual hive of activity in the main square known as free speaker's corner. An Organiman known as "Mystic Alluishus Cobhorn," or "Mac" for short, was preaching, as usual, the downfalls of the Planetary home they had found in Earthanon. However this starlectoid was different. This starlectoid he had an audience and what was worse they appeared to be taking great interest in what he had to say. After all, there was much common talk and speculation throughout all districts of Earthanon as to who the unknown Flotilla forces were, and what they were planning.

"The end is nigh," shouted Mac. "And our time is up," he continued. "In that there is no mistake. We do not, have never and never can belong here. It is too far from our loved ones, our roots and our history.." he shouted as a heckler drowned his voice.

"If it weren't for this Planet in which you say we don't, have never, and never can belong. Then we would not exist, so what is the point of listening to you anyway umm answer me that?" shouted a Plumacriate from the crowd. An Organitron from the Planet Plumbaba in the Fruitanutes plexus.

"Even if your body is here, there are those among us that think your mind left ages ago; tell me have you got any Macadamian blood in you Mac?" shouted another member of the crowd, an Organiwoman from Guavailian descent of the Planet Guavertutu in the Fruitalia quadrant.

"Oh mock me if you will but remember this! When the aliens arrive from that distant place, you heard it here first, and I tell you now, I will lead us to salvation, protect you from their evil actions and we will drive them from our communities." he said shaking his finger at the young Organiwoman.

"So you get to do the talking, and we get to do the fighting." cried an outraged Sun-Fleet security guard, Ensign Lattro Apricotlear, joining him on the rostrum.

"Listen to me all of you!" shouted the Ensign directing his attention to the crowd. It is true, we do not know exactly who they are; but we are quite sure that they are indeed Fasterfoids and as usual we Organitrons will deal with them if, and when it is necessary. When have we let you down umm? Please don't take the logic of this troublesome Cornmaizerite cuckoo. Now disperse and return to your homes. Trust me," he pleaded. "You are safe. You have Commodore Cu-Cumbala's and Admiral Ducarrotain's word for that and we all know that their words are worth a lot more than this bilge spouting mobile sewerage system."

Gradually the crowd dispersed and Mac turned to the young Officer.

"You fool, can you not see that you are being duped by the powers that be. I demand my freedom to speech." he shouted stamping his feet.

"That I can promise you!" laughed Ensign Apricotlear. "You can talk as much as you like to explain yourself to Ground Commodore Cu-Cumbala and if required, Admiral Ducarrotain." he said grabbing his arm and pulling him along.

"I will protest to the highest authorities you can be sure of that!" wailed Mac as what was left of his audience laughed at him being pulled away like a school Organiboy.

"Well unless you have a private communication frequency to Widdup the wise or Helios himself, you will just have to settle for Ground Commodore Cu-Cumbala for now. And my little paranoia preaching parasite friend, any more struggling from you Mac and you can talk a whole lot more to yourself; in the main brig house until you cool off! Is that clear?" said the fiery young Ensign.

Mac saw the look in his eyes. It was definitely time to shut up and resist no more. "Not another word shall pass my lips." he said going through the motions of zipping his mouth.

"If that were true," said the Ensign. "We could all rest easy and pull out our ear plugs once and for all.

Part two (2)

A real Pea souper!

Sundate 2.999,999,999/ 330 Biltechtoids. Time 14.00 starhectoids.

Captain Beetrouly and Captain Sunfleur were having breakfast in the O.S.S.S Milkymarrow way's ward room, when FO Twizzlepasta and FO Yamura Entered at some speed.

"Well of course the Fasterfoids are up to something. The last confirmation came from the Robopod relay some twenty four starlectoids ago. It confirmed they are still there at the same co-ordinates. In fact I think Captain Sunfleur, we are about to get the next relay report." said Captain Beetrouly.

"Thank Helios! This whole situation is becoming quite troublesome on the planetary surface. Shouts of "the end is nigh," are becoming quite common place in the market place. The other starlectoid I even heard some-one say that it was a new life-form observing us ready to pounce at anytime. I mean, really." said Captain Sunfleur.

"They are worried and maybe quite rightly so." said Captain Beetrouly. "It is not like the Fasterfoids to hold off attack. They are only thinking about their families and loved ones. After all, we cannot even confirm that they are not right." he continued

"Captain Beetrouly, Captain Sunfleur." said FO Yamura. "We apologise for interrupting your meal, but I'm afraid we bring bad news from the Robopods in the Bervado quadrant." winced FO Yamura.

"Oh really, well now why am I not surprised I wonder." Sneered a very smarmy Captain Sunfleur.

"Carry on FO Yamura." said Captain Beetrouly, glaring at Captain Sunfleur.

"It would appear one of our Robopods has gone missing. We think it may have tackled an Asteroid mine belt trying to get closer to the Flotilla.." she continued as Captain Sunfleur interrupted her flow again.

"Oh well that is unfortunate, I mean we can't even rely on our Robopods to hold orders now. Holy Helios, whatever next Captain Beetrouly?"

"Captain Sunfleur," continued FO Twizzlepasta. "We have got several Robopods in the sector sweeping the immediate area for any traces of calorific emissions or wreckage."

"Why bother? It is only a Robopod." sniped the Captain Sunfleur. "Keep your eyes peeled on those Fasterfoid blighters." he continued.

"We bother Captain Sunfleur, because if they have open fired and destroyed the Robopod, then, they will have initiated unfriendly warfare. We could not ignore such action."

"Ahh.. hum." coughed FO Twizzlepasta, "As far as keeping the enemy Flotilla under observations that.. That might be a bit of a problem." continued FO Twizzlepasta. "We have lost them, the Flotilla that is, not the Robopods."

"How in the blazes did you lose an entire enemy flotilla?" asked Captain Beetrouly.

"We didn't; the Robopods did." said FO Yamura. "The Robopods are programmed to automatically divert attention to the lost Robopod to recover its protocol box. While they were doing so the Flotilla force must have slipped away."

"Do we have them heading our way FO Twizzlepasta?" asked Captain Beetrouly.

"No Sir, they have disappeared completely." confirmed FO Twizzlepasta.

"Well that's some consolation I suppose." said Captain Sunfleur.

"I suppose you are right Captain Sunfleur, but I don't know. It doesn't make any sense." reasoned the Captain. "Why waste valuable time credits and resources on a training programme in a notoriously dangerous uncharted territory, just to turn about and go home? FO Yamura." he continued. "Excluding our present position and along an axis of one hundred and eighty blimits, what is the nearest star system or Planetary formation? He asked.

FO Yamura walked up and down thinking very hard for a moment. "Well Sir." he chirped. "A fraction to their right about two or three starlectoids away from their last known position is the "Asteroid crush basin" also known as "Sector F4" beyond that nothing, I see no point to their heading in that direction. Beyond that and to the left is the abandoned planetary system known as the "Nomadic Laylow grounds." A collection of largely uninhabitable, small Planet configurations. To the best of our knowledge there are no minerals to speak of and no sustainable life stabilising atmospheres. The only people desperate enough to go in there are Pirates in hiding and, or, those seeking to evade Admiralette Xion Ru Roser." reasoned FO Yamura.

"Very well, FO Yamura. I want you to ensure that the news of our lack of control doesn't reach the blabbering mouths of the scare mongers of the Earthanon surface."

"Aye Sir." said FO Yamura.

"FO Twizzlepasta, place all Sun-Fleet defence systems on green alert but be discreet. Panic must be avoided at all costs." said Captain Beetrouly thoughtfully.

"Aye Sir." agreed FO Twizzlepasta

"FO Twizzlepasta, have we any news on Commander Marrachinello's Star Fighter?" asked Captain Sunfleur.

"No Sir. It has been nine starlectoids since he left Captain. If he had arrived on time and delivered the vidiscript and turned back immediately then he should appear on our Gyroscope, but to date he and his ship have made no appearance." confirmed FO Twizzlepasta.

"Well at least no news is good news!" said a nervous Captain Sunfleur mopping his plate with his finger.

"That is all. You are dismissed, both of you." said Captain Beetrouly. "But keep me informed as to any changes to the situation. I smell a rat and I don't want to be the cheese in this trap!"

"Aye, aye Sir." said both FO Twizzlepasta and FO Yamura offering the Organitron salute.

As they left Captain Sunfleur picked up his dish and licked it clean. Making Captain Beetrouly feel quite queasy at his counterpart's table manners.

"Tell me Captain Beetrouly, do you want that last portion of Dindivallta compote?" Asked Captain Sunfleur with his face covered in the remnants of his last portion.

Captain Beetrouly looked at him and shuddered in disbelief at the mess sitting before him.

"No thank you Captain Sunfleur," said Captain Beetrouly. "Suddenly I appear to have lost my appetite. Frankly I find it difficult to stomach anything under these conditions of chaos and confusion. It looks like I picked the wrong day to make clear decisive moves towards dealing with the enemy, who-ever they are! Particularly when the enemy make the conditions of observation so foggy with the aid of that dashed Asteroid belt. Then to top it all, the whole situation becomes well and truly clouded by the actions of our own Robopods! No Captain Sunfleur, this is turning out to be no ordinary cloudy day, this is turning out to be a real pea souper." he winced. "And between you and me I hate pea soupers. It's as good as working in the dark or with a blindfold on, only the dark in space is infinite and the blindfold spans the universe!"

Captain Sunfleur put down the last portion of food and wiped his face with a cloth. "You know?" he said. "Suddenly I'm full up too."

Then they sat in silence as the feeling of helplessness and uncertainty fell upon them.

Part three

The liberation of Garlicazure.

Sundate 2,999,999,999/ 332. Time 09.20 starhectoids.

In the Vegitamisation suit, FO Potatree carried out the final checks on the equipment and supplies that were to accompany them on the journey through the Voidwell; hopefully their destination to be that of the lost Planet of Garlicazure. When all the checks were complete he began pacing up and down the Vegitamisation platform, the tension running through him like a dose of cod liver oil. Pirate Milnedew sat in silence watching the pacing Chief Engineer with an almost captivated glance. They were suited up for space walk conditions in case the Garlicazure atmosphere was not as it was expected; and frankly to the keen eye of Pirate Milnedew, FO Potatree looked as comfortable and gracious as a beached Whalon. Captain Carrot de-energised the doors and entered with FO Marrowlar, FO Cornelius, Professor Goosegorgon also accompanied by Dr Kiwitranus and Viceroy Councillor Au Paw-Paw.

"Is it time to go Captain Carrot?" said FO Potatree launching himself off the Vegitamisation Platform.

"No Chief," said the Captain reassuringly looking at his timepiece. "It is not; we are now at **09.20 starhectoids**, you leave in V Minus ten starmins! Chief, Pirate Milnedew ah.. Ah Kenthal, we your fellow crew have come here to wish you luck in your newest path of destiny. I, as your Captain, but, more as your friend; come to offer you, no to beg of you to let me go in your places. What you do for the noble good of the Organitron is indeed brave and with full heart but it is I that should take this path to the bitter end." Said the Captain genuine in his words.

"Be-Helios Captain," said FO Potatree. "What would you be waan'tin to do that for? You talk about destiny as if you could change our paths. Believe me Captain, our paths are already written, our arrows already shot, and where they land, we will be!" Then he smiled at Captain Carrot. "Captain," said FO Potatree. "All of you listen up, for once only I shall say this. I cannot speak for Pirate Milnedew but if he wishes to change his mind then frankly, I would be happier. No-one should have to go in there. Nobody, has to go in there, and very few of us want to go in there but my destiny tells me that I am one of those few! So for my part, we'll be having no more on these emotional blackmails to change my mind, no Sir."

"And that goes for me too; here-here, just the two of us; we can make it if we try! You'll see." said pirate Milnedew giving FO Potatree a comical but meaningful hug.

"Ahh wisht away wit ya, you sloppy Marrow-mush." said the Chief as they all laughed. Captain Carrot de-activated the doors again and in walked Leisurelando Pinnelexo the wily old Soda-bar tender pushing a trolley loaded with glasses of FO Potatree's favourite fruit-shake.

"I didn't think you would change your mind and Viceroy Councillor Au Paw-Paw tells me you are expecting the universes biggest fruit-shake when you come back. Well," said Captain Carrot lifting a shake off the trolley. "This isn't the biggest but it is the best." acknowledging Leisurelando and handing everyone a glass. "Chief Potatree, Kenthal Milnedew. I give you health, wealth, luck and life. More valuable than this I give you your favourite fruitshake!"

"Captain, you don't mean pistachio, caramel, rum-raisin and chocky fudge toffee with those crispy flakes of chocolate on top?" said FO Potatree, his jowls leaking with moisture at the much thought.

"The very same Chief." Giggled Captain Carrot.

"In that case Captain." Continued the Chief taking a slurp of his Fruitshake and re-appearing with a blob of cream on his nose. "In that case Captain. I give you the O.S.S.S Earthanon and her crew, happiness and the magical hand of Leisurelando Pinnelexo; Cheers!"

"CHEERS!" They all said collectively as Leisurelando Pinnelexo winked at FO Potatree in recognition of the honour of the compliment that his old friend had bestowed upon him. After they had all consumed the fruitshakes, Captain Carrot offered them both the Organitron Salute and handed FO Potatree a documentation declaration for the leader of the Planet Garlicazure, Queen Oilyio Perfumo Garlialla, outlining the rescue plans and telling her of the new life awaiting them beyond the realms of Blottmeager. Then he turned to exit the Vegitamisation suite and de-energised the doors. Just before he left, he returned to the Chief who had now mounted the Vegitamisation Platform with Pirate Milnedew and gave him a firm embrace. "Grow with the flow my friend. I'm with you all the way. Make it happen for the Space Tracers of Organitron and for the people of Garlicazure." FO Marrowlar saluted them and awaited the Captain's departure. As they left a sudden feeling of imminence crashed through the mind of FO Potatree. "Well!" he said to the rest of the crowd. "Haven't you got any work to be getting on with now?" He gave a nervous laugh as the time approached 09.26 starhectoids; just four minutes to go. Everyone had gone except for Leisurelando Pinnelexo who simply walked up and gave both Pirate Milnedew and FO Potatree a small package. They both opened them up and inside were two pendants carved from the rare Plato of Templevegarial.

"Where there is Widdup there is a way, and may the way be clear and uninterrupted." said Pinnelexo quietly. "For bravery beyond the call of duty you deserve these more than I." He continued. "Helios be with you my friends." He whispered immediately turning and leaving without saying goodbye. The two of them stood alone with only their thoughts and Ensign Broccleman for company. "Who is he?" said Pirate Milnedew. As he said that the pendants started to glow, floated out of their hands and placed themselves around their necks.

"Magic that's who Kenthal, pure magic!" said FO Potatree with an affectionate admiration. "Millions of startechtoids ago," he reminisced. "As legend would have it, the Space Nations of Organitron uncovered a tablet on the Plato of Templevegarial. It was a sister to the Templevegarial altar in shape and size but appeared not to hold any of the magical powers of its brother. So for acts of bravery and leadership these pendants were carved and presented to those who risked life it's very self to help others. Only one for each act is awarded and they are awarded rarely." FO Potatree stopped and mulled over the facts running through his mind. "If I am not mistaken, only two thousand and sixty eight have been awarded to Sundate." He said kissing his pendant. Pirate Milnedew listened quietly then felt a surge of guilt.

"That means these belong to Leisurelando Pinnelexo." he said. "He has obviously earned them. Why, it would be like surfing on somebody else's wave if we were to take them with us; he can't give them to us." reasoned a thoughtful Pirate Milnedew.

"Believe me," said FO Potatree. "He has not given them to us but merely lent them for the duration of this mission. If they don't return he feels we would deserve them more than he did." Then FO Potatree placed his space helmet on as did Pirate Milnedew. "Fear not Pirate Milnedew these are on loan, not for keeps. Something tells me that if he gets them back on our return then we will be receiving pendants of our own." said FO Potatree.

"But to give your two most treasured possessions away must be awful; too awful to contemplate." Noted Pirate Milnedew.

"But you are not in possession of all the facts Kenthal." smiled FO Potatree. "If you knew the man you would know that no possession means more than life. You would also know that he has received three such awards for bravery, so he still has one tucked under his belt." He continued.

"What did he do to earn these pendants? From what I can gather he is only a Soda Barman." questioned Pirate Milnedew.

"That my friend is another long story that he himself may tell you one day. All I can tell you is that it is not who he is, but what he is: pure magic." said FO Potatree.

"V minus sixty starsecs FO Potatree, Pirate Milnedew. Prepare to Vegitamise and good luck both of you." said Ensign Broccleman interrupting the conversation.

"Take a good look Pirate Milnedew. That could be the last face you see for a long time." chirped FO Potatree.

"If we miss our target FO Potatree, it could be the last face we see ever!" laughed Pirate Milnedew.

"Oh dear, it doesn't bear thinking about. No insult intended Ensign Broccleman, but, your mug isn't exactly an oil painting..." chuckled FO Potatree as Pirate Milnedew giggled profusely.

"Don't you worry Chief," interrupted Ensign Broccleman. "I'll get you there" he continued. "As for my face being your last vision, it could be worse." smirked Ensign Broccleman cheekily

"You mean it could be that loony tune Professor Goosegorgon's eh?" enquired FO Potatree.

"No Chief; you could be looking in a mirror." Laughed Ensign Broccleman as Pirate Milnedew offered his hand to FO Potatree.

"Good luck FO Potatree, I'll see you on the other side!" he said slowly as they shook hands.

"V minus thirty starsecs." confirmed Ensign Broccleman.

Captain Carrot stood on the bridge as FO Marrowlar Counted down the mark.

"V minus thirty starsecs, Captain Carrot," he continued. "The O.S.S Capsicumby and the O.S.S Ommelettra will activate the R.E.C.D on my mark. Five, four, three, two and one. Mark." Between the two ships the reverse electron catapult dragnet lit up the space as it linked between the two ships as they fired up the K factor Californic proton reactors awaiting the rehearsal of the arrival of the Planet Garlicazure.

"All stations as before monitor as if your life depended on It." said the Captain.

"V minus twenty starsecs Captain." confirmed FO Marrowlar.

"Captain Carrot to FO Cornelius. Activate Radion-ring on my mark." said the Captain.

"Aye, aye Sir. Hatchooo.. Hatchooo.. Thud!" Confirmed FO Cornelius in his usual way.

"V minus Fifteen starsecs Captain." confirmed FO Marrowlar.

"Mark FO Cornelius; initiate Radion-ring." said the Captain.

"R.E.C.D on line and functional, the O.S.S Capsicumby and Ommelettra confirm all systems are go." confirmed Ensign Strawballis.

"Radion-ring on-line Captain." confirmed FO Cornelius over the communications channel.

"V minus ten starsecs Captain." confirmed FO Marrowlar.

"Very good, FO Cornelius. Fire Satellite Phaser Housing." ordered Captain Carrot. The Radion-ring lit brightly as the Satellite Phaser Housing shot its powerful beam into the expulsion point of the Voidwell which immediately began to stir with the energy intake.

"Viceroy Rhubarblatt, stand by with Califoric K factor three. On activation increase in five second intervals by one K. Traverse pivotal thrusters on my mark. Visaid enhancement Ensign Strawballis!"

"Aye, aye Captain, Visaid on line now Sir." confirmed Ensign Strawballis.

"V minus Five starsecs." confirmed FO Marrowlar activating the security com tracking device.

"Captain Carrot to Ensign Broccleman. Fire Oudag capsule now! Good luck FO Potatree, Kenthal." said the Captain firmly.

"Aye, aye Sir," said Ensign Broccleman. "Oudag expelled Captain. Three, two and one Sir." said FO Marrowlar. "Oudag breaching the Voidwell.. Now."

"Vegitamise now Ensign Broccleman." ordered Captain Carrot. On screen in front of them they could see the Voidwell illuminating at the expulsion point, gradually opening up for the whole universe to see inside its vast expanse.

"Status reports Nav Com." said the Captain.

"Holding trajectory Sir." confirmed Ensign Viola.

"Vegitamisation initiations complete Captain," confirmed Ensign Broccleman. "Tracking the Oudag and Vegimatter transfer, all systems Ay'Ok, they are in and on their way. All life functions are on line and read normal." he continued. At the steering column Viceroy Rhubarblatt alerted the crew to the problems he was beginning to have in stabilising the ship's course heading.

"We are starting to feel magnetic suction Sir. The steering is becoming light and unruly but controllable for now Captain." confirmed Viceroy Rhubarblatt adjusting his steering com to counteract the strain the ship was beginning to encounter.

"As soon as you feel danger Viceroy let me know." said the Captain.

"All ship's systems are fully functional Captain." confirmed SO Tulipina monitoring the ship's systems analyser.

"Open all line inter-ship communication, Ensign Strawballis. Initiate scrambled frequency." Ordered Captain Carrot.

"Aye, aye Sir, all line inter-ship communications are operable Captain." said Ensign Strawballis.

"Now hear this, now hear this!" said the Captain, addressing all on board the O.S.S.S Earthanon and all Sun-Fleet ships in the area. "This is Captain Gillespie J. Carrot of the O.S.S.S Earthanon. Monitor all frequency transmissions. Do not, I repeat, do not off-line your energy sources until we have received confirmation of the landing parties' static position. It could start to get a little rough so secure all movable objects. Captain Carrot UFO and out." announced the Captain. "Ensign Strawballis, punch up Ensign Broccleman's tractor geographical simulation." ordered Captain Carrot taking to his Command Com seat.

"Aye, aye Sir, on Visaid!" On screen the Voidwell showed as a cloud mass with two blips following the same course; one in white the other in red. The white representing the Oudag capsule, the red representing the Vegitamisation molecules.

"Ensign Broccleman to Captain Carrot." came Ensign Broccleman's voice over the communications channel. "Captain Carrot, Sir, the Oudag is approaching the last known co-ordinates of the previous capsule Sir, V Minus fifteen starsecs!" confirmed Ensign Broccleman.

"Captain," interrupted Viceroy Rhubarblatt. "Increasing thrusters to maintain position. Proton output increased by fourteen-percent, eighteen-percent, twenty-two percent. She is becoming very sluggish, Captain." continued Viceroy Rhubarblatt.

"Ship's structure approaching breach point Captain." said SO Tulipina at the ship's analyser.

"Calorific reactors at full displacement Sir; approaching overload." confirmed FO Marrowlar.

"Hold it just a little longer Viceroy Rhubarblatt." Said the Captain gripping his seat with anticipation.

"V minus ten starsecs Captain." Confirmed Ensign Broccleman.

On board the O.S.S Ommelettra Captain Macoronite was in communication with Captain de Fleetrap.

"We are starting to feel the strain Captain de Fleetrap, how do you wish to proceed?" enquired Captain Macoronite.

"Yes, it is definitely becoming very difficult to manoeuvre. Let us increase proton out-put at one thousand emissions per starsec to maintain position. They are nearly there if we can just hold out a little longer give them a fighting chance at least!"

"Affirmative Captain de Fleetrap; increasing ratios from now!"

Back on the bridge of the O.S.S.S Earthanon, Captain Carrot monitored all stations with a wary and watchful eye. "The O.S.S Capsicumby and Ommelettra are increasing proton emission by one thousand out-put to the starsec Captain." confirmed FO Marrowlar. "V minus five starsecs for Oudag and V minus eight starsecs for Vegimatter completion." He continued.

"Thrusts at maximum out-put Captain, barely holding steering tract; preparing to switch to Califoric K Factor three." confirmed Viceroy Rhubarblatt.

"Hold off if you can Viceroy. It's imperative." said the Captain.

"Three, two, one Oudag is static and homer device operational. Three, two and one Vegitamisation complete and off line. It would appear Captain, that they have made It." confirmed Ensign Broccleman. "All ships Communications, all ships communication. Off line R.E.C.D, off line Radion-ring, off line Satellite Phaser Housing, disengage Califoric K factor." Ordered Captain Carrot.

FO Marrowlar observed from the security com as all systems were shut down.

"R.E.C.D off line," called FO Marrowlar. "Radion-ring off line, Satellite Phaser Housing off line. All systems are clear. Califoric K Factor disengaged Captain." confirmed FO Marrowlar.

"Steering tract back in full control Captain, decreasing proton out-put to normal levels." confirmed Viceroy Rhubarblatt.

"Voidwell closing up just as before, Captain." confirmed SO Tulipina.

"It is sweeping the system for energy source location, Captain Carrot." said Ensign Viola at the Particle scanner.

"All ships; all ships." interjected Captain Carrot. "Close down all but life- support systems and switch to auxiliary power." He ordered as the bridge sank into relative darkness. "It would appear that they have made it. Well done everybody; you all did very well. Now we just have to sit and wait. All systems back on line in exactly three starhectoids fifty eight starmins. Cease all ships communications!" continued Captain Carrot. "It's time to play dead so silent running if you will. This is Captain Carrot. UFO and out, end transmission. Good work everybody," said the Captain to his bridge crew whilst signing the ships analytical log. "Prepare final checks for the liberation of Garlicazure. FO Marrowlar, you have Command Com, I will be with Dr Kiwitranus in the Medilab!" he confirmed.

"Aye, aye Captain," said FO Marrowlar at the Command Com as Captain Carrot disappeared into the elevation chamber.

"Pheweeeeee.. Phewoooooh." Piped Ensign Melonture.

"Captain off the bridge." shouted Ensign Rasperillo. Then the doors closed and the Captain was out of sight.

"Stand easy on the bridge, all eyes alert on stations and keep them peeled, seedlings." said FO Marrowlar.

"The Voidwell has stopped sweeping the sector FO Marrowlar!" confirmed Ensign Viola.

"Good, that's just the way we want it." he smiled in secret admiration of the bold and courageous aura of the Organi-Captain that could still be felt even though he had just left the bridge. He felt somehow envious of the two intrepid explorers in the form of FO Potatree and Pirate Milnedew. They were the real heroes of the hour and for some strange reason, FO Marrowlar missed the very presence of his old advisory in the Engineering department and could only hope that the both of them would return from the situation in tact to be graced with every honour that Sun-Fleet could bestow.

In the Centre of the Voidwell, FO Potatree and Pirate Milnedew Vegitamised in between the dummy Oudag and the actual Oudag used to cut them a path through to Garlicazure. FO Potatree could not believe what he saw.

"Holy vegmoley it's a desert," said FO Potatree, observing the dry crust on which he was standing. "Kenthal.. Kenthal" he repeated looking around to check that he had made it but with no success. "Kenthal was right," he muttered under his breath. "You can't see further than your nose." he continued, becoming worried by Kenthal's absence.

"Of course I was right FO Potatree," came Kenthal's voice on the internal communication system. "That shouldn't bother you though, FO Potatree; not with a conk like yours should be able to see for starmillo's." He continued as he tapped FO Potatree on his space helmet. FO Potatree smiled pleased to see that his companion had made it. The jibes of his nose size becoming unimportant by comparison to his surviving the Vegitamisation process.

"Kenthal my boy," said the overwhelmed Chief. "I'm glad you could make it. Better late than never, sonny. Better late than never indeed." laughed FO Potatree taking an atmospheric reading.

"Can we survive without the suits FO Potatree?" asked Kenthal. "Only these really are beginning to cramp my sense of fashion." he said hooking a line onto FO Potatree's utility belt to avoid them becoming separated again.

FO Potatree tested the atmosphere inspecting the mobile particle scanner readings.

"Well, it's breathable Kenthal, but with this much raw energy around I'm more concerned with being struck by stray energy protons." he confirmed. "We ought to keep the suits on for now, just to be on the safe side." he continued moving over to where the tools and sleeping draughts had arrived?

"It doesn't appear that we have a greeting party, FO Potatree. I would have thought that the first Oudag would have alerted them to our presence." he reasoned.

FO Potatree looked around again and slowly turned back toward Kenthal. "Judging by the restricted vision, we could be surrounded and not know. Besides, if you have been stuck in this place on your own for millions; billions of startechtoids you are hardly likely to meet strangers with open arms until you know exactly who and what they are!" said FO Potatree. "One thing is for sure Kenthal," he continued. "If they are here they would have picked up the shock-waves from the Oudag landings. I'll wager they are watching us before they make any moves towards making contact. I know I would." he said picking up his tool capsule.

"Where to now FO Potatree? Find shelter or make contact?" asked Kenthal, picking up the rest of the tools.

"Hopefully both Kenthal, hopefully both; because one thing we haven't got on our side is time!" he replied as they walked towards a rock formation that could just be made out in the distance when the lightning flashed and reflected off of its angled face.

"What's that over there Chief?" said Kenthal pointing at the foot of the mountain in the final approach to what they hoped would be shelter.

"It.. it.. it's a cave entrance." he said clearing the dust from his visor and fighting to remain standing in the wind, as all around bracken bush was flying about the surface battering them indiscriminately. Hurriedly they fell into the cave and lay very still while focusing their eyes to the new environment. It was surprisingly light in the refuge they had stumbled upon.

"Look!" said Chief Potatree pointing towards the ceiling.

"What is it Chief? It's beautiful" said Kenthal looking in amazement at a painstakingly precise mosaic of what must have been the original positioning of the Bubbleonion Squeak Vegitalis Solar system.

"That my dear boy, is history." said FO Potatree lighting a Carotene flare which also acted as a small heat providing bonfire. FO Potatree checked the mobile particle scanner again then took off his helmet.

"Well!" he laughed "It say's we will live without the space suits. Now is the time to get things right so cross your fingers as soon as I tell you it's OK, then follow my lead. Is that clear, Kenthal?" Said FO Potatree grasping the locking devise on the helmet.

"Phewtshhhhhhh." Came the noise of the air escaping from his space suit as he released the catch and removed the headgear, while taking a deep breath. "Ahh.. Phew that's better. It's all right. Kenthal slow deep breaths when you come out now." he said starting to remove the rest of his suit.

"Phewtshhhhhhh." "Wow, am I glad to be out of that thing Chief! It's like an oven in there." said Kenthal, unhooking the link line between them.

FO Potatree looked at his timepiece wondering when or if, the first signs of the Garlicallian Space Race would show themselves. If they were aware of the Oudag capsule's arrival then the Garlicallian habit of "need to know" would surely bring them out of the woodwork.

"Right Kenthal." he said. "We have three point five starhectoids; that doesn't give us much time. The sleeping draught must be administered within two starlectoids and it will take me at least one starhectoid to alter the atmospheric gravitational reactors on to a timing device, so the first thing to remember is that they must only take the draught after they have secured themselves to a fixed surface away from loose material. That will be your job to organise. You can leave me with the climatic equaliser."

He said, biting his bottom lip, uneasy that there were still no signs of the residents of Garlicazure.

"That is of course provided they show themselves?" said Kenthal searching the cave perimeters for other exits. Suddenly, as they turned to face the cave entrance, a huge stone tablet blocked it off sealing them in.

"What is it Chief a rock fall?" asked a claustrophobic Kenthal Milnedew at the thought of this, their new home, becoming their tomb.

"I hope not otherwise we, my boy, are in serious trouble. No, this my friend means that they know we are here. I believe this is some kind of holding room. For observation purposes, perhaps?" said FO Potatree, hoping he was right. Then the floor started to revolve and began to go in a downward spiral for at least two hundred staryards. Kenthal took out his blazer gun and FO Potatree held his arm, effectively saying that he wouldn't be needing it.

"Come now, Kenthal. They are scared enough as it is; let us not worry them with our strange new ways, umm? We want them to trust us not truss us!" he laughed. Putting the gun back in his holster he smiled nervously at what they were about to meet face to face; in Helios knows how long since a Garlicallian had met an alternative civilisation. Gradually the cave floor broke light at the bottom of a tunnel and FO Potatree and Kenthal Milnedew were both overcome with emotion as a massive group of Garlicallian people stood before them. At the front of the pack stood the proud Queen of the lost Space Race. Queen Oilyio Perfumo Garlialla. From his tunic FO Potatree pulled the oldest flag that he could find in the O.S.S.S Earthanon that represented the Organitron Races; an emblem of the sun with water and a tree set inside a large zero. As he unrolled it, smiles broke on the faces of the hesitant crowd and laughter began to fill the air as they knew that friends, not foe, had joined their flock. Unaware of the bid to save them, they were merely pleased to know that Organitrons of any race, existed elsewhere and they were no longer alone. As the cave floor stopped, FO Potatree stepped forward and knelt in front of the Queen whose tears flowed with joy. Then he handed her the envelope from Captain Carrot.

"Your Highness." Said FO Potatree. "I am First Officer Chief Engineer Potatree of the Potanto Space Race, loyal subject of the Planet Potatoorimar. This is Sun-Fleet Envoy Kenthal Milnedew of the Marrownillaz Space Race, loyal subject of the Planet Marrowavax. We represent the Space Tracers of Organitron on behalf of "The United Foliage of Organitron." This is a communication from Captain Gillespie J. Carrot of the O.S.S.S

Earthanon. Ma'am, we are here to liberate Garlicazure from Blottmeager and return you, your Planet and your Space Race to its rightful place in the heart of the Bubbleonion Squeak Vegitalis Solar System." he said thrilled to deliver such news to such a scared and frightened race.

"I am Queen Oilyio Perfumo Garlialla. Welcome, and on behalf of my subjects, I thank you FO Potatree; Kenthal Milnedew." She said opening the envelope and pulling out the mobile pre-programmed visaid, and then a vague look seemed to overcome her face. Seeing that she was confused with the envelopes contents its meaning, FO Potatree stepped forward.

"May I Ma'am?" He said, taking it from her and placing it on the ground after pressing the activation switch."

As if by magic, a three dimensional figure appeared in front of the Queen and her people as they sighed in disbelief at the vision and technology in front of them.

"Greetings Queen Oilyio Perfumo Garlialla and the brave subjects of Garlicazure. I am Captain Gillespie J. Carrot of the O.S.S.S Earthanon, Mother ship of the United Foliage of Organitron; a Sun-Fleet Organisation. If you are listening to this Visaid communication then, FO Potatree and Envoy Milnedew have made contact with a living nation of Garlicazure. Time is short so regrettably this communication must be brief. The fact that you have survived is half the battle. The other half of the battle is more complicated; there is much to do for our intended plan of the Planet Garlicazure rescue. I must ask you to place your full trust in me and my representatives who are with you today. I must be honest your rescue is in no way a certainty, but we have covered all angles of danger to minimise the risk of failure. I will leave my colleagues to explain the details and I trust you will do everything in your power to assist in this. This most daring attempt of rescue in order to minimise the risks from your end and enable the plan to become a complete success. I cannot stress too importantly the need for your complete co-operation in this matter." He continued. "Until we meet face to face on the other side. This is Captain Gillespie J. Carrot of the O.S.S.S Earthanon ever your loyal subject. FO Potatree, Envoy Milnedew; grow with the flow. UFO and out, end transmission" then giving the Organitron salute, the vision disappeared.

"We always knew someone would come." said Queen Garlialla. "We always hoped it would be true. Whatever you require of us FO Potatree, Envoy Milnedew; we will do." She said wiping her eyes.

"Out on the surface," said FO Potatree. "We have a special respiratory draught that we must organise for everyone on Garlicazure to take at the same time in exactly?" FO Potatree looked at his time piece. "Two starhectoids." he confirmed. "But first everybody must be in a secure hold, as I am going to have to stunt the energy output on your planetary gravitational vitamin reactors; so if you have any valuables, I suggest they go into a safe place where they can't float away." Said FO Potatree awaiting a response.

"How many Organimen do you need to go to the surface FO Potatree?" asked Queen Garlialla.

"Twelve Ma'am." he said as she turned and picked a working party.

"Then," continued FO Potatree. "You will need a hundred and seventy Organipeople to issue the sleeping draughts and make sure that the people are strapped into their vegewells. Will that be possible Queen Garlialla?" enquired Chief Potatree. "Remember Queen Garlialla, everybody must be secured in their Vegewells and take the sleeping draughts in exactly two starhectoids." he insisted.

"Trust me." said Queen Garlialla. "You are the first ray of light to touch this Planet in an eternity. As your Captain quite aptly says, we will grow with the flow. You have my word, we will be ready." she said softly.

"Envoy Milnedew will see to the sleeping draught allocation. Could you please have somebody direct me to the artificial gravitational atmosphere reactors. Preferably somebody who understands them! I'm afraid my vitiminal fusion theory is a little rusty." Said FO Potatree.

"Bulbouey." shouted Queen Garlialla, as a small squat figure bounced toward them. "Bulbouey is the Planetary Maintenance expert. Anything you need to know, he is your Organiman." She said smiling and rubbing his forehead.

"Yes Siree, Bulbouey is my name and fixing is my game." he said as he hopped over to FO Potatree and held his hand. He seemed no more than an Organi-child but FO Potatree could see that he was an underdeveloped Garlicallian male who for some time must have been doing an Organiman's job in a seedling's body. Queen Garlialla saw the look on FO Potatree's face, and glanced at him discreetly.

"Come on then; what are you waiting for FO Potatree? Hee.. Hee. It was you that said there was work to be done so let's get to It." said the bubbly little fellow, dragging him off the cave floor towards a dark passageway.

"Will he do, FO Potatree?" said Queen Garlialla smiling.

"Aye, aye, Ma'am. If he is as skilled as he is energetic he'll do just fine, just fine. All right I'm coming, I'm coming." As they disappeared down the passageway, Envoy Marrowmilne went back up to the surface while Queen Garlialla rallied the troops in the settlement Catacombs in which they all lived together.

Sundate 2,999,999,999/ 332 Biltechtoids. Time 10.00 starhectoids.

Across the galaxy beyond the "Asteroid crush basin" bordering the abandoned "Nomadic Laylow grounds", in sector F4 of the uncharted Bervado Quadrant General Satuese and Principle Gammachip addressed the Fasterfoid task-force on the interships communications channel for the last time before departing for the Planet Earthanon, and the unsuspecting Organitron Sun-Fleet.

"Gentlegrills and Gentlefrills." said General Satuese addressing the complete crew of all ships. "The time has nearly come," he continued. "To unleash and put into practise our beliefs and vengeful souls; indeed vent our frustrations that have been bottled up for billions of startechtoids. Originally we were to have eight starlectoids of battle manoeuvres but as usual you have responded beyond the call of duty. It would appear that we are running some twelve starhectoids beyond our timetable and both I and Principle Officer Gammachip here, are very pleased with the skill and determination that you have shown in the testing times that have been placed upon you in recent starlectoids. I... We have every confidence in your ability to carry the Fasterfoid banner. Delivering it to the Organitron with forceful supremacy, causing the ultimate chaos to their Sun-Fleet network, showing them once and for all that we, the Fasterfoids, are the most intelligent, most powerful Space Race in existence. Given that you have performed so well, I propose that you all take the next twelve starhectoids to relax and if you wish? Party the time away in true pre-battle Fasterfoid style. Gentlegrills, Gentlefrills we depart for Earthanon in exactly five starlectoids twelve point five starhectoids. Keep up the dedication and in five starlectoids, you will have yet another relaxation period before our departure for Earthanon. Our journey to the outer boundaries of Earthanons Atmosphere, will take approximately twenty eight starlectoids then battle stations will be called and finally, we will activate our cunning plan to teach those Organitron namby pamby's a lesson they will never forget. This is General Satuese closing transmission." The crews of the Fasterfoid fleet stood in silence as the communications line went off and gradually an air of excitement filled sector F4 and party time became imminent.

Back on board the O.S.S.S Earthanon as the bridge was in relative darkness, Captain Carrot was seated at the Command com deep in thought when FO Marrowlar interrupted his brief respite from the turmoil of uncertainty surrounding them.

"Ahh.. Hum. Captain Carrot Sir." he said awaiting a response. Captain Carrot turned toward him and looked straight into his eyes.

"I don't know FO Marrowlar!" Said the Captain rubbing his hands slowly.

"But you don't know what I was going to ask Captain. Do you?" asked FO Marrowlar confused.

"You want to know what will happen if we go ahead as planned and they are not ready on Garlicazure, am I correct?" asked Captain Carrot calmly.

FO Marrowlar looked stunned, as the Captain was spot on with his pre-emptive analysis.

"Yes Sir," said FO Marrowlar. "But how did you know?" he continued.

"Because, my friend," smiled the Captain. "it is the only question that I have been asking myself that remains, as yet, without a sufficient answer to satisfy my nervous system enough to calm it." he said thoughtfully. "I am afraid," he added. "From the bridge we can do only so much, the rest is in the hands of FO Marrowlar and Envoy Milnedew. If it's any consolation, FO Marrowlar. That question is probably most prominent in the minds of them and the people of Garlicazure as we speak. I have every confidence in FO Potatree that he will not let them, us, or himself down by failing." laughed Captain Carrot gently.

"Of course," acknowledged FO Marrowlar. "I forgot that failure is not a word that appears in FO Potatree's vocabulary or in his dictionary come to think of It." he continued. "It isn't even allowed in his training classes." he giggled.

"Well, FO Marrowlar." said the Captain looking at the starhectoid glass, we only have one point five starhectoids before we find out for sure." Then he stood up and signed the ships analytical log. "FO Marrowlar, I feel now is as good a time as any to update the Widdup chronicles, in case something goes wrong. Have a Robopod prepared for departure to Carridionaries in one half starhectoid. You have command com!" He said as he entered the elevation chamber."

"Captain off the bridge." shouted Ensign Rasperillo.

"Pheweeeeee... Phewoooooh." piped Ensign Melonture.

"Stand easy on the bridge." said FO Marrowlar, "All systems checked with a fine tooth comb please crew. Ensign Strawballis, have Engineering prepare a Robopod in accordance with Captain Carrot's instructions." he said sitting back slowly.

"Aye, aye Sir." said Ensign Strawballis, turning to the Communications com.

Back on the Planet Garlicazure, FO Potatree was deep in the chambers of the artificial gravitational atmosphere reactors with Bulbouey when Envoy Milnedew came through on his personal channel.

"Envoy Milnedew to FO Potatree, come in please." said Envoy Milnedew as Bulbouey looked around the chamber for the owner of the voice.

"FO Potatree here, Envoy Milnedew." he said, crawling out from under the vitamin reactor housing and activating the communicator.

"Wow!" said Bulbouey, amazed at the technology that came with the strangers of the new worlds.

"FO Potatree, we are ready to administer the sleeping draughts. Chief, are you OK down there?" he asked.

"I'm having a bit of a problem securing the timing device to cut in at the right time. I'm afraid the new technology is not as compatible as we would have hoped. I'm going to have to operate it manually when the time comes. But don't worry." he continued. "I'll wear a space suit." he confirmed. "You're running late Envoy Milnedew, we depart in one starhectoid and twenty starmins; why the delay?" Asked FO Marrowlar.

"Some of them were unsure, FO Potatree. They have grown accustomed to this existence and fear the consequences of our actions." He reasoned.

"What changed their minds Envoy Milnedew?" asked FO Potatree.

"I told them that the Macadamians claimed they were the stupidest race in the entire universe and therefore had no right to live. Now there isn't one of them that don't want to take the draught." He said laughing.

"Poetic licence it might be, but well done." said FO Potatree. "When they are all secure, you find a safe place and take the draught. Envoy Milnedew let me know when they are all under before you go to the land of nod!" He added.

"Negative FO Potatree. I'm staying with you!" he said. "We are in this together remember?" he continued.

"I remember, Envoy Milnedew." remarked FO Potatree. "But if something happens to me then it will be necessary that you are safe and sound to take over the running of the operation. There may be much confusion and panic; they will need you." He reasoned.

"One thing you are forgetting, FO Potatree. If something, as you say, does happen to you, who will return the gravitational atmosphere back on to a sustainable level?" he asked. There was silence momentarily as FO Potatree knew that Envoy Milnedew was right.

"I'll stay with you." said Bulbouey. "We have breathing apparatus for outside excursions on the planetary surface!" He continued.

"Are you sure Bulbouey?" Asked FO Potatree.

"Are you kidding me FO Potatree? I wouldn't miss this much excitement for the universe." he said tapping him on the leg.

"OK Bulbouey, you're on the team." laughed FO Potatree. "Go and get your apparatus and my suit from Envoy Milnedew. Hurry though, we are running out of time. Envoy Milnedew." He replied on the communications channel.

"Yes FO Potatree I am still here!" Said Envoy Milnedew.

"Bulbouey will work with me on this one. He knows the system and explaining it to you would take a lifetime. I'm sorry but you're going to have to sit this one out, but that doesn't in any way, shape or form detracts from the importance of your responsibility to come." Explained FO Potatree.

"Of course FO Potatree. As usual you are wise and I am hasty. It will be done as you request." Confirmed Envoy Milnedew.

"Thank you Envoy Milnedew. Bulbouey is on his way to fetch my suit. Please see to it that he gets everything I need. Oh, and you had better pack me a spare oxygen cylinder; just to be on the safe side you understand?" reasoned FO Potatree.

"It is done, FO Potatree. Until later my friend." he confirmed.

"Potatree out."

"Milnedew out."

Then FO Potatree disappeared under the reactor once again.

Back on the Flight deck of the O.S.S.S Earthanon. Commander Marrachinello checked his Star Fighter ready for departure as soon as the Garlicazure Project was complete. As he wiped the emblem on the side of his trusted ship, a picture of his wife with a rolling pin. Ensign Broccleman brought him the stat reports of the ship's momentum drive service charts.

"Here you are Commander Marrachinello. She is all ship shape and Bristol Fashion Commander. Commander are you all right, Sir?" said Ensign Broccleman.

"What? I say, what old bean? You'll have to excuse me old fruit; starmillo's away don't you know." quipped Commander Marrachinello.

"I asked if you were all right Sir?" repeated Ensign Broccleman. "If you don't mind me saying so, you look rather out of sorts." He continued.

"Oh don't you worry about that, Ensign Broccleman. If you must know I was just thinking about the enormity of the situation. If we pull this thing off Ensign Broccleman, it will be the best news I could possibly take home to Earthanon." said the Commander smiling.

"I'm not so sure the "Mad Macadamians" will agree with you there, Commander." replied Ensign Broccleman.

"Do you really think not? I should have thought that finding a new Planet, irrespective of which one, would be sterling news, giving rise for hope of our other missing compatriots. Wouldn't you agree?" asked the Commander.

"Indeed I would Sir! But then I am neither mad nor a Macadamian." reasoned Ensign Broccleman.

"You're certainly no Macadamian Ensign Broccleman, but I think in all of us there exists a touch of madness. Somehow I think that is what it takes to survive this ambiguous, complicated playground we call a universe." said Commander Marrachinello, placing an arm over his shoulder as they walked towards the service elevation chamber. But," he continued. "All the while we have a playground there is a game at hand, and all the while there is a game at hand there is a chance of winning." he laughed. "This game Ensign Broccleman, pays the biggest prize of all, freedom and hope." Added Commander Marrachinello.

"Yes, I think I see what you mean Commander," said a thoughtful Ensign Broccleman. "Oh well, I had best get back to the Vegimatter room. By my reckoning this game kicks off in V minus five starmins. Captain Carrot asked me to invite you to the bridge if you wish?" Said Ensign Broccleman.

"If I wish indeed! The Planet of Macadamia couldn't keep me away, I'll be there; in fact I'm on my way now-and Ensign Broccleman," said the Commander as they stepped into the elevation chamber.

"Yes commander?" replied Ensign Broccleman.

"When you fire those activated proton torpedo's, remember you are destroying an evil phenomenon for the good of the universe and to avenge the Planet of Garlicazure! So make sure the first hit hurts for good." said Commander Marrachinello.

"Aye, aye Sir." said Ensign Broccleman. Then the doors de-energised and they were out of sight.

Sundate 2,999,999,999/ 332 Biltechtoids. Time 11.25 starhectoids.

FO Potatree walked through the Catacombs making sure that all the inhabitants had taken the sleeping draught. As he looked upon the faces of the young and old Garlicallian race he felt tears welling in his eyes. Then at the corner of his eye, he spotted Envoy Milnedew sleeping with a group of seedlings, stuck around his body like metal to a magnet, in a domed communal Vegewell sucking their thumbs and deep in a world of dreams. He looked at his time piece and saw that zero hour was fast approaching. Then confident that all was well and no one was conscious, he began to speak.

"People of Garlicazure, you can't hear me but I hope my words transmigrate into you world of dreams. I'm scared but I am not alone in that feeling. I'm not scared of dying but of failure. I don't want to let you down, any of you. Life has let you down enough. I must go now and see to it that this mission is a success but I just wanted to tell you this. The fact that you have survived this long is a miracle and tells us, the Organitron, much that is hidden in your souls and character. You are all heroes in my book and believe me, my book is short and with few entries, but today you move to the top of my list with the very elite. Captain Gillespie J. Carrot, Envoy Milnedew and a special place of courage goes to two people from within your fold. Your strong and Courageous Queen whom I have no doubt has helped to carry you to this day with much personal heartache, and to Bulbouey, who's bravery and determination is helping us all to have a fighting chance of success. Organigirls and Organiboys until we meet again on the other side, sleep tight and soon we will all awaken to a new, more hopeful future. Helios knows you could use it. I, FO Potatree, on behalf of "The Space Tracers of Organitron." salute you and strive to deliver us all to a better way forward." Then he departed for the chambers of the artificial gravitational atmosphere reactors where Bulbouey awaited his return. Pirate Milnedew opened his eyes drowsily and opened his hand, kissing the pendant which Leisurelando Pinnelexo gave them on the O.S.S.S Earthanon.

"Don't leave your name out of that little book my friend, you.. Yo... you are the Organiman of the hour and a fine hour I know you will make.

See you on the other side, FO Potatree. Of that I am sure!" Then unable to resist any longer, he fell asleep.

"How does it go?" asked FO Potatree entering the chambers. "Is she ready?" he continued.

"As ready as she'll ever be. As soon as the hour comes, we are ready when you are!" said Bulbouey patting the reactor with confidence.

"OK my friend. Strap yourself to that pillar and keep your hand on that solenoid screwdriver. When I give you the signal, turn it clockwise until the core element rises above that magnetic housing. As soon as she is clear I'll give you the signal to throw that switch to your left." said FO Potatree, strapping himself to a pillar and placing his space helmet on.

"Then what?" Asked a nervous Bulbouey.

"Then Pray. Believe me, once I've halted the lector oscillator. I'll be doing the same on this side. Now get your breathing apparatus on Bulbouey, and thank you for all that you are doing." He said smiling and giving him the Organitron salute.

"Any time FO Potatree! Anytime." Then he slipped on his helmet and fumbled his salute in return. "FO Potatree," he said. "When we get through this can you teach me how to do that blessed salute? I'll be giggled if I can get my fingers around it and it looks so cool." He laughed.

"You bet ya." He said nodding. "V minus sixty starsecs and counting. All aboard for liberation or obliteration. Whichever way, it will be one Helios of a ride." said FO Potatree grasping a solenoid wrench. "Now Bulbouey! Now!" Frantically they both worked away at their tasks. As the cores rose out of the main vitamin reactors, a sharp humming seemed to surround them. Its source from the very centre of the Planet as its tectonic plates drained of all gravitational qualities and the atmosphere gradually became lighter and lighter, sending debris floating into space. Soon the core elements floated in the Plasma tubes above their heads.

"V minus thirty starsecs, Bulbouey. Flick the switch!" Shouted FO Potatree above the din. Then the Planet began to shake and tremble as the magnetic field was withdrawn from the planetary surface, clearing loose rock and artefacts and sucking them into space with incredible force.

On board the O.S.S.S Earthanon Captain Carrot sat at the helm as the packed bridge watched the visaid with eager anticipation.

"V minus thirty starsecs." confirmed Ensign Broccleman. Captain Carrot stood on the bridge as FO Marrowlar counted down the mark.

"V minus thirty starsecs Captain. Captain Carrot," he continued. "The O.S.S Capsicumby and the O.S.S Ommelettra will activate the R.E.C.D on my mark. Five, four, three, two and one. Mark." Between the two ships the reverse electron catapult dragnet lit up the space linking between the two ships as they fired up the K factor Califoric proton reactors awaiting the arrival of the Planet Garlicazure.

"All stations repeat as before, monitor with absolute precision as this time our lives truly does depend on it." Said the Captain.

"V minus twenty starsecs, Captain." Confirmed FO Marrowlar.

"Captain Carrot to FO Cornelius. Activate Radion-ring on my mark." said the Captain.

"Aye, aye Sir. Hatchooo.. Hatchooo.. Thud!" Confirmed FO Cornelius with his usual style.

"V minus fifteen starsecs, Captain." confirmed FO Marrowlar.

"Mark, FO Cornelius; initiate Radion-ring." said the Captain.

"R.E.C.D on line and functional. Captain O.S.S Capsicumby and Ommelettra confirm all systems are go and good luck." confirmed Ensign Strawballis.

"Radion-ring on-line Captain." confirmed FO Cornelius over the communications channel.

"V minus ten starsecs, Captain." confirmed FO Marrowlar.

"Very good, FO Cornelius. Fire Satellite Phaser Housing." ordered Captain Carrot. The Radion-ring lit brightly just as before while the Satellite Phaser Housing shot into the expulsion point of the Voidwell which immediately began to stir with the energy intake, but this time its velocity far more ferocious.

"Viceroy Rhubarblatt, stand by with Califoric K factor three. On activation, increase in five second intervals by one K. Traverse pivotal thrusters on my mark. Visaid enhancement Ensign Strawballis!"

"Aye, aye Captain, visaid on line now Sir." confirmed Ensign Strawballis.

"Come on FO Potatree, wind that baby down and make it burp." said the Captain gripping his seat.

"V minus Five starsecs." Confirmed FO Marrowlar activating the security com tracking device. "On line and awaiting Radion ring sonic perambulator detonation module alignment."

"Anti-Matter Acidulated Califoric Proton Torpedoes armed, co-ordinates set."

Confirmed Ensign Broccleman.

"Zero hour," said FO Marrowlar. "Running at full energy output Captain, she's taking all that we have got. All systems are running clean and clear." he confirmed.

"As soon as that Planet comes out of there, SO Tulipina, I want speed ratios set and calculated for a distance of one point two million starmillo's. FO Marrowlar, when that distance has been achieved by the Planet Garlicazure and all Sun-Fleet ships in the vicinity are clear of the explosion zone, fire A.M.A.C.P.T!" ordered Captain Carrot. On screen in front of them they could see the Voidwell illuminating at the expulsion point, gradually opening up for the whole universe to see inside its vast expanse.

"Status reports, Nav Com." said the Captain.

"Holding trajectory Sir." Confirmed Ensign Viola.

At the steering column, Viceroy Rhubarblatt alerted the Captain to the problems he was beginning to encounter in stabilising the ship's course heading. Only, unlike last time, the force began sucking them in towards the mouth of the Voidwell.

"We are starting to feel magnetic suction Sir," shouted Viceroy Rhubarblatt. "The steering is becoming light, momentum shaft running at top enhancement. Uncontrollable now Captain, we are in its grasp and it's pulling us in." confirmed Viceroy Rhubarblatt adjusting his steering com to counteract the strain the ship was beginning to encounter.

"Divert all available auxiliary power to frontal shields, FO Marrowlar." said Captain Carrot.

"Aye, Aye Captain. Frontal shields now operable at one hundred and fifty two percent and falling. Full auxiliary diversion complete."

"As soon as you see the point of no return approaching, Viceroy Rhubarblatt, let me know." Said the Captain.

"All ship's systems are fully functional Captain." confirmed SO Tulipina monitoring the ship's systems analyser.

"Frontal shields at ninety-three percent and falling." confirmed FO Marrowlar.

"Open all line inter-ship communication, Ensign Strawballis. Initiate scrambled frequency." ordered Captain Carrot.

"Aye, aye Sir. All line inter-ship communication are operable, Captain." said Ensign Strawballis.

"Now hear this, now hear this." said the Captain, addressing all on board the O.S.S.S Earthanon and all Sun-Fleet ships in the area. "This is Captain Gillespie J. Carrot of the O.S.S.S Earthanon. Monitor all frequency transmissions. Do not, I repeat do not off-line your energy sources until we have Garlicazure in our sights and beyond the explosion safety zone. O.S.S Capsicumby and Ommelettra, standby on K factor three. Jump as soon as you get Garlicazure on your particle scanner. Increase your speed when you feel the need. Remember, when she comes, she will come hard and fast. Speed and course co-ordinates will be sent on instant relay, so take your mark from them.

Captain Peabazzare, I need you to get behind the O.S.S.S Earthanon and lock on tractor beam. We are being sucked in and need more power to pull clear. No matter how close it seems we are to the Voidwell, stay with me. Fire up Califoric K factor and set jump for K factor five. Initiate on my mark. Good luck everybody Captain Carrot UFO and out end transmission. Ensign Strawballis punch up Ensign Broccleman's tractor geographical simulation." ordered Captain Carrot, taking to his Command com seat while Commander Marrachinello held onto the hand rail in front for dear life.

"Come on you great gob stopper, fire that cannon ball, hey what?" He shrilled.

"Aye, aye Sir, on Visaid now Captain!" Said Ensign Strawballis.

On screen, the Voidwell showed as a cloud mass with one blip, presumably representing the Planet Garlicazure.

"Ensign Broccleman to Captain Carrot." came Ensign Broccleman's voice over the communications channel. "Captain Carrot the Oudag homing device is approaching the Voidwell expulsion point Sir, ETA Planetary expulsion in V Minus fifteen starsecs!" confirmed Ensign Broccleman.

"Trajectory and speed Ensign Broccleman?" Enquired Captain Carrot.

"Expulsion estimated at forty seven point five blimits, speed K factor four and increasing, approximately Four hundred and seventy thousand starmillo's a starmin.." confirmed Ensign Broccleman.

"Captain.." interrupted Viceroy Rhubarblatt. "Increasing thrusters to maintain position. Proton output increased by twenty-five percent, twenty-eight percent, thirty-two percent; she is becoming extremely sluggish Captain." continued Viceroy Rhubarblatt. "I'm shifting ratio displacement to forward thrusters. Red lining, I repeat, red lining at forty percent. Captain she's slipping, I can't control her!"

"Captain," said FO Marrowlar, "O.S.S Satsumuroo is in position and locking on to target. Tractor beam on-line, she's holding us back Captain." confirmed FO Marrowlar.

"Yes but you can be sure that we are not out of the compost heap just yet. Status Viceroy Rhubarblatt." Quipped Captain Carrot.

"I have established minimum control Captain, but I don't know for how long." Said Viceroy Rhubarblatt keying in instructions to the steering column Computron at hyperspeed. "Proton output at twenty percent over-ratio and holding." Confirmed Viceroy Rhubarblatt.

"Ship's structure approaching breach point Captain." said SO Tulipina at the ship's analyser.

"Calorific reactors at full displacement Sir, approaching overload." confirmed FO Marrowlar.

"Hold it just a little longer Viceroy Rhubarblatt. I'm going to need at least two minutes of your time and skill!" Said the Captain, gripping his seat with anticipation.

"V minus ten starsecs Captain." Confirmed Ensign Broccleman.

On board the O.S.S Ommelettra, Captain Macoronite was in communication with Captain de Fleetrap.

"We are starting to feel the strain, Captain de Fleetrap. How do you wish to proceed?" enquired Captain Macoronite.

"As before, Captain Macoronite, let us increase proton out-put at one thousand emissions per starsec to maintain position. They are nearly there, if we can just hold out a little longer; they are in sight of the target!" said Captain de Fleetrap.

"Affirmative Captain de Fleetrap, increasing ratio's from now!"

"Sighted confirmation, speed and trajectory receiving on line Captain." said Ensign Ramputinder at the Communications com.

"Fix and log to the computer." ordered Captain de Fleetrap. "Coming ready or not!" He Shouted.

Back on the bridge of the O.S.S.S Earthanon, Captain Carrot monitored all stations with intrepid expectations and watchful eye. "O.S.S Capsicumby and Ommelettra are increasing proton emission by one thousand out-put to the starsec Captain." Confirmed FO Marrowlar. "V minus five starsecs for planetary expulsion" he continued.

"Thrusters at maximum out-put Captain. Barely holding steering tract; preparing to switch to Califoric K Factor three." confirmed Viceroy Rhubarblatt.

"Hold off if you can Viceroy. It's imperative. When the Voidwell burps up Garlicazure it will lose the dragnet power source. It might concentrate on us." said the Captain.

"Aye, aye Sir." said Viceroy Rhubarblatt.

"FO Cornelius, full power to the Radion ring and phaser housing. Give it everything it's got. Halt firing as soon as the Planet comes out and continue when she is clear." said Captain Carrot. "Ensign Broccleman, arm and make ready A.M.A.C.P.T." He continued. "Captain Peabazzare, more power; all you have got and on-line your Califoric K Factor to five, initiate on my mark." confirmed Captain Carrot.

On the visaid the Voidwell opened up and within the sights of the collective Sun-Fleet were the first sightings of the lost Planet of Garlicazure for billions of startechtoids, and by Helios, was it amazing; one might even say beautiful.

"Look Captain! I do believe she's a coming old bean!" said an excited Commander Marrachinello.

Suddenly the Planet Garlicazure was expelled from the Voidwell sending shockwaves through space. Leaving a trail of electric protons that lit up the whole sector, making an explosion that made the sun look like nothing more than a camp fire; except without the comfort that a campfire brings. The crew were thrown around like Vegetables at a poor rendition of an old Vege-Vaudeville musical.

"We are breaking up Captain." shouted SO Tulipina. "Structural overload at maximum crumplezone specification. Nine thousand blimits to the square star-inch." she confirmed.

"Radion ring re-activated at full output, Captain." confirmed FO Marrowlar. "We have expulsion of Garlicazure," he shouted as he was thrown to the floor.

As the Planet sped off into the distance the O.S.S Capsicumby and the O.S.S Ommelettra. Jumped into K Factor five ahead of the universes largest active meteorite.

"Activate full transverse pivotal thrusters, Viceroy Rhubarblatt. Initiate K Factor three now!" Shouted Captain Carrot as his chair span round and round.

"K Factor three initiated, Captain. We are pulling away, but only just Sir." confirmed Viceroy Rhubarblatt.

"Carrot to Peabazzare, go! Repeat go! K Factor five." ordered Captain Carrot as the O.S.S.S Earthanon creaked and moaned under the strain of the Voidwell's grasp.

"Negative Captain Carrot. We are here for the duration. Hold on Captain Carrot, we are chaining our computer data banks; that should give you the ability to draw from our energy shields." Confirmed Captain Peabazzare.

"Captain Carrot, the O.S.S Satsumuroo has initiated her security matrix code the link is irreversible." confirmed FO Marrowlar.

"Captain Carrot." said So Tulipina. "Structural overload specification has dropped to eight thousand blimits to the square starinch. It would appear we are back in the game." she confirmed.

"You're nuts Captain Peabazzare, but I like you, you're just like you're Organidaddy a real chip off the old pod." cried Captain Carrot. "FO Marrowlar. Distance status of Garlicazure?" he ordered. FO Marrowlar tapped into the security com with vigour.

"Six hundred and twenty three thousand, one hundred and six point four starmillo's, Captain. At current rate of travel they will be clear of the explosion zone in one starmin." he confirmed.

"Okay, here's what we do." said the Captain. "Viceroy Rhubarblatt, increase K Factor by one K in five starsecs on my mark, FO Marrowlar, lock on our tractor beam to the O.S.S Satsumuroo from the ship's Satellite phaser housing. She is effectively dead in space, a barnacle on our hull. We are going to have to tow them out with us. Let's give that thing a throat lozenge it will never forget!"

"Aye, aye Sir." said FO Marrowlar.

"Ensign Broccleman, pre-set the A.M.A.C.P.T delayed detonator at one starmin thirty starsecs. Activate on my mark. Viceroy Rhubarblatt; distance from the Voidwell?" asked Captain Carrot.

"One hundred and eleven thousand starmillo's Captain, retreating at fourteen thousand starmillo's per starmin. The Voidwell suction is slowing our departure considerably.

"Captain Carrot," called FO Cornelius. "The Radion Ring and Phaser housing is on the move. E T A in Voidwell twelve seconds." confirmed FO Cornelius.

"Ensign Broccleman, activate A.M.A.C.P.T now." said the Captain, getting back in the Command com chair as the ship's controls stabilised.

"Aye Sir. A.M.A.C.P.T armed and activated.

"Viceroy Rhubarblatt one K in five, mark!" said the Captain.

"Aye Sir, K factor three and increasing distance one hundred seventy thousand starmillo's."

Down on the Planet Garlicazure, FO Potatree and Bulbouey struggled with the G force to contain their body movements with any degree of sense.

As they left the Voidwell, a huge explosion rocked the Planet and suddenly FO Potatree's mobile particle scanner lit with the confirmation that they were free of the Voidwell. He signalled to Bulbouey to re-activate the core elements into the magnetic housing then they both frantically fought to control their limbs to complete the task.

On the bridge of the O.S.S Ommelettra, Captain de Fleetrap monitored the Planet Garlicazure as it approached the dragnet.

"Viceroy Chrysanthenna, activate buffer shield. Garlicazure will make contact in V minus twenty three starsecs." said Captain de Fleetrap, operating the gyroscope.

"Dragnet buffer shield activated. Garlicazure speed, five hundred and seventy three thousand starmillo's per starmin. Dragnet speed, Five hundred and fifty thousand starmillo's per starmin."

Back on the O.S.S.S Earthanon, Captain Carrot plotted the course of the Planet of Garlicazure with Ensign Viola at the Navigation's com.

"Two, one. K Factor five, distance three hundred and Ninety thousand starmillo's from Voidwell; Satsumuroo in tract." confirmed Viceroy Rhubarblatt. On the Visaid the Phaser housing could be seen entering the Voidwell expulsion point. As the bridge crew looked at the visaid in excitement, Professor Goosegorgon and Dr Kiwitranus stepped on to the bridge with Captain Carrot's wife, Viceroy Councillor Au Paw-Paw and Mushroids Fungola and Funguy.

"A.M.A.C.P.T Entering Voidwell, three, two and one, Now!" confirmed Ensign Broccleman.

"Captain Carrot," said SO Tulipina. "The Voidwell is closing and scanning for energy source."

"A.M.A.C.P.T activation in V minus seventy starsecs." Confirmed Ensign Broccleman. There was now an air of excitement that flooded the bridge as Viceroy Rhubarblatt gave the ship's vital statistic readings.

"K Factor six, mark. Five hundred sixty thousand starmillo's and increasing speed." confirmed Viceroy Rhubarblatt.

"O.S.S Satsumuroo in tract." said Ensign Viola taking over at the scanner.

It was going to be a close thing if they were to clear the explosion zone. Some on board felt it too close for comfort.

On the Planet Garlicazure, FO Potatree and Bulbouey had completed the element core insertion and were ready to flick the switches. As they did so the magnetic housing activated along with the electro oscillator effectively acting as a brake on the Planet. Without warning, all Helios broke loose as flying debris flew across the chamber, smashing into the walls; fortunately nothing that would crush them.

On board the O.S.S Ommelettra, Viceroy Chrysanthenna, gave out the vital statistics. Garlicazure contact in V minus five starsecs, distance from Voidwell. Nine hundred and eighty-four thousand starmillo's, Speed equilibrium at Five hundred and fifty thousand starmillo's per starmin. Speed descent at ten thousand starmillo's per starmin. Two, one. We have bagged the ball. Garlicazure is harnessed and controlled. Clear of the explosion zone in twenty-six point five starsecs.

On the bridge of the O.S.S.S Earthanon, Viceroy Rhubarblatt carried on the countdown.

"K Factor Eight, mark. Eight hundred fifty thousand starmillo's from Voidwell expulsion point and increasing speed." confirmed Viceroy Rhubarblatt.

"O.S.S Satsumuroo in tract." said Ensign Viola at the scanner.

"All systems clear and on line." said SO Tulipina.

"A.M.A.C.P.T activation in forty starsecs." Confirmed Ensign Broccleman.

"Garlicazure is slowing, Captain Carrot. It will be clear of the explosion zone in V minus twenty starsecs." confirmed Ensign Viola.

"Here we jolly well go, hey what?" cried Commander Marrachinello.

On Garlicazure, FO Potatree and Bulbouey appeared to have fainted under the strain of the pressure on their bodies. But the atmosphere had returned to normal and all was well in the catacombs where the population lay in enforced hibernation.

On the bridge of the O.S.S.S Earthanon, Viceroy Rhubarblatt carried on the countdown as time started to run out.

"K Factor ten, mark. Nine hundred seventy thousand starmillo's from Voidwell expulsion point. Speed levelling at one point four million starmillo's per starmin." confirmed Viceroy Rhubarblatt.

"O.S.S Satsumuroo in tract." said Ensign Viola at the scanner.

"All systems clear and on line." said SO Tulipina.

"A.M.A.C.P.T activation in thirty starsecs." confirmed Ensign Broccleman.

"Garlicazure will be clear of the explosion zone in V minus ten starsecs." confirmed Ensign Viola.

"K Factor Ten and holding, one million, one hundred thousand and ninety starmillo's from Voidwell expulsion point, speed confirmed at one point four million starmillo's per starmin." Confirmed Viceroy Rhubarblatt.

"O.S.S Satsumuroo in tract." Said Ensign Viola at the scanner.

"All systems clear and on line." Said SO Tulipina.

"A.M.A.C.P.T activation in twenty five starsecs." Confirmed Ensign Broccleman.

"Garlicazure will be clear of the explosion zone in V minus five starsecs." confirmed Ensign Viola.

On the bridge of the O.S.S Ommelettra excitement was high with the situation.

"We are clear of the Voidwell explosion zone Captain de Fleetrap." said Viceroy Chrysanthenna as the ship's crew gave a jolly cry of jubilant relief.

"Visaid split, Voidwell and Garlicazure Ensign Ramputinder." Said Captain de Fleetrap.

Aye, aye Sir." He replied.

Back on the bridge of the O.S.S.S Earthanon sighs of relief were rife.

"K Factor Ten and holding. One million two hundred thousand and sixty starmillo's from Voidwell expulsion point, speed holding at one point four million starmillo's per starmin." Confirmed Viceroy Rhubarblatt.

"O.S.S Satsumuroo in tract." Said Ensign Viola at the scanner.

"All systems clear and on line." Said SO Tulipina.

"We are out of the explosion zone Captain." Confirmed FO Marrowlar.

"A.M.A.C.P.T activation in five starsecs." Confirmed Ensign Broccleman.

"Garlicazure is clear of the explosion zone Captain." confirmed Ensign Viola, as a cry of excitement came from the lips of Commander Marrachinello.

"Yippee!"

"Five, four, three, two, one. Activation." Confirmed Ensign Broccleman.

On the visaid the Voidwell could be seen exploding with humongous force and the ship rocked silently but vibrantly. The skies lit up with a frightening splendour and then there was nothing. Silence prevailed on the bridge.

"Status report of ship FO Marrowlar?" asked Captain Carrot.

"All systems are clean and clear; minimal damage sustained Captain." he said smiling. "Satsumuroo is free and clear." he continued. "Garlicazure?" he said pausing. "Life signs on Garlicazure read very strong; approximately one hundred and seventy thousand strong Captain Carrot." he said. "The mission is a complete success and you Sir, are a genius. I would offer to shake your hand but something tells me you would rather hug your Organiwife." He said as the tears of joy started to flow throughout the Sun-Fleet flotilla force. Garlicazure had been liberated and the universe was better for it; much better! Carrelda ran into his arms and the bridge crew surrounded them and joined in a group hug. Today was a good day, long but satisfying. Just the way the Organitrons liked it.

"FO Marrowlar let's get down to that planet and crush FO Potatree with a bear hug." said Captain Carrot the happiest Organitron in the universe, with the possible exception of one hundred and seventy thousand the Garlicallians, FO Potatree and Envoy Milnedew that is!

"Aye, aye Sir," said FO Marrowlar activating his personal channel. "Ensign Broccleman prepare to Vegitamise a landing party, destination Garlicazure!"

"With pleasure FO Marrowlar ready when you are." he confirmed.

"Ensign Strawballis, open inter-ship communication." said Captain Carrot as he prepared to address them.

"Inter-ship communication on-line Captain." Confirmed Ensign Strawballis.

"This is Captain Carrot to all Sun-Fleet crew. Quite simply, I salute you. This day will go down in history as our finest triumph. Your finest triumph. All Captain's and FO's, prepare to board Garlicazure, full battle dress. And pack Vegimatters for all, something tells me a party is needed. Guests of honour. FO Potatree, Envoy Milnedew and the Garlicallians. All crew will be allowed a visitation as soon as we are sure they are ready to receive them. Thank you, all of you this is your day as well as theirs. I for one will never forget that. Captain Carrot UFO and out, end transmission."

"Captain Carrot Sir." said a worried Ensign Strawballis. "I cannot raise FO Potatree or Envoy Milnedew on their personal channels."

"I want four medical teams Dr Kiwitranus, Professor Goosegorgon you will attend and oversee all emergency medical requirements."

"Yes Capatano, I will 'a do my best 'a." Said the professor looking for his monocle.

"Ensign Strawballis." Continued the Captain in full flow. "Have each O.S.S ship delegation accompanied by a medical team and medical equipment."

"Aye, aye Captain." she agreed manning the Communications com.

Then Captain Carrot kissed Carrelda on the lips and whispered in her ear.

"When I know it is safe will you join me on Garlicazure?" he asked.

"Try stopping me, just you try stopping me." She said hugging him. "Now go they will need you down there."

"FO Marrowlar, FO Cornelius, FO Melonicord, Commander Marrachinello. To the Vegimatter room.

SO Tulipina, you have command com. Ensign Strawballis keep trying to raise FO Potatree and Envoy Milnedew on the communications channels." he said heading for the elevation chamber.

"Aye, aye Sir!" said Ensign Strawballis.

Part four

With Garlicazure secure, Earthanon calls.

Sundate 2.999,999,999/ 332 Time 13.20 starhectoids

On Garlicazure, FO Potatree and Bulbouey were still unconscious as the Sun-Fleet delegation Vegitamised on the planetary surface. Batch after batch of Vegimatters appeared as the delegation stood in wonder of the sight set before them. The planetary surface was bleached dry and covered in a substantial and dense form of crust. Even the deserts of Earthanon appeared to look healthier, more appealing, and more homely. It was hard to imagine survival on such a bleak and unforgiving terrain, without the added hindrance of a Voidwell. But with it, it could only have been a pure and unstoppable nightmare.

Present were Captain Carrot, FO Marrowlar, FO Cornelius, FO Melonicord, Commander Marrachinello, Professor Goosegorgon, Dr Kiwitranus and Viceroy Au Paw-Paw along with four emergency medical teams. Also present were Captain Macoronite and FO Swedeuroo of the O.S.S Capsicumby, Captain de Fleetrap and FO Cornytiela of the O.S.S Ommelettra, and Captain Peabazzare with his second in command FO Pepperat, of the O.S.S Satsumuroo Each of the O.S.S class ships brought with them a medical team to aid in coping with the possibility of a large amount of casualties.

Under the Planetary surface in the chambers of the artificial gravitational atmosphere reactors, FO Potatree stirred as Ensign Strawballis's voice echoed in his sub-conscious.

"This is Ensign Strawballis to FO Potatree. Come in please. O.S.S.S Earthanon to FO Potatree please come in." Still there was no reply.

Bulbouey was still sparko after receiving a knock on the head from a stray foreign body, leaving a slight cut to his forehead. FO Potatree came round slowly and tapped his chest activating his personal com.

"FO Potatree here I think Ahh.. Hum..' answered FO Potatree feeling the effects of the dusty atmosphere. "Glad to hear your voice Ensign Strawballis. Tell me, is this a dream or did we make it." He asked dazed.

"It's a dream FO Potatree." Laughed Ensign Strawballis.

"Well.. At least that means I'm sleeping and I'm still alive.' He chortled.

"FO Potatree, Captain Carrot and his landing party have Vegitamised to the planetary surface with medical teams and supplies. Request directions." She continued. Just then FO Potatree noticed that Bulbouey was hurt and rushed towards where he had strapped himself in.

"Bulbouey, Bulbouey are you all right?" He whispered tapping him in the face, but with no response. "Helios, please don't let him be hurt. I'll do anything, anything to make him good; do you hear me!" He shouted untying him and carrying him in his arms.

"Ensign Strawballis, tell Captain Carrot to head for the Oudag capsules. Turn on a bearing of forty seven point five blimits due north towards the rock formations about two hundred staryards away. There they will find a cave. Get everyone in the cave and have them stand well clear of the entrance. I'm on my way. Have a medical team ready we have a casualty; and hurry. Let me know when they are all in the cave." Shouted FO Potatree concerned for the well being of his new found friend.

"Aye, aye, FO Potatree. They are on their way." Confirmed Ensign Strawballis.

FO Potatree ran from the chambers grasping Bulbouey for dear life. Quickly he dodged and weaved his way through the sleeping inhabitants toward the cave elevator on which he and Envoy Milnedew had previously arrived. Looking around for a control leaver, he activated the spring coiled locking device on the door to the cave on the surface. As Captain Carrot approached the rock formation he and the landing party spotted the cave opening and ran as fast as they could. Quickly they reached the cave and once all were inside Captain Carrot contacted FO Potatree then they waited hesitantly for something to happen.

"Captain Carrot to FO Potatree, we are ready when you are!" He said looking for an alternative exit.

"Glad to have you aboard Captain. Stand well clear of the cave entrance Captain." Said FO Potatree, activating the counterbalance mechanism. Slowly the cave entrance closed and soon the floor was revolving and heading down into the heart of Garlicazure. It seemed to take forever as far as FO Potatree was concerned and he paced back and forth trying to get through to Bulbouey without success.

"Bulbouey, Bulbouey come on my friend, please. Talk to me, you can do it; come on." He said, as Captain Carrot and the landing party came into sight. He rushed towards them, and as the cave floor came to a halt, he laid Bulbouey down on the floor.

"Dr Kiwitranus, help him. His name's Bulbouey. He received a bump on the head but I don't know what with. He hasn't been conscious since I came round. Do whatever it takes, Dr Kiwitranus, he's a real hero." Quickly Dr Kiwitranus and the medical team worked to revive the little Garlicallian. Captain Carrot walked up to FO Potatree and shook his hand. Sensing FO Potatree was anxious for his new found friend he reassured him that all would be well.

"Hello Chief," said the Captain. "Don't worry he is in the best possible hands. He'll be fine now. Come here and let me have a look at you. Are you OK?"

"I will be when I know Bulbouey will be OK!" Said FO Potatree sitting at Bulbouey's side and holding his hand. "What do you say doc? Is it serious? Is he going to be OK?" Asked FO Potatree. Dr Kiwitranus scanned Bulbouey from head to toe and took his vital readings.

"I think so, chief, mostly superficial cuts and abrasions. A mild concussion at worst; no serious damage to the brain tissue. Yes, our friend here is going to be fine." Confirmed Dr Kiwitranus smiling with relief.

"Are there any other injured parties FO Potatree?" Asked a concerned Professor Goosegorgon.

"I haven't checked but on my way through everything seemed OK. The damage to these people I'm afraid will run a lot deeper than cuts and bruises. At the end of this row are the sick and infirm. They will need your help when they come round in about thirty five starmins." Confirmed FO Potatree looking at his timepiece.

Bulbouey stirred and FO Potatree was the first face he saw as he opened his eyes.

"FO Potatree are you all right? Did we make it? Are we safe? The others; are they OK?" He said, dizzy and confused by the sudden realisation of the new strange faces around him. "Oh, I guess we made it then." He continued lying back down and fainting.

"Yes Bulbouey, we made it. Now you rest. Get some sleep; you look like you could use it." Said FO Potatree mopping his brow.

"Ha.. Haaaaum." yawned Bulbouey. "Sleep, get some sleep; a much overrated pastime. But, if you insist, sleep it is." Then as suddenly as he had come round, he fell asleep.

FO Potatree stood and looked into Captain Carrot's eyes. Nothing needed to be said, the relief in all their faces told the whole story. Captain Carrot hugged FO Potatree and FO Marrowlar put an arm over his shoulder. Gradually the whole of the landing party shook FO Potatree's hand and dispersed to deal with their duties. Viceroy Councillor Au Paw-Paw was the last to hug FO Potatree and as she did so he whispered in her ear.

"Helios that was scary, I don't ever want to have to do that again. Look at me. I'm shaking like a leaf and.. And; I can't stop it."

FO Potatree, cried into her shoulder as she comforted him. It was tears of joy, but tears nevertheless.

"That's OK FO Potatree, you are entitled to let it out. Today is your day and anything you want to do goes." She said, understanding the cocktail of emotions drowning poor FO Potatree's soul. "You have done a great thing and, well, the rest goes without saying. Just remember this, we are all very proud of you and Envoy Milnedew. What you have achieved is to bring the Organitron one step forward toward a complete body of space nations."

Commander Marrachinello walked amongst the sleeping inhabitants of Garlicazure. They looked happy in this state of enforced relaxation. Soon he would have to depart for Earthanon but before he did, he so much wanted to see the faces of the Garlicallians as a collective free nation. This would be a sight for sore eyes and help to bolster his spirits in the long journey home. He felt humbled by the sights set before him and filled with admiration for what this race had endured and conquered. As he walked he happened across the domed Vegewell that encased Envoy Milnedew with a dozen or so Garlicallian seedlings. Leaning forward, touched by the view that pulled at his heart strings, he could see Envoy Milnedew open his eyes. FO Potatree appeared over his shoulder just in time to see a beaming smile across the face of Envoy Milnedew. Together they opened the dome and pulled Envoy Milnedew clear of the Vegewell.

"Chief, Commander I take it we made it," he said slowly, still under the influence of the sleeping draught. "The Garlicallians? Bulbouey? Did all go as planned?' he asked yawning.

"Like clockwork my boy. By all accounts it was a text book rescue." said FO Potatree.

"Only this time you had to write the text book first." laughed Commander Marrachinello.

Captain Carrot followed behind Commander Marrachinello after seeing them pull Envoy Milnedew from the Vegewell.

"And what a terrific ending it has got." He said. "All the heroes survived and the baddy, "Blottmeager," wiped from the face of the universe forever.

Well done Envoy Milnedew, you're a star. At one time, as Garlicazure shot out of the Voidwell you were a veritable shooting star at that." He chuckled as they all joined in with the light relief of jovial Camaraderie that was feared lost forever. If they were honest with each other.

On the bridge of the FF Francaisfry across the galaxy. General Satuese took pride of place at the helm with Principle Officer Gammachip at his side.

"Prefect Roistered. Open communication to the flotilla force Command ship." said the General, anxious to get underway with the second phase of the testing programme.

"Aye, fry General. This is the FF Francaisfry calling the FF Shallow fryer."

"FF Francaisfry, this is the FF Shallow fryer. Major General Ickychick Fattyspot here. Flotilla force assembled and ready for departure. All final checks are complete and we are running at one hundred percent efficiency; apart from a few tired and weary crew. That was one humdinger of a party. Just what we all needed." said the Major General, nursing a headache of his own.

"Indeed Major General Fattyspot, a welcome break for all deserving troops of the elite, but the biggest party is yet to come. The victory celebration of the defeat of the Earthanon Organitron defence network." jeered General Satuese. "Course heading and formation confirmation. Heading, one hundred and seventy two blimits from current position. Formation, diamond, FF Shallow Fryer to spearhead formation. We will commence our five starlectoid formation rehearsal, our departure is set for **Sundate 2.999,999,999/ 337 Biltechtoids. Time 18.30 starhectoids.** Minimise radio contact, we have to read each other's mind like we have never done before. Radio silence to be maintained upon departure for Earthanon, until final attack position accomplished, ETA Earthanon twenty eight Starlectoids and mark. ETA time of arrival **18.30 starhectoids. Sundate 2.999,999,999/ 365**. Marking all course and trajectory for Flotilla fleet communication. Please confirm receipt and compliance." asked General Satuese.

"Course pre-set and logged receipt and compliance acknowledged." confirmed General Fattyspot.

"This is General Faturno Satuese of the FF Francaisfry, over and out ending transmission."

"Until we speak again General Satuese, this is Major General Ickychick Fattyspot of the FF Shallow fryer. Over and out. End transmission."

General Satuese stood at once and turned toward Principle Officer Gammachip.

"PO Gammachip, transfer course logging to flotilla force on board computers." he said sternly.

"Aye, fry Sir." Responded PO Gammachip.

"Vice Principle Waffleat, crank up the reactors and let's get this show on the road. Steady as she goes and set speed to E factor two."

"Aye fry General, Course heading logged and computed, crystalline reactors on line and speed setting E factor two. Mark. All momentum systems are on line and functional General." Said Vice Principle Waffleat.

"Vice Principle Fritz, initiate the particle scanner and scan the solar system. Any sign of an Organitron ship and we need to cloak immediately. You may need to take a few facts into account when we get under way for the Earthanon Space sector. We should be OK for twenty Starlectoids on our approach. But as soon as we are within one starlectoid of breaching the Organitron Silicone sphere scanning range, I will give you the matrix coding for the parental cloaking device." Said General Satuese as the confused bridge crew were unaccustomed to this new development in Fasterfoid terminology.

"A what General Satuese?" Asked a bemused Vice Principle Fritz.

"You heard Soldier, you may not understand but you all heard." He said looking around the bridge. "When these trials are over you are going to be amazed, enough for now let's get back to the job in hand. Vice Principle Roastie," continued General Satuese. "Monitor that ships systems equaliser like it was your Wifeoid. Any fall out of synchronisation I want it reported and rectified toot sweet."

"Aye fry General, all systems register one hundred percent and Ay'Ok." He said.

"Prefects Beefychip, Crinklet." smiled General Satuese. "Keep your eyes on VPO Roastie! I happen to know his Wifeoid pulls the wool over his eyes at every possible occasion." He laughed. PO Gammachip paced the bridge wondering about one or two key points of interest to the mission.

"Yes PO Gammachip? You have a question for me?" asked General Satuese.

"Yes General I do." he said slowly. "I realise this mission relies on the fact that we appear to be beaten, but for some time I have wondered how we are to get close enough to Earthanon to maintain the element of surprise. We can remain cloaked, but surely the flotilla force will stick out like a sore thumb in a pair of wire gloves?" enquired PO Gammachip.

"Indeed PO Gammachip, and we have got it covered. Fear not, all will be revealed in our final approach." said the General. "Anything else?" he continued.

"Yes Sir, there is. Again I have to question the route we are embarking on. Fourteen starlectoids from here lies a Slithervoid that would deliver us to the heart of the Earthanon central defence network. Why are we taking the long- winded approach?" he asked. General Satuese smiled and placed a hand on the shoulder of his second in command.

"PO Gammachip, there is much that you need to learn about the way's of battle and honour. I beg of you to watch the master and learn. I cannot give you all the details now but let me tell you this: there are three reasons we are not taking the Slithervoid option; one, we really want to throw a spanner in the works of any millennium celebrations that those health hooligans are planning, that is why we are not setting off immediately, we may as well be point perfect in our attack strategy so we will practise these Manoeuvres until everyone can perform their duties with their eyes shut. Secondly, the activation of the Slithervoid will alert them to our presence and can disable our cloaking capability whilst in the Slithervoid transportation. And the third, well, when I introduce you to my trump card up the sleeve you will understand perfectly. So trust me, it's very, very exciting." said General Satuese.

"Aye, fry Sir, but I still do not understand why we don't just go straight in, surely the amount of time from emerging from the Slithervoid to reaching our objective will merely be a matter of starmins." said an unhappy PO Gammachip, who was growing tired of being kept in the dark.

"As I said Principle Gammachip soon you will understand!" Whimpered General Satuese holding his head in his hands, growing weary of his second in commands lacking capability to learn, but more importantly to reason.

Time 14.30 starhectoids.

Back on the Planet Garlicazure Queen Oilyio Perfumo Garlialla, awoke in her Vegewell to the artificial light from the gravitational atmospheric vitamin reactor. FO Potatree and Envoy Milnedew had gone to the chambers to shore up the core elements. It had been a long time since they were in full operation and the risk of them breaking down was reasonably good. It went without saying that to come through this rescue just to be sucked into outer space seemed rather idiotic. Captain Carrot entered the chamber and inspected the legendary vitamin reactors, the likes of which he had never seen before.

"Holy Vegmoley!" he said, as the daunting array of tubes, switches and levers astounded him. "For something so primitive it all looks very complicated." he gasped.

"You're right there, if it wasn't for young Bulbouey, I think we just may have been in a bit of a muddle. Do you know that little fella has been running this unit since he was thirteen starlectoids old Captain?" Exclaimed FO Potatree.

Captain Carrot swallowed the lump in his throat and pulled the two brave Organitrons closer to him.

"Listen." he said. "While I have you alone I just wanted to say something. I know that you won't want any fuss and would prefer for business to get back to usual as soon as possible, but this has to be said. There are many things in life that we cherish and nothing more so than life itself. Envoy Milnedew, we all know of your past and pray that your future is less fraught. Sun-fleet will hear of your bravery and I would like you to consider a place in the crew of the O.S.S.S Earthanon. Don't answer me now. Mull it over and think about it a while. The position I want you to consider is one of Star Fighter technological advancement advisor. I believe, through your experiences, you have much to pass on. It will be an FO Status and you will be a very good example of what can be achieved if you just persevere. FO Potatree no one can thank you enough for your trouble in this affair and I am sure that honours will be forthcoming from Sun-Fleet. I would like you to talk some sense into this young Organiman with a view to accepting the position that I have mentioned. And finally to both of you I must say this. There are few occasions where an Organiman can count himself fortunate in life, but to have you both as friends, irrespective of Sun-fleet, makes me more proud than you could possibly imagine. On behalf of the Garlicallians and Sun-Fleet division of UFO I salute you both." Then he saluted them and gave them two small parcels. "I order you not to open these until you are given permission." he said as his personal channel activated.

"Viceroy Councillor Au Paw-Paw, to Captain Carrot."

"Captain Carrot to Viceroy Councillor Au Paw-Paw." He replied.

"Queen Garlialla and Bulbouey have come round and are anxious to meet you, and thank FO Potatree and Envoy Milnedew." she confirmed.

"We are on our way, Carrot out." said the Captain smiling. "Come now, let us meet your new found fan club." he continued laughing.

In the habitation Catacombs, Garlicallians were milling around by their thousands. Excitement filled the air as the realisation of freedom became too much to bear. Fainting was rife and floor space was becoming short. The differential in the air quality was a major factor in the light headed reception they were getting. Queen Garlialla opened her arms as FO Potatree, Captain Carrot and Envoy Milnedew stepped forward from the chamber entrance. Bulbouey jumped up into FO Potatree's arms and Queen Garlialla hugged them all in turn.

"Thank you Captain Carrot. We owe you our lives and will be forever in your debt." She said with tears in her eyes.

"Thank you ma'am, but you owe me... Us, nothing. It is we who owe you thanks, thanks for surviving, thanks for being strong, thanks for your courage as a Race and determination as a Nation. For showing us that good will always triumph over evil."

"Evil, Captain Carrot? Blottmeager may have been uncomfortable, but even we could not blame an elemental phenomenon for actions that it was neither in control of, or capable of moderating." She said surprised by Captain Carrot's statement.

"Perhaps you are right Ma'am forgive me, but there is much of which you are unaware about the recently dearly departed, natural elemental phenomenon "Blottmeager" but nothing that need concern us for now. Tonight Ma'am, with your permission, we will throw a party to celebrate your new found independence. I think you.. We, deserve to indulge in a treat of that nature and I, for one, can't think of a better reason for letting our hair down. What do you say?" asked the Captain.

"It has been a long time since we have had cause to celebrate, Captain Carrot. We may not exactly be the best company for a party. I'm not sure we could remember what to do?" she answered honestly.

"FO Potatree." shouted Captain Carrot.

"Aye, aye Sir." he replied.

"The Queen here is worried about what a party might involve. Do you think the Garlicallians have cause for concern?" Smiled Captain Carrot.

FO Potatree walked up to Queen Garlialla and took her by the arm and began to sing a little ditty.

"If you can dance and you can sing then you can party with a zing,
Yes, you can swing it with a hullabaloo.
So fear not my dears, for the party king's here.
And that party is in honour of you.
I will croon while you swoon to a merry old tune,
Celebrate the Organitron way.
So all come dancing with us, place in us your full trust.
For tomorrow we work, but tonight we can play."

Queen Garlialla looked upon the faces of her subjects and her heart melted with joy. She began dancing on the cave floor and sent its revolving action flowing.

As her court musicians struck up a tune and she began to perform a ballet, a quartet of Garlicallian singers gave song in the back ground.

"Aaah.. Hum... hum... la.la.di.da.dum.do,
Let us sing while our Queen flows along.
To the music that we bring,
Show the universe we can be strong,
Put our feelings into song.

We are free and there's nothing to say,
Except "thank you" and to Helios we pray.
You have turned our lives upside down,
And our problems chased them away.
Turned our darkness and cloudy existence,
Into a bright new sun shining day.

So yes we can dance, we can sing, join the party with zing,
And thrive on the hullabaloo.
So let your King join our Queen on the dance floor and sing,
To the Organitron, the Organitron,
For we are back in the fold good and new.
Again we are Organitrons, Organitrons... free just like you."

Queen Garlialla stopped dancing and gave a bow to the applause and walked toward the Sun-Fleet delegation.

"Well FO Potatree, will we do for this party of yours?" she asked quite out of breath.

"Oh yes, indeed you will Ma'am, and the party is ours." he laughed. "Only I'm afraid my dancing is not quite as angelic as yours." He guffawed as the rest of the party agreed loudly.

"Dr Kiwitranus." said Captain Carrot. "Will Queen Garlialla and her entourage be fit to travel in the Vegitamisation beam to the O.S.S.S Earthanon."

"I see no reason why not Captain. They are all remarkably healthy considering the trauma they have endured for so long." answered Dr Kiwitranus

"Entourage Captain Carrot?" said Queen Garlialla. "We are all equal on this Planet I have no need for superior treatment. What is this Vegitamisation beam that you speak of?" she said.

"Oooh.. Oooh.. I know. FO Potatree has told me all about it. You must try it; you simply must! Of course I will try it first if you like, just to make sure that it is absolutely safe, if you wish?" insisted Bulbouey.

"Well Captain." Chuckled Queen Garlialla. "It looks like I have found an entourage after all. I will leave my council here whilst I am gone." she said holding her hand out to Bulbouey.

"Very well Queen Garlialla. I will leave our medical and technical teams on the planetary surface to prepare for the forthcoming events and secure the atmospheric chambers. Commander Marrachinello. I know you are anxious to return, but would you consider staying for the celebrations this evening and depart early next starlectoid? This will give me the opportunity to update my report. I would appreciate it if you would deliver it to Admiral Ducarrotain upon your arrival at Earthanon."

"Well, as long as you are sure, Captain, that we will arrive in time to prevent the you know who from creating havoc. I would be honoured and delighted Captain." said Commander Marrachinello, careful not to mention the Fasterfoids for fear of creating anxiety to the Space Race of Garlicazure.

"Earthanon, Captain Carrot? Where is this Earthanon?" asked Queen Garlialla.

"If you will permit me to explain all once we leave for the O.S.S.S Earthanon?" he asked as she nodded, sensing the delicacy of the matter.

"Captain Carrot to Ensign Broccleman, come in please." said the Captain activating his personal channel.

"Ensign Broccleman here, Sir." He replied.

"Commander Marrachinello, Captain Peabazzare, Captain Macoronite, Captain de Fleetrap, FO Potatree, Envoy Milnedew, FO

Marrowlar and I will Vegitamise back on board immediately. Have you fixed and computed our positions?" he enquired, as they all stood on the cave entrance elevation floor, leading Queen Garlialla and Bulbouey with them.

"Also, lock on two Garlicallian subjects in immediate proximity and Vegitamise." he continued.

"Vegitamisation Tract on line, fixed and computed. Vegitamising now." said Ensign Broccleman.

To the amazement of the other Garlicallians they sighed as Queen Garlialla and Bulbouey disappeared from sight and seemed to have gone in a puff of air.

"What in Blottmeager was that?" asked an old Garlicallian Organiman sitting down with the shock of what he had witnessed.

"It's a long story, but fear not, they are safe it is just a matter of molecular transportation." said FO Melonicord assuring him.

"Molecular transportation, hey I have seen it all now!" Then looking where the party were standing, he winced. "But then maybe I haven't?" He chuckled as the rest of the teams joined him in the realisation that the slightest thing they seem to take for granted. Was a huge step forward in the experiences of the Garlicallians.

In the Vegitamisation suit room on board the O.S.S.S Earthanon, the Garlicallian transferral party appeared and stepped off the platform into the main reception area, making room on the Vegitamisation platform for the rest of the party to Vegitamise. When all were present, Captain Carrot activated his personal Channel while the two visitors from Garlicazure stood captivated by the surrounding decor, technology and sounds of their new friends and their ship.

"Tooty fruity." Said Bulbouey as they watched the rest of the party appear. "That was Cooooooowell." He giggled with excitement. "Can we do that again sometime?" he said tugging at FO Marrowlar's tunic.

"I'm sure there will be plenty of time to play later, little fellow." said FO Marrowlar smiling.

"Captain Carrot to Ensign Garlizamto."

"Ensign Garlizamto here, Captain Carrot."

"Meet me in the strategy room on the double please, Ensign Garlizamto." asked Captain Carrot.

"Ay'Ok and I are on my way, Captain."

"Carrot out." He replied. "Ensign Broccleman we are on our way to the strategy room. Inform SO Tulipina that I will require a full report and course specification for Earthanon. Have Ensign Viola run comparatives through the Nav com. All options covered." He said de-energising the doors.

"Aye, aye Captain." he replied.

Then Captain Carrot accompanied them all to the strategy room. With Garlicazure secure, it was now time to divert the main focus of attention, albeit reluctantly, on the Planet of Earthanon and the potential threat of a Fasterfoid invasion.

Seated in the strategy room was Ensign Garlizamto, who hurriedly stood to attention as Captain Carrot and the party entered.

"Ensign Garlizamto may I introduce you to your rightful Queen. Queen Oilyio Perfumo Garlialla, leader of the Garlicallian space race of your home Planet of Garlicazure. And this is the hero of the hour, Bulbouey, who helped FO Potatree to free Garlicazure from the evil clutches of the Voidwell Blottmeager. Queen Garlialla, Bulbouey, this is one of several Garlicallian descendants based here on the O.S.S.S Earthanon, Ensign Garlizamto. I will, of course, arrange for you to meet them all as soon as it is physically possible, but as I hope you will understand this is a very big and busy ship with over five hundred thousand in- habitants." He continued. Ensign Garlizamto knelt on the floor on one knee and kissed the hand of Queen Garlialla.

"At last we are reunited Ma'am." he said slowly with immense feeling. "I.. We have always been and will always remain true to our roots, and true to our race. I am honoured to be the first to be received by you Ma'am." Then he stood and offered a hand to Bulbouey which Bulbouey shook and said. "Tell me, it's really good to meet you and all that but, can you do that Coooowell salute?"

Ensign Garlizamto saluted Bulbouey with the Organitron salute. "Good enough?"

"Like I said. Coooowell!" He said fumbling at the salute again. "Oh well. I'm pleased to make your acquaintance Ensign Garlizamto." He chuckled.

"Ensign Garlizamto." said Captain Carrot. "Could you take our young friend here on a tour of the ship? I think he will have a particular interest in the gravity equaliser and the Californic reactors. FO Potatree will locate you when we have finished with our business here."

"It will be a pleasure. Sir. This way Bulbouey." he said pointing towards the door.

"Catch you later veg and potata's." he said cheekily bouncing his way out.

When the strategy doors closed behind Ensign Garlizamto and the boisterous Bulbouey Captain Carrot pulled the chair back for Queen Garlialla to be seated, then the rest of the party sat down and awaited Captain Carrot to begin. As he did so Queen Garlialla knew instinctively that he was going to break some bad news and prepared herself by pre-empting his embarrassment or guilt, whichever it was that troubled him.

"Captain Carrot, brave and gallant crews of Sun-Fleet, times have changed since the days of our ancestors were part of your Solar System. Something tells me that you have to go Captain, and soon. This place Earthanon calls you and, if they are in trouble, then go you must. We will survive, now we have more than a fighting chance." She said trying to soften the blow for the Captain.

"Queen Garlialla, you are a wise and strong Organiwoman. Yes, it is true. With regret, we do have to leave you. But now that we know where you are, we will return to Earthanon and contact UFO Carridionaries to arrange for your Planet to be returned to the Bubbleonion Squeak Solar System, repatriated with other surviving Garlicallian descendants and the space nations collective. Shortly I will escort you to the Widdup archives where the whole of our history can be better explained and you may ask questions that will fulfil the hunger of a knowledge seeking mind. I, and my crew, will do our very utmost to satisfy your needs with knowledge and manpower and supplies." He added. "Commander Marrachinello, you and your Star Fighter will board the O.S.S Capsicumby. Captain Macoronite, you will convey the news through Commander Marrachinello to Sun-Fleet Earthanon and arrange for the O.S.S Cruditae and the O.S.S Mousseline to return with you immediately to this sector, and begin the transportation of Garlicazure back to our beloved homelands. They will require a full complement of crew with a complete science party to establish a farming programme and eco system. You will need ten thousand ground troops for planetary surface defence. I would estimate Organipods to house them in until we can get you supplies to re establish the colony above the surface. For this purpose, I propose you requisition a Vege-cruiser to carry plentiful stocks of Vege, Meater and Fishy Matters, as well as armaments and mining equipment for the colony infrastructure. I would suggest two thousand civilian Organitron to start with and a detachment of two squadrons of

Star fighters. Commander Marrachinello, I will leave you to organise this, and a fleet of shuttle ships, shall we say twenty? I would also suggest you requisition one hundred Robopods for scout reconnaissance and security." Captain Carrot stooped to re-access the needs of the Garlicallian people, and the requirements for the new way forward. He did not want them to feel that they were on their own, soon to be forgotten. They must feel coveted and cherished. "Captain Carrot to Ensign Viola." said the Captain.

"Ensign Viola, here Captain." She replied.

"Ensign Viola, have you worked out those Course trajectory time tables yet?" He asked.

"Yes Sir," said Ensign Viola punching up the data on the Computron. "Captain, if we plot course for the Earthanon Atmosphere to arrive over Arcticus through the nearest available window; without activating the Slithervoid and assuming you would want to travel at top speed of ten K on the return, I would estimate a time spectrum ETA of twenty two starlectoids. If you choose to use the Slithervoid option, engineering informs me that we would be wise to run at six K maximum, to allow the structural and reactor checks to be completed. The Slithervoid may disintegrate the O.S.S.S Earthanon if we do not rectify all areas of structural fatigue as a safety precaution. That would take nine starlectoids, ETA Slithervoid expulsion seven Starmins. ETA Earthanon then accessing a window that will bring us out over the Europetriennes Hemisphere three starmins, ETA Arcticus twelve starmins Captain." Captain Carrot turned to FO Potatree who nodded in agreement with Ensign Viola's reasoning.

"Commander Marrachinello." said the Captain in mid-train of thought. "The Fasterfoid flotilla was positioned in sector F4 of the Asteroid crush basin is that correct?" he asked.

"Spot on old bean, I would say at top E Factor they are, or, were at twenty eight starlectoids away from Earthanon." he confirmed.

"Very well, Commander Marrachinello, I know you have been concerned with the Earthanon situation, but I am sure you will agree that two Mother ships and five squadrons of Star Fighters are more than enough to cope with a substantial battle situation? And anyway, I think I know them well enough to feel reasonably comfortable in the guess that they are still there." Said Captain Carrot smiling. "Aye Captain I would, besides old bean, Garlicazure had no real defence at all. Their need was far greater!" Said Commander Marrachinello. "Though, I wish I had your confidence as to their whereabouts."

"Yes, indeed I would agree Commander. As for my air of confidence I will explain. Now, it is the third starlectoid since you came aboard and your journey lasted ten starlectoids, it should have taken six starlectoids let's call it seven to be safe. This gives us a total of thirteen starlectoids since your Earthanon. This means that at the outside, the Fasterfoids first opportunity to attack Earthanon will be in fifteen point-five starlectoids. Captain Macoronite," said Captain Carrot. "You will depart for Earthanon immediately, fly like the wind and don't stop for anyone or anything. At top Calorific speed you should make the Slithervoid in five starlectoids, I want you fully loaded, fully fuelled and the troops and civilian workforces ready to return within two starlectoids of your arrival at destination Earthanon. With a vege-cruiser in transportation, your return journey will take six starlectoids. We will allow two starlectoid to disembark all personnel and equipment whilst the Vege-cruiser will remain on Garlicazure for conversion to a regeneration chamber. That will take fifteen starlectoids to reach that stage. Which is exactly how many days the Fasterfoids will have until they can make their first move. That takes us up to, **Sundate 2.999,999,999/ 347 Biltechtoids.** Everyone agreed?" He asked as they all nodded. "Good then this is my proposal. The O.S.S.S Earthanon will depart from Garlicazure Sundate **2.999,999,999/ 359 Biltechtoids.** It will take us six starlectoids in which to make it back to Earthanon on **Sundate 2.999,999,999/ 365 Biltechtoids.** Organigirls, Organiboys, which means that we will surprise them with a visit for the Millennium celebrations, which if I know the Fasterfoids? That will be the time they will least expect any outside help, and would find the most satisfaction in the attack if indeed they are planning an attack. Agreed Captain Macoronite?" Asked Captain Carrot who was looking mightily concerned.

"Agreed Captain Carrot, but I hope you are sure of the Fasterfoid strategy, we will be ready for departure in one starhectoid in any case. May I be dismissed Captain? We have many final preparations to make!" Asked Captain Macoronite.

"As you wish Captain Macoronite, I will see you prior to your departure Commander Marrachinello. I'm sorry, but, this means you will miss the celebrations later I'm afraid. I will speed up processing my report for Admiral Ducarrotain ready for your departure." Said the Captain apologising.

"Never mind Captain, my heart will be with all of you and I really couldn't be happier." he said standing. "I too have much to organise.

Captain, Queen Garlialla may I be excused too?" Said Commander Marrachinello kissing the hand of Queen Garlialla.

"Yes Commander, you may, until later." said Queen Garlialla as Commander Marrachinello and Captain Macoronite left the strategy room.

"So, Queen Garlialla." Said Captain Carrot. "We will do whatever we can to make your Planet secure and perhaps sow the seeds of a new beginning. We only have twenty seven starlectoids, but, that is better than none at all." he smiled.

That night much fun was had by all and the O.S.S Capsicumby had departed as planned. Gradually, the citadel of Garlicazure stretched its tentacles to the planetary surface. Bulbouey and FO Potatree became inseparable and Envoy Milnedew had agreed to become the new FO on board the O.S.S.S Earthanon. First, he was to take a well-earned sabbatical to gather his thoughts and strength but not until they reached Earthanon. Queen Garlialla had become close friends with Carrelda Carrot and many of the seedlings on board the O.S.S.S Earthanon. Much music and celebration filled the air, and dance, become the second language. When the O.S.S Capsicumby returned with the troops, civilians and supplies, sadness dawned on the Planet, as if old friends were to be dragged screaming from each other, never to meet again. On the twelfth day after the O.S.S Capsicumby's return. The O.S.S Capsicumby, the Ommelettra and the Satsumuroo awaited the arrival of Captain Carrot and the departure party as they flanked the vast mother ship up above the Planet of Garlicazure. Down on the planetary surface, Queen Garlialla and Bulbouey said their goodbyes to them and watched as the group prepared for Vegitamisation.

"Wait, wait a minute." shouted Bulbouey. "This is for you." he said handing Captain Carrot a large piece of Garlicazure rock. "Wherever you go we are with you and forever you're compatriots of mind. Until we meet again the Planet of Garlicazure salutes you." With that Bulbouey and the rest of the planetary inhabitants gave a perfect Organitron UFO salute. "See, I told you we would get there in the end." he chuckled.

"Thank you, all of you; it has been a privilege and an honour. Until we meet again may Helios guard you well and deliver you to a happy and righteous path." Then they returned the salute.

"Ensign Broccleman," said Captain Carrot activating his personal channel the emotion of the moment being sensed by all who witnessed the transferral party departure. Ensign Viola set course for Earthanon, Viceroy Rhubarblatt, and K factor six on SO Tulipina's mark." Captain Carrot took one last look around him at what they had built, and the people that they were leaving behind. Tears were welling in all eyes and sadness filled the air as FO Potatree winked at Bulbouey, whilst Envoy Milnedew smiled on all before them. "Vegitamise." croaked Captain Carrot, and they were gone, heading for as far as the Garlicallians were concerned, the strange Planet of Earthanon of which they knew nothing except for Queen Garlialla's teaching. She had much to pass on and she had all the time in the universe. Yet she felt disturbed at the departure of their new found friends and niggling at the back of her mind, she was doubtful that their paths would ever cross again. These thoughts though were to remain quiet and unspoken, but hopefully, to be proven wrong.

CHAPTER EIGHT

A turn for the worse?

Part one

O.S.S.S Earthanon saves the day.

Sundate 2,999,999,999/ 364 Biltechtoids. Time 19.30 starhectoids.

The Fasterfoid Flotilla force arrived within one point-five starlectoids of the silicone sphere's scanner range as vice principle Fritz alerted Principle Gammachip as to the situation.

"Excuse me Principle Gammachip; we are approaching the Earthanon scanning zone. I have picked up a Robopod in the immediate area. It has not locked on our ships yet, but, we will be in its scanner range in two point five starmins."

General Satuese listened with relish as he pulled from around his neck a booklet on a chain and opened it.

"Did you hear that Sir?" said Principle Gammachip. "We have to take evasive action or we will be spotted and plotted." He continued.

"Prefect Roastard," said the General. "Open interships communications; link all on-board computers to the FF Francaisfry. This is where we take the initiative. Show Flotilla force on screen all bridge visaid's, activate." He smiled.

"Aye, fry Sir. On board computers linked and on line, interships communications established and all bridge visuals activated." he said.

"Principle Gammachip," continued the General. "Enter the following matrix into the ship's defence system synchroniser and boost frequency to interships relay to all on-board computers." Said the General moving to the edge of his seat.

"Computers standing by for relay General." Confirmed Principle Gammachip.

"Matrix initiation as follows: C slash, P slash, F.F dash, **5** dash, 1 P.C.D Sat 1, enter!" Laughed General Satuese excited at what was about to happen.

The Flotilla bridge crews looked on with anticipation at what was to follow, and then one by one all of the ships in the Flotilla force disappeared. Gasps of amazement filled the Solar System as Principle Gammachip tried hard to look as if he were part of the secret all along but failed dismally.

"Vice Principle Waffleat, place reactors at full thrust E factor ten. Vice Principle Fritz, are we within range of the Robopod?" he asked.

"In ten starsecs Sir." He said locking on the scanner isolator. "Five, four, three, two, one. In range General. Robopod negative response, she can't see us, any of us." He repeated with excitement. "They are blind."

"All ship's systems running at one hundred percent Captain. Parental cloaking device modulator holding and powered at source. At current levels we have thirty starlectoids of reserved energy then we will have to convert to FF Francaisfry singular cloak only." Confirmed Vice Principle Roastie.

"ETA Earthanon, PO Gammachip?" Asked General Satuese.

"Twenty starhectoids at E factor ten General." he confirmed.

"Very well. Vice Principle Fritz, set course for the Arctolimba district. Bearing one, five, three, by one, seven, four blimits. Prefect Roastard, send message on scrambled frequency. Find me some sand and we will land. As soon as we have touched down, F.F Flotilla force will begin camouflage manoeuvres, and remember, as soon as we are completely covered, the cloaking device on your behalf is defunct. So you are on your own, make it look as though the battle was intended and limp away damaged. Maintain radio silence and good luck, General Faturno Satuese out etc... Etc... Etc!"

"Aye, fry Sir." Said prefect Roastard.

"Now, do you understand Principle Gammachip? If we were to take the Slithervoid route we would not be able to maintain a group cloaking device through the Slithervoid transportation. That, combined with the Slithervoid activation, would effectively eliminate our advantage of surprise." he said calmly. "Yes General, now I understand." Confirmed an agitated Principle Gammachip still disgruntled at the level of secrecy used by his commanding officer.

Sundate 2.999, 999,999/ 365 Biltechtoids. Time 04.30 starhectoids.

Back on the Planet Earthanon, preparations for the celebrations were in full flow and Commander Marrachinello was preparing the defence systems and flight formations for the expected Fasterfoid invasion; only there was no sign of a Fasterfoid presence as yet. "But," he thought, "When Captain Gillespie J. Carrot has a hunch you would be unwise not to follow it." If all was going according to plan the O.S.S.S Earthanon would be in the Earthanon Arcticus hemisphere in a little under eleven starhectoids. A great deal of celebration was expected on their arrival. The liberation of Garlicazure was a surprising and pleasant change from the humdrum normality of Earthanon. News of another Planet found under such circumstances, and the ingenious way in which the rescue was undertaken, had elevated Captain Carrot and his crew to new levels of respect. Even the Admiralette Xion Ru Roser was eager to commend him, FO Potatree and, unbelievably, accept Pirate Milnedew into the ranks of Sun-Fleet. She had arrived for the changing of the guard ceremony, which had been brought forward due to recent events of the Fasterfoid activities bringing Captain Carrot and the O.S.S.S Earthanon back prematurely. As well as to hear first hand from Captain Carrot the full details of the rescue and the condition of the Garlicallian race themselves.

On board the O.S.S.S Milkymarrow way, ordinary engineer Marrowmilne was distraught at the news of his estranged son's arrival. He did not know how to feel. He felt shamed by his own actions but that was not a new development. On the contrary, he had been fighting with his conscience since he had sent his son into the wilderness of space. His mother could not control nor hide her eagerness to be reunited with her first born. If Kenthal could see his way to forgive his own father for certain, then deep down engineer Marrowmilne longed to hug his son and heal the rift between them that he had caused. He had misjudged and insulted his son's honour. By his actions of bravery on the Planet Garlicazure, he had proved that he was a better Organitron than his father. All he could do was await his arrival with his mother, and hope that upon their meeting Kenthal could find forgiveness in his heart.

On board the O.S.S.S Earthanon, Captain Carrot was seated at the helm as Ensign Viola scanned the Solar System for Fasterfoid presence.

"Nothing Sir, Fasterfoid free." confirmed Ensign Viola.

"I see, Ensign Viola. How long until we reach the Slithervoid entry point?" He asked.

"Ten starhectoids nine starmins, Captain." She confirmed.

"FO Marrowlar, phasers at full capacity and on line. Blazer guns fully charged and on preliminary activation mode. Activate Blazer tractor beam on automatic tract. Arm and align fifty Oudag capsules and have defence control prepare two thousand cluster bug units. We want to be ready and I am taking no chances with those sneaky snackettes." He said calmly.

"Aye, aye Sir." Said FO Marrowlar keying in the relevant requirements to the security Computron. "Defence specifications loaded and under way, Captain."

"Good! Viceroy Rhubarblatt, full speed ahead and all spare power to the fore. A new millennium is dawning and there is a party with our name on it." He laughed.

"Aye, aye Captain. Full speed ahead and all systems are clean and clear." Confirmed Viceroy Rhubarblatt as the O.S.S.S Earthanon shot off into the distance heading for home flanked by the O.S.S Satsumuroo, the O.S.S Ommelettra and the O.S.S Capsicumby.

Time 13.20 starhectoids.

General Satuese paced the bridge of the FF Francaisfry as VP Fritz locked on to the co-ordinates and the Flotilla force headed for the abandoned lands of the Arctolimba mining district.

"Re-entry point in five, four, three, two, one." Said VP Fritz as VP Waffleat handled the steering column. "One hundred forty thousand starfeet, one thirty, one twenty, lowering speed to E factor six. One ten thousand starfeet, one hundred thousand and clearing danger zone, ninety, eighty, seventy, sixty thousand starfeet and levelling. ETA Arctolimba, one starmin twenty starsecs." Confirmed VP Fritz.

"Engaging reverse thrusters." Informed VP Waffleat. "Steering Ay'Ok E factor six confirmed and holding, dropping by one factor in five starsecs. E factor five, E factor four, E factor three, E factor two, E factor one. Switching to auxiliary crystalline momentum. Fifty starsecs to touch down." Said VP Waffleat.

"All systems clean and clear cloaking intact, no confrontation in sight." said VP Roastie at the ships equaliser.

"Flotilla force breaking off as planned General." He continued.

As the Flotilla broke off, the FF Francaisfry reached the touchdown co-ordinates and began skimming the desert surface, scooping the top layer of sand into its large, waffle shaped compartment situated in the middle of the fuselage. Like a powerful Hoover it sucked the silicone into the hold and the FF Francaisfry then transferred the sand into the awaiting ships above using their equivalent of the Vegitamisation process, flash vaporisation. When the Flotilla Force holds were full, the FF Francaisfry touched down and cut all engines and energy outputs, except for the cloaking device. One by one, the Flotilla force dropped their loads of sand onto the FF Francaisfry until she was completely covered and obscured from sight. When the FF Francaisfry was completely Submerged, General Satuese ordered for all power output systems to be cut to the minimum and placed the crew on silent duties.

"Principle Gammachip circulate silent running scenario, cut power to minimum auxiliary." Then he paused momentarily and a gleaming smile crossed his face and he gave a small but definite chuckle and sigh of satisfaction. "Then send me Ground General Crinkle ark, have him report to my bunker room tell him to place his troops on standby. Now is the time for phase three of the operation." As the Francaisfry cut its power and the sand blocked its cloaking transmission waves. The Fasterfoid Flotilla ships became visible and alarm bells began to ring from the Silicone Sphere satellite, to ground station Arcticus and on board the O.S.S.S Milkymarrow way and Junipitaris.

Inside the caverns of the Silicone Sphere Commodore Bramblebush gave the turbulent alert to the Sun-Fleet Admiralty of Earthanon.

"This is direct line communication, Silicone Sphere Commodore Bramblebush to Admiral Ducarrotain, attack alert, repeat, and attack alert. Four enemy vessels heading toward Arcticus region; one Mayo-class star station and three flash-cruisers. Defence analysis systems indicate, they are armed and locked preparing to strike at Mother ships. Gunge gun phaser banks initiated locked on target transmissions. I don't know where they came from, but come they did. We didn't spot them; maybe our satellite receiver modules have been sabotaged, but they are all reading normal." He reasoned checking the command module.

"Thank you, Commodore Bramblebush. We have picked them up on our Robopod reconnaissance system. They seem to have appeared from thin air. Warning received and understood, Admiral Ducarrotain out." Admiral Ducarrotain had been in a meeting with Ground Commodore Cu-Cumbala when the shock alert came through and they wasted no time in activating their defence systems.

"Ground Commodore Cu-Cumbala alerting Commander Marrachinello. Red sector leader, scramble ground force defence and intercept enemy vessels. I repeat..."

"No need Ground Commodore," interrupted Commander Marrachinello who was already airborne. "Message received and understood. This is Red Sector Leader, chocks away over and out."

On board the O.S.S.S Milkymarrow way, Captain Beetrouly had activated the ship's Star Fighter squadron, but it was too late. The FF Shallow fryer locked on its Gunge gun phasers and fired on them without warning.

"SO Sweetpea, increase energy shields maximum output." shouted Captain Beetrouly. "Viceroy Cornkeepey, evasive action. Get us out of here! We are a sitting target engage full transverse thrusters!" He shouted.

"Aye, aye Sir." Confirmed Viceroy Cornkeepey.

As Viceroy Cornkeepey fed the Computron with the desired instructions, a massive blast of electron protonic ray from the Gunge tractor beam of the FF Shallowfryer star station, drained the Milkymarrow way's energy shields then blasted it with a high density Gastric acid Ketchup plasma beam.

Captain Beetrouly was thrown to the floor as the O.S.S.S Milkymarrow way rocked to its foundations and the electron protonic ray sent a live charge of electricity through all metallic surfaces.

"Damage report, SO Sweetpea! Ow... ow... owee" shrilled the Captain as electro-static charges ran through him and the crew at every available opportunity. "Quickly Sweetpea we haven't got much time to lose!" shouted the Captain picking himself up off the floor, only to be thrown again as the Gastric acid Ketchup plasma struck the ship on the starboard flank disabling the forehead starboard momentum thrusters.

"Shields down to thirty six percent, outer hull breached at levels 13 and 14 deck C, securing teams are at the scene and making good. Ship's particle scanner clogged beyond working order, Captain, we are fighting blind. Phaser housing port aft and forehead fully operational, starboard forehead phasers barely registering at sixteen percent and falling. Sir, if we take another blow in that quarter the chances are that we will be dropped scones within the starsec. Height falling by thirteen hundred staryards to the starmin and increasing, entering re-entry zone. Crash course, Earthanon. ETA fifteen starmins."

"SO Sweetpea, revert auxiliary momentum engines to main thrusters," ordered Captain Beetrouly. "Switch auxiliary proton reactors to defence shields. Viceroy Cornkeepey, activate pivotal thrusters to angle our approach of entry. Let's see if we can't unclog our systems the hard way and burn that gunge off at re-entry. Ensign Starfruiteena, boost up the power conduits to concentrate balsa guns firing over a five hundred staryard net surface area. FO Twizzlepasta, Fire Oudag capsule by using the gyroscope particle Grid Finder. Concentrate on the enemy ship's phaser expulsion point, and fire on those co-ordinates. Raise all protective plasma shields." Said the Captain taking to his seat at the helm. If they were going to go down it would not be because they hadn't tried everything within their power to survive.

"Aye, aye Sir." Shouted FO Twizzlepasta picking himself off the floor.

Outside the O.S.S.S Milkymarrow way, the FF Shallowfryer lined her sights on the Organitron Sun-station and began a new approach on the Port side. From the bridge of the Star-station, Major General Ickychick Fattyspot looked on the O.S.S.S Milkymarrow way and smiled wholeheartedly. His second in command, General Ghi Chickydigit, stood at the ship's systems equaliser drawing the statistics on the state of health of the O.S.S.S Milkymarrow way.

"Major General Fattyspot." the General said. "Our scanners indicate a breach in her outer hull on the starboard fore quarter. Tell me, how do you find it possible to resist so easily finishing her off when it would be so gloriously invigorating and simple to do so?" he asked.

"But I don't find it easy General Chickydigit. Captain Beetrouly and I are old enemies. I assure you, there is no love lost between us. Ever since he doused my Fasterfoid cousin, Griscillian Fattyspot, in gravy plasma in the Bapmacdo striates, he has been at the forefront of my mind. Revenge, however is sweet, but not in our remit today. No, we will switch our attack to the port side and level their already significant headache. Prefect Mocknugget, lock on Gunge phasers, charge to full power and strike when you see the colours of their eyes." grimaced Major General Fattyspot.

"Aye fry Major General." acknowledged Prefect Mocknugget setting his range for the final blow.

"Of course Major General." Said General Chickydigit. "Tell me what did happen to your cousin in the end?" He asked nervously.

"Ahh. It's a long story General Chickydigit but the outcome of it is this. Now, whenever Griscillian Fattyspot so much as smells a gravy globule, he reverts to a childish state of panic and hysteria. He constantly scratches himself, pulls off his clothes and masquerades as "Granular man," Fasterfoid hero of the spatial planes. His quest, to rid the universe of gravy forever. When he has one of these fits he tends to think he can fly and leaps off the nearest raised surface armed with only a large pair of underpants with a big G on them, a coloured grease proof cape, and a mask made of two wooden spoons with holes drilled in them tied to his head. I'm afraid General Chickydigit, he is as mad as a Vege-Pattie at a Fasterfoid banquet. I am ashamed to say he is the Fasterfoid equivalent of the mad menace Pirate Milnedew; only much nuttier I fear." he said gripping his teeth and slapping his chair.

Back on the O.S.S.S Milkymarrow way, FO Twizzlepasta sounded the green alert as the F.F Shallow fryer came in for another striking blow on the troubled ship.

"Ship identified: FF Shallow fryer, Mayo-class Star Station, locking on blazer phaser's port side." he said desperately switching all energy conduits to the port defence shields. "Firing now!" He confirmed.

"Captain Beetrouly." said Ensign Starfruiteena. "There has been Slithervoid activation, but, I don't know who or what it is. Our particle scanner is blocked and the gyroscope particle Grid Finder enhancer is locked onto phaser expulsion tracking."

"So it is my old friend Major General Fattyspot. What in Helios is he playing at?" shouted Captain Beetrouly as again he was thrown to the floor while the electron protonic beam whipped around the port side of the ship, rapidly followed by a huge deposit of yet more gastric acid Ketchup plasma. "Why didn't he go for the starboard again? Maybe our Major General Fattyspot has lost his marbles," sneered Captain Beetrouly sick of playing mouse in the trap with such an obvious buffoon. "Retaliate, FO Twizzlepasta. Mellow them with Gello and baste them with the gravy!" Shouted Captain Beetrouly moving towards the steering column.

"Firing Oudag Capsules, one, two, three. Locking on Blazer phasers, full energy dispensation and fire." confirmed FO Twizzlepasta.

Four hundred starmillo's away the O.S.S.S Junipitaris struggled under the strain of the attack from the FF Fatpan and the FF Lardlip. Blazer phasers were doing their best to cripple the Sun Station class vessel but the smaller ships had neither the firepower nor skill and speed of the Mayo-class star station. Suddenly Commander Marrachinello and his squadron of Star Fighters came into the area with a determination that would have made a grown Fasterfoid fill his boots with the usual fatty substance they purport to be sweat. Then the Fasterfoids legion of Flash-flyers launched from the FF Hotbox moved in to greet them as the Organitron elite hit the scene.

"Righty ho, chaps." laughed Commander Marrachinello, preening his moustache. "This is Red Sector Leader control. Reading seventy Flash-flyers on a bearing of zero, six, two blimits by Zero four-three. Red sector leader two, three and four follow my vapour trail. Five and six peel off and flank at port and starboard respectively. Set phasers for capture mode. Cluster bugs armed and ready, fire at will." said the Commander as they confirmed orders and compliance. The surrounding space filled with sprout gas and Ketchup plasma mixed with a gloupy gravy cloud formation. Flash-fryers that were hit had been seen tumbling towards Earthanon presumed captured on impact. The Star Fighters however, suffered minimal casualties in the exchange to date. Damaged Star Fighters managed to return to the relative safety of the O.S.S.S Junipitaris. Their pilots however, were not so fortunate. The affects of coming into contact with the electron force field that accompanied the ketchup plasma, almost drove them out of their own skin with irritation, reducing them to a shivering pile of nervous Vegetation's, unable to control normal body reflexes or vocal controls.

The O.S.S.S Milkymarrow way had reached sixty thousand starfeet from the Earthanon surface. Captain Beetrouly activated the graviton buffer defence shield but the calorific reactor housing had been damaged by the last phaser blow on the port side.

"Captain Beetrouly to Chief Engineer Cateloupe comes in." He said opening his personal channel but with no reply. "SO Sweetpea, get down to Engineering and see how bad the situation is. We need the activation of the Calorific Graviton force field if we are to stand any chance at all."

"Aye, aye Sir. I'm on my way." She shouted Vegitamising off the bridge.

Down on the Planetary surface of Earthanon the O.S.S.S Milkymarrow way could just be seen with the naked eye. Commodore Cu-Cumbala was suffering under a deluge of thirty or so Flash-flyer crash sites that needed securing and organising, their pilots to be taken prisoner as well as dealing with the unlucky troopers in the Sun-Fleet defence Star Fighters that had been forced from the skies unable to return to the Mother ships. The millennium celebrations had been rudely interrupted, bringing much chaos to the citizens of Arcticus and the surrounding townships. As sporadic fires erupted, dousing parties were dispatched to ensure the safety of the mining infrastructure. The population clearing the streets heading towards the safety of the battle bunkers as they desperately dodged and dived to escape the falling stray Ketchup beams. Then good news came forth from Commodore Cu-Cumbala's second in command, FO Onionack, via Admiral Ducarrotain's command centre.

"Commodore Cu-Cumbala, Sir. I am receiving an emergency coded transmission from Admiralette Xion Ru Roser. Commodore, the O.S.S.S Earthanon is two starmins from Arcticus and has acknowledged the battle at hand via her particle scanner. Captain Carrot is dispatching his Star Fighter defence force along with the O.S.S Capsicumby and the O.S.S Satsumuroo to bolster the defences of the O.S.S.S Junipitaris. He is coming along-side the O.S.S.S Milkymarrow way with The O.S.S Ommelettra to bring her down to Earthanon in safety. They are going to use their tractor beams to sustain a rapid and controlled landing at the following Co-ordinates. Captain Carrot requests emergency ground teams on standby with a full Fire and medical brigades at the ready." Said the excited and relieved FO Onionack. He was also relieved at the thought that the O.S.S.S Milkymarrow way would not be crash landing on the citadel of Arcticus or any other Populated area. That would bring chaos and confusion into a whole new ball game, not to mention the risk to Organitron lives.

"Get everything we have got that is spare to those co-ordinates and Helios bless Captain Carrot and his crew. Heroes of the hour for their bravery in the Garlicazure affair, but now proving their hero status in the hour of need in the Earthanon saga." Said the Commodore plotting the co-ordinates for the Sun-ship landing site.

On the bridge of the O.S.S.S Earthanon, Captain Carrot and his crew were heading for the troubled O.S.S.S Milkymarrow way when she became fired upon by the FF Lardlip. The O.S.S Ommelettra peeled off and rallied to her defence striking a critical blow to the Fasterfoid wimps, sending them limping off into space, their attack systems obliterated by a direct hit on her mid-ships where the Ammunitions housing was stored. Great cries of joy filled the crew as Captain Carrot hailed the O.S.S Ommelettra in congratulations.

"Excellent shot, Captain de Fleetrap. Well done but, quickly, we must reach the O.S.S.S Milkymarrow way before she breaks up in mid-air," said the Captain.

"Aye, aye Sir. We are right behind you." Confirmed Captain de Fleetrap.

"Ensign Viola." Said Captain Carrot hurriedly. "How long before the O.S.S.S Milkymarrow way is within tractor beam range?" He asked.

"Twelve starsecs Sir." She confirmed.

"FO Marrowlar." said the Captain. "Dispatch all Star Fighter Defence forces to the O.S.S.S Junipitaris. She is taking considerable flack. Let us lighten her load somewhat. Have them co-ordinate attack strategies with the O.S.S Satsumuroo and the O.S.S Capsicumby." He continued marking the course trajectory.

"Affirmative Captain Carrot. Star Fighter command dispatched and on route." Confirmed FO Marrowlar inputting data to the security command com.

On Board the O.S.S.S Milkymarrow way, SO Sweetpea contacted Captain Beetrouly on her personal channel.

"SO Sweetpea to Captain Beetrouly, come in please." She said, deep in the gut of the ship where the engine room was situated.

"Come in SO Sweetpea, Captain Beetrouly receiving." He answered.

"Captain." She continued. "Engineering has been hit badly, Sir. A proton reactor has fractured its drive shaft and the calorific computer bank is on fire. FO Cateloupe is badly hurt. I'm afraid there will be no extra power coming from this quarter Captain. We are barely maintaining auxiliary power. Maximum output estimated at one and one half pulse speed, Sir." She reasoned as the commotion could clearly be heard in the background.

"Maintain that power whatever it takes. Get all injured to the Medilab on the double. Secure all stations for crash position, Beetrouly out." he said with a note of dejection in his voice that was impossible to cover up.

"Aye, aye Captain. SO Sweetpea out."

"Captain Beetrouly." shouted Viceroy Cornkeepey at the steering column. "Ships momentum falling to one and one quarter pulse speed, descent rate increasing to seventeen hundred staryards per star min. Hull integrity is becoming dangerously compromised Captain; the gravitational pull is taking its toll, at this rate we will break up before we even get a chance of landing." Said the Viceroy at the controls.

"Do the best you can Viceroy Cornkeepey, that's all anyone can ask. FO Twizzlepasta, systems status?"

"All main line reactors down Captain. Back up reactors running at thirty percent, defence shields down to sixty one percent and falling. Phasers are defunct, Torpedo outlets are functional on the port side but blocked on the starboard." confirmed FO Twizzlepasta

"Captain Beetrouly," shouted Ensign Starfruiteena, attracting the Captain's immediate attention. "I am picking up another presence on the Particle scanner it, it... its. I don't believe Sir, it's the O.S.S.S Earthanon and the O.S.S Satsumuroo; they are coming to the rescue. Receiving coded transmission now." Said Ensign Starfruiteena unscrambling the transmission at the communications com.

"Prepare to drop energy defence shields. They are going to carry us to Earthanon Surface by utilising a linked tractor beam. Acknowledge receipt and compliance." She said turning to Captain Beetrouly.

"Confirm, Ensign Starfruiteena. Receipt and compliance." Smiled Captain Beetrouly, glad that, at last, help was at hand to pluck them from certain peril, as Ensign Starfruiteena replied to the communication in coded transcript.

"Drop defence shields in five starsecs Captain, four, and three...." said the Ensign Counting down.

"On Ensign Starfruiteena's mark, FO Twizzlepasta." Ordered Captain Beetrouly.

"Two and one mark." Continued Ensign Starfruiteena.

"Defence shields de-activated." FO Marrowlar we are in their hands Captain."

"Maintain pulse speed and go with the changes, we're heading for Earthanon, hitchhiker style thanks to Captain Gillespie J. Carrot." Said the relieved Captain Beetrouly, above the cheers and furore of the bridge crew.

Meanwhile, the Fasterfoid Flotilla force were busy revelling in the success of their surprise attack as they gathered together for one final attack on the O.S.S.S Milkymarrow way. Major General Icky Chicky Fattyspot had decided that as the Milkymarrow way's destruction looked imminent, they may as well take the glory and bring her down in style. As the FF Shallowfryer, the FF Hotbox, the FF Fatpan and the FF Lardlip joined forces in their final assault approach formation, the O.S.S.S Earthanon and the O.S.S Satsumuroo registered on their particle scanners. Suddenly they became under attack from underneath and behind from the O.S.S Capsicumby and the O.S.S Satsumuroo, along with a mighty task force of Star Fighters spearheaded by the devilishly daring Commander Marrachinello. They had all but obliterated the flash-flyer squadrons, the remainder sent scuttling into the distance. As the FF Shallow fryer was struck from behind, almost melting the rear phaser housing, Major General Icky Chicky Fattyspot began to cry in disbelief as the O.S.S.S Earthanon plucked the Milkymarrow way to safety and forced the tide of change upon his, until recently, superior strategy.

"That blasted Carrot is at it again." He shouted lying on the floor kicking and punching at the carpet with all his might.

"Shall we fight, Major General?" Enquired General Ghi Chickydigit, praying that the Major General would not agree to do so.

"No... No... No... No, retreat! We must retreat. Every time that orange skinned, elongated, great lump of compost fuel comes on to the scene, he steals the show. Well this time we will let the Organitron think they have scored a resounding victory, but we know that our mission is a success. But next time I will not let them rest so easy. Call off the flash flyers, pull back the defences and let's get out of here. It's time to head for the rendezvous in the no fry zone whether we like it or not." Cried Major General Icky Chicky Fattyspot in a crumpled and dejected heap on the floor.

"Aye, Fry Major General." Said the relieved General Chickydigit looking at the Grid finder. "I'm afraid General we have lost all but a handful of flash fryers Sir!"

The on-coming Organitron defence forces watched in amazement as the Fasterfoids flotilla force departed as rapidly as it had entered the scene. As they left they fired several minor shots at the O.S.S.S Earthanon with minimal affect; almost as though it was an act of desperation; a venting of frustration. Commander Marrachinello and his task force Star Fighter squadron followed the Fasterfoid fleet, returning fire, until the Fasterfoids had crossed the no fry zone and then returned to Earthanon to welcome the last minute arrivals that had not only saved the day of the millennium change over from the old to the new, but had saved the O.S.S.S Milkymarrow way, her crew and the inhabitants that it would have fallen on.

Captain Gillespie J. Carrot and the O.S.S.S Earthanon had returned and secured the futures of the Organitron Earthanon Space Races yet again and had truly saved the day. When all the ships had returned, the celebrations continued and honours were placed upon Captain Carrot, FO Marrowlar, FO Potatree and the newly appointed FO Milnedew. There was much music and dancing. Fireworks dominated the skies and the crews of the various star ships had to prepare for the lengthy hand over procedure which would take place as soon as all repairs were complete. The news of the Liberation of Garlicazure sparked much excitement on Earthanon, and the Admiralette was anxious to travel to their Planet with an army of aid and eco workers to help them re-establish full integration for their arrival in the Vegitalis Solar System. FO Milnedew, as he chose to remain named, met in private with his perennials and many tears were spilt in the weeks that followed. They would all depart from the Organitron complex and try once again to understand each other and heal the rifts of the past. They all knew that it would be a long road of discovery and they all knew that there was much pain and anguish ahead. His Mother, perennial Molara Marrowmilne, was just glad that they were once again reunited. Her tears spoke a thousand volumes and she became mediator, soother and healer in the time to follow. She was an Organiwoman with much hidden strength and both engineer Marrowmilne and FO Milnedew were glad that she was there to pave the way for forgiveness.

There was much to be done on Earthanon before the O.S.S.S Milkymarrow way could depart for refit at the Spaceark academy. And no time was wasted getting down to the business of the changeover. Commodore Cu-Cumbala and Admiral Ducarrotain set in motion the schedule of events and Captain Carrot set in motion the hand over sequence. Before he sent FO Milnedew away with his family, he asked them all to consider transferring aboard the O.S.S.S Earthanon. FO Potatree would enjoy the company and skills of Engineer Marrowmilne in his department, whilst the Captain felt that it would be good for Kenthal to have his loved ones around him after such a length of isolation. The decision of course was theirs, only to be decided upon their return.

Part two

Volcadis doom and gloom.

Sundate 3,000,000,000/ 060 Biltechtoids. Time 10.00 starhectoids.

FO Marrowlar stood with pride at the Command com of the O.S.S.S Earthanon. It was a beautiful space day, the Millennium had past with a memorable bang in one way or another. The repairs to the O.S.S.S Milkymarrow way were nearing completion in airspace above Earthanon and the changing of the guard ceremony had gone extremely well. The hand over period was ending its duration and the O.S.S.S Earthanon was now in charge of all space and ground activities in and around the Earthanon Solar System. The only slight blemishes on the Horizon were the lost contact situation with the satellite Volcadis. Volcadis was a space transmission booster relay satellite that handled the exchange frequencies and de-coding mechanisms between Earthanon, Silicone sphere and the Bubbleonion Squeak Vegitalis system. And a rather disturbing blip in the Gamma quadrant that appeared to be the start of a Sodium Star belt. A space Particle dust Hurricane, a mixture of Graphite and Radiation particles blended with a space salt. FO Marrowlar on the other hand, was not overly concerned as his shift would soon be ending. He would return to his quarters and spend some time with his family. His wife Tripolina, as well as Dordia and Tricton, their twin sons. Perhaps they would take a trip to Earthanon for the benefits of their day time cycle, meander along the coastal front or just settle for a lavish picnic in the Europetriennes region.

The elevation chamber doors de-energised, and from the chamber emerged Captain Carrot, fresh from a spot of relaxation shore leave after the Fasterfoid encounter they had recently endured, upon an early and unexpected arrival back to the Earthanon Solar System ahead of schedule. To the uneasy mind of a trained Sun-Fleet Organitron Captain, the victory was sweet, but, somehow too easy by far. They had sent them scurrying home in time for tea without even breaking into a sweat, although they had very nearly destroyed the O.S.S.S Milkymarrow way, on closer inspection of the battle criteria they had missed a sure-fire opportunity to finish her off but then for some reason changed tactics and reverted to attacking the starboard side. "Most unusual really." Thought Captain Carrot as Ensign

Rasperillo announced his arrival on the bridge and Ensign Melonture piped him on board.

"Captain on the bridge." he shouted giving his best salute.

"Pheweeeeee... phewoooooh." confirmed Ensign Melonture with his whistle, right in the Captains ear, much to his annoyance.

"Thank you Ensign Melonture. I think the cobwebs are cleared now, don't you?" he asked sarcastically."

"A thousand apologies Captain Carrot." He said as the Captain interrupted him.

"On top of the thousand apologies I got last time that makes rather a lot of apologies wouldn't you say...? Umm? Much better you just didn't do it in future! Holy vegmoley man, if wealth were judged by deafness and apologies, I would surely be the richest Organitron in existence." snapped Captain Carrot half heatedly.

"Yes Captain I'm Very...." Ensign Melonture stopped immediately. The last thing he needed to do right now was apologise, so he just smiled, nodded and saluted, clicking his heels as smartly as he could while standing to attention.

"You have Command com." Said FO Marrowlar as he handed over the ship's log after signing it.

"Thank you FO Marrowlar and you have a gravy stain on your tunic. Messy lunch was it?" asked Captain Carrot.

"No Sir, lunch with FO Cornelius and his infernal nervous system! He answered, ashamed that the Captain had spotted the blemish on his otherwise shining record.

"Very well FO Marrowlar, Ensign Strawballis status report if you will, don't hold back on the punches and give it to me straight." ordered Captain Carrot as he sat in his Command com chair. "Oh," he continued. "And make ready the photon back-up pilot. I want its surveillance satellite ready for departure in one starhectoid."

Ensign Strawballis removing her head set, closed down the ship's rapid communications module, and then proceeded to deliver her report.

"Yes Captain right away. The O.S.S Satsumuroo has just departed to the Gamma quadrant to collect the orbital satellite Volcadis. The systems communication relay indicates that there is terminal damage to its outer hull and the on-board, in flight organiser is not responding, making it impossible to attempt a routine re-entry to the Earthanons atmosphere."

Ensign Strawballis paused as she punched up the co-ordinated data, then, brought the structural layout of the satellite Volcadis on the communications, "Diagraphic Observation Consul." "D.O.C on Graphical Sir." she confirmed, as she began dimming the bridge lights, whilst a hologram table rose from the deck floor; the ceiling began beaming down a glittering sapphire and diamond like cluster of levitating Electrons, swooping and diving. Rapidly they formed a perfect sphere, then most dispersed into static mist while some streamed off in the direction of Ensign Rasperillo.

"I can never get over seeing that," whispered Ensign Rasperillo with a smooth glow of satisfaction on his face, his eyes fixed in a trance. "The appliance of science in all her beauty. Wow! What a sight." He shrieked as a stream of electrons passed right through him. "Wow man! What a feeling. I've got goose bumps on my goose bumps." Slowly as the stream of electrons dispersed, his face beamed with a smile wider than his shoulders.

"Are you all right Ensign Rasperillo?" Asked Captain Carrot.

"I feel fine Captain, it's only static." He sighed.

"Judging by the look on your face, I would say ecstatic is more like it!" Giggled Ensign Melonture. Captain Carrot turned to face the D.O.C, which was now showing a three dimensional hologram of the Satellite Volcadis.

"Nevertheless," he said. "SO Tulipina, have Chief Potatree re-calibrate the D.O.C electro static energy field. Carry on Ensign Strawballis."

"Aye Sir." Confirmed SO Tulipina.

"Captain, our calculations indicate," continued Ensign Strawballis. "if standard re-entry is attempted the satellite Volcadis would suffer mass meltdown at the entry zone, due to a breach in the lower front section of the outer hull nose cone Sir."

"Do we have any information as to the cause of the damage?" Asked Captain Carrot calmly.

"No Sir, the on board computer transmission system closed down before it could send the information analysis, in order to enable itself to maintain Pulsar speed." Ensign Strawballis took readings from the communications com then turned to the Captain somewhat flustered.

"Sir, if we don't get to Volcadis within twenty four starhectoids, her on board reactor will reach a critical power deficiency and invoke the self-destruct mechanism!" she exclaimed.

"Very good Ensign Strawballis, communicate to the O.S.S Satsumuroo they must make all haste." Captain Carrot turned to FO Marrowlar, stroking his chin with his thumb and forefinger. "FO Marrowlar. I want to know why a sun class satellite fitted with an automatic space particle guidance oscillator, appears to have had a collision? More importantly, what with, and why did it not alter its course or initiate its defence systems?"

"Indeed Sir, there is much that lies uncertain in this matter, very odd indeed." Noted FO Marrowlar cautiously.

"Excuse me Sir," interrupted Ensign Strawballis. "Ground Commodore Cu-Cumbala is requesting a shore to ship transmission. He says it is of the utmost importance Sir!"

"Very well Ensign Strawballis, transmit to visaid." Captain Carrot straightened his tunic as the visual screen came on line.

"On line now Sir." Confirmed Ensign Strawballis.

Commodore Cu-Cumbala was a well-weathered figure with a craggy voice and endearing eyes that glowed a warming rosy red; a common trait of the Space Race Cucumputranes. Normally a calm and calculating character, it was obvious by his jumpy disposition that there was something niggling at the back of his mind. It was clear to the bridge crew of the O.S.S.S Earthanon that Commodore Oswald D. Cu-Cumbala was unaware that the visual screen was activated.

"Now you listen to me FO Onionack; when I request a full report, I expect it to be full. Where, pray tell, are the conclusion and summary elements?" screamed Commodore Cu-Cumbala, as he started to go ballistic.

"I regret to inform you Sir," reasoned FO Onionack. "It was consumed by our pet Plutterbunny at the breakfast table this morning. Another copy will be with you within the half starhectoid, Ground Commodore." Replied an embarrassed and cringing FO Onionack.

"I regret it was eaten by my pet Plutterbunny Sir," mimicked Ground Commodore Cu-Cumbala in the voice of a child. "Why, that is the sort of excuse that I get from my Grand siblings when their school work is late! I don't accept it from them, so tell me why on Earthanon should I accept it from you?" Commodore Cu-Cumbala suddenly noticed that he was performing to an audience on board the O.S.S.S Earthanon, and his face reached new peaks in scarlet flushing.

"Oh, oh Captain please excuse me, I." Ground Commodore mopped his brow with his handkerchief. "That will be all FO Onionack. We will continue this farce later!"

"Aye Sir, once again, I do apologise Sir. It will never happen again, you have my word."

"Yes... Yes, now please, you may leave." Said Ground Commodore Cu-Cumbala, as FO Onionack left the room at great speed.

"I'm sorry; we are having some personnel problems down here. Greetings Captain Carrot, this is Commodore Oswald D. Cu-Cumbala of the Ground Station Arcticus." Bellowed Commodore Cu-Cumbala, being very formal and offering Captain Carrot the Organitron Salute.

"Greetings Commodore Cu-Cumbala," said the Captain returning his salute. "Well my friend, judging by the svelte texture of your complexion it would appear that the Earthanon atmosphere serves you well these days? Like the Millennium you must improve with age!" Chortled the Captain sarcastically. Commodore Cu-Cumbala's face switched to a stiff and drawn grimace. Usually, there would be a rally of jibes between the two friends and colleagues. It was not the case today as Captain Carrot became aware that his old friend was genuinely worried.

"I'm sorry Captain Carrot, but I have not the energy to rise to the bait. Believe me; I would like nothing more than to enter into jovial rhetoric with you." He said, as a half-hearted smile perched on the lips of the weary commodore.

"Of course Commodore Cu-Cumbala. Tell me, what worries you so?"

Commodore Cu-Cumbala held his head in his hand scratching nervously.

"We are very concerned about our Atmospheric Triabulator Captain. It is indicating a sharp drop in temperature of nearly fourteen blimits in a little over three starhectoids. It's not much I know; we often experience drops of temperature, but these were designed to happen in the night cycles, aided by the construction of the silicone sphere for our rest periods. Drops in temperature are common place, sometimes as much as a forty blimits decrease has occurred, but we have never experienced such a radical and sustained drop inside the daylight cycles."

Captain Carrot turned to first officer Benzo Marrowlar who was pawing his chin in silence, obviously unnerved by the recent turn of events of Volcadis and the Sodium Star belt, now this. "Could they be connected?" Thought Captain Carrot, "If so, what was the missing connection? What could cause such a change to the atmosphere? Worse still, was it confined to the Arcticus Hemisphere?" Raising himself from the chair, he calmly asked FO Marrowlar for his opinion.

"Do you have any suggestions that might explain this irregularity FO Marrowlar?"

FO Marrowlar moved to the particle scanner and keyed in several analysis elements.

"It might be possible," he suggested, "that there is a build up of Isotronic gas clouds Captain, but my primary scans do not indicate any abnormal clusters Sir!" Confirmed FO Marrowlar. "There is however adverse moisture builds ups in sporadic formations around the globe, though they are not the usual example of storm composition it could be the start of an early tropical rain storm."

"I see." Captain Carrot said, as he peered into the gyroscope. "FO Marrowlar, recall all data from the Earthanon Mechanoid probes. Let's see if this blimit loss situation is isolated to the Arcticus Hemisphere, or, whether perhaps we are dealing with a Global epidemic?" Captain Carrot turned back to address Commodore Cu-Cumbala.

"Fear not my good friend, I will send down a science party to investigate the situation. You have my word that we will get to the root of the problem. Only my best crew will be hand-picked for this expedition. Be prepared to receive a landing party of six. They will be led by Science, First Officer Cornelius and Chief Engineer, First Officer Potatree. There is always the possibility that it is a minor problem; perhaps the Planetary light equaliser sensors for instance."

"Very well Captain, when can we expect their arrival?" Acknowledged a very tired and frustrated Commodore Cu-Cumbala.

"We are configuring the co-ordinates as we speak. I will gather the team together and brief them personally. They will Vegitamise down to the Earthanon surface within the half starhectoid." Said Captain Carrot, trying his best to reassure his friend.

"Message received and understood, until we next communicate Captain" said Commodore Cu-Cumbala softly, now with a familiar affection brought on by the fact that help, was on the way. The Commodore and Captain Carrot had both gone through training at the Star fleet Pioneer Space-ark Academy together. There was much history between them. Commodore Cu-Cumbala had always viewed his friend of old with much respect. Even in the days of the Spaceark Academy, the then Pioneer

Private Gillespie J. Carrot, was the driving force and calming influence behind all his colleagues looking to excel in the ranks of Sun-Fleet.

Captain Carrot smiled. His old friend had always been of a nervous disposition. Deep down, he knew there was a mind and constitution of solid rock.

"Until then my friend, UFO and out." Said Captain Carrot, as they offered each other the Organitron salute. Commodore Cu-Cumbala then ended the transmission.

"UFO and out, end transmission!"

The screen cleared and Captain Carrot stared into space briefly. The O.S.S.S Earthanon was following the Orbital tract of Arcticus, some sixty five starmillo's above the Earthanon surface, its view breathtaking. Hanging there like a champion marble in stupendous Technicolor, surrounded by a silk like abyss. If the light caught at the right angle, a rich dark blue, tinted infinite shroud, speckled with rich and mysterious, soothing, yet untouchable diamonds could be seen. Every sparkle as refreshing as the first flick of an eye dawning on the new day. Then he turned to FO Marrowlar.

"FO Marrowlar, please assemble officers," He paused briefly whilst remembering his promise to his old friend and colleague, Commodore Cu-Cumbala. "Yes," he continued. "Officers Cornelius, Potatree and Melonicord. Assemble them in the strategy room. Have they pick one crew member each to accompany them to the Earthanon surface," Captain Carrot again paused momentarily. "Navigator Viola, when the co-ordinates are configured to establish Vegitamisation transmission, cross match them into the Vegimatter room computer to run surveillance mode on the landing party. Have them maintain radio contact with the ship every half starhectoids."

The ship's Navigator, Organigirl Ensign Viola, a bright crimson blue flower born of the Space Race Violatrianic, from the Violatrax colony based on the Planet Flowertura in the Herba Flowturu Quadrant, turned to the navigation command panel and resumed inputting data for the Co-ordinates.

"As you wish Captain," said Viola just as the particle alarm com rang. "Sir. I'm picking up traces of Prima Mustard Gas Electron particles on the Earthanon surface; of a particular high density in the Arcticus region."

Captain Carrot moved across to the Nav com and looked into the particle gyroscope again. Immediately he turned to Ensign Viola.

"I want a full particle scan, covering the whole of Earthanon surface."

"There are also traces of, as yet, an unknown substance Sir." Stated Ensign Viola.

"Can you be more specific Viola?" Enquired the Captain.

"I will do my best Sir, but without sample matter, it will at best be a guestimate Captain." She replied shrugging her shoulders.

"Very well. Confer with Science Officer Cornelius before he departs to the Earthanon surface. Ensign Strawballis, have Professor Goosegorgon meet us in the strategy room, immediately."

"Aye Sir," confirmed Ensign Strawballis turning to the communications com. "Professor Goosegorgon, report to the Strategy room immediately. I Repeat, Professor Goosegorgon, please report to the strategy room, immediately."

Captain Carrot stood at the elevation chamber and turned to address the bridge crew as the doors de-energised.

"When you have some answers for me Ensign Viola, you can transmit your report to me on the Strategy room Computron." Second Officer Tulipina approached Captain Carrot, handing him the systems analysis log. Scanning through the sheets of information, Captain Carrot signed the log and handed it back to S.O Tulipina. "Very good S.O. Tulipina" he said. "Keep a close eye on all systems everyone, maintain full energy shields and sweep the Gamma Quadrant for any unusual activities."

"Aye, aye Sir, we have already carried out a preliminary Gasamatronic scan with nothing to report yet Captain.

We are approximately half way through the Matter Anti-Matter activity tracer." she acknowledged.

"Very good, if you find anything, you know where I am?"

"Aye Sir." Said SO Tulipina taking her position by the ships analyser to relieve FO Marrowlar.

Captain Carrot then directed his attention towards the steering column.

"Viceroy Rhubarblatt, maintain your current position, keep your eyes on the Grid Finder, if there are any foreign bodies around here, I want to know about them, preferably before they know about us!"

"Aye Sir, scanning now."

"FO Marrowlar. You have Command Com," Captain Carrot pointed at his chair. "Send a brief coded transmission to the S.F.A, outlining our situation. All repairs from the Fasterfoid attack complete, Volcadis satellite recovery under way, the Earthanon surface temperature deviation and course of direction. Oh, and you had better make mention of the prima mustard gas."

"Aye Sir, thank you Captain." FO Marrowlar stood at the Command Com whilst the crew stood to attention.

"Would you mind very much delaying your duty stand down a little longer FO Marrowlar?" Asked Captain Carrot.

"Of course Captain." He replied.

Captain Carrot entered the elevation chamber. "Computer, consultation suit Observation deck A."

The doors re-energised and the Captain made his way to the strategy room.

"Captain off the Bridge." Announced Ensign Rasperillo. Ensign Melonture signalled his departure with the ships whistle. "Pheweeeeee... Phewoooooh."

FO Marrowlar took pride of place at the Command Com. "Stand easy on the bridge. Ensign Strawballis," ordered FO Marrowlar. "Secure me a channel to the Sun-Fleet Admiralty. Apply full voice communication transcripts and enter them into the Captain's Log."

When the doors to the strategy room opened on Captain Carrot's approach. Officers Cornelius, Potatree and Melonicord were already seated. They stood as the Captain entered the strategy room and took his place at the head of the table. The doors opened again and bouncing into the room came the gibbering Professor Goosegorgon. **Boing, Boing, Boing**. Eventually he came to rest with a **Splatt!** In the seat between Officer Cornelius and Captain Carrot.

Professor Goosegorgon as you know was the "Ships Science and Technology Advisor." Born to the Space Race Gooseberrulax a Space race Organitron from the Planet Gooseberrantea in the Fruitanutes Plexus. Though considered by all on board the O.S.S.S Earthanon as a Genius, he often gave the impression of being something of an absent minded nut case, at least it was always expected, and to be fair he never let the expectation down.

He was a very rounded Organitron fruit, green in skin colour with thin white vertical flashings, and as usual his white wispy hairstyle and goatee beard seemed fuzzy and shot all over the place as if charged with electricity Removing a handkerchief from his pocket, then searing his breath across the lens, he proceeded to clean his Monocle. Emitting a high pitched whistle as his fingers encircled the glass; it began visibly causing much irritation to the ears of those assembled in the strategy room. In the centre of the table, stood a Macadamia crystal drinking vessel which suddenly started to shake violently. Then, one by one, all the glasses around the table started to shatter, sending the crew, except for the fearless Captain, hurtling behind their seats only to appear armed with Blazer Guns set to stun. As the glass of grape juice in front of Captain Carrot exploded soaking him to the skin, Captain Carrot grabbed Professor Goosegorgon on the shoulder, disabling his cleansing arm. Professor Goosegorgon, noticing that Captain Carrot was wet, looked around the table, and saw the carnage that had been created, blissfully unaware that his antics were the cause. Professor Goosegorgon began, he thought, to understand the disgruntled and vexed look upon the face of the Captain. Turning up his new hearing aid and re-placing his monocle quickly, he said sheepishly.

"Why Capatano, you're all wet! You had best get 'a yourself down to sickbay when this is 'an over, I will check 'a you out personally, no?" Professor Goosegorgon grabbed his hand taking the Captain's pulse. "Will you look at 'a this mess. The ship's Mushroids must be experiencing 'a problem with is 'a cleansing program. And 'a your pulse! Mamma Mia you should 'a lie down." Captain Carrot's gaze fell on the Professor, his nostrils flaring. "Ha... Umm, I'll get on it as soon as'a we hav'a finished no?" continued the professor nervously.

Wiping his face with his other hand, Captain Carrot silenced the professor.

"Enough Professor! Enough!" He said in a deeply agitated manner. "We have serious matters to discuss. Time is of the essence so I would like to be as brief as possible. FO Marrowlar is on the bridge as you know, and for the moment at least, he will not be joining us. He is still working hard to find us some crucial answers to some rather complex questions!"

"Amma sorry amma late Capatano, I have 'a been checking on the trace elements found in'a the Prima Mustard Gas. I do have 'a theory, but I have left Dr Kiwitranus running some experiments to make sure, yes? Now, I just find 'a pen and I'm 'a hockey, dockey, ready to go. Yhi! Aye, aye, now where did I put 'a my pen?" He mumbled, fumbling in his coat. "Its 'a my good luck charm, early Organitron Centuriat you know? Primitive but affective." As Professor Goosegorgon looked around the room, under all the chairs and then the table, bouncing up and down in search of his pen, he muttered to himself again.

"I know I have it 'a here somewhere, I had it only seconds ago." Finding it hanging around his neck where he left it, he bounced back into his chair and sat waiting for the Captain to begin.

"Are you quite comfortable now Professor Goosegorgon?" Enquired Captain Carrot. "May we continue?"

"Amma ready if 'a you are Capatano!" Replied the Professor, cowering in his chair. By now; all that could be seen poking out from his white coat was a clump of wispy white hair and a small chin jutting out, adorned with spiked hair filled with static.

Captain Carrot turned to the Computron.

"Computer, open hologram Earthanon sequence!" ordered Captain Carrot. Within starsecs, hovering above the centre of the table was a breathtaking visual display in three dimensional proportions. The global map of the Planet Earthanon appeared its full colour glory stunning to the eye, highly detailed and accurate to the minute precision. The Arcticus region was highlighted with the O.S.S.S. Earthanon circling in a fixed position above Arcticus, and the O.S.S.S Milkymarrow way above the Europetriennes, with the O.S.S.S Junipitaris situated over Urasiar.

"Organigirls, Organiboys." Began the Captain. "In the last half starhectoid, we have received disturbing reports from Ground Commodore Cu-Cumbala, in the Arcticus mining region on the Earthanon surface. Arcticus has, according to all reports, endured a rapid drop in blimit levels. At the moment it is not an emergency, but you will no doubt be aware, as soon as the blimit levels reach a reduction total of forty blimits, we will have to suspend all mining activities.

A drop of forty blimits in itself is not unusual in the rest periods during the night cycles. This is different. We have already experienced a drop of fourteen blimits in a little under three starhectoids. Reports from all Earthanon regions on the light side are coming in now. FO Marrowlar will collate all the information, either confirming or dismissing the Global epidemic theory. Personally, I believe if the Arcticus hemisphere is undergoing a radical climatic change, then, I'm afraid we will find that it is not an isolated occurrence! As you will appreciate, during the day cycles it makes life very difficult for our crews to operate with heavy losses of energy, which is inevitable if our Photosynthesis cycle is interrupted for any significant length of time. Computer, halt hologram Earthanon sequence." Captain Carrot leant forward gazing around the table.

"In short, Organimen, Organigirl." He said acknowledging First Officer Melonicord. "This is how I see it! We will have no choice but to suspend all mining operations if we cannot solve this problem within shall we say a total reduction of thirty blimits?"

"Capatano Sir, please..?" Interrupted Professor Goosegorgon.

"Yes Professor, I pray this is something constructive?" Said the Captain with a sigh.

"Well Sir, we have a little over ten starhectoids of 'a daylight in'a cycle left. At the current rate of 'a blimit descent. That gives us only three starhectoids and twenty-five starmins, yes?"

"Go wherever it is you are going Professor, just hurry up and get there!"

"Of 'a course Capatano. Closing down a 'the mining operations will 'a cause a 'no problem. This can 'a be done swiftly and securely. Our re-generation chambers can sustain both cycle simulations for up to ten startechtoids on reserved generation reactors alone. But, if 'a we suffer sustained blimit loss, then it would be necessary to consider the evacuation procedures, and 'a, the time and energy limitations in'a carrying those procedures out."

First Officer Cornelius turned abruptly, facing the Captain and Professor Goosegorgon. FO Cornelius who was born to the volatile space race Cornmaizonite, from the Planet Cornmaizerite in the Vegitalis Plexus, who spoke in a high pitched Urasiar accent (Australian to be precise), was an unusually nervous and shy character, as you know. This was due to, in theory, according to his fellow crew members, his chosen solitary profession; the lonely world of Science. Although he was the chief Science Officer, his speciality was Organatronopamy. In short, the theory of the Organitrons existence, and scientific studies into their evolutionary futures. As you will also be aware, FO Cornelius had been graced with an unfortunate twitch. Every time he had a panic attack, his right leg kicked into the air and with his head shooting forward, he would release an almighty sneeze.

Being the ships Science Officer, he had an incredible capacity to understand the complex, but an uncanny efficiency in being flummoxed by the obvious.

"**Woah... Woo... Hatchooo**!" **Thud!** As FO Cornelius's knee, came up and thumped the underside of the table, he yelped as his funny bone shot what seemed like an electric charge through his body.

"**Ow... owee**. "**Whoooo, wha... Ha. Ha. Hatchooo**." **Thud!** As his knee struck the underside of the table again. The vibration knocking yet more grape juice into the lap of Captain Carrot.

"Holy Helios FO Cornelius! Exclaimed Captain Carrot, as the cold sensation in his lap sent shivers down his naturally rigid spine.

Then, Professor Goosegorgon and Captain Carrot ducked simultaneously as a stream of spray shot over their heads.

"Phew that 'a was a close call Capatano." Quipped Professor Goosegorgon as he measured his own pulse rate. "I do 'a wish you would cure this a 'messy business FO Cornelius. Some poor soul is 'a going to have a dickey ticker if 'a you don't learn to control this... this... this 'a thing!" He shouted sweating profusely and pointing to the centre of his chest were all Organitrons hearts are located.

FO Cornelius, taking a drink of grape juice as Professor Goosegorgon passed comment on his sensitive affliction, choked mid-gulp spurting the grape juice over FO Melonicord who was sitting opposite. Clearing his throat he turned to Professor Goosegorgon.

"I'm not the ship's Medical Officer Professor. Dr Kiwitranus has tried everything in his power to solve the problem, I might add to no avail. Then, he told me that he would have to speak to you. Surely Professor, this places the onus of responsibility in your hands. Yes, it is your obligation to cure me?"

"But..." Professor Goosegorgon started to defend his position.

Captain Carrot thumped the table and stood on his feet. Everyone stopped and stared in silence as the Captain circled the table.

"Firstly Organigirls and boys, this is a briefing session, and might I add, until now, it has resembled a Monkey nuts tea party;" (Monkey nuts being very close allies to the Mad Macadamians), "utter chaos. Secondly, we could be on the verge of a major catastrophe for the Organitron race. We have a total of four million, one hundred and eighty thousand crew on the Earthanon surface, not to mention some eight hundred thousand on various Mother ships and Sun-Fleet carriers in the Orbital tract." Captain Carrot calmed himself. "This was no time to lose my cool," he thought, "even if those around him made it difficult to prevent." Returning to his seat, he leant forward on his forearms and viewed the group assembled in silence.

"And thirdly" he continued, deciding to lighten the atmosphere, bringing a smile to his face. "FO Cornelius, I appreciate you have a problem but the very least you could do, is put your hand over your face when you're sneezing, I expect it from my children. They seem to manage without any problems, so I'm sure you can cope with such a small request?"

FO Cornelius apologised to Captain Carrot and the other Officers.

"I apologise," he said. "But I cannot control my knees Captain. It seems my arms have a mind of their own as well. I will try to control it Sir. Now, getting back to the point in question. Isn't it being a little over reactionary pre-empting a mass evacuation?"

"I hope it is 'a." Said the Professor, "but 'a we cannot ignore the possibility that we are dealing with 'a several unknown forces here. These's may be totally isolated incidents that have occurred. FO Cornelius, you, as'a the Chief Science Officer should realise, if they are all somehow connected, what 'a we are potentially trying to defend against is 'a the unknown. Territorial enemies until now unheard of perhaps. Who knows? But one 'a thing is 'a for certain, we can and should take nothing for granted. These enemies could take on a form as'a yet un-encountered. It could be an intelligent phenomenon in a mineral, gas, or even electron form. The fact is, we don't know. So I would 'a suggest that all angles of protection should be taken into account; even the unthinkable. Retreat!"

Chief Engineer Potatree shuddered where he sat. FO Potatree was an Organitron born to the Potanto race from the Planet Potatoorimar, in the Vegitalis Legume. As you may have gathered the Potanto, a usually jovial race speak with an Irish tongue. Potatree's hair, jet black and in a curious bowl-cut sheened with a layer of hair oil, made him the object of some ridicule within certain ranks of the ship's crew, always behind his back and always with a sneaking respect. It didn't make life any easier of course, having great unruly, bushy eyebrows resting on his big bulbous red-streaked eyes, and an incredibly misshapen nose. Since the Blottmeager affair though, he was enjoying a period of Idolisation from his immediate crew and the Sun-Fleet Premier Seed Consul!

Potantos' are known as a fierce fighting race when they are cornered; also they are viewed as the second most respected race in the Bubbleonion Squeak Vegitalis Solar System. With his russet coloured skin and pitted complexion giving away his respected, but quite considerable age advantage, he began clearing his throat then, asked if he may speak.

"Ahh... hum, excuse me Sir. If I may add to the discussion?" asked FO Potatree.

"Of course FO Potatree, grow with the flow." Said the Captain.

"We have three Space Stations in the Earthanon vicinity; our own, the O.S.S.S Earthanon, the Junipitaris and the Milkymarrow way. Between us we have the capacity to carry two point five million in deep regeneration mode. Our life support system can sustain five hundred thousand crew members indefinitely. Both the Junipitaris, and the Milkymarrow way, have the capacity to sustain four hundred thousand crew members indefinitely."

FO Potatree stopped to peruse his calculations. "Captain Sir, by my reckoning, that leaves us still to find places for one million two hundred thousand Organitron. What are we going to do about them? It surely has to be all or nothing at all Captain?"

Captain Carrot turned to FO Melonicord who was working out some calculations on the Computron.

"FO Melonicord, you're the transportation supply genius, what is the current crew status of the three O.S.S.S Mother ships?" enquired Captain Carrot.

"Well Sir, we have on board O.S.S.S Earthanon, seventy thousand crew in operational mode and ten thousand on shore leave. The Junipitaris and Milkymarrow way have between them, one hundred and twenty thousand crew in operational mode; and twelve thousand on shore leave." FO Melonicord punched in some more data and asked the computer for transportation freighter ship passenger capacity.

"Computer, numerical analysis of all ships within one starlectoid, passenger capacity data please."

"Analysis underway," confirmed the Computer. "Awaiting configuration confirmation, please stand by."

"Sir," stated FO Melonicord as the readout began to appear, "between the three O.S.S.S Mother ships, we can carry two million five hundred thousand Organitron in deep regeneration, and one million eighty eight thousand operational extra crew. In all Sir, with existing ship's compliment; we can sustain indefinitely, one million three hundred thousand operational crew. This gives us a rescue capability of three million eight hundred thousand in all. This means we will have to ensure transportation for a further, one million one hundred and eighty two thousand Organitron."

The Computron completed printing the information on screen, and FO Melonicord access filed the information as it came to an end. Then the computer came over the personal channel.

"Computer analysis complete. Please confirm for additional information requirements?" It asked, pending such requests.

"Sufficient data requirements reached." Confirmed FO Melonicord de activating the computer mode.

"Well FO Melonicord what do you have for us?" Asked Captain Carrot.

Pulling the read-out from the Computron, FO Melonicord passed the information to Captain Carrot.

"We can just do it Sir, in the sector there are thirty one Tuber class cargo Sun Freighters. These have the capacity to carry twenty thousand Organitron in Minimised stature Formulation. Three science farm storage transporters, which can carry one hundred thousand Organitron each.

There are two Star Fighter Space Stations in the Gamma minor quadrant; they can convert to carry one hundred and fifty thousand Organitron each. This gives us excess capacity of thirty three thousand within the main ship's rescue fleet. You will also observe Captain, that there are some two hundred private trading ships and freighters that we can enlist; should we have any problems with our own emergency rescue plan. I estimate a further rescue capacity of some one point eight million, Sir." FO Melonicord said casually, who just loved having the information at her fingertips for instant appraisal.

"Excellent FO Melonicord, you have done well. Let's just hope that we need not bring these emergency plans into force."

Dr Kiwitranus came through on the professor's personal channel.

"Dr Kiwitranus to Professor Goosegorgon, come-in, please."

"May I Capatano?" Asked the Professor. Captain Carrot nodded silently.

"Yes Dr Kiwitranus, Professor Goosegorgon here. So tell me, what 'a do you have to report eh?"

"I'm sorry Professor," announced Dr Kiwitranus, "but I fear your initial thoughts are confirmed. It would appear, the unknown trace elements found in the Prima Mustard Gas, are a very close, but, not an exact copy of Tomaldonite Plasma. As you can see, the generic chain has been altered to contain acidulantas ore elements. Oh, one more thing Professor, your initial theory followed the thought, that to maintain the field they would need a mobile electrical rampage flux fluctuate. However, on closer inspection of the Gasamatronic equaliser test results it would appear they have formulated a static Electron self generating photon simulator."

"What 'a brings you to that conclusion Dr Kiwitranus?" Enquired Professor Goosegorgon curiously. "As'a yet, this is a dream of an idea. Why, it is not yet realised in our own laboratories; let alone in'a the laboratories of our enemies." Laughed Professor Goosegorgon nervously.

"Until this morning I would have laughed with you, but take a look at this!" remarked Dr Kiwitranus. The look on Dr Kiwitranus's and more importantly, Professor Goosegorgon's face, told a very disturbing story; sweat visibly ran down his brow.

On all the Computrons a generic chain appeared. The look on Professor Goosegorgon grew into a bright crimson red, steam almost shooting from his ears as he jumped up and down on his chair, frantically somersaulting, and then finally coming to rest in tears. Cradling his head on the table, he began banging it with his fists. He was reduced to a quivering nervous wreck, as he lifted his head he could visibly been seen sucking his thumb.

"Contain yourself Professor Goosegorgon, this is a time to stick to our guns and maintain our composure, not sucking our thumbs and crumpling under pressure!" Said Captain Carrot looking around the table, smouldering with anxiety.

Professor Goosegorgon looked down and saw his thumb in his mouth, quickly pulling it out making a loud popping noise. "POP! Excuse me Capatano, mamma-Mia, this is 'a no good for my blood pressure, all this work and they beat 'a me to it. Capatano," cried Professor Goosegorgon. "I'm a sorry to add to the complexity of the situation but," he continued, "it would appear our enemies have infiltrated the Earthanon surface." Said the Professor now under some considerable stress.

Looking at the Computron, Captain Carrot scratched his head and stated nervously, a little like at school, when the teacher asks you a question and you only think you know the answer.

"My chemistry is a little rusty Professor, but is that the D.N.A breakdown of a substance called, "Eggello sulphur gas?"

"Dr Kiwitranus" said Professor Goosegorgon. "I have tried Eggello sulphur gas; it works for a brief period of time, but wowee, what a stink! Put me out of my misery, what is the missing ingredient?" begged the professor.

"To all intensive purposes Professor," explained Dr Kiwitranus. "It would appear to be Eggello sulphur gas, but it is simulated sulphur gas. I would assume it has been screened and filtered through a Gamma ray particle nebuliser, then fine blasted with Cochinello gas protons."

"Of course, Gamma ray nebulisation." Interrupted Professor Goosegorgon, slapping his head with the palm of his hand. "Capatano, as exciting as this is. This means in all probability, one of our enemies has come up with a mobile particle enhancement cloaking device; this can mean only one objective, to infiltrate Earthanon. Oh I want 'a my Mamma." cried Professor Goosegorgon with a gaunt reflection of defeat in his face and a tear rolling down his cheek.

"Holy vegmoley," said Captain Carrot jumping to his feet. "Professor Goosegorgon, you said one of our enemies, why not a coalition force infiltrating the Earthanon surface?"

Professor Goosegorgon pulled himself together blowing into his handkerchief, rolled his eyes and scratched his head, then tapped into the Computron the particle breakdown analysis. After a short while turning toward Captain Carrot, he looked a little overwhelmed by the whole affair.

"Well Capatano, I will try to explain as briefly and simply as I can. Is 'a like this. The force field would have to be limited in its uses, simply because of its likely power source limitations. One would assume that 'a the power source is self-regulating in accordance with the levels of solar energy in the atmosphere. To extend the life span of the cloaking device, the enemy would try to minimise the energy field proximity to preserve the proton output. We already have certain clues that indicate to us there may be a coalition plan to infiltrate the Earthanon surface, but not necessarily directly involving all four of the Fasterfoids.

For instance, the Chickonaldirs and the Burgerites have a stark dislike to any form of sulphur gas; combine that with Eggello particles which would irritate their skin, I think we can safely say that 'a the infiltrators are the Faster Fritters or the Crinkleozones maybe both! We already know that 'a because of the chemical breakdown of the cloaking device force field the infiltrators must appear as a red Organitron; a Tomatron, or an Appleoneon for example.

The Chickonaldirs and Burgerites are too large in stature, given that the energy field would have 'a to encapsulate the life form entirely. They would have to blend in with the Organitron race. Therefore my Capatano, I would assume it 'a more likely that the Faster Fritters, and or, the Crinkleozones could activate the force field; whilst still of course, remaining a reasonable size. This of course making it'a possible to go about their business undetected. So you see Capatano, if this whole situation is true then oh boy, are we in'a big bag of.. of booboo." And with that, Professor Goosegorgon sat in silence, and awaited the Captain's response.

"Ahh.. to be sure Captain," squawked FO Potatree. "We all know the Faster Fritters and the Crinkleozones can't stand each other, but, they might join forces if the booty was essential to both of them."

"Booty FO Potatree?" enquired Captain Carrot, his face showing signs of deep confusion.

"Aye Sir, booty, you know, booty; swag," Captain Carrot was still looking a little vague.

"You can bet your bottom credit, that if either of those two blighters are involved they are out to steal something!"

"Ahh indeed booty, I see where you are coming from FO Potatree. Yes, but what could they possibly be after in the Arcticus region? Minerals, Fuel?"

Within moments, Captain Carrot activated his personal channel communicator. "Ensign Strawballis," said the Captain hurriedly.

"Yes Sir, Ensign Strawballis here." she replied.

"I want you to send a communication to Earthanon Arcticus, Military and Civilian divisions. Please request all co-ordinates and data on the following areas of concern. Ammunition, fuel and food storage areas! When you have received all the information, send it through on the strategy room Computron, thank you Ensign Strawballis. Captain Carrot out."

"Aye Sir, Ensign Strawballis out."

Captain Carrot sat back in his chair, his mind working out all possibilities for the reasoning behind the infiltration plan.

"Professor Goosegorgon. Tell me, what is your reading of this situation? What, in your opinion, is their objective?"

"Well Sir, the Organitron-Fasterfoid treaty was signed, sealed and delivered by our ancestors; only after, I might add, giving all the information that was required of us. Even then, after allowing the Fasterfoids time on the Earthanon surface to carry out a spectral analysis, which occurred when Earthanon was originally discovered. The settlement wars that followed were relatively short, but they certainly had long enough on the Earthanon surface to complete full mineral surveys. The climate was simply not suitable for their existence on Earthanon. As we already know, there were no minerals of interest for use in Fasterfoid technology, besides, Fasterfoids consider minerals and vitamins of any kind, far too healthy.

To the best of our knowledge, all the Fasterfoid Fryfleet are still running on Acidulation proton reactors." Professor Goosegorgon stopped in his tracks and pulled out his notebook. Flicking through the pages anxiously, he found exactly what he was looking for. "Eureka!" he shrieked. "Capatano do you remember at the last confederation meeting of Space Nations we saw the Fasterfoids new Mayo class Star Station?"

Captain Carrot searched his memory banks. As far as he could remember the new Mayo class Star Station was a beast of a machine. Gaudy in its design, rather like a large plate of patties in sesame seeded baps on a fuselage of latticed waffle work with three thruster tube engines, designed to look like deep fried croquette potatoes. Admittedly smooth in its acceleration, but it left a vapour trail of grease across the galaxy, and if Captain carrots memory served him correctly it was distinctly cumbersome in its steering.

"That's right Professor, we did didn't we. Tell me, weren't you doing some kind of testing programme on our last batch of recognisance data from that scuttled flashfry cruiser we found in the Bapmacdo Aurora?"

"This is 'a the results, yes. We have only just finished the trial run on what we believe is their new Bio-atmospheric rejuvenation chamber. From the test results coming back from the lab, I can calculate it's a fake! It's principle is within the perimeters of realism, but I don't a 'know Capatano. There is an element missing somehow, something just doesn't gel?"

FO Cornelius coughed to gain the attention of Captain Carrot, who was in deep concentration at this point. "And the plot thickens," he thought to himself. "Have the Fasterfoids boo-booed in a major way? From where the Captain was sitting; time, money, blood, sweat and tears had been invested in this so- called, top-grade technology. Not to mention the vast reputation that they claimed to have carved for themselves in the advanced science superiority stakes."

"Ahhh.. Ahhh. Excuse me Captain, may I be permitted to offer a theory?" asked FO Cornelius, eager to interject.

"What?" Captain Carrot snapped out of his trance. "Of course, I can only repeat, grow with the flow FO Cornelius. All angles must be viewed rigorously." Captain Carrot waved his hand at FO Cornelius, signalling him to continue.

"Thank you Sir. Where the Fasterfoids are said to have developed new and advanced technology in space power momentum their claims to have constructed a new chamber for the purposes of regeneration is, I think, a blanket screen for the heart of their real problem; if you will, follow my train of thought. We have known for some time that the Fasterfoids are running perilously low of their natural starch oil reserves. The old method of regeneration required vast amounts of the raw starch oil product for a complete emersion process. Our sources have reported the refinery storage capacity tanks are as little as half full. Natural reserves are as little as one star-million barrels on Friezarchion, three quarters of a star-million barrels in Crinkletura, some two star-million barrels on Burgeratis, and one star-million five hundred thousand barrels on Chickenora."

"I'm not sure that I follow your point FO Cornelius?" enquired the Captain.

"Well Sir, the Bio-atmospheric rejuvenation chamber lays claim to the fact, that they no longer require raw starch oil based regeneration fuels. Instead, they claim they can now undergo the rejuvenation process in half the time, using, crystalline olio plasma. My tests have shown, that although the process works in principle the affect is very short lived, and they are required to rejuvenate as much as three times more often. We also have reason to believe the crystalline olio plasma breaks down sooner than the traditional starch oil compounds. This makes the process very expensive and time-consuming.

My theory, is that the Fasterfoids are after our olive oil reserves, as well as our olive, maize, corn and peanut stockpiles in order to refine the olive oil crystalline plasma theory, and bolster their flagging starch oil reserves with the other Vegimatter BI-products."

"That sounds very plausible FO Cornelius." said the Captain as the Computron came on line with a message from the bridge.

"Ensign Strawballis to Captain Carrot, come in, over."

Activating his personal channel, Captain Carrot turned to the Computron and switched to visual. On the screen, was a map of the Arcticus region, with three high-lighted areas in red, three in blue and two, in yellow.

"This is Captain Carrot, come in Ensign Strawballis!"

"Sir," continued Ensign Strawballis. "The red high-lighted areas on the map are the food storage tanks, the blue areas are the ammunition strongholds, the yellow areas are the mineral and ore deposit holding zones. Now watch this. Here, is the final analysis of Ensign Viola's particle scan." As Captain Carrot watched the Computron, a second map of Earthanon Arcticus region appeared, super imposed over the top of the first map. With the second map, the high-lighted areas of mauve indicated where the particle scanner had picked up the foreign trace elements.

"The Prima mustard gas particles," explained Ensign Strawballis. "are concentrated around the food storage areas, and as far as Ensign Viola can make out, the unknown substance is a variation of Eggello sulphur gas. We can also detect small traces of, what we consider to be Cochinello gas protons."

"Very good Ensign Strawballis, very good indeed. Ensign Viola has done well. Have her key in the tractor beam instructions. I want all the fixed positions logged then monitored for movement where there are external particle build-ups of those substances. Then, send a communication on a closed line, to Commodore Cu-Cumbala and the Captains of all O.S.S.S Mother ships. Have Commodore Cu-Cumbala step up security on the food storage tanks. Issue all personnel with blazer guns, stand all Arcticus and ships personnel on green alert.

All red-skinned personnel, are to carry their identification insignias and must be searched without exception, even disregarding rank, before entry to the food- storage zones. Alert security to the possibility that the Fasterfoids may have developed a cloaking device. Make it clear,

Ensign Strawballis, I want no singular heroics. This is a time for sensible observation, where, direct action could endanger any out-numbered Organitron. We must not alert them to the fact that we are on to their little scheme so check the yellow skins as well. Just tell them it is a routine personnel activity study, but only go through the motions with the yellow skins, make that clear.

We believe that they are likely to appear as Tomatron or Red Appleoneon Organitrons, approach with caution and set blazer guns to stun. That is all with regard to the Earthanon communication. Tell me, are we ready to launch the proton back-up pilot, Ensign Strawballis?"

"Yes Sir, it is waiting on standby at launch pod one."

"Hold the launch for now, the O.S.S Satsumuroo should be able to cope with the Volcadis recovery." Captain Carrot paused, "If they are after the Vegimatter stockpiles," he thought. "then it would be sensible to assume that they will have a flotilla battle force on stand-by somewhere. "Yes, hold back the proton pilot," he continued. We may have to key in some black box protocols. Should any problems arise in the possible battle plans, but keep it under your crown Ensign Strawballis. It's a possibility, but hopefully I am reading too much credit into the Fasterfoid's plan. If the Fasterfoids are around, they will be ready for battle. Inform SO Tulipina, I want her to scan the Solar System. If there is a battle force flotilla out there then I want to know where. At the very least, I want us to be on our toes and have all scenarios covered. Captain Carrot out."

"Aye Sir, Ensign Strawballis out."

Captain Carrot swivelled in his chair to address the party of Officers and Professor Goosegorgon, who, entangled in the pen holder around his neck, fell off the chair and rolled around the room trying to free his leg, which had lodged behind his neck. As he bumped into chairs, tables and walls like a frenzied pin- ball game out of control, he began sounding off cries of anguish and pain with every collision. For a moment laughter filled the strategy room, breaking the stress-riddled atmosphere with some light and welcome relief, whilst Professor Goosegorgon, received welcome help from FO Melonicord and FO Cornelius, who promptly untangled the much flustered Professor.

Taking back to their seats at the conference table, Captain Carrot settled his laughter, and taking a drink of grape juice in order to regain his composure, prepared once again to deal with the stressful rigours of Sun-Fleet business.

"Thank you Professor." said the Captain, the smile on his face beaming from ear to ear, "I think you have missed your vocation in life, Professor."

"Really Capatano, tell me, you mean a comedian no?"

"You're right; no! I mean you should have been a court jester or a village idiot perhaps."

"Very cruel Capatano," whinged Professor Goosegorgon, crossing his arms in a huff. "Very cruel indeed. Hhmmm."

"No cruelty intended my friend. Now, after a welcome respite, we must get back to business. FO Potatree, when you Vegitamise down to the Earthanon surface, check the planetary light sensors circuitry. It's just possible that it is something as simple as that responsible for playing havoc with the blimit levels; have you decided who you will take with you to assist?"

"Aye Sir. I have, I'll be taking Ensign Fennelter, he's been working closely in liaison with the ground crew power Engineers for several starlectoids. His familiarity with the grid system should save us valuable time."

"Good thinking FO Potatree. The time element may be crucial.

FO Cornelius. I want you to see if you can find anything in the Arcticus region atmosphere that might cause this drop in temperature."

"Yes Captain, I have already started to gather the various equipment requisitions that we will need."

"Good, who are you taking with you?"

"Ensign Bananra Sir, his skills with a molecular atmospheric anjanogram, may come in very useful."

"Very good, FO Cornelius. FO Melonicord."

"Yes Sir?"

"I want you to make preliminary plans for an evacuation. A word to the Widdup; go quietly about your business all of you, we don't want to create a panic. FO Melonicord consult only with the Commodore Cu-Cumbala. Who are you taking with you to the Earthanon surface?"

"Ensign Never Sir. His geographical knowledge of the communities will be invaluable."

"I agree, well done FO Melonicord. Professor Goosegorgon, can you construct some kind of device that will enable us to detect the infiltrators? We will need enough for ourselves and for the Earthanon security forces."

"I guess 'a so, now that we have 'a the chemical breakdown. I can convert a mobile particle scanner to read for a specific proton wave."

"Excellent. If you started immediately, when can they be ready for the crew on the Earthanon surface?"

"Twenty starmins Capatano, the landing party will have them ready in time for their Vegitamisation down to Earthanon surface Sir."

Captain Carrot closed the files in front of him, tapped the logging instructions into the Computron and removed a voice transcript box. As he did so he looked upon the assembled team.

"That is all Organigirls and boys. Be careful, keep your wits about you. And remember, maintain radio contact with Ensign Strawballis every half starhectoid. That is all, you are dismissed. Good luck and good hunting." he said giving them the Organitron salute. Captain carrot activated his personal channel, as he stared out into the vast open space.

"What is going on?" he thought, "Could it be, the Fasterfoids are desperately low in energy resources? Was it possible, that after all these years, they were possibly trying to re-stake a claim on the mining rights of Earthanon? Even worse, was it possible that a new chapter in the saga of the settlement wars was about to raise its ugly head?"

"Captain Carrot to SO Tulipina, come in please." he said, his deep concerns growing.

"SO Tulipina here Sir." she replied swiftly.

"SO Tulipina. Status report on the ships analyser scans, any signs of prima mustard gas on board O.S.S.S Earthanon?"

"No Sir, We have carried out full scans in all Sun-fleet ships, negative response in all areas. It would appear that so far it seems confined to the Arcticus region on the Earthanon surface. Captain, we are picking up what appears to be an Aqua Asteroid cluster in the Gamma quadrant, approximately fifteen degrees from the last known co-ordinates of the orbital satellite Volcadis, before the collision occurred."

"You said, "appeared" SO Tulipina, can you not confirm?"

"Well Sir, we have been monitoring, a hurricanous Sodium Star belt for the last thirty six starhectoids, as you know. It has only been possible to internally scan the Star belt in the last ten starmins, as there is an apparent respite in the storm. However Captain, that is not my immediate concern."

"Expand if you will SO Tulipina, quantify your concerns."

"Captain, at the Star belt's current course, it's on a direct collision course with the Aqua Asteroid cluster then they will join forces and at the current course head straight for Earthanon." Captain Carrot's ears pricked immediately. "At its present speed of one hundred thousand starmillo's per starhectoids, I estimate that collision is imminent within thirty six starhectoids." SO Tulipina awaited the response of Captain Carrot. Deep down she knew the frightening truth in the possibilities of being caught in either a Sodium star belt, or an Aqua Asteroid field. Mixing the two together was nothing short of an explosive cocktail; both unpredictable and uncontrollable. Captain Carrot stood examining the star charts in the strategy room. As he worked out the co-ordinates of the Sodium Star belts trajectory, the full extent of the danger become most uncomfortably obvious, bringing a whole new sense of urgency to the situation.

"Holy Helios." he muttered under his breath. "SO Tulipina, taking into account the Earthanon orbital tract would I be right in my prognosis that when the Sodium Star belt hits Earthanon, the Arcticus region will take the brunt of the collision?"

SO Tulipina, after taking several deep breaths, calmly informed the Captain of the terrible truth that was to be the certain fate of Earthanon.

"Arcticus will certainly be the first region to become affected Sir," she said slowly "but, as I was about to say Sir, I estimate that the Star belt is some five hundred thousand starmillo's deep, and twenty thousand starmillo's wide. My calculations show that there will be no region of Earthanon unaffected." Captain Carrot sat down and steadied his nerves. "This is a time for strength and calm." he thought as his hand trembled in front of him. "First Volcadis, now a whole new hotchpotch of doom and gloom. What next?" he wondered.

"SO Tulipina," he continued, after gathering his composure. "keep monitoring the Star belt and inform me as to any significant changes immediately."

"Aye Sir, SO Tulipina out."

"Captain Carrot to Viceroy Rhubarblatt."

"Rhubarblatt here Captain."

"Are there any signs of Fasterfoid vessels in the vicinity?" enquired Captain Carrot.

"No Sir, all scans are negative. The only activity on the Grid Finder is the Sodium Star belt." confirmed Viceroy Rhubarblatt.

"Keep your eyes peeled, Viceroy. If there are any blips on the Grid Finder that you cannot identify, keep me informed. Captain Carrot out."

"Viceroy Rhubarblatt, over and out."

"Ensign Strawballis come in." Captain Carrot left the strategy room and made his way along the corridor.

"Ensign Strawballis here Captain carrot."

"Ensign Strawballis, I will be back at the helm in fifteen starmins, I want you to patch me a line of communication to the Sun-Fleet Admiral, use a secure line and initiate scrambler frequencies. I will be in my quarters should any problems arise. Captain Carrot out." Captain Carrot stepped into the elevation chamber and the doors de-energised.

"Aye Sir, Ensign Strawballis out."

"Captain Carrot to FO Marrowlar."

"FO Marrowlar here Captain."

"I will relieve you in fifteen Starmins. I just have to make a little detour. Acknowledge."

"Confirmed Captain." said FO Marrowlar.

"Captain Carrot out." said Captain Carrot. "FO Marrowlar out." he replied.

CHAPTER NINE

An Organiman's home is his castle, his memories, in its dungeons he keeps.

Captain Carrot entered his quarters and stood watching his Organiwife, Carrelda, as she played with their young son Carab.

"Gillespie darling," she said, pleased yet surprised to see him. "This is unusual, it's most unheard of to find you playing truant from the bridge! Look darling, Daddy is here."

Carab turned and ran towards Captain Carrot, as he did so, his nappy slithered around his ankles.

"Hello my little one." he said at the jolly vision of his son's struggling steps as he tried to reach out to him. Suddenly, Captain Carrot felt his heart melt as the child's eyes glistened with mischief. His tongue circling his mouth, as every step showed the concentration and determination of the little tyke. "Give Daddy a big hug my brave little soldier."

As he scooped the child in his arms he held him close, their heartbeats in perfect time. Captain Carrot's eyes closed, the little bundle of flesh in his arms seemed to fill him with warmth and love, momentarily draining him of the troubles that vexed him so.

"Helios knows he needs a big hug." he whispered into Carab's ear. "Where is your sister eh? Where is your big Sis... umm? Where is Caroon darling?" he asked Carrelda quietly.

"She's gone on the hologram deck with the school trip to Rasperon. Honestly Gillespie your mind is like a sieve sometimes." she joked.

"What time do you expect her return?" His conversation taking a more concerned tone.

"Oh, they will be back in about two starhectoids. I have to go and collect her." Just then, she turned and saw the face of her dear husband, his eyes swelling with emotion, holding Carab's face close to his cheek. Stroking his small green tufts of hair, he turned and joined Carrelda in a group hug.

"It seems like only yesterday that the children were just seedlings, babes, in arms of doting parents, parents agog at the spectacle of such tiny little beings." he said with a sad but calming, warm face.

"Gillespie you old romantic, you," she said pinching his cheek, as if he were a child. "I hope you're not getting all broody on me. Why I've got little enough energy as it is!" laughed Carrelda. Captain Carrot took her hand and held it tightly. As much as he tried, he could not raise a smile.

It was then, Carrelda knew that something was wrong. She had been married to this Organitron for too long not to know when he was under pressure, or when he was troubled. She did not want to push him. She knew he would tell her if it was serious, or when he was ready, whichever came first. Stroking his face she whispered lovingly in his ear. "Trouble not my darling, when you are ready, I will be strong. When you need me; need us, we will be here, but for now, just tell me this. Should I collect Caroon early?"

"No darling," said Captain Carrot trying to lighten the concern. "I hope we are worrying about nothing. We are in no immediate danger believe me, we are probably in no danger at all. It's just that I have to think of all possible scenarios, It's my responsibility to do so. Sometimes though, it seems such a heavy responsibility to bear." With that he kissed them both on the lips and handed Carab back to his mother.

Walking to the main doors he turned and looked at Carrelda and Carab. "Don't worry about me my loved ones. Whatever happens, I am sure it will all come good in the end! I love you my darlings; more than life itself."

"I love you too Gillespie. Whatever the problem is, we know that we are in the safest, bestest possible hands, don't we Carab?" whispered Carrelda lovingly.

Carab chuckled and waved goodbye to his father, his little green eyes even seemed to smile as he fumbled with the Organitron salute.

"Wuv ooh Da da." he said, with his cute, high pitched baby talk.

"Be happy my little one. I will see you soon." he whispered.

With that, he turned and de-energised the doors, blowing a kiss as he left his quarters. Meanwhile in the Vegimatter room the landing party were finalising their preparations to Vegitamise down to the Earthanon surface.

Professor Goosegorgon bounced in and issued the landing party with the Cochinello proton scanners.

"Here you are," said the Professor, "as 'a promised, you can detect the infiltrators within five hundred Staryards. You will have to re-power the units in twelve starhectoids, so I have prepared spare units, one each whilst the others are re-charging, There is also ten spare sets for the Earthanon security forces. If you need 'a more, just a'letta me know. I will Vegitamise them down to you personally. Let us hope you don't need to use them, and we can solve this little problem swiftly and quickly, hum?"

Chief Engineer FO Potatree, turned as he mounted the Vegitamisation platform.

"Us? we? You wouldn't be planning on coming with us now would you professor?" he laughed.

"I will have you know FO Potatree, that if I were ordered on this detail it would be, how 'a you say, easy peasy." demanded Professor Goosegorgon, infuriated by the slur on his bravery, and his importance to the running of the ship.

"Easy peasy" is it Professor? I wonder if you would consider marching into the sights of a blazer gun with such "easy peasy" eagerness?" said FO Potatree, dismissing Professor Goosegorgon's hollowed ego.

With that, the landing party collapsed in a heap with laughter, much to the disgust of Professor Goosegorgon.

"So, this.. this 'a spud brain is 'a so brave and fearless is he? Please, let 'a me tell you about the time, this fierce, brave, Organitron came 'a to the Medilab with a toothache. Eh? As'a soon as I switched on the drill he fainted. Hmm... some 'a hero you are." retorted the scorned Professor.

FO Potatree sloped onto the Vegimatter platform, his face becoming boiler red with indignation. "Landing party, prepare for Vegitamisation." he ordered in a child-like tantrum. "Come away wit you now, we haven't got all starlectoid."

Again the landing party's raucous laughter, rippled through the Vegimatter room.

"Now." he ordered, his fuse becoming shorter and shorter. The landing party stepped into the bright blue power beams and waited for the Vegitamisation chamber to reach full power. When the room turned violet. FO Cornelius gave the command to Vegitamise.

"Ensign Broccleman, set co-ordinates and Vegitamise."

"Vegitamising now." On command the power beams turned neon orange and the landing party disappeared, leaving Ensign Broccleman to contact Captain Carrot and confirm the completion of landing party transfer.

"Ensign Broccleman to Captain Carrot." he called bidding farewell to Professor Goosegorgon, whom by the way, considered himself one up in the latest gotcha round with his old verbal sparring partner, FO Potatree.

"Captain Carrot here, Ensign Broccleman, what do you have to report?"

said the Captain in the elevation chamber on his way to the bridge.

"Landing party Vegitamisation transmission to Earthanon surface is complete Sir. Ensign Viola has cross-matched the co-ordinates and loaded them into the Vegimatter room computer. We have also confirmed the tractor beam surveillance mode is fully functional and operational Captain." confirmed Ensign Broccleman running diagnostics into the Vegitamisation consul.

"Very good Ensign Broccleman, any problems, and I mean anything at all, you fix positions immediately and Vegitamise the landing-party back on board, is that clear?" he asked.

"Aye Sir, as a bell, loud and clear." agreed Ensign Broccleman.

"Captain Carrot out," said Captain Carrot.

"Ensign Broccleman over and out." he replied.

As the elevation chamber approached the bridge, Captain Carrot was thinking longingly about the beloved family he had just left, and his family back on Carridionaries; his birth Planet. "Now for that little detour." he said. Stopping the elevation chamber he cast his mind back, back to the place of his childhood, the place of his early days of adolescence, before he and his family settled in the Brocclequazerite nebular. This was where his father had been assigned as Ground Station Commodore, and his mother was Chief Science Officer for the Vegitalis plexus Vegimatter farming programme.

Carridionaries held a very special place in the Captain's heart. It was there that he found his first and as it was to transpire, his one and only love. A smile gashed his face, as visions of a very young Carrelda flooded his mind. There was nothing this thirteen Startechtoid old Organitron, would not do for the Organigirl of his heart. He reminisced about the day he carried Carrelda's books home from school for the very first time. "What was my approach? Oh yes, that's right." he remembered, fondly talking aloud with a slight chuckle. Carrelda was in the Startechtoid above him at school. She was also very popular with the upper Organitron, much to his annoyance. One day, just as school had finished, he as usual, followed in Carrelda's slipstream, just to catch a whiff of the sweet aroma of Verbena scent. Nobody wore Verbena scented perfume quite like Carrelda could. Her perfectly groomed crown, with green tufts, lovingly manicured into French plaits and her dress flowing in the slight breeze. She was truly, in his eyes, a vision of splendour. As he blindly followed, she quickly turned and before he realised it, he had walked straight into her, lost in the trance set in motion by her beauty. The dust had settled and they were both sitting on the ground, as their books lay strewn on the floor around them. He remembered they sat looking at each other for what seemed like an eternity as words of brilliance rushed through the brain of Gillespie J. Carrot. He had decided that ignorance was his best defence, he would tell her that he was sorry, and that he was starmillo's away, in deep thought. That was it that would break the ice.

"Well," said Carrelda trying desperately to sound miffed about the collision.

"Are we going to sit here all day or shall we buy this plot of land and have someone build an Organipad around us? Perhaps never bother to move again?"

"Oh, yes please," he said, as the sunlight caught her complexion perfectly, the breeze carrying the sweet aroma of Verbena perfume, "Ahhh," straight to his nostrils.

"I beg your pardon young Sir?" asked Carrelda, with a scalding, but half-hearted tone. Gillespie snapped out of his love Lorne stupor correcting his last comment quickly.

"Oh but the trees," he said, trying to disguise his embarrassment. "We would have to uproot the trees. We wouldn't want to do that, would we?" he expanded, desperately trying to hide his red face.

Gillespie stood up, helping Carrelda to her feet. Their hands touched for the very first time, the palms of his hands perspiring, as Goosebumps ran down his spine. Gradually, he felt warmed by her smooth, velvet touch. Carrelda blushed with anticipation of Gillespie's next words of wisdom.

Gillespie looked into her eyes, feeling his knees turn to jelly, as his mouth dropped, in homage of her very presence. Helios only knows what he must have looked like. Certainly not the image he wanted to portray, not unless appearing like a tongue tied puppy was the order of the day.

"What was the matter Gillespie," enquired a curious Carrelda, playing games with what, to all intensive purposes appeared to be a tongue tied puppy. "Were you blinded by the sun perhaps? Umm?" she continued.

Gillespie remembered his response and cleared his throat, ready for its smooth, calm and impressive delivery.

"Ahh... Ahh. N. no of course not, I'm starmillo's," he said. "I was sorry away, deep in thought. I mean err.. well I mean." The more he tried to correct himself, the worse his predicament became as his ready prepared ice breaker had well and truly sunk. Carrelda laughed, brushing herself down and rubbed her behind. "Oooh, I'm sorry too." Carrelda looked at Gillespie, as he relentlessly tripped over every word. "It's all right," said Carrelda holding his arm. "I understand, well, at least I think I do!"

Then Gillespie gathered up her books and slotted one of his books into her pile. This would give him an excuse to call by her Organipad the next morning, collect his book and offer to walk her to school, telling her of course, they it must have got mixed up by mistake.

"P... P... Please," stammered Gillespie, "the least I can do is carry your books home, You're not seriously hurt, are you?" he asked.

"Nothing that won't mend, young Gillespie J. Carrot."

So together they walked off into the distance, talking about everything to do with nothing, just so long as they talked. Gillespie was the happiest of Organitron's in all of Carridionaries. It was to be a further two and a half startechtoids of happy friendship, a period where all memories for both of them would be set in stone forever.

It was a day of mixed emotions when the news of his father's promotion came from Sun-fleet Admiralty. A double celebration in fact, with his mother's head-ship of the new Farming Programme. It seemed as though the whole City turned up to offer their congratulations at one point or other. Gillespie would have to move to the Brocclequazerite nebular with his parents. Despite everything, the pride that he felt in his parents achievements, only served to quash any sadness he felt for his own loss. Carrelda, he remembered, took him aside that day, sat him down on a log firmly holding his hand. As a tear fell from her cheek, she caught it in a locket of her hair and kissed the inside. Closing the locket then placing it around his neck, she started to sing.

(What will be will be, will be you and me.)
"Take this locket with all of my love,
There is a light for us that shine up above.
You see that star it will shine for all of our lives,
That star that burns bright in the deep of the night.
Yes it's shining for us, shining for our hearts tonight.
What will be will be, will be you and me,
So take this locket with all of my love.

So babe, if you're ever feeling truly lonely,
Or feeling downright blue unhappy and sad.
Well just look to that star and tell me,
My mind will come looking for you, and make you glad.
Can you hear me, look to that star and tell me,
And my mind will come 'a looking for you.
Bring a smile to your face and make you glad.

Darling, so strong is the bond between us,
I'll feel your warmth travel through space.
Believe me honey, I'm missing you now,
But in my heart, for you is a special place.
Please believe me, when I tell you,
I'll always be dreaming of your face.
Because, so strong is this bond between us,
I will hear your thoughts in outer space.

So wherever, wherever we are.
We just look to the sky and search for that star.
I'm telling you distance, it don't matter,
No matter how near or how far with light speed I will shatter.
I will be there for you, to my heart you are true,
And there's nothing I wouldn't do for the love of you.
Oh what will be, will be, and will be you and me.

Baby just remember this day, every word that I say,
As long as we have our star, then true to our hearts we will stay.
Then we who are two, I hope and I pray someday,
That this two, you and me, this two can truly be.
Can become one, and fly away.

So take this locket, with all of my love,
There is a light that shines for us up above.
You see that star it will shine for all our lives,
That star that burns bright in the deep of the night.
Yes it's shining for us, shining for our hearts tonight.
What will be it will be, will be you and me,
So take this locket you see, with all of my love.

So strong had the bond between Gillespie and Carrelda become, no distance had been contemplated, that could stand in the way of their true paths of destiny.

"Oh what heady days they were." he thought to himself, stroking the Purtanium locket of her green tufts, she had given to him as a parting present from the Planet Carridionaries. The simple inscription saying. "From C.C to G.J.C, what will be, will be you and me." Then, his mind turned its attention to the early days of settlement in the Brocclequazerite nebular. As visions of his happy, mischievous youth surfed across his tightly closed eyes, so real was the vision deep in his subconscious, he held his hand out to grasp his mother's.

Gradually, his whole being seemed to transmigrate back to his happiest memory, as she, his mother, guided him safely through the swamp fields of the farm's tropical rain forests. The sweet smiling face of his sister Carrolowl, catching the corner of his sights as she dived with shrills of glee, into the Rasperon cordial lagoon. It was truly an oasis, a place of paradise in every sense, the lagoon a well of deep red expanse set in an enclosure of tropical palm trees. Looking up, he saw chatterbox worker butterflies filling the bright turquoise green sky.

Named chatterbox, because of their non-stop gossiping in the tree tops, they were used for the natural cross fertilisation and upkeep of the native foliage. The cascading cordial falls fed the lagoon, while sparkling reflections imaged the sun, almost blinding, as its angular ricochets, bounced off the torrid splendour set before them, rather like a huge cut ruby chandelier, reflecting every ray of light like shards of glass.

"Gillespie, catch me if you can?" echoed the playful jibes of Carrolowl surfacing from his sub-conscious. In his mind's eye he saw her jumping off the precipice, as she began her descent from the top of the falls with absolute elegance, her arms were spread out, like a giant Chatterbox surfing the thermals. As her body silhouetted the sun she was like an angel in flight, For a split second appearing to hold her position. Then, plummeting towards the lake, her arms stretched out in front, she hurtled down, disappearing into the abyss of pink and white rapids that crashed into the very heart of the lagoon, sending shock wave ripples to the very edge of the cordial lake. He could remember feeling the exact wondrous tension of awaiting her re-appearance. How the hairs on his neck stood on end, every second passing becoming more tense. Slowly moving towards the edge of the lake, looking for his dear sister, he started to worry. "Where was she?" he remembered churning over in his mind. "was she all right?" he thought looking around at his mother, who could be seen laying out a picnic on a nearby bank.

As it turned out his worries were quite ill-founded as his beloved sister, Carrolowl jumped out of the cordial water, pulling Gillespie into the lake with her. And the picnic, umm.. Ahh what a banquet that was. Truly a feast set for premier consul. Every form of Vegimatter you could imagine passed his lips that day, followed by his favourite, Carridionaries cake with lashings of Fruitalia Ice cream. "Ahh yes indeed," he sighed licking his lips and rubbing his tummy. Opening his eyes he composed himself, tearing himself away from his brief indulgence in fantasia, and back to facing the real world. How he would dearly like to take a trip down memory lane in the Holodeck programme. Perhaps revisit all his old childhood haunts, taste the very simpleness and innocence of his youth that at the time, he now, felt within himself, he had taken fore-granted. Pushing the pulse pad Captain Carrot re-activated the elevation chamber.

Suddenly he was back at the bridge. As the doors de-energised, he knew that his dreams would have to wait. Those that he loved in life were at his various homes around the Solar Systems, of the universe. The home that he had just left was his castle now, and it was time to place his memories back in the Pandora's box of his castle's dungeons. There were more urgent, pressing matters at hand.

"Pheweeeeee... Phewoooooh" piped Ensign Melonture.

"Captain on the bridge." announced Ensign Rasperillo.

Again the bridge stood to attention awaiting the Captain to take up his position at the Command com.

"You have Command com Captain!" said FO Marrowlar swiftly.

"I thank you FO Marrowlar." Taking his place at the command com, Captain Carrot called upon the services of Viceroy Rhubarblatt. "Nav com?"

"Aye Sir," answered Viceroy Rhubarblatt.

"Alter course seven degrees starboard and take us down to fifty thousand feet, One quarter pulse speed, steady as she goes and hold position."

"Aye, aye Sir, code indexing for primary descent." confirmed Viceroy Rhubarblatt.

"Automatic air pressure is set for secondary positioning, Viceroy Rhubarblatt." said SO Tulipina, standing at the ships analyser.

"Secondary pressure readings computed and logged. Thank you SO Tulipina." acknowledged Viceroy Rhubarblatt.

"Ensign Strawballis." added Captain Carrot.

Ensign Strawballis swivelled on her chair, her eyes alluring with the warm comfort of familiarity. Ensign Strawballis was the longest serving member of the O.S.S.S Earthanon. She was specifically requested for transfer from Captain Carrot's previous command, the O.S.S Soufflé. Indeed requested by the Captain himself. Captain Carrot is a firm believer that communication is everything, as far as he was concerned, Ensign Strawballis was the finest most reliable and loyal communications, Officer in the whole Sun-Fleet organisation.

"Aye Sir." replied Ensign Strawballis.

"Ensign Strawballis," continued Captain Carrot. "Please contact Captains Beetrouly and Sunfleur of the O.S.S.S Mother ships Milkymarrow way and Junipitaris. Instruct them to maintain trajectory but alter altitude to Fifty thousand feet. If we have to initiate the evacuation plan, then we can save some valuable time in the transportation distance."

"Yes Captain Carrot. Oh Captain," said Ensign Strawballis. "I have taken the liberty of loading the back-up proton pilot with a basic programme of protocols Sir."

"Well done Ensign Strawballis. What would we do without you? Let's hope it won't be necessary to initiate it!" smiled Captain Carrot.

Slowly Ensign Viola manoeuvred the ship into position under the watchful eye of Viceroy Rhubarblatt.

"One quarter pulse speed, steady as she goes." announced Ensign Viola. "Frontal heat reflector shields activating, now. Re-entry tract fixed and computed, ready when you are, Ensign Viola. On your mark."

"Entry angle set at one three five blimits, all systems are clear commencing descent. Three, two, one. Altitude on your mark if you will, Viceroy Rhubarblatt, entering the Earthanon Atmosphere now."

A slight juddering could be felt at the re-entry point, quickly dissipating to a calm tranquillity as Ensign Viola took the O.S.S.S. Earthanon into descent from the steering column.

"One hundred and fifty thousand feet," confirmed Viceroy Rhubarblatt. "Anti-graviton field on line now," he continued. "Leaving Earthanon re-entry point, now Sir. Heat shields holding, no compromise apparent. All systems are Ay'Ok. One hundred thousand feet, anti-graviton field holding at one hundred percent, eighty thousand feet, seventy thousand feet, sixty thousand feet," as Viceroy Rhubarblatt marked the altitude descent, Ensign Viola made preparations for the stabilising procedure.

"Fifty five thousand feet." marked Viceroy Rhubarblatt.

"Activating pivotal thrusters on one." informed Ensign Viola.

"Fifty Five.... Four.... Three.... Two.... One." marked Viceroy Rhubarblatt.

"Firing thrusters now, and ignition." confirmed Ensign Viola activating the thrusters' throttles. The ship's engines droned to low pitched humming with no vibration at all. "Fifty thousand feet and static. Thank you Ensign Viola," said Viceroy Rhubarblatt. "Captain our position is fixed and computed, all systems are clean and clear, anti-graviton field at full displacement. Switching to auxiliary power; auxiliary power on. Remote and calorific reactors are off line, now. auxiliary power has linked in, auto gravity pilot in place, all systems remain clear and fully functioning Captain."

"An excellent manoeuvre Viceroy Rhubarblatt," said the Captain. "Ensign Viola, I could have slept through that approach, well done."

"Thank you Captain." replied Ensign Viola.

"Viceroy Rhubarblatt is teaching you well. Maintain trajectory and switch the calorific reactors to auxiliary pulsar control auto gravity pilot. We may need to get out of here in a hurry. It is possible there will not be time to waste re-booting the calorific reactor computer terminals!"

"Thank you Sir, as you wish. Switching Calorific reactors to auxiliary pulsar control auto gravity pilot, on line, now Sir."

"S.C.R to A.P.C.A.G.P. Confirmed on line Viceroy Rhubarblatt." announced SO Tulipina at the ships Analyser.

"Ensign Strawballis," said Captain Carrot. "Patch me through to Sun-Fleet Admiral Ducarrotain. Secure channel if you will, image to Visaid?" requested the Captain examining the ship's star chart.

"Aye, aye Sir," confirmed Ensign Strawballis. "O.S.S.S Earthanon to Admiral Ducarrotain over, I Repeat O.S.S.S Earthanon to Admiral Ducarrotain over." said Ensign Strawballis. "Captain Carrot Sir, Admiral Ducarrotain is in rejuvenation mode but his schedule indicates his return in thirty Starmins. she confirmed.

"Very well Ensign." he replied. "No message, re-establish contact in thirty five Starmins."

CHAPTER TEN

Better late than never!

Part one

All aboard for the O.S.S Satsumuroo

Time 11.30 starhectoids.

Captain Carrot stood at the ships Security com discussing the Volcadis oddity and its implications for the future communication transmissions to the home Planetary system.

"Sir, the Satellite Volcadis was are only link with the home Planets, we cannot get confirmation from the Premier Seed Council for the evacuation. We are going to have to hope that Admiral Ducarrotain relaxes his stance on the retreat front." said an unhopeful FO Marrowlar.

"He will see reason FO Marrowlar." said a thoughtful Captain Carrot. "If he doesn't then we stay and suffer the consequences of the unknown." he continued.

"No change there then." laughed FO Marrowlar.

"That's the spirit Benzo, that's the spirit." chuckled the Captain.

"Captain Carrot." Interrupted Ensign Strawballis. "I have Admiral Ducarrotain's office on the line." she confirmed. "Ahh Admiral." she continued. "I have Captain Carrot standing by Sir."

"Admiral Ducarrotain has always got time for Captain Carrot," came a cheery response. "It is a pleasure to hear from you, Ensign Strawballis if I am not mistaken?" asked the Admiral.

"Indeed Admiral you are correct, Captain Carrot wishes to make direct communication with you on a scrambled frequency Sir." confirmed Ensign Strawballis her cheek's blushing profusely.

"I thought so, recognise those tonsils anywhere!" said a playfully flippant Admiral Ducarrotain with more than an element of tenacity and jealousy in his voice, the Admiral had tried on many occasions to get Ensign Strawballis on his personal staff, but, alas without success.

"Flattery will get you almost everything except me as your Communications Liaison Admiral." chirped Ensign Strawballis.

"Very well Ensign Strawballis," laughed the Admiral. "but I warn you, I will not give up. It will be a pleasure to Communicate with Captain Carrot initiating scrambler now."

"Aye, aye Admiral, switching Image to Visaid Communication. On line now Sir, you are through to Sun-Fleet Admiral Ducarrotain Captain."

Admiral Ducarrotain was the Bubbleonion Squeak Vegitalis Master-at-arms on special attachment to the Planet Earthanon. It was his destined to be his responsibility to give the order for the Sun-Fleet to abandon Earthanon. The Captain knew that it would be difficult to persuade him to do so. The Admiral, a very proud Organitron, was the youngest ever Admiral appointed to the main council of the United Foliage of Organitron. His reputation for being a hard headed tactician was gained in the great battle of Macadamian conquest. The Macadamian Planet in the Fruitanutes plexus was taken siege some thirty Startechtoids ago by the Burgerites, in an evil attempt to hold the nutty eccentrics hostage in return for ten million credits and four million tons of sesame seeds, plus one million gallons of peanut oil. The then Captain Rillo T Ducarrotain of the Famed O.S.S Grapefruiterang, out-smarted the Burgerites by showering the Planet with cluster bugs. An invention of his own, these would explode in the atmosphere above the Planet Macadamia, releasing a candy floss mine belt that would cover the entire Planet, acting as a blanket preventing the secondary explosive capsules containing sprout gas from escaping. Thus, trapping the Burgerites under the threat of sprout gas so they were faced with an embarrassing, ego bashing certain doom. The bad baby Burgerites agreed to vacate the Planet Macadamia with their gloupy fat filled heads hung low in the shame of defeat, taking to their ships in droves. The final agreement reached in negotiations under the terms and conditions of the then Organitron- Fasterfoid treaty were; once clear of the Macadamian surface, the Fasterfoid fleet would be escorted out of the Fruitanutes plexus, until they reached the outer perimeters of the Bubbleonion Squeak Vegitalis Solar System. From there, they would be monitored until they were two hundred and fifty thousand starmillo's clear of the fifty thousand starmillo's wide "No-fry Zone."

Once clear of the mine belt, they reneged the agreement formed and based on trust almost immediately, and turned their Gunge-guns on the Sun-Fleet convoy. As the ships came under fire with highly concentrated ketchup globules, their protective shields started to clog up and drain of power. Captain Ducarrotain gave chase in the face of adversity and returned fire with his yet untested secret weapon, the "Oudag capsule." These capsules contained Organitronic Uni-Vegimatter De-Acidulating Gellogas.

The Oudag Capsule was designed to firstly penetrate the ships energy defence shields, to do this it would release an electro proton acidulant via an advance heat guided laser missile as it made its approach. allowing the missile to effectively burn a hole through the energy defence shield and creating an entry tunnel for approximately five seconds. The tunnel was maintained by outploading the energy field in the tunnel with positive electrons, creating a molecular disturbance. This channel would be held open for the secondary missile, the legendary Oudag capsule.

The nose cone unit of the capsule would have attached to it, an electromagnetic plunger which would suck onto the outer hull of the enemy vessel. Upon impact from within the missile, a diamond studded drill would breach the outer and inner hulls. Then once the hull penetration was complete, it would release the noxious cocktail of Gellogas rib tickler throughout the ship. Carried by a high pressure release of CO^2 this would be an extra treat for the meat filled no necks. The second most thing that drives them crazy is the cold.

If there is one thing that drives a Fasterfoid crazier than the cold, its being happy, and with a ship full of Gellogas (a very pungent laughing gas). There was guaranteed an abundance of the aforementioned. From that time forward it reflected in the law of the Fasterfoids, a law that outlawed laughter. Anything more than a chuckle was strictly forbidden; although they have been known to bend the rules and use it as a punishment method within their own ranks.

Rather than be captured in a state of ecstatic rapture they retreated into the night, as the Sun Ship convoy gave chase. If you listened very hard above the sound of the engines you could hear the pain of their laughter echoing across the Fruitanutes plexus. As it later transpired, over two thirds of the Burgerites were hospitalised on their return to Burgeratis. A variety of ailments were said to blame. Our sources revealed to us that the two major culprits on the hospital wards were inflamed tonsils and bruised ribs.

Recognisance reports of the time revealed the Principle General of the Fasterfoid Fleet who spear-headed the invasion, became so addicted to the happy gas and became so depressed after his hospitalisation, it was necessary to demote him and restrict him to non-active duty. Even when the General made a quick and full recovery, the doctors would not sign him over to active duty in the field of battle; so untrusting were the doctors of his miraculous recovery.

On the screen in front of Captain Carrot, appeared a huge frame of an Organitron, quite larger than the usual size of a Carridionaries. Sniggers were hard to contain on the bridge of the O.S.S.S Earthanon, seeing those bold green pointed eyebrows, intimidating, and somehow out of proportion with his head; though this was never mentioned to his face, it was widely commented on in private. He was looking tired and shaded in the eyes, not with his usual fiery glow at all.

"Greetings Captain Carrot, I wish it were better circumstances for this communication." said Admiral Ducarrotain offering the Organitron salute.

"Greetings Admiral Ducarrotain, alas some wishes are longer in the granting than others." replied Captain Carrot returning the salute.

"I have already received your preliminary report Captain Carrot." he said browsing through the documents in front of him. "Yes indeed most strange, tell me, do we have any answers yet? The report is very thorough, but all it seems to offer is questions and possibilities, no solutions!" replied Admiral Ducarrotain.

"I think we can satisfy your quest for answers Admiral!" stated the Captain reassuringly. "We believe that the Fasterfritters and, or the

Crinkleozones, have infiltrated the Earthanon surface. We also believe with a view to stealing our olive oil stocks and or our stock piles of Olives, Corn, Maize and peanuts for the purposes of converting their oil properties into energy. As you know our sources divulge that their starch oil reserves are dangerously low." Captain Carrot stopped mid-flow as Admiral Ducarrotain interrupted him.

"I think perhaps you are forgetting that the Fasterfoids have created a new rejuvenation chamber? Thus making the oil reserves reports irrelevant." noted the admiral scratching his bushy eyebrows.

"Professor Goosegorgon thinks that he can disprove the working theory of the new rejuvenation chamber, not because it doesn't work perhaps, but certainly on the grounds that the rejuvenation chamber is ineffectual in both time and expense." Captain Carrot paused to gather his thoughts. FO Marrowlar was right, the Admiral was going to be a tough nut to crack. "We believe however," he continued, "that we face a more serious and pressing problem, Admiral. There is now no doubt that the Fasterfoids have developed a cloaking devise and are masqueraded freely as Organibeings on the surface of Earthanon." Captain Carrot hoped that the news of the cloaking device would make the Admiral view his report with more urgency. On the Visaid Admiral Ducarrotain perused the report again, then mopping his head and chin with his handkerchief turned to his Computron and began inputting some data.

"Surely all you need to do is Vegitamise all the relevant food stockpiles into the ships stores Captain carrot." reasoned Admiral Ducarrotain.

"I agree Sir, but Earthanon is about to be struck by a Sodium Star belt. We have already suffered a collision with the Sun Satellite Volcadis. Our most recent estimate is this; at its current speed and trajectory, the Sodium Star belt will be within the Earthanon Atmosphere within thirty-four starhectoids, Admiral. Possibly less?"

"Then remove the problem, Captain Carrot. You surely have enough firepower between the Mother-ships, not to mention five squadrons of Star Fighters at your disposal. One would assume they are ready and able on the Earthanon surface?" said the old warrior smugly as if to indicate that Captain Carrot was somehow running scared instead of standing up and fighting.

"I'm afraid that will not be enough Admiral. The Star belt is some five hundred thousand starmillo's deep and twenty thousand starmillo's wide. It looks as though we will have no option but to evacuate the Earthanon surface until it blows over. You see Sir," continued Captain Carrot. "we have reason to believe that the Star belt is the least of our problems. Within the star belt there are confirmed Grid Finder particle readings showing that contained inside is a vast bombardment of Aqua Asteroids; some of them up-to one eighth the size of Earthanon." Captain Carrot thought if that didn't make the Admiral sit up and take notice, then nothing would breach the old warriors grey cells.

"Five hundred thousand starmillo's by twenty thousand starmillo's eh? Aqua Asteroids, Eighth of the Planet umm? Thirty four starhectoids indeed. An estimate you say?" asked the Admiral obviously rocked by its enormity.

"Affirmative Admiral Ducarrotain. You see the evacuation process really is our last and I think our only option." confirmed Captain Carrot

"I see, Captain. This shows everything in a whole new light," said the Admiral struggling to control his Adam's apple. "Holy Helios Organiman that is not the common size of your average Sodium Star belt. More like the size of your average universe, I.. I assume you have a feasible evacuation procedure in mind?" enquired the wide eyed Admiral.

"Yes Sir, but it does include leaving the stockpiles of Vegimatter behind, unless you can issue a general order commandeering all civilian space freighters in the Earthanon Atmosphere to rendezvous in the Arcticus Hemisphere. Also all ships in the Gamma Quadrant Minor to report to the O.S.S.S mother-ships immediately." requested the Captain.

"Leave it with me Captain Carrot," replied a pensive Admiral Ducarrotain. "I will issue the necessary writs and Vegitamise over to O.S.S.S Earthanon immediately." he confirmed.

"I look forward to your arrival Admiral." agreed the Captain breathing a sigh of relief.

"Until then Captain, end transmission UFO and out." Then Admiral Ducarrotain gestured the Organitron salute and the screen cleared as Captain Carrot ended the transmission.

"Captain Carrot UFO and out, end transmission."

Leaving the command com, and turning to the Gasamatronic gyroscope he checked the particle scanner for any indications as to the size of the Aqua Asteroids.

"Still no clear reception, Viceroy Rhubarblatt. Those storms appear to be blinding the ship's triabulator." grunted the Captain, trying to re-calibrate the particle scanner to compensate for the interference clogging up the transmissions.

"My calculations indicate that the winds are in excess of three hundred starmillo's per starhectoids Captain" confirmed Viceroy Rhubarblatt.

"Thank you Viceroy Rhubarblatt that is just what I wanted to hear. Ensign Tulipina. See if you can re-configurate the ship's analyser to override the static created by the storm. Whatever we do, we must know what it is we are up against!"

"Aye, aye Sir, I will try to re-direct the transmission frequencies via the ship's satellite booster banks." replied SO Tulipina.

FO Marrowlar turned to Captain Carrot, he knew that he would be on edge having the Admiral on board at such a time of crisis. Admiral Ducarrotain may have been a fierce warrior of the Organitron once, but there have been recent concerns raised with regards to the Admiral's failing health. FO Marrowlar could not help feeling how his presence might somehow unbalance the performance of the crew.

"Captain Carrot Sir," said FO Marrowlar searching for the most diplomatic approach to air his concerns, "with respect Captain Carrot the Admiral does not look well. Would it not be better for his excellency to stay where he is on board the O.S.S.S Junipitaris and rest? We could keep him fully briefed on the situation via the Visaid, perhaps send a personal envoy to convey the civilian writs from the Admiral." he reasoned.

"You know Admiral Ducarrotain, FO Marrowlar. When his people are in trouble, he would gladly give his last breath to help. No, he will be a good stabilising factor aboard the O.S.S.S Earthanon. We have a lot of young and inexperienced Organitron in the ship's crew. They may find some comfort in having a real live legend on board. If that is so, I for one welcome it."

Captain Carrot looked to the stars for some degree of comfort. Somehow that particular barrel seemed rather empty of comfort rations.

"No, FO Marrowlar," he continued. "something tells me we are heading for some very testing and turbulent times. Take my advice my friend, spare your concerns for the more pressing matters which we are about to endure."

"Aye Sir." agreed FO Marrowlar sloping off with his tail between his legs, the truth of the matter being that Admiral Ducarrotain frightened the very life out of him.

"Ensign Strawballis." summoned the Captain with a renewed vigour. "Alert cancellation of all Organitron shore leave with immediate effect. All duty personnel are to report to their work stations, all Sun-Fleet ship's crew as well as the Earthanon surface Engineers; UFO or civilian. Alert the Holodeck that all simulations are cancelled, and recall all travellers immediately."

Captain Carrot looked to the Planet Earthanon for strength, as the stars had seen fit to offer no hope, maybe he could find some form of solace in the Planet so many of his kind had come to know as home. He always managed to find inspiration from it in times of trouble, but this time the hidden energy so often found within, was strangely cold in its absence. Leaving him to find the inspiration he needed from within himself.

"Ensign Viola," snapped Captain Carrot, deeply vexed by the surrounding feelings of nothingness. "do we still have a firm fix on the Earthanon Landing party?"

"Yes Sir, they are due to make contact in a little under five Starmins."

Responded Ensign Viola checking the Arcticus map for the tracking blips.

"Ensign Strawballis, when the Earthanon landing party report comes in transfer their communication transcripts to my personal channel in my quarters."

"Aye Sir." said Ensign Strawballis breaking off to receive a transmission.

Ensign Strawballis alerted Captain Carrot to a message coming though on the Communications com.

"Captain Carrot Sir, I have Captain Peabazzare of the O.S.S Satsumuroo on the line, I'm afraid the contact is very weak, Visaid is not possible due to cross particle electron interference."

"Can you secure and clarify the link Ensign Strawballis?" interrupted Captain Carrot.

"It might be possible to improve verbal clarity by boosting the Satellite receiver proton wave conductor." said Ensign Strawballis. "Coming on line now Sir." she confirmed as the bridge crew stood poised for the message coming from the storm struck vessel that was sent to recover the stricken Sun Satellite Volcadis.

"Ensign Strawballis, patch this through to Professor Goosegorgon. We may need his advice." instructed Captain Carrot taking his place at the command com. There was panic in the voice of Captain Peabazzare. The reception was indeed weak, breaking up intermittently.

"This is Captain Peabazzare of the O.S.S Satsumuroo We have been struck by a barrage of small Aqua Asteroids. Our shields are down to thirty percent power.

T*- ship's lasers are stretched to their l*m-t, some of the Asteroids are as big as the ship itself. The Grid Finder is going crazy. Captain there g*tt-ing bi*ger, be prepared. At the current speed of the Sodium Star belt, this is increasing as it approaches the Earthanon Gravitational pull. We estimate it hitting the E***han** *urfac* *n aproximat**y twe**y **ur Star*****id*." The communication line began to break up.

"Captain Peabazzare you are breaking up. I repeat, you are breaking up, repeat your transmission." Captain Carrot shouted, his concern for the O.S.S Satsumuroo and her crew taking precedent to any information they could give. "Ensign Strawballis can you re-establish contact?" he asked as Ensign Strawballis fought frantically to regain contact. After a brief period contact was resumed. Captain Peabazzare's voice still faint, meanwhile, Ensigns Rasperillo and Melonture were arguing over who's turn it was to take charge of the ships whistle blissfully unaware of the commotion.

"But it's my turn, you promised you would give it to me." said Ensign Rasperillo stamping his feet.

"Well I lied. You couldn't play a tin whistle let alone the ships whistle!" laughed Ensign Melonture.

"Oh go on, give it to me please." pleaded Ensign Rasperillo like a child denied of his favourite toy.

"Will you two Juice brains pipe down, or rest assured I will let you both have it, personally!" shouted Captain Carrot struggling to make sense of the communication." Ensign's Rasperillo and Melonture jumped speedily to attention, not another word passing their lips as silence fell on the bridge of the O.S.S.S Earthanon.

"The sodium Star belt is gaining speed, as it approaches the Earthanon atmosphere Gravitational pull." repeated Captain Peabazzare. "We estimate it will be with you within twenty four starhectoids. Shields down to twenty-five percent power. Laser reactors are approaching meltdown," he confirmed.

Captain Carrot rose sharply as he leant on the handrail before him, his knuckles turning white.

"Captain Peabazzare abort your mission, head for home. I repeat, abort your mission and head for home." ordered Captain Carrot breaking into the transmission from the O.S.S Satsumuroo Then came the penultimate communication from Captain Peabazzare of the much troubled O.S.S Satsumuroo

"We are breaking up, the ship's analyser and life support systems barely operational. There's no air Captain, auxiliary power failing fast."

"Abort your mission head for home that is an order Captain Peabazzare." Captain Carrot mulled over the thoughts running through his mind he must hold up their spirits at all costs.

"Stand by Captain Peabazzare help is on its way. Ensign Strawballis I'm counting on you to keep this line open, whatever it takes."

"Ahh.. Ahh.. Ah. We'll do our best Captain, but please hurry!" Captain Peabazzare did his best to sound defiant and strong, but the bridge crew of the O.S.S.S Earthanon could tell, although its sentiment was delivered with confidence and forceful strength, the underlying tone was one of deep insecurity and fear of the unknown. Sweat was now pouring down the face of Captain Carrot. Somewhere, somehow, he had to find a solution to the predicament of Captain Peabazzare and the crew of the O.S.S Satsumuroo Captain Carrot had bolstered the flailing confidence of Captain Peabazzare by offering the assurance of a plan already in its implementation. Captain Carrot could only hope that while Captain Peabazzare may disapprove of his method, there would be understanding for his reasoning. Offered a life line of hope he did, false hope admittedly, but Captain Peabazzare didn't know that. In Captain Carrot's book, where there was no hope, there was no reason to fight on under extreme pressure. Even the finest of Organitron Sun-Fleet officers had given up and died, not for the good of the cause but because the cause was out of their control or lost.

"FO Marrowlar scan the galaxy, are there any ships within firing range of the O.S.S Satsumuroo?"

"No Sir, all ship's flight plans have been grounded awaiting instruction. We are only awaiting three civilian freighters to arrive, There are two ships on a heading from Gamma Minor but they are well out of range Captain."

"Distance FO Marrowlar?" rebuffed the Captain.

"They are one and a half starhectoids out of range from the O.S.S Satsumuroo's current position."

"Can we fix co-ordinates on the crew, and Vegitamise the crew back to O.S.S.S Earthanon?" enquired Captain Carrot.

"I am trying to fix co-ordinates now Sir. Co-ordinates fixed and logged. Sir, they are still relatively well placed on the outer perimeters of the Sodium Star belt," FO Marrowlar paused, his face showing signs of concern. Wiping his brow with his sleeve and with a heavy heart, he brought to the attention of Captain Carrot, a startling, ominous realisation.

"but there is a risk Sir." he continued. "If the storm in the Star belt intensifies we could lose the link..."

"Meaning FO Marrowlar," interrupted the Captain. "if the link is broken during Vegitamisation, those in the system will be lost forever!"

"Yes Sir that is the inevitable risk." confirmed FO Marrowlar slowly.

It was when choices like this needed to be made, where the buck of responsibility was ultimately the Captain's, he found himself having no envy for the Captain's authority, and the rush to follow in his impressive footsteps subsided into a slow trot. It was not a question of choice any longer to the Captain. It was a no other option last ditch attempt if they were to save Captain Peabazzare and his crew, it was now a matter of necessity nothing short of complete success would be a failure!

"FO Marrowlar, send the co-ordinates through to the Vegimatter room, I will take full responsibility for the decision, and Benzo," said Captain Carrot smiling. "I want you to bolster the link from the ship's analyser, both computers on line working in unison will add a rather comforting safety net; frankly you're the best officer for the job."

"Aye, aye Sir, I hope your trust in me is justified Captain. Sending them through to the Vegimatter room computer now." he said punching in the co-ordinates at his Computron com.

"Sir, I have the automatic Vegimatter Vegitamisation beam systems programme loaded." replied FO Marrowlar calmly.

"SO Tulipina, contact the Vegimatter room and instruct them to Vegitamise the crew of the O.S.S Satsumuroo now!" ordered the Captain.

"Aye, aye Sir. SO Tulipina to Ensign Broccleman."

"Ensign Broccleman here." came the reply.

"Ensign Broccleman, activate the automatic Vegimatter Vegitamisation beam now, and prepare to receive a lot of visitors. When I say a lot Ensign, rest assured that's an understatement."

"Aye Sir, activating now! A.V.V.B on line and activated. Please inform Captain Carrot, S.F.A Ducarrotain is on his way to the bridge." confirmed Ensign Broccleman. Captain Carrot heard Ensign Broccleman, but the news of the imminent arrival of a Superior Officer on the bridge was not his greatest concern.

"Ensign Strawballis, what is the ship's complement of the O.S.S Satsumuroo?" he enquired.

"One thousand six hundred and seventy two, sir." she replied at lightning speed.

"Maintain that line of communication Ensign Strawballis, it is vital that they do not feel alone and abandoned." insisted a now flowing Captain Carrot, as the doors of the elevation chamber de-energised and on to the bridge stepped Sun-Fleet Admiral Ducarrotain, accompanied by Mushroid Fungola.

"Admiral on the bridge." announced Ensign Rasperillo as Ensign Melonture piped him on to the bridge as the crew stood to attention. "Pheweeeeee.. Phewooooh."

"Stand easy on the bridge." said the Admiral quickly. He had been monitoring the O.S.S Satsumuroo situation since he Vegitamised on to the O.S.S.S Earthanon compliments of Fungola's mobile bridge communication's transmitter and could see there was work to be done. Work that he could see made his presence insignificant by comparison.

"Thank you Mushroid Fungola, I think I can manage from here, you are relieved." Mushroid Fungola gave the Organitron salute.

"My pleasure Admiral Ducarrotain," he crawled with little or no self respect. "Maybe we can get together later, perhaps discuss various battle tactics I have been working on. Your professional input would be most gratifying your Excellency."

"Thank you Mushroom Fungola, maybe sometime later when the situation is a little less fraught." he replied.

"Captain Carrot to Ensign Broccleman, how many crew have Vegitamised on board O.S.S.S Earthanon?" asked Captain Carrot opening his personal channel.

"Ninety seven Sir, the Sodium Star belt is making the link very erratic." said Ensign Broccleman hurriedly.

"How much time do you need for another one thousand six hundred Organitron?" enquired the Captain mopping his brow.

"Holy Helios Sir, we c.." Ensign Broccleman paused to contain his shock. "Twenty minutes at least Sir, which is assuming the link holds." came Ensign Broccleman's flustered reply.

"Keep on it, we will do our best to see that you get the time you need, Captain Carrot out. Captain Carrot to Professor Goosegorgon come in." said the Captain switching channels.

"Yes Capatano, Profe..."

"There's no time for joviality Professor. Have you been monitoring the transmission from the O.S.S Satsumuroo?" asked the Captain interrupting the Professor.

"Yes Capatano!" replied the Professor.

"I need to buy some time Professor and I need it now! Have you any suggestions?"

"Yes Sir, I think if you override the O.S.S Satsumuroo's ships computer using the emergency Sun-Fleet security index, you can divert their power from the Calorific reactors and the auxiliary powers to the energy shields. That would buy you some time and protection from the Sodium Star belt. Then, try switching the laser beam power source to the automatic space particle guidance oscillator. This should create a guidance heat shield to protect them from the Aqua Asteroids for a short while." reasoned the Professor. "It's a long shot Capatano," he continued. "but then blow all emergency oxygen tanks through the air ducting and pray that it lasts long enough! The instructions and the override codes are on their way to FO Marrowlar's Computron, but only you can give the final matrix code to set the security system override programme in sequence. Capatano Carrot. I must remind you that once initiated, the programme sequence cannot be altered in any way." stated the Professor.

"Good work Professor. Tell me, is the Medilab and emergency medical facility ready and able?"

"Yes Capatano. We have set up the spare Star Fighter hanger on deck C as an emergency Medilab, Dr Kiwitranus is on hand and standing by for the rush." confirmed the Professor.

"Let's prey it won't be necessary. Stand by, we may need you again!" said Captain Carrot turning swiftly to FO Marrowlar. "Have you received the information FO Marrowlar?" asked the Captain.

"Aye Sir, the matrix code is all that we need!"

"Very well compute as follows; O.S.S.S.E dash, dash, S.F.A slash, C.J.C dash, dash, ZERO dash 3." dictated the Captain.

FO Marrowlar punched in the Command code and awaited the computer confirmation. "Computer emergency override sequence programme activated voice recognition sequence please." confirmed the computer awaiting the Captain's confirmation Code.

"C.J.C dash, dash, ZERO 3, 2, 1. Slash ORANGE." said the Captain in reply.

"Emergency override sequence programme standing by, activate at your security Command com."

Captain Carrot nodded at FO Marrowlar.

"Grow with the flow, FO Marrowlar," he said. "and pray to Helios that we are in time."

"Aye Sir," said FO Marrowlar punching in the clearance sequence.

"Emergency override sequence programme activated in 3, 2, 1. Sequence in operation." commanded the Computer.

Out in space on the edge of the Gamma Quadrant, the O.S.S Satsumuroo was being thrown around in the outer boundaries of the Sodium Star belt. On board Captain Peabazzare and his team struggled to maintain a sensible management of the ships functioning capability. Outside the ship small Aqua Asteroids pelted the defence force field, and instantly vaporised as the heat shield took the force.

Back on the bridge Captain Carrot looked at his time piece, it had been fifteen Starmins since the emergency measures had been employed. He could feel that time must surely be running out.

"Ensign Strawballis, how is that communication line?" asked Captain Carrot.

"Still holding Sir, barely but surely; putting you through now Sir. You are on line now Captain."

Captain Carrot sat at the Command com and attempted communication with the O.S.S Satsumuroo.

"This is Captain Carrot of the O.S.S.S Earthanon calling Captain Peabazzare of the O.S.S Satsumuroo come in, over." Silence loomed as Ensign Strawballis tried realigning the Communication's com again. Suddenly from amidst the buzzing came the voice of Captain Peabazzare.

"Thank you." said Captain Carrot under his breath looking back towards the sun which now took pride of place in the bridge's observation window.

"Captain Peabazzare here Captain Carrot, we are still being thrown around like a pinball and have suffered many losses in the ship's crew, but our shields have increased to seventy percent and holding. We have lost auxiliary power, our lasers are down and we appear to be surrounded by some kind of heat emulating buffer shield. The air situation has improved, but the ship can't take much more of this. We have a major breach in the engine room Captain; so we are sitting dead in space. Life support systems are functional, but we have had to close down the ship's back-up proton pilot to maintain it. Much of the improvements I'm afraid are impossible to explain, I can only assume that Helios is looking kindly on us today."

Captain Carrot cleared his throat ready to brief Captain Peabazzare of the actions that he had taken.

"Captain Peabazzare, we have had to override your ship's computer in order to provide some protection for you from the Star belt. We don't know how long it will last. We are Vegitamising your crew on board the O.S.S.S Earthanon slowly but surely."

A scream came over the communication line as an explosion could clearly be heard in the background along with the ships general alarm. Frantically Captain Peabazzare could be heard shouting orders.

"Ensign Kamqauter man the systems analyser, FO Pepperat see to the fire in the main computer bank. Hurry Captain Carrot; Ahh.. Ahh, we don't have much time."

"Hold on Captain Peabazzare we are doing all that we can, Ensign Broccleman status report?" said the Captain activating his personal channel.

"I am finding it very hard to maintain the link Captain, we have taken on board nine hundred and sixty-seven crew so far, with respect it's bedlam down here Sir." The noise in the background proving the point Ensign Broccleman was trying to make. A mixture of cries could be heard, pain, anger and relief. Still running through the mind of Captain Carrot was this lone thought; traumatised, hurt and angry they may be, but they were safe, that was the important thing. However they must be aware that some of their colleagues were as yet, not so fortunate. This would be sufficient to cause anguish and anxiety amongst the crew. Organitron's were by tradition an extremely compassionate, protective, caring and sensitive collection of Races.

"If you want to imagine bedlam Ensign Broccleman, try putting yourself in the position of the crew on the O.S.S Satsumuroo." responded the Captain.

"That's not what I meant Sir, but I take your point. Don't you worry Sir, they haven't invented a Sodium Star belt that can beat Ensign Bart Broccleman. There are substantial numbers of injured Captain, the Medilab is reaching saturation point Sir." replied Ensign Broccleman.

Captain Carrot directed his attention back to the Captain and Crew of the O.S.S Satsumuroo

"Keep hanging on Captain Peabazzare, we are nearly there, just hold on."

Captain Peabazzare was coughing heavily now and the sense of urgency on the bridge was becoming electric. S.F.A Ducarrotain was sitting pensively in FO Marrowlar's secondary Command com chair.

"The heat is becoming unbearable, hard to breath, Ahh.. Ahh. Ah, please hurry Captain, Ahh.. Ahh.. Ahh hurry." came the desperate response of a choking Captain Peabazzare.

Captain Carrot was sitting tentatively on the edge of his seat.

"FO Marrowlar can you give me any indications as to how many people are left on board?" enquired the Captain, desperately aware that time was running out, without any indication of fatalities they were struggling in the dark.

"No Sir, we are too far from the ship, the Sodium Star belt is blocking our scanners." reasoned FO Marrowlar.

"Captain Peabazzare we are nearly there. You must hold on. Do you hear me?" Just to keep him talking would help, thought Captain Carrot.

"I hear you Captain, but it is running late and I fear our time is nearly up." confirmed Captain Peabazzare.

"Hold on my friend, we will get you out of there I promise, just hold on." said Captain Carrot awaiting his reply, but there was nothing but flames crackling in the background.

"Captain Peabazzare keep talking to me, we've come this far don't give up on us now!" shouted Captain Carrot anxiously.

Then, within seconds there was an explosion. It seemed to last forever over the Communications com, the faces of the bridge crew showing every shock wave. Viceroy Rhubarblatt confirmed slowly that the ship had disappeared off the Grid Finder.

"I regret to inform you Captain, the O.S.S Satsumuroo no longer registers on the Grid Finder," Viceroy Rhubarblatt turned to offer his condolences to the stone faced Captain. "I'm sorry Sir, if it's any consolation Captain, you did everything you could and more."

Captain Carrot sat back slowly in his seat holding his head in his hands, a tear breaking the surface of his face.

"FO Marrowlar," enquired Captain Carrot. "do you confirm?" he continued.

"Sir," said FO Marrowlar with great sadness. "the Particle scanner confirms a Calorific Electro Proton explosion at the exact co-ordinates of the O.S.S Satsumuroo"

"You tried your best Captain, frankly under the circumstances what you achieved was nothing short of a miracle, both you and your crew did sterling work." expressed Admiral Ducarrotain holding his head.

Then he sat up and tried to bring the bridge crew back to reality.

But," he continued. "you my dear friend broke the third rule of Organitron, never make a promise you cannot keep." continued the Admiral. Captain Carrot raised his head slowly then clearing his throat and activating his personal channel, he called Ensign Broccleman.

"None of us are perfect Admiral, believe me, I only wish we were, just maybe life would sometimes not be quite so hard and for once, be oh so simple."

Admiral Ducarrotain nodded with quiet respect for the Captain's sentiment.

"Ensign Broccleman come in." commanded Captain Carrot activating his personal channel.

"Ensign Broccleman here Sir," he said with a chirpy voice. "The final count of Vegitamised crew before the ship blew, was one thousand two hundred and thirty six."

"Thank you Ensign Broccleman, you did well I'm proud of you!"

"There was just one more thing Sir?" added Ensign Broccleman.

"Yes Ensign Broccleman, what is it?" enquired a sullen Captain Carrot.

Suddenly the voice that was last heard on the bridge of the O.S.S Satsumuroo came over the communication channel.

"The one thing that I like about you Captain Gillespie J. Carrot, is that you always keep your word, for that, I and the crew of the O.S.S Satsumuroo owe you everything!" announced the voice of Captain Peabazzare

The bridge crew jumped in jubilation as the Captain lunged from his chair.

"Welcome aboard Banier, I mean Captain Peabazzare!"

S.F.A Ducarrotain smiled at Captain Carrot softly.

"It looks like I broke the second rule of the Organitron," said Admiral Ducarrotain." Think before you speak and never speak too soon." he said shaking the hand of the proud and jubilant Captain. Mushroid Fungola got so excited, he scooted around the upper bay of the bridge straight into Ensign Melonture, carrying him for the remainder of his journey, One full circuit, then came to a sudden stop. Unfortunately, forcing Ensign Melonture to complete the last leg of the journey single handed, flying with fearful screams straight into the arms of Ensign Rasperillo.

The shock of Ensign Rasperillo's face bringing the bridge crew to a rapturous applause.

"A fine catch Ensign Rasperillo." laughed SO Tulipina. "It must be love." cried Mushroid Fungola.

"Why, I never knew you cared Ensign Melonture?" chuckled a rather dishevelled Ensign Rasperillo.

"I do believe it must be fate that draws us together Ensign Rasperillo?"
cried Ensign Melonture.

Captain Carrot, who was whisking Ensign Strawballis with a waltz at the Communications com, seemed to stop in his tracks, the look on his face changing to a cold and empty stare. The feeling of electricity soon changing to one of stark humility.

"I know what you are thinking." said Admiral Ducarrotain. "Captain Carrot you did well for those who were living, you cannot ponder on the loss of a crew that you could not help."

"We have just lost four hundred and thirty six Organimen and Organiwomen. We will have to prepare full reports and dossiers at once, their families must be informed as soon as possible. "Ensign Strawballis put me on the ship's communicator."

"Aye, aye Sir, you're on line Sir."

"This is Captain Carrot, welcome aboard the O.S.S.S Earthanon." Captain Carrot addressed the ship quietly marking the respect of the Crew of the O.S.S Satsumuroo that were not fortunate enough to make it back.

"As you are no doubt aware," he continued "some of your friends and colleagues did not make it back. The Sun-Fleet Admiralty commend your bravery. You were strong and resilient but unfortunately time ran out. They will be remembered as they were, heroes to our cause. Those requiring medical attention report to Dr Kiwitranus in the emergency sickbay on deck C where the emergency Medical team are standing by. The time is now Twelve hundred starhectoids. All able bodied personnel, please report to Ensign Kamqauter in the accommodation sector on deck I. I'm sure you would all like time to freshen up and perhaps rest a while. All those pronounced fit for active duty, please report to SO Okralate at fifteen hundred thirty starhectoids in the observation deck where you will be issued with work stations according to your experience. In honour of those lost from the crew of the O.S.S Satsumuroo all Personnel will observe a two minute silence at fourteen hundred thirty starhectoids. It is our intention to initiate the mass evacuation of the Earthanon surface as of fourteen hundred thirty two starhectoids. Recent unfortunate events have dictated that your path of destiny lies here with us on the O.S.S.S Earthanon. Here you will stay on board as active crew members for the duration of the evacuation." Captain Carrot paused momentarily to gather his thoughts.

"If any of you feel it necessary to talk to someone about your experiences, then by all means make full use of the ships Councillor, Viceroy Au Paw-Paw. This is Captain Carrot UFO and out."

Sitting down in the Command com chair Captain Carrot activated his personal channel.

"This is Captain Carrot to Ensign Broccleman come in." he said slowly.

"Ensign Broccleman here Sir."

"Is Captain Peabazzare still with you in the Vegimatter room?" enquired the Captain.

"Yes Sir he is," confirmed Ensign Broccleman. "shall I put him on line?" he enquired.

"Yes please Ensign Broccleman."

Captain Carrot sat back and awaited Captain Peabazzare.

"This is Captain Peabazzare. Thank you for those kind words Captain Carrot, but please do not carry such a heavy heart my friend, the crew had already perished. The bridge is always the last station to be Vegitamised. The ship's computer would have scanned the whole ship looking for signs of life. You know that, it comes with the job."

Captain Carrot knew that he was right, and yet somehow, deep inside he also knew the job was not always the most pleasant of positions. At times like this he would gladly swap with a civilian.

"Thank you Captain." he said half heartedly. "Captain Peabazzare I will have Ensign Broccleman settle you and the bridge crew into the guest suites as soon as possible. You should be most comfortable there. I am sorry to press you Captain Peabazzare, but time is of a premium. I wonder if you and the bridge crew could join me in my strategy room at fourteen hundred thirty starhectoids for a de-briefing. I'm sure any information you can provide will help us in the evacuation process."

"Of course Captain Carrot." came his reply.

"Until then Captain Peabazzare, Captain Carrot out."

Captain Carrot turned to Admiral Ducarrotain who was looking very tired at this point.

"Ensign Broccleman come in." ordered Captain Carrot.

"Aye Sir. Ensign Broccleman here."

"Have the Admiralty guest suite prepared for Admiral Ducarrotain would you?"

"I already have Ensign Spinacher on that detail Sir, it's ready when the Admiral is Captain."

"Very good Ensign, Captain Carrot out."

"Ensign Broccleman out Sir."

"Come Admiral Ducarrotain," said the Captain, "let me show you to your quarters. I'm sure you would appreciate the opportunity to write your reports in peace?"

"Yes that would be most gratifying Captain Carrot thank you."

"I will see you at the de-briefing Sir?"

"Indeed Captain, I am as anxious as you are to hear what we are up against."

As Admiral Ducarrotain struggled out of his chair. Captain Carrot took his arm as he helped him up the stairs. When they reached the elevation chamber, Captain Carrot addressed the bridge crew.

"You have all served Sun-fleet and UFO well today. I am proud of all of you. It is my genuine belief that I am the most fortunate Captain in Sun-Fleet. When it comes to crew determination and perseverance, take it from me, you are the tops. And that is an under estimate." Captain Carrot gave them the Organitron salute and turned to Ensign Strawballis.

"Ensign Strawballis, is the report from the landing party ready?"

"Aye, aye Sir. It is ready when you are."

"Very good I will receive it in my quarters."

"Captain Carrot, here are the writs for the civilian freighters you required." gruffed the Admiral with the writs in his out-stretched, shaky hand.

"Thank you Admiral," said Captain Carrot taking them from Admiral Ducarrotain and handing them to FO Marrowlar.

"FO Marrowlar. Will you contact the freighter Transportation unit on Earthanon surface, and prepare to start the Vegitamisation of the Vegimatter stockpiles into the civilian freighter holds. Maintain a secured frequency channel. I will leave it to you to organise the fighter squadron formations in order to protect the convoy. Might I suggest that you update your statistics on the fighter squadron's capabilities with Commander Marrachinello. We must leave nothing to chance. If this operation is to be a success every detail must be set in concrete and we must be aware of our limitations."

"Aye, aye Sir." retorted FO Marrowlar as Captain Carrot turned his attention towards Ensign Viola.

"Ensign Viola. Can you plot a course around the Sodium Star belt with its estimated position at twenty two hundred starhectoids."

"Aye, aye Sir, I will have it ready in one Starhectoid, Captain." agreed Ensign Viola. SO Tulipina approached the Captain handing him the ship's log which he signed and handed back to her.

"Very good SO Tulipina. FO Marrowlar, if there are any problems I will be in my quarters."

"Yes Captain." said FO Marrowlar standing to attention.

Captain Carrot de-energised the elevation chamber doors. Leading the Admiral in to the chamber, Ensign Rasperillo announced their departure bringing the bridge to attention.

"Admiral off the bridge." he Shouted as Ensign Melonture piped them off the bridge. "Pheweeeeee... Phewoooooh."

"FO Marrowlar, you have Command com." confirmed Captain Carrot.

"Thank you Captain." said FO Marrowlar taking control of the Command com as the doors to the elevation chamber closed.

"Stand easy on the bridge." he muttered sitting in the chair.

"Ensign Strawballis, get me the transport unit on Earthanon Surface, then contact Commander Marrachinello. Have him draw up the available statistics for the squadron Star Fighter fleet. I want a breakdown of all grounded ships undergoing repair, complete with a time table to get them in flying in the air no matter what it takes. When the report is complete inform him to stand by his Computron and await further contact from myself."

"Aye, aye Sir."

After showing the Admiral to his quarters, Captain Carrot made his way towards his personal quarters. It was time for him to take a well-earned regeneration period. He decided that he should take the opportunity to receive a double dose of photosynthesis radiatory particles. "Who knows," he thought, "I may not get another chance before this is all over." De-energising the doors to his quarters, he activated his personal channel.

"Captain Carrot to FO Marrowlar come in please."

"FO Marrowlar here, Sir."

"FO Marrowlar, have all personnel roistered to double photosynthesis regeneration breaks, then afterwards have them report to the minimisation suite. In order to conserve energy, have them operate at seventy five percent stature. This could save valuable energised proteins, besides," he continued, "we can't be sure that the previously set roster will be maintainable. The last thing we need is to concern ourselves with the ship's crew going down in mass with non- eneringeritis."

"I will get on to it immediately, Captain." replied FO Marrowlar. "Captain Carrot," he continued. "might I suggest Sir? It might be wise to reactivate the Calorific reactors to increase our energy output capability. This will allow us to activate the regeneration intensifier and cut down the regeneration period by half."

"Very good FO Marrowlar I will leave it in your more than capable hands. I will be taking my regeneration period now. You can expect me back on the bridge in three starhectoids."

"Aye, aye Sir, will you be requiring an alarm call?" said FO Marrowlar.

"No, that won't be necessary thank you. Until then, Captain Carrot out."

"FO Marrowlar out."

Carrelda, Caroon and Carab were sitting at the table eating supper when he sneaked up behind Caroon and placed his hands over her eyes. She shrieked as her world sank into darkness and her pretty pink ribbons bobbed with excitement.

"Well now who is this sitting in my chair? Perhaps a little Appleoneon dumpling? I think not. I have it, you're the roving Pirate Radishared of Radichgrub. No; no, far too big. Why, it's the delectable Caroon Carrot, daughter of the strikingly handsome and debonair Gillespie J. Carrot. Adonis of the Space Race Carridionaries."

Caroon turned and jumped up into her father's arms nestling her nose into the shoulders of his slender frame.

"Oh father," she shrilled loudly. "you didn't really know who I was, did you?"

Captain Carrot looked lovingly into her eyes. Rubbing her nose with his, he whispered.

"Of course not my darling. I would spot the most beautiful Organigirl within ten thousand starmillo's without any problem at all."

Caroon smiled and whispered into her father's ear, as they both laughed loudly. Gillespie's Organiwife Carrelda Carrot turned scornfully, playfully poking him in the ribs.

"What are you two plotting now?" she enquired.

"Our beautiful bright little button here has quite rightly pointed out that you my love, are the most beautiful Organigirl in the Earthanon Galaxy. So if I want any supper like a good Organiboy, I should demote her to the second most beautiful Organigirl within twenty thousand starmillo's." he said, proceeding to tickle Caroon on her tummy.

"I should think so too." said Carrelda.

Their laughter could be heard echoing in the passage way outside the Captains quarters. The ship's crew walking past trying desperately to ignore the loud shrills emanating from the Captains quarters.

"Huh, difficult life this Captain lark." laughed the Ensign Gingertree as he mimicked the famed walk of the Captain.

"Don't let the Captain catch you Hugo. He will have you in the brig for sure!" said Ensign Garlicatara.

"Good I could use the holiday." he retorted as they both chuckled their way to the accommodation block.

Part two

Oh what an Atmosphere!

Meanwhile, down on the surface of Earthanon in the Arcticus district, FO Potatree was in the inspection tunnels within the vast complex of the Planetary light sensors, which were situated at the top of the communication tower high above the Earthanon surface. From a distance, they resembled great shiny mushrooms covered in magnified plasma reflector panels that directed and stored the Sun's Solar energy in vast Trio-anthellite coils that run up the central column.

"Ensign Fenneltra." boomed FO Potatree's voice as his head was stuck in a small access point in the main hub of the Planetary light sensors and the acoustics exaggerated his tone. "Hand me the binary climatic solenoid wrench please." he continued. Ensign Fenneltra was looking over the vast expanse set before him. It was beautiful; luscious in its evergreen plantation splendour. Then mistakenly looking down, his nerves wavered forcing him to steady himself on a nearby handrail, as the slight breeze brushed through his hair and he become light headed at the dizzy sight set below him.

"Oh my goodness," he yelped with shock. "such a long drop. Have you seen how far it is down to the ground FO Potatree?" he asked with his eyes clamped shut.

"Aye sonny I have, and if you don't keep your mind on the job I'll help you measure it, the quick way." said FO Potatree.

"There's no need to be like that Sir," said Ensign Fenneltra. "I was only making an observation. Honestly, ever since you emerged from that Voidwell you have been so tetchy. he continued."

"Ensign Fenneltra," snapped FO Potatree. "I may be getting on a tad; some might argue that my mind is not what it used to be. However, I must tell you something that may shock you." he said coming down the ladder waving his finger towards Ensign Fenneltra as if to whisper into his ear. Stepping forward to receive the hush-hush information, Ensign Fenneltra placed his ear within close range. FO Potatree looked around, cunningly aware that walls have ears.

"What is it Sir?" enquired Ensign Fenneltra with baited breath.

"I'm not blind you know, my vision is as good today, as it was the day I was born!" he shrilled into Ensign Fenneltra's ear almost making him jump out of his skin so that he banged his head on the plasma steel girder above where he was standing.

"Ow. Ow. Ow oooh! There's no need to be so touchy Chief." commented Ensign Fenneltra observing stars flying around his head.

FO Potatree shrugged his shoulders, then looking around in the tool bag he started to mutter to himself.

"I ask for a simple tool! And all you offer me is you, I could hardly call you anything other than simple sometimes. I don't know! Might as well get it myself now that I'm here!" grumbled the Chief

"Get what Sir? If you wanted something you only had to ask!" moaned Ensign Fenneltra.

"I did ask you great lump of aniseed weed." snapped FO Potatree.

"Oh well, if you are going to start being rude." said Ensign Fenneltra stamping his feet. "I'll leave you to search on your own! It is quite windy up here you know. You were probably mumbling as usual. I mean, how I can be expected to hear you up here if you mumble?" shrugged a defiant and hurt Ensign Fenneltra.

"So," said FO Potatree. "Not only am I blind, but," he continued. "I'm incoherent now. Ensign Fenneltra have you ever stopped to think that you might simply be deaf, umm... umm, well?"

"Nonsense Chief. My hearing is perfect!"

"OK Smarty pants. If your ears are perfect let's test your eye sight. Tell me! Where is the binary climatic solenoid wrench, eh?" quipped the Chief Engineer as he smirked tapping his foot. "You haven't packed it have you?" he continued.

"It's err, well Chief it's like this, how can I put this?" paused Ensign Fenneltra. "No there's no other way, I'll just have to come straight out with it. It's in your pocket." said Ensign Fenneltra desperately trying to curb his laughter.

FO Potatree looked in his back pocket and found the wrench. Slowly a smile crossed his face and he turned to climb the ladder. Gingerly he turned to Ensign Fenneltra.

"Ensign Fenneltra, will you make a mental note that I think I need my eyes tested? Oh, and in case my memory is failing, remind me when we get back on board the O.S.S.S Earthanon, but quietly you understand, mum's the word!"

"Aye Sir." said the Ensign.

FO Potatree activated his personal channel.

"FO Potatree to FO Cornelius, come in please."

"FO Cornelius here. Yes, FO Potatree what do you have to report?"

"I have overhauled the Planetary light sensors, but short of a little corrosion on some of the contacts they are in perfect working order. The problem isn't here."

"Have you checked the solar panel directional energy banks?" enquired FO Cornelius.

"Aye Sir, all systems are Ay'Ok. We are down to 17 blimits below usual levels." confirmed FO Potatree.

"Can you think of anything that could be causing this deficiency FO Potatree?" asked FO Cornelius.

"It's a long shot Sir, but we are going to run some diagnostic tests on the ultra ray reflector shields. It is possible that the shield has condensed itself somehow and is blocking the heat as well as the ultra violet rays."

"Go to it my friend, keep me informed won't you? As soon as you find anything, I mean anything at all, let me know understood?"

"Aye Sir, rest assured when I know, you will be the first to hear."

"Very good FO Potatree. Carry on, FO Cornelius over and out."

"FO Potatree out." Pausing, he consulted the Earthanon charts.

"Right," snapped FO Potatree. "let's get over to the filtration reactors over in section C 17 and see if we can't find this little bug in the system."

Ensign Fenneltra packed the tool bag then they set off carefully down the long shaft towards the Earthanon surface.

Back at the command module, at the hub of the Arcticus mining operation in the City of Arcticon, Commodore Cu-Cumbala and FO Melonicord were preparing the preliminary plans for the mass evacuation of the Earthanon.

"Viceroy Marrachellan, have your security forces found any infiltrators among the communities?" asked Commodore Cu-Cumbala on his personal channel.

"Not as yet Sir, but we are checking all areas as fast as we can!" confirmed Viceroy Marrachellan.

"Very good, keep me informed as to your progress. Any infiltrators found must be held in the brig house under the strictest security. This is Commodore Cu-Cumbala over and out."

"Aye, aye Sir, Viceroy Marrachellan over and out."

"Carry on FO Melonicord." asked Commodore Cu-Cumbala.

"Thank you Sir. As I see it Commodore Cu-Cumbala, with the re-organisation of the freighter fleet, combined with all Sun-ships and the Mother fleet; we can initiate the evacuation and have the manoeuvre completed in six starhectoids."

"Is that not going to strain the power supply FO Melonicord? Surely, we could seriously overload the proton reactors to near melt down if we run the Vegitamisation suits, the regeneration reactors and the minimise stature chambers fluctuation energy banks to full capacity. Is that not so FO Melonicord?" reasoned Commodore Cu-Cumbala.

"I think we can avoid this Sir," said FO Melonicord. "but it means organising ourselves with absolute precision. If we begin to reduce the workforce to minimise stature immediately, then we should be able to complete the reduction programme in a little under one and a half starhectoids. Then, we divert the minimisation fluctuators' energy banks power source to the regeneration reactors. These will be coupled to the mother ships back-up Proton reactors in the auxiliary banks. Leaving the Earthanon Proton reactors free, thus allowing them to deal solely with priority Vegitamising of the Earthanon crew to all standby ships. The ships by this stage, will be positioned at set co-ordinates within the Atmosphere of Earthanon. The Mother-ships main Vegimatter computers will be pre-loaded with the transfer ships co-ordinates, then networked for maximum efficiency; automatically calculating the destination ship's capacity by linking with that ship's main computer." explained FO Melonicord.

Commodore Cu-Cumbala, was now looking deeply disturbed, feeling the tension running through his body faster than a Splutterbun stampede, he began to reminisce of things past and present of Earthanon.

Splutterbuns were his favourite of the Soya carnivore breeds that the Organitron bred from Soya / Vegimatter / Meatermatter substitute. A cross between a kangaroo, a dog and a rabbit, all cuddly with floppy ears and massive feet. As FO Melonicord informed him of the planned evacuation proposals his mind wandered to the things he loved about Earthanon and the sights he would miss. Sights such as the Rugerplotts grazing the plains much more graceful and far less energetic than the Splutterbun it's a sort of cross between a horse and a cow, and Dindivar; (a cross between a horse and a camel with a touch of giraffe thrown in for good measure) roaming freely on the Earthanon surface, surviving on the naturally sown vegetation and wild-life native to Earthanon.

"FO Melonicord," said Commodore Cu-Cumbala, snapping back to reality. "Do you honestly think it is better to minimise now, why not when they get to the ships?" questioned Ground Commodore Cu-Cumbala.

"Three reasons Commodore; firstly; this way as soon as the ship's capacity is reached, they can depart at hyperspace K Factor speed from the

Earthanon Atmosphere immediately. Something that we could not do in full stature, due to the weight ratios placing dangerously high stress factors on the ship's structure. Secondly;" she continued. "the Sodium Star belt is increasing its speed as it approaches Earthanons gravitational pull. We may need the hyperspace K Factor capacity to out-manoeuvre the Sodium Star belt in a hurry. Thirdly; FO Marrowlar is convinced after talking to Professor Goosegorgon, that the infiltrators cannot alter the perimeters of the Eggello sulphur gas energy field that makes the cloaking devise possible.

In short," she continued. "Vegitamisation wouldn't work on them. The field would block the affects of the Vegimatter particle beam. This will enable us to round up the infiltrators quickly, without diverting manpower resources from the task ahead." explained FO Melonicord.

Commodore Cu-Cumbala sat back in admiration of the organisation and the calmness in which all angles were covered as a matter of course.

"FO Melonicord you have done an excellent job." he admitted. "I have every faith in the abilities of you and the ship with which you serve. Captain Carrot is the most respected Captain in the UFO organisation. Frankly I am amazed at the efficiency with which the O.S.S.S Earthanon operates. Tell me, how much of that is his guidance, and how much is your natural abilities?"

FO Melonicord stood silently pondering the question. She turned to Commodore Cu-Cumbala smiling wryly.

"Commodore Cu-Cumbala." she said Captain Carrot's infinite wisdom and ability to lead with compassion and firm direction has become the directional beam for all our natural abilities. "In short Commodore Cu-Cumbala; our abilities are just an extension of his."

Commodore Cu-Cumbala stood up from his desk and walked towards the observation window. The Earthanon skies were bright blue, tinged with brilliant orange ridges of cloud setting off the natural beauty of the carefully landscaped natural foliage. "All this work;" he thought, "it would indeed be a wrench to leave such an idyllic and tranquil paradise.

"Do you know Earthanon and its history well FO Melonicord." asked the Commodore.

"I have only been stationed on the O.S.S.S Earthanon for two Startechtoids Commodore but what I have seen of it is beautiful. As for its history? Well, let's just say it was not my favourite subject at school." she said slightly embarrassed.

"It had been a good home for thousands, millions of Startechtoids, to generations of Organitron's." stated Commodore Cu-Cumbala. "Billions of Startechtoids if one took into account the first two settlements of our long past pioneering ancestors. You see FO Melonicord, history has a nasty habit of repeating itself. For example, the first inhabitation ceased abruptly by the onslaught of what became known as the big freeze Ice age. What we are facing now is the return of Aqua Asteroids. The second evacuation was caused by the sudden introduction of a particularly fierce breed of Dinosaur, known as the Tyrannosaurus Rex. Unlike the other Dinosaur's who were very friendly and had learnt to communicate Tyrannosaurus Rex was to become a real blighter. Hiding behind it's old clothes and principles of friendly ally and yet harbouring a secret agenda. Becoming rather partial to the Organitron race as a food supplement, it forced the Organitron to flee in desperation once again. Only returning under top security to maintain the Vegimatter programmes. Such was the importance of this place that we take for granted. Oh, of course we are no longer under threat of the Dinosaurs but we have Fasterfoids to contend with masquerading as something they are not. Organitron's, of all the nerve! and there agenda may not be so underhand as the Dinosaurs yet they are as equally filled with arrogance and false notions of supremacy. In both cases the Organitron's, switching their main operational base to the underground star station of Silicone sphere, and the new Planets of Minestrone, Mixed Vegaris, Fruitalia Salaard, Crushtonutes, and Casserule. Thinking about it though, the Dinosaur's inhabitation probably saved many Organitron lives. Although it was true they managed to live in harmony for nearly three million years, Tyrannosaurus Rex reared its ugly head, forcing the Organitron to vacate the Planet. The Dinosaurs were to inhabit the Planet for nearly one hundred and sixty million years. The climate of Earthanon grew to such intensity, finally comets rained down bombarding Earthanon, ridding the Planet of the Dinosaurs forever. Who knows what might have happened if the Organitron's were sharing Earthanon too? Would we still be here I wonder?" proposed Commodore Cu-Cumbala. "It was unfortunate that it wiped out all living things, foliage included but in hindsight, was it faith that prevented our race from following the same path? The Organitron's are a feisty and stubborn breed of races. It was a further Eighty two million years before Earthanons blimit levels had cooled sufficiently enough to re-inhabit. Leaving the Organitron's the massive task of establishing the new ecosystem that exists and flourishes today. The third new start to Sundate. Yes indeed, this Planet had given up much of its natural minerals and resources. Unwittingly and unreservedly, allowing the construction of the new Planets to house the ever increasing population and over spill of the Organitron Space Races. Now, Earthanon looks certain to be wiped of all life again in yet another big freeze perhaps, some two hundred and twenty million years after the Dinosaurs departure. The work-all that work washed away in one foul swoop. Yes history repeats itself all right, mark my words FO Melonicord!" then Commodore Cu-Cumbala sank into a far and distant land at the back of his mind. The land of what once was.

FO Melonicord tried to gain the attention of Commodore Cu-Cumbala.

"Commodore Cu-Cumbala," she said. "excuse me Sir?" Still there was no reply. "Ahhh.. Ahhh." spluttered FO Melonicord.

Commodore Cu-Cumbala snapped out of his trance.

"I'm sorry FO Melonicord, what were you saying? I'm afraid my passions run high for this place. Many of us have come to know it as home. Many of our children were born here and have grown to love it. Many of our ancestors died in the settlement wars protecting it, not forgetting the hard but fruitful labours of the Foliage Farming establishment programme. To evacuate and leave it to face the elements again with almost certain destruction is such a wrench." said Commodore Cu-Cumbala feeling the warmth and anxiety of reminiscing the good old days.

"I was merely seeking confirmation of your agreement to the plan of evacuation Sir?" responded FO Melonicord.

"Indeed FO Melonicord, you have my full backing and admiration. It is a brilliant plan, well thought out and covering all possible scenarios."

"Thank you Commodore Cu-Cumbala. If you have no objections I will inform FO Marrowlar of the finalised plan." Commodore Cu-Cumbala nodded in agreement as he gazed at the picture of his family that took pride of place on his desk.

FO Melonicord activated her personal secure channel.

"FO Melonicord to FO Marrowlar, come in please."

"FO Marrowlar here, what do you have to report FO Melonicord?"

"We have completed and agreed provisional plans for the Earthanon evacuation Sir." said FO Melonicord.

"Is Commodore Cu-Cumbala happy with the proposed plan?" asked FO Marrowlar.

"Yes Sir, we worked on it together! Would you like to communicate with Commodore Cu-Cumbala, FO Marrowlar?" enquired FO Melonicord.

"It would be an honour FO Melonicord!" said FO Marrowlar.

"An honour indeed FO Marrowlar," interrupted Ground commodore Cu-Cumbala, "you obviously don't know my Organiwife Sir. Let me tell you this! She does not think so highly of me sometimes!" he said laughing. "I have agreed the plans FO Marrowlar, and I must say, they are of the most genius proportions thanks to FO Melonicord and Ensign Neeper's thorough research. I just hope they are achievable and there isn't something hiding in the background that we haven't covered." said commodore Cu-Cumbala.

"Good, I am pleased that you have reached agreement and so quickly," noted FO Marrowlar. "let us hope that all elements of the evacuation can be achieved as quickly without mishap or misjudgement., Captain Carrot has requested that you attend a meeting on board the O.S.S.S Earthanon Sir?" he continued.

"Indeed it will be a pleasure FO Marrowlar. When is the meeting to be scheduled?" asked Commodore Cu-Cumbala

"Fourteen hundred thirty starhectoids Sir, in the Captain's strategy room!" replied FO Marrowlar.

"Very well, I will attend. Prepare to receive me at thirteen forty five starhectoids FO Marrowlar. I will Vegitamise on board as I'm afraid all the shuttles are on leave recall repatriation duties." confirmed the Commodore.

"We look forward to your visit Commodore, until then Sir." said FO Marrowlar.

"Until then FO Marrowlar." confirmed Commodore Cu-Cumbala.

"FO Melonicord, will you be heading back to the O.S.S.S Earthanon now?" enquired FO Marrowlar.

"As soon as Ensign Neeper returns with the security clearance codes from the commandeered civilian freighters. We felt it necessary to check them thoroughly Sir. The possibility that one or more of the freighters is an undercover secret work base of the infiltrators is a realistic threat." responded FO Melonicord.

"Good thinking. It would be rather ironic if we were to deliver the Vegimatter straight into their holds. I will expect you then FO Melonicord, FO Marrowlar over and out."

"FO Melonicord over and out."

Across Arcticus City in the science block modules, FO Cornelius and Ensign Bananra were running Gasamatronic tests on the Earthanon Atmosphere in the laboratory. Trying to establish a natural elemental reason for the rapid blimit descent and / or to find a cure.

"Ensign Bananra. Could you place the tubes in the centrifugal cylinder?" shouted FO Cornelius above the noise of the proton chamber whilst placing the protective goggles around his neck.

"Certainly Sir." replied Ensign Bananra. "Shall I carry on running the Ionised laser particle scan on the Eggello sulphur gas or will you require my assistance?"

"Yes and no," replied FO Cornelius. "but when you run the scan make sure that you increase the energy field to allow for the Earthanon gravity factors! We don't want the sulphur gas to explode do we?" he chuckled.

"Will do FO Cornelius!" confirmed Ensign Bananra disappearing into the still room as FO Cornelius cranked up the proton reactors and moved behind the plate steel for protection from the ultra violet rays. Slowly the reactor began to increase its power while FO Cornelius moved his safety goggles into place. The centrifugal chamber started to glow inside with a bright red haze. Suddenly a loud explosion shook the laboratory filling it with dust particles as Ensign Bananra ran from the still room into the main lab to investigate.

"Are you all right Sir?" shouted Ensign Bananra loudly, searching for his superior Officer amongst the strewed wreckage.

"FO Cornelius. Talk to me! Where are you?" said Ensign Bananra listening for any signs of life from his colleague.

"Ensign Bananra? Who turned the lights out? I can't see a thing." answered the distressed voice of FO Cornelius.

As Ensign Bananra struggled to clear the broken furniture and building debris away from the damaged area when he did so, he revealed a very dirty and shaken FO Cornelius with a large bucket stuck over his head.

"What on Earthanon was that Sir?" asked Ensign Bananra trying to prize the remainder of the debris away from the immediate area.

"Oh Bananra, thank Helios you are OK. Be careful now, the power is down; there are likely to be live cables all over the place. Watch your step, are you all right?" he asked struggling to his feet banging his head against several fallen girders and roof sections, the resonance and vibrations causing him much ear splitting distress. Gradually the vibrations travelled the length of his body causing him to collapse in a gibbering heap as his knees turned to jelly.

"Yes thank you Sir," answered Ensign Bananra fighting to contain his laughter. "D. d.. d.. don't worry Sir the power is still on its just that you... ,"

"You mean I am blind?" interrupted FO Cornelius. "This is awful!" he continued growing very distressed. "Oh Helios, why me? Will mine eyes be denied the spectacle of a setting sun forever? Hatchooo!" Boing. "Ow!.." Shall my gaze never fall just once more on my sweet homelands of Cornmaizerite or your Bananjous; and perforated eardrums to boot, oh, oh woe is me. Hatchooo.. Hatchooo.. Thud, bang, wallop, ooh!" he cried.

"No FO Cornelius, now calm down. Come along now." exclaimed Ensign Bananra grasping the fearful shoulders of the panic stricken FO Cornelius. "Rest assured you are not blind. What you can hear is merely an echo, not the result of perforated eardrums believe me." shouted Ensign Bananra reassuringly.

"Thank you Ensign Bananra you are very kind, but please, tell me the truth no matter how awful it will be for me to bear." begged FO Cornelius.

"So you want the truth do you FO Cornelius?" asked Ensign Bananra giggling. "Well the truth is this, you have a bucket stuck over your head."

Then unable to resist the temptation any longer he broke down with an uncontrollable fit of hysteria, as a shocked and embarrassed FO Cornelius felt his head.

"Well then why didn't you tell me you great oaf? Ensign Bananra I hope you are not laughing at my misfortune? If you are, rest assured once this thing is off you will face the full force of my displeasure!" shouted FO Cornelius, causing yet more vibrations and deafening sound. "Ba... Ba... Ba... Bananra," he whispered. "get this blessed thing off me will you? Please." said FO Cornelius calmly. Ensign Bananra stood over FO Cornelius as he collapsed on the floor.

"Yes. I think perhaps you are right FO Cornelius besides you do look a little pale." he laughed placing his knees on FO Cornelius's shoulders and pulling at the bucket, "Aaaaahhhhh... Pop! Owee shmowee!" cried FO Cornelius rubbing his eyes then adjusting his sights on Ensign Bananra. "For once I do believe Ensign Bananra, I am pleased to see you." said FO Cornelius smiling.

"Thank you FO Cornelius," said Ensign Bananra nervously. "I do believe I am glad to see you safe and sound Sir." he continued crawling to his utmost capacity.

"However Ensign Bananra," sneered FO Cornelius. "if I hear you tell a soul about this little episode, then I will be pleased to see only the back of you. Have you posted to the Bapmacdo Aurora observation post perhaps, is that clear?" threatened the ruffled FO Cornelius as Ensign Bananra brushed off the dust from FO Cornelius's tunic.

"You have my word FO Cornelius. Not a soul!" confirmed Ensign Bananra offering FO Cornelius the Organitron salute. FO Cornelius walked towards the charred remains of the proton reactor which was bellowing smoke like the oil in a Fasterfoids week-old rejuvenation chamber. He reached inside and pulled from it the remains of the centrifugal chamber.

"Blast." exclaimed a bemused FO Cornelius.

Ensign Bananra looked around the destroyed Laboratory. "A-1 one for observation FO Cornelius. Nothing gets past you does it!" he said under his breath.

"What did you say Ensign Bananra?" growled FO Cornelius.

"What was the experimentation Sir; quite something of a blast, what caused it I... Ah... I won... der, I wonder?" he reasoned quickly.

"Oh yes well, It's simple really," explained FO Cornelius. "You see, I can't find anything in the Earthanon Atmosphere that could possibly cause the blimit level reductions. So I thought that if tried to find something to put into the Atmosphere that would protect the Earthanon surface, it might be possible to reduce the heat loss or stop it all together. Just to stabilise the situation would be acceptable. You know, by creating a sort of chemical ecosphere; an invisible hot-house environment you see?" explained FO Cornelius.

"Isn't the protective layer gas belt theory that you and Professor Goosegorgon are working on anywhere near completion FO Cornelius?" enquired Ensign Bananra.

"We are having some teething problems with the mixture of elements. We can create a protective belt to replace the old Planetary light sensors, and the ultra violet protective shields. Then when there is a fluctuation in the oxygen levels it breaks down and becomes fragile." choked FO Cornelius as he continued to brush himself down.

"So what caused the explosion Sir?" asked Ensign Bananra.

"Let me see if I can make this simple." FO Cornelius paced up and down as he began to explain. "Well," he continued. "at the moment we have an atmosphere of seventy percent Nitrogen, twenty nine percent Oxygen, point three percent CO^2 the remaining point seven is a mixture of other inert gases; helium and so on." he said. "When Earthanon was discovered by our ancestors, it was ninety five percent nitrogen and five percent inert gases. Not perfect for our inhabitation, but adaptable. So the new formula was arrived at in accordance with those used on our home Planets. The mixture was at first pumped out to create a constant Atmosphere, then after planting various natural ecosystems, the entire Atmosphere became supplied by one hundred percent natural foliage." continued FO Cornelius in his element. "However, because we could not and still cannot contain this layer of Earthanon Atmosphere, it rapidly dissipates into space leaving cracks in the protection layer. The result allowing the more undesirable elements through the protective layer from outer space; such as Ultra Violet and Gamma rays as well as Radiation particles, all of which are extremely harmful to the Organitron and the ecosystem farming programme. Now that the air's natural balance is totally provided by the natural foliage during the light cycles, we still have to top up the natural production to shore up any cracks that start to appear, but these are generally confined to the night cycle when photosynthesis levels are at a minimum. For generations," continued FO Cornelius as Ensign Bananra felt sorry that he asked the question. "we have tried to create a corridor of heavier air, about a half mile wide to effectively sit on top of the lighter air, holding it down while the lighter air atmosphere holds it up, If you like, the perfect partnership, a zoning layer!" FO Cornelius looked around the dishevelled lab that now looked more like a municipal tip than a laboratory.

"That is what I was trying to achieve." he said sitting down and holding his head in his hands. "I tried using a Hydrogen gas mixed in very small quantities with pure oxygen to act as a stabilising agent. But, as you can see that didn't work. One doesn't have to look too hard to establish the results were a little, shall we say, shocking!"

Both Ensign Bananra and FO Cornelius looked around the laboratory and laughed as a large globe fell of its stand and rolled backwards and forwards eventually coming to rest at their feet.

"I think you mean rocking Sir." Eventually, containing the laughter FO Cornelius pulled himself together and activated his personal channel.

"FO Cornelius to Professor Goosegorgon. come in over."

Professor Goosegorgon was sitting in his laboratory running diagnostics on the Eggello sulphur gas.

"Why does it'a stay in is'a perimeters to an exact specification? The infiltrators must'a be able to breathe. Maybe they are using artificial breathing apparatus? No, that would only serve to limit the amount of time they might remain cloaked." he reasoned to himself

"FO Cornelius to Professor Goosegorgon come in over!" repeated FO Cornelius.

"Professor Goosegorgon here, what'a can I do for a 'you FO Cornelius?" replied the Professor.

"Professor Goosegorgon." said FO Cornelius. "we can't find any reasons in the Atmospheric condition to suggest that it could be the cause of the blimit reduction problem. I think," he continued. "this calls for a change of direction as to where we are looking Professor. I was wondering if you had come up with any ideas with the gas layer we are working on. Working on the prevention being better than the cure syndrome you understand. I have tried to add one percent hydrogen as a stabilising agent, with seventy percent nitrogen twenty nine percent pure oxygen and two percent CO^2." he confirmed.

"Did the layer hold under the ultra violet particle test?" enquired Professor Goosegorgon.

"No Professor, it blew up the Laboratory." said FO Cornelius, with an embarrassed tone to his still shaky voice from the shock of the explosion.

"No doubt the hydrogen ignited under the pressure of ultra violet rays combined with radiation. I have been thinking along these lines myself FO Cornelius. After examining the Eggello sulphur gas, it has become obvious to me that the inner chamber, in which they must breath to survive, is filled with a substance to keep the sulphur gas from their respiratory organs." reasoned Professor Goosegorgon. Just then Ensign Bananra came running from the still room in excitement.

"FO Cornelius! Look at the spectrograph reading from the Ioniser." he said handing the scroll to FO Cornelius.

"Professor Goosegorgon, we think we have found something in the Ioniser spectrograph. What is it Ensign Bananra?"

"Oxygen, in a crude but simple form; a three molecular combination. They are attracted to each other yet remain individual in their own right, holding very tight together." said Ensign Bananra.

"Did you hear that Professor? Oxygen Molecules That is how they maintain the cloaking field. It appears, Professor, that they encapsulate air somehow carrying a constant release source. Surround it with the Eggello sulphur gas which is slightly lighter, due to its fine blasting with Cochinello protons. Then Wrapped in this Oxygen molecular mixture which is almost the same density but non-compatible, in turn held in place by the proton energy field, this simulates the Earthanon gravitational pull, keeping it all exactly in place."

"Oxygen molecular chaining, umm?" said the Professor. "Leave it with me FO Cornelius. I would like to run some comparitory tests. FO Cornelius if your right that means our zoning layer is closer to reality than we thought." Professor Goosegorgon thought momentarily and thumped the table. "It also means my friend that those dratted Fasterfoids have come up with it first yet again! I'll get back to you, over and out."

"FO Cornelius over and out." Then diverting his personal channel to the O.S.S.S Earthanon Communication's com, he called Ensign Strawballis.

"FO Cornelius to Ensign Strawballis come in, over."

"Ensign Strawballis here FO Cornelius."

"Please inform Captain Carrot and FO Marrowlar that, as yet we have not managed to find any abnormality in the Earthanon Atmosphere. We think however, we may have stumbled on a formula for the protective gas belt layer. Myself and Ensign Bananra will join up with security forces to retrieve their reports. As soon as they are complete we will Vegitamise back to the Mother ship in time for the de-briefing meeting at fourteen hundred thirty starhectoids. Please log this call as our monitored half Starhectoid check-in." requested FO Cornelius.

"Your message is received and understood, and your request is logged and acknowledged."

"Thank you Ensign Strawballis, this is FO Cornelius over and out."

"Ensign Strawballis over and out." Closing down the communications com, Ensign Strawballis turned toward FO Marrowlar who sat quietly over lording events on the bridge of the O.S.S.S Earthanon.

"Excuse me FO Marrowlar,"

"Yes Ensign Strawballis." asked FO Marrowlar.

"All three sections of the landing party have called in Sir. With your permission I will compile a report for your meeting at fourteen hundred thirty starhectoids."

"As you wish Ensign Strawballis. Tell me, are all shore leave personnel confirmed for recall?" enquired FO Marrowlar.

"All except the science party in the Europetriennes region Sir. I have issued a May-day call, it should only be a matter of time before they receive and acknowledge." confirmed Ensign Strawballis

"Keep me informed Ensign Strawballis, If they have not acknowledged within the next Starhectoid, we will take the precaution of sending out a Robopod!"

"Yes Sir, I have already taken the precaution of activating a Robopod. Its situated in the Port Launch pod section on alert. The transport Engineers are in possession of the necessary co-ordinates and are awaiting instructions to proceed."

"Very good Ensign Strawballis, make ready the probe on board computers. Instruct the Engineers to load the co-ordinates and place them on launch stand by."

FO Marrowlar nodded with satisfaction at the crew. It was a shining example of Captain Carrot's leadership quality that made the O.S.S.S Earthanon and her crew the envy of the UFO organisation. He was proud to be his, "No. Two" as well as, he hoped, his good friend and respected colleague. All he could think of was that one day he would Captain a Sun-class Ship himself; who knows maybe even a Mother-ship? If that path of destiny were to transpire then he certainly hoped his crew to be, were as proficient and dedicated to him as the good Captain Gillespie J. Carrot could command. Even in his absence he seemed to be present and in this there was a comfort. The Atmosphere of the Planet Earthanon was as fragile as that of the Organitron themselves. If either of them could be contained then Captain Carrot was the man to carry it through.

CHAPTER ELEVEN

For the good of all kind!

Part one

The beginning of the end!

TIME 13.30 starhectoids.

In Captain Carrot's quarters, the Captain and his family were deep in regeneration mode. Organitron's do this by sleeping in soil lined Vegewells (holes), soil from the individual's home Planet as a reminder of home and as a mark or respect to their roots. Sleeping with rainbow filaments pulsating overhead, this activates their energy cycle of photosynthesis rejuvenation. In the corner of the room there was a platinomic hour glass gradually running out. Organitron's sleep parallel in the ground as have generations before them since the beginning of time.

At exactly 13.30 starhectoids the last grain of platinum fell through the Starhectoid glass. As it did so, the Captain's Mushroid valet, Funguy, activated, propelling itself across the room with a tray of Verbena tea, pumpkin muffins and a selection of fresh crisp Vegimatter. Carrots, Lettuce, Broccoli and Cucumber. Fruits such as Melon, Grapefruit, Pineapple, Paw-Paw, Guava and Grapes. Funguy stood over the sleeping family and sighed as they stirred to the aroma of the feast that he had prepared. The first to awake as usual was Captain Carrot, his eyes sparkling with energy. He jumped out of his Vegewell disengaging the rainbow filaments and brushing down his silky green pyjamas.

"Happy awakening Captain Carrot," chirped Funguy as Captain Carrot stretched out his arms and yawned. Then after rubbing his eyes Captain Carrot proceeded to bend and touch his toes, followed by his usual twenty press-ups.

"Your shower is running and your clothes are set out in the anti-room. Will you take sustenance with your loved ones or shall we let them rest Sir?"

Captain Carrot looked upon his family. They looked so peaceful. Carrelda was talking in her sleep slowly, almost inaudible. It wasn't a bad dream by all accounts. Carrelda smiled as her dream took over her senses.

"No. No. Carab take the saucepan off you head." whispered Carrelda. "No, don't be silly darling, Daddy never wore a saucepan when he was a boy pretending to be a Sun-Fleet Officer. Oh no, Daddy used a colander and a wooden spoon for a blazer gun." Then she gave a little giggle and fell back into a deep sleep.

"Let them rest a little longer Funguy." said Captain Carrot trying to cover Carrelda's mutterings. Funguy disappeared into the anti-room laughing. "Colander and wooden spoon eh, now that I would love to have seen." tittered Funguy.

"Stop laughing Funguy, and might I add," said the Captain looking for Funguy. where are you Mushroid Funguy?" he said as Mushroid Funguy re-appeared under a tea towel at the service hatch. "Ahh there you are. As I was saying, you will forget what you have just heard or I will have Professor Goosegorgon erase your memory chips." teased the Captain.

"Me Captain?" shouted Funguy, "Why I never heard a thing Sir."

Carab was stirring now. Sucking his thumb loudly he turned away from the Captain. Caroon's bright green tails drooped over her face tickling her nose. Every now and then she would blow them clear and they would return. "Go away, phewoooooh, phewoooooh! It tickles go away. Naughty that's what you are. Yes, very naughty." said Caroon mumbling scornfully.

"So no, leave them for now Funguy and wake them in the half Starhectoid please. They will need all the energy that they can muster in the turbulent times ahead." confirmed Captain Carrot.

"Are we really in a serious trouble Captain?" enquired Funguy.

"Yes my little Mechanoid friend, I fear it is more serious than even I estimated." admitted Captain Carrot.

"Shucks Captain, If you underestimated then things are surely in a tough spot. Still look on the bright side Captain." said Funguy cheerfully.

"You can see a bright side Funguy; tell me please what is it?" smiled the half hearted Captain Carrot.

"Well Sir, look at it this way. If you can underestimate, you can over estimate! Therefore it is possible is it not, that you over estimated your under estimation meaning that the situation could probably be normal. Status quo intact; business as usual, yes?" reasoned Funguy.

Captain Carrot looked at Funguy with some confusion as he tried to make sense of the Mechanoids analogy.

"I thank you for that Funguy; at least I think I do. Whatever you are saying, let us hope it is true, I think." smiled Captain Carrot, deep down no wiser for Funguy's theory. "Funguy my friend," continued the Captain lowering his voice. "We must keep this to ourselves for now Funguy. You must act as if nothing is wrong do you understand me? Nothing at all. Any misplaced sign of trouble and panic could spread throughout the ship like wildfire!" stressed Captain Carrot.

"Jeepers creepers Captain you can trust me to be strong. When have I let you down before?"

"Of course Funguy. I forget that you are not fitted with the emotional programmes."

"And don't forget it," chuckled Mushroid Funguy. "as far as I am concerned mum is the word. Rest assured Captain Carrot, I will remain my usual, fearless non-emotional self." Insisted Mushroid Funguy leaving the Captain to his vitals.

"Thank you Funguy I knew I could trust you." winked Captain Carrot activating his Computron; he had much to catch up on and little time in which to do it. Shooting across the room, Funguy disappeared into his service cupboard. Closing the door behind him, he stood himself into the corner placing a blanket over his head, shaking himself into a state of panic. What he had not told anyone on board the O.S.S.S Earthanon, was that he had secretly programmed himself with emotions by sneaking into Professor Goosegorgon's laboratory and linking up with his Mechanoid data processor memory banks. Funguy didn't like to break the rules, but it was the only way he could successfully play games with the children. Charades was not the easiest game in the world to play without emotions. As for doctors and nurses, well, in Funguy's, book, it was essential. Captain Carrot stepped out from the shower and dressed himself.

"Ahh now," muttered Captain Carrot slowly sitting down at the table. Staring at the food in front of him he prepared to tuck into the feast set before him. "Well Gillespie Jethro Carrot." he said under his breath, "You may not feel like it, but something tells me this could be the last chance to gain sustenance in relative peace and quietude for a long time."

Little did Captain Carrot know of the truth that lay in those words. The de-briefing was no less than forty five Starmins away. The ship's crew were starting to feel on edge. Already the Earthanon surface was experiencing infrequent but intense storm winds, swelling to almost hurricane proportions. Then, within the bat of an eyelid it would be gone, and Earthanon would return to its usual tranquil paradise. Whispers could be heard in every corner of the ship. Reasons for the winds varying from a bad batch of beans, to a new secret electron propulsion engine undergoing tests. Captain Carrot knew he must soon end such speculation, but, for now it was easier for them to bear blind ignorance, than the as yet uncertain truth.

Time 13.45 starhectoids.

On the bridge FO Marrowlar stood studying the star charts with Viceroy Rhubarblatt. SO Tulipina and Ensign Viola were finalising the planned evacuation route around the Sodium Star belt when Mushroid Fungola entered the bridge via the service elevation chamber.

"Oh no, here comes the intellectual parasite!" sniggered Ensign Rasperillo. Ensign Melonture laughed loudly as he stood with his hands resting on his stomach. Mushroid Fungola swivelled round, opening the small circular flap on the top of his head. Out of it came a large hand attached to a coiled spring, its forefinger extended as it shot across the room in the direction of Ensign Rasperillo.

"Here we go again," said Ensign Melonture. "What is it up to now?" he muttered. Suddenly, the forefinger launched itself up the nose of Ensign Rasperillo. Lifting him off the ground, pulling him towards Mushroid Fungola. Ensign Rasperillo cried out in pain as he was launched off his feet.

"Oweeeeee... Ahh.. Ahh.. Wowser.. No. N. No.. Put me down at once!" he demanded hovering ten foot off the ground above the Captain's chair.

"O.K! But remember this, intellectual I am, but parasite, I am not!" said Mushroid Fungola logically.

"Sure thing," said Ensign Rasperillo. "whatever you say. I'm sorry, just put me down please." agreed Ensign Rasperillo pleading with Mushroid Fungola.

"Pretty please sounds much more acceptable wouldn't you agree Ensign Melonture?" asked Mushroid Fungola grinning gleefully.

"Absolutely Mushroid Fungola," laughed Ensign Melonture nodding. "I couldn't agree more." continued Ensign Melonture covering his nose.

Ensign Rasperillo was beginning to get very flustered as Ensign Viola looked over her shoulder and smiled at him discreetly, giggling as she spotted Ensign Strawballis trying to hide her laughter in response to the commotion.

"Pretty please." said a rather ill-tempered Ensign Rasperillo.

"Better, much better!" Jeered Mushroid Fungola dropping him from where he was elevated. As he landed crashing into the Captains chair in a crumpled pile, FO Marrowlar turned and saw him sitting at the Command Com station.

"Ensign Rasperillo!" Called FO Marrowlar. "What on Earthanon do you think you are doing?"

"Well Sir I..." whimpered Ensign Rasperillo.

"Why are you not at your station?" interrupted FO Marrowlar.

"Because Mush..." began to reason Ensign Rasperillo.

"And might I add," interrupted FO Marrowlar again. "Helios may see fit that your destiny will carry you to the position of Captain one day. Let us hope that by then, you will have learned to wear your tunic with pride.

"But Sir you see..."

"No buts Ensign, as I was saying, until then, might I request that you vacate the Command Com, return to your station and spend some quality time on your appearance. Oh and Ensign Rasperillo, preferably before the Captain returns to the bridge! We would hate him to find you there and have him think you were a whoopee cushion or something." smiled FO Marrowlar.

Silence fell on the bridge as Ensign Rasperillo jumped out of the chair and straightened his clothes running towards the elevation chamber. Then standing to attention he saluted FO Marrowlar.

"I am very sorry Sir, it will not happen again. You have my word on it FO Marrowlar." he said gritting his teeth at Mushroid Fungola.

"Very good Ensign Rasperillo, I will remember you said that, and hold you to it; now secure your station and get on with it."

Mushroid Fungola stood behind FO Marrowlar giggling, FO Marrowlar called his name sharply without making eye contact.

"Mushroid Fungola." he said

"Yes FO Marro..."

"Where there is disruption on the bridge, you my little mechanised menace are usually somewhere around the scene. If you have a problem with any member of Sun-Fleet, you will do well to use the proper channels in making your complaint. It would be a great shame if we were to have you converted into a toaster, or perhaps even a garbage disposal unit. Do I make myself clear Mushroid Fungola?" asked FO Marrowlar.

Mushroid Fungola shook on his casters at the thought of being a garbage disposal unit. That was the lowest possible position attained by a Mechanoid in the Sun-Fleet.

"Yes Sir, message received and understood," he said nervously. "I will be the bestest Mushroid in the Sun-Fleet crew. Please Sir," he continued. "I beg of you don't turn me into a garbage disposal unit, my fellow Mechanoids will send me to the cleaners. FO Marrowlar I would never be able to hold my head high in Mechanoid circles again." pleaded Mushroid Fungola.

"After a spell in garbage disposal that would be the best place for you, you great big rust bucket of nuts and bolts." whispered Ensign Rasperillo.

"Did you say something Ensign Rasperillo?" snapped FO Marrowlar.

"Ahh. Ahh. Just clearing my throat Sir." said Ensign Rasperillo cowering at his post.

"I see. Well Mushroid Fungola, you're on the bridge? I assume you have a reason for being here?" enquired FO Marrowlar.

"I do, I mean yes Sir, indeed I do. One of my fellow Mechanoid surveillance probes was picking up a strange power source Sir. It was emanating from the abandoned mining district Arctolimba, on the outer perimeters of the Arcticus region." he said activating the Arcticus map on the Visaid.

"*Was*, Mushroid Fungola," commented FO Marrowlar uneasy with the past tense. Tell me, has it disappeared, stopped or perhaps it has just changed its mind?" jibed FO Marrowlar taking his place at the Command com.

"I don't know FO Marrowlar. We lost contact with the Mechanoid probe as of twenty Starmins ago. We have been trying to re-establish contact but as yet, we cannot pick up its frequency transmissions. There is a storm ripping through that sector at the moment. This could be the cause of the transmission displacement."

What sort of storm is it Mushroid Fungola, electrical or elemental?"

"Elemental Sir. It is also bringing with it severe cold spots."

"Sir," interrupted SO Tulipina. "that could incur a much more rapid drop in the blimit levels." confirmed SO Tulipina analysing the Arctolimba region atmospheric readings. "FO Marrowlar, the blimit readings for Arctolimba are on average three point seven blimits below Earthanons current levels. If the storm path widens, it may mean bringing our original estimates for the evacuation timetable forward quite considerably." she confirmed.

"Do you have any estimated spectacle analysis data that would offer any indication as to a revised timetable SO Tulipina?" asked FO Marrowlar.

"No Sir. I would have to monitor all storm times over a considerable period to establish a mean average." she explained.

"Thank you that won't be necessary SO Tulipina. What about your central on- board spectacle Analysis programme Mushroid Fungola?" he enquired.

"No. As yet Sir, my memory chips are still collating data from over two thousand such probes. It is a little early to confirm, but it would appear that the storm in the Arctolimba region is not an isolated phenomena. My sources tell me that there are several such storms around the Earthanon surface. These are roughly situated in the Arctolimba, Urasian, Europetrienne and the Anonarcticle regions." he said.

FO Marrowlar walked to the ship's system analyser and checked the log that SO Tulipina had compiled. Browsing through it he strolled across the bridge and sat at the Command Com, signed and closed the manual. He did not like the way events appeared to be shaping up. Hard facts were short in supply. As yet untraceable infiltrators were roaming the Earthanon surface, apparently their aim to plunder valuable Vegimatter stockpiles; not to mention the rapid appearance of storms that wreck any firm plans of evacuation. No indeed, this did not bode well with the thinking of FO Marrowlar, and it showed.

"Mushroid Fungola." said FO Marrowlar. "I want you to report to Professor Goosegorgon in Dr Kiwitranus's Laboratory. Instruct him to patch you through to the ship's main Analytical collation equaliser. Let's see if we can't speed up the information gathering, collation and confirmation process. Ensign Strawballis,"

"Yes Sir," said Ensign Strawballis.

"Contact Dr Kiwitranus and Professor Goosegorgon and alert them to the arrival of Mushroid Fungola. Then, contact Engineering SO Sproutette. Have her switch the polarity chamber that feeds from the auxiliary reactor into the main dialysis microproton memory bank computer. That should free up the system to speed up Mushroid Fungola's Collation cycle."

"Aye Sir, Ensign Strawballis to Professor Goosegorgon, come in please."

FO Marrowlar looked at the Starhectoid glass. It was time to prepare the bridge for his departure to the strategy room for the de-briefing meeting.

Rising to his feet, he handed the Captain's manual to SO Tulipina, walking to the Grid Finder for a final observation in the particle scanner.

"SO Tulipina you have Command Com." he said turning towards the elevation chamber awaiting the door de-energisation.

"Should you have any problems, you may direct them to the Captain in the strategy room. Failing that you will be able to locate me I am sure. If anything comes up that you feel specifically requires my attention, contact me direct on my personal channel." he confirmed.

"Aye Sir, thank you FO Marrowlar." acknowledged SO Tulipina standing to attention.

"First Officer off the bridge." shouted Ensign Rasperillo as the bridge crew stamped to attention. Ensign Rasperillo and Ensign Melonture gave the UFO salute as FO Marrowlar stepped into the elevation chamber, and the doors re-energised.

SO Tulipina sat at the Command com giving her first order.

"Stand easy on the bridge. SO Tulipina to Viceroy Graperon, come in please." she said activating her personal channel.

"Viceroy Graperon here Sir." came the sharp high pitched reply.

"Viceroy Graperon, please report for duty at the ship's systems analyser Command Com on the bridge immediately." This would make Viceroy Graperon her FO for the duration of her stint at the helm.

"Aye, aye Sir, Ay'Ok and I'm on my way." confirmed Viceroy Graperon.

"Very good Tulipina out." SO Tulipina was eager to prove her competence at the Command Com. In her mind, re-establishing communications with the Mechanoid Probe would be a plus point in her performance. "Ensign Strawballis," continued SO Tulipina. "Can you try and make contact with the Mechanoid probe in the Arctolimba district by using the high density Silicone-sphere communications satellite?" asked SO Tulipina.

"Aye, aye Sir, I will try to establish contact now." confirmed Ensign Strawballis.

"Ensign Viola," continued SO Tulipina. "get to work on scanning the Arctolimba district. Concentrate on cross ambulating the Grid Finder with the particle scanner electron booster Triabulator. If we can't make contact with it, we can at least pin point its last position and retrace it's route by picking up the probes calorific magnetic emissions."

"Aye, aye SO Tulipina, initiating cross ambulation synchronisation programme now." acknowledged Ensign Viola as she proceeded to key the instruction into the Particle scanner consul.

In the heart of the ship down on deck J, the recreation rooms were a hive of speculation. None of the crew beamed on board from the O.S.S Satsumuroo were anywhere to be seen. Not since they had boarded had any of them made themselves familiar with the ship. What the crew of the O.S.S.S Earthanon were not aware of, was that Captain Peabazzare had instructed his crew to keep themselves to themselves and confined to their quarters until after the de-briefing. Rumours of terrible disease wiping out the crew were rife. Dr Kiwitranus made his way to the recreation area and was so busy talking to himself, that the odd looks he received from passing members of the crew went unnoticed.

"Do this Dr Kiwitranus!" "Do that Dr Kiwitranus!" "Rest Dr Kiwitranus? Rest is for inferior intellects. Frankly Dr Kiwitranus. I am 'a beginning to doubt 'a your ability to cope 'a with 'a the changing face of science. Don'ta start what'a you cant'a finish Kiwitranus. Ask 'a before you start 'a the task Kiwitranus." "Yes Professor Goosegorgon. No, Professor Goosegorgon, three bags full Professor Goosegorgon. I hate to tell you this Sigfreed Kiwitranus, but you are nothing more than a whipping boy, a punch bag for the holier than thou megalomaniac Professor Goosegorgon." he continued muttering to himself. Dr Kiwitranus walked into the soda bar and sat on a stool at the fountain springs.

Leisurelando Pinnelexo, a rather stout and jolly pineapple from the Planet Pinilsues was born to the space race Pinnopleat. The wisest of Organitron's aboard the O.S.S.S Earthanon, whose distant home lies in the lesser quadrant of the Fruitanutes plexus. As usual Leisurelando could be found on duty standing at the far end of the bar, reliable as ever present at the station of his calling. Leisurelando or Vege-babes as he was more affectionately known was the typical beacon of knowledge.

Hearing all and saying nothing, he was often viewed as some kind of wise guru of spatial intellect. Even Captain Carrot referred to him as the agony aunt of the Organitron's. Everybody's friend and nobody's enemy. That was Leisurelando Pinnelexo's calling. Dr Kiwitranus often came here to escape and unwind today of all days was no exception. Spotting a weary Dr Kiwitranus behind him in the mirror's reflection, he turned slowly at first with his hands emitting a bright blue then effervescent haze. Levitating between his fingertips was a luxurious Fruitalia bocker glory. An eighteen inch glass frosted with green sugar. The base of the glass was filled with chocolate crisp biscuit bits, topped with seven flavours in a rainbow formation of Vegimatter ice cream, lavished with fresh fruited Vegimatter in between each layer. Then topped with smouldering hot fudge sauce and crowned with toasted marshmallows and caramelised strawberry and toffee Vegimatters. Then as if by magic the lights dimmed and four sparklers ignited and as it came to rest in front of Dr Kiwitranus a spoon Vegitamised in his hand.

"Wow," said Dr Kiwitranus in astonishment of the spectacular sight before his now bright and child like eyes.

"What on Earthanon is this my fine wise old friend?" asked the astounded Dr Kiwitranus.

"I like to call it my pick-me-up-special." said Leisurelando Pinnelexo. "Just taste it, you will see what I mean, I promise you!" he said smiling.

Dr Kiwitranus delved into the delightful treat. As he took his first mouthful, his eyes closed and his mind started to tingle. Gradually the tingling sensation travelled all the way down to his toes. Opening his eyes he realised that he was floating above the soda bar, over the head of Vege-babes and in full view of the rest of the crew. Slowly, he drifted back to his chair and could not help sighing with a deep sense of relief. His body overcome with an innate sense of relaxation. Not until Dr Kiwitranus had scraped the vessel clean and slumped back in his chair with complete satisfaction did he utter one word.

"Vege-Babes that was truly Earthanon shattering, Just what..."

"The Doctor ordered." interrupted Leisurelando.

"That's right," said Dr Kiwitranus agog with Vege-Babes accuracy.

"You know, you are one cool dude Vege-Babes. I don't know what it is about you, but whenever I come in here feeling a little low or tired.... I can't put my finger on it, you just seem to perform some kind of special magic. In fact, between you and me," Dr Kiwitranus stopped, leant over the soda bar and quietly whispered to Leisurelando. "Short of Captain Carrot himself, you are probably the most important person on this ship!"

"Oh, come now Dr Kiwitranus," rebuffed the shy but thankful pineapple. "I am just a humble servant to the needy and I hope a friend to all." he said.

"You sure got that right Vege-babes." agreed Dr Kiwitranus thankfully.

"Now that my ego is inflated to bursting point, why don't you get it off your chest, umm?" asked Vege-Babes.

"You can tell huh?" moaned Dr Kiwitranus remembering all of a sudden that he had problems.

"Oh no, but I can listen, be assured I will never tell." replied Leisurelando.

Dr Kiwitranus held his head in his hands playfully sobbing, then flung his hands in the air and screamed momentarily losing control.

"Ahhh... Sassle, frassle, crassle, nassle, aka-chaka-naka-chaka-duka-na-ka- kaaaaa."

Then he slumped in silence as Leisurelando handed him a Banana and kiwifruit Vegimatter shake.

"Frustration is a terrible thing Dr Kiwitranus," said Leisurelando. "Let me give you the benefit of my experience if I may?" he continued as Dr Kiwitranus waved him on. "I don't know whether it is relevant but if it helps, well, my guess is that it will be worth it!" reasoned Leisurelando.

"Sure, go ahead, but you will never guess what's bothering me." challenged the defiant Dr Kiwitranus.

"I provide no Guarantees my friend," chuckled Leisurelando, "but perhaps just a glimmer of hope." he continued closing his eyes and sinking into an apparent trance. When his eyes opened he said.

"The thing you must do is remember the **"Organitron Jazz Tattoo."** Then he began to sing a little jingle.

"Run when you can, sleep when you must,
but in your ability you must trust.
You cannot run before you can walk,
to avoid a false start, then first you must talk.

Dr Kiwitranus looked at Leisurelando with amazement.

"So what you are saying is that I can achieve anything provided I make the correct preparations, make the right decisions and follow the rules."

"Rules were made to be broken my friend, just get their permission first. Those that push you to your limits have more faith in you than you do!"

"Thank you Vege-babes, thanks a lot." smiled Dr Kiwitranus. "You don't know how much that has helped." Suddenly Dr Kiwitranus stopped in his tracks looking back at Leisurelando reservedly. "On the other hand." he said. "Maybe you do? but Vege-Babes, what's with the Organitron Jazz tattoo?" Leisurelando stepped up onto the stage where Frankie Satsumatra and the Vegettes had just finished a number called. "I have got you under my skin." Leisurelando whispered into Frankie's ear and after a short while the band struck up a tune. Frankie handed Leisurelando a spare trumpet and microphone and soon was snapping his fingers to the beat. The lights dimming low, Dr Kiwitranus sat in captivation of the hip swinging spectacle on stage before his very eyes. All around him a crowd gathered with the irresistible tapping rhythm in their feet. Dr Kiwitranus and the gang didn't know what was about to happen, but the general air of excitement spelt out that whatever it was, it was going to be special. Leisurelando turned to the band and gave them his hip swinging instructions.

"Okay boys and girls, what we have here is a serious situation, nay, more. What we have here, is a situation of frightening magnitude. I hear tell that this man and this here gang are in for an awakening nothing short of bang. So hold on to your hats you cool Organicats for the Organitron Jazz Tattoo. Okay Organiboys' and girls' follow me on the count of three, make sure you ring with the changes.

Strike up the band, one, two, three."

"The Organitron Jazz Tattoo."
Are you happy, are you snappy, tell me, are you feeling blue?
What a beautiful day, I'll chase your troubles away.
C'mon get in hip with the tune.

It's time to sing, to get with the zing, of the hip swinging hullabaloo.
So pick yourself up, brush yourself down, get it together under the moon.
It's time for the only, holy Vegemolly, Organitron Jazz Tattoo.
So strike up the band don't it feel grand? Yes, this one this is for you.
Tell me babes are you ready, guys are you steady?

Here comes the music up-up and away.
Look to the sun in the sky, wipe the tears from your eyes,
Getta ready to brighten your day.
Yes gang look, look to the moon and strike, strike up this tune,
Cause it's the Organitron jazz tattoo way.

Doggone and dognabbit, no Siree this ain't no bad habit,
So follow me and you will see, look life in the eyes and grab it.
C'mon and cut your stuff loose, being blue ain't no use,
Put a smile on your face, We're the Organitron race.
I say, can you hear me-hold this song to your hearts and cheer me.
Got my sights stuck on you, here comes the music lasso.
The Organitron jazz tattoo

I'm a happy and strapping full of vitamin "c". See; see,
Take a tip from someone who's a real bizzy bee. Bee; bee
If you don't believe it, take a good look at me, Me; me
I'm a shooting star, a moonbeam from Mars this is the you see.
No this ain't no ruse, this is the news.
Of the Organitron jazz tattoo

I'm a fruiting, rooting tooting,
A fiery shooting, hooting grooving.
Man I'm a spoofy loving hublin and bubbling,
Organitron jazz tattoo fan.
Yes, I'm a zootin moving, slinky rinky dinky.
Shrinky dinky Organitron clan.

Strike up the tune and dance under the vroom vroom moon.
And make ready, get steady, for the Organitron jazz tattoo.
Run when you can, sleep when you must,
But in your ability you must trust.

You cannot run before you can walk,
To avoid a false start, then first you must talk.
Got my sights stuck on you, here comes the music lasso,
And make ready, get steady for the Organitron jazz tattoo.

"I am here to serve and observe, if I can help just give me a yelp, adios amigos." said Leisurelando from the stage with a twinkle in his eye.

As Dr Kiwitranus made his way back to the Medilab with a spring in his step and a bounce in his stride he sang a little ditty of his own.

"It's time, to get back to work,
No time to shirk, got to get with it,
No rest for the wicked, So move out of the way.
Cos no Siree I've no time to play.
And that is as we say, a rap jack here today."

As he stood in front of the elevation chamber, the doors de-energised and out came a party of children on their way to the amusement deck. Dr Kiwitranus picked up one of the Organitron children as the rest gathered round him clutching at his coat, and he carried on singing.

"So you see how I'm moving,
I'm hot and I'm grooving.
Got to shake it, this worlds in a rush,
So slap me some skin, cause I'm coming on in,
Got me a problem that I have to crush.
Now keep that smile on your face,
And my heart it will race.
And your glow, it will light up the moon,
You kids make this world go around with a vroom,
Where ever you are you light up the room.
So for you we will strive, to face life with a pride.
You're our future and we grown up's are just along for the ride.
Chow, tootle pip, tatty bye, Au rouvoir, not goodbye.

Putting the little Organitron down with the rest of the group, he stepped into the chamber.

Till we meet again my heart it will cry,
Just keep smiling and be happy, let's grab life and be snappy.
Chow, tootle pip, tatty bye, Au rouvoir, not goodbye."

Dr Kiwitranus blew them a kiss. The children returned the gesture and sang the last line.

"Chow, tootle pip, tatty bye, Au rouvoir, not goodbye."

"Teacher Orangite." said Dr Kiwitranus. "If you would like to take the children into the soda bar, tell Leisurelando the pick-me-ups are on me."

"Why, thank you Dr Kiwitranus." replied Teacher Orangite.

"No Teacher Orangite, thank them."

He waved as the doors re-energised leaving the children running for the soda bar.

Part two

To reach the point of no return.

Time 14.25 starhectoids.

Standing in the strategy room were FO Marrowlar, FO Cornelius, FO Melonicord and FO Potatree of the O.S.S.S Earthanon. Commodore Cu-Cumbala, the ground station Arcticus controller. Captain Peabazzare, FO Pepperat, SO Courgiett, Viceroy Tomaldy and Chief Ensigns Kamqauter and Fusiana, the bridge crew of the ill fated O.S.S Satsumuroo

"Viceroy Graperon to FO Marrowlar come in please." came over FO Marrowlar's personal channel

"FO Marrowlar to Viceroy Graperon." he replied.

"Sir, I am sorry to disturb your meeting." she continued. "SO Tulipina has placed me on the ship's analyser and has asked me to contact you with reference to several issues."

"Proceed Viceroy Graperon, you have my undivided attention." said FO Marrowlar.

"Thank you Sir. I have just completed a ship's security particle scan, Sir, we have detected a high concentration of Prima mustard gas within the ship's Recreational quarters on deck I, section fourteen." she confirmed.

"Have SO Okralate seal off the area, no one must leave that area unless I give permission personally. Step up to full security alert on decks H, I and J. Is that understood Viceroy Graperon?" he asked.

"Aye Sir, we have also confirmed the last known position of the Mechanoid probe in the Arctolimba region. I am sending through to the Computron its last information transcripts retrieved from mushroom Fungola's data banks. We have confirmed communication on the recall May-day distress call. The shore leave party in the Europetriennes region have acknowledged and confirmed."

"When is their ETA Viceroy Graperon?" asked FO Marrowlar

"One point two five starhectoids Sir." confirmed Viceroy Graperon.

FO Marrowlar strolled across to the Computron. Reading the information as it came through, he called on FO Cornelius to join him at the monitor.

"Stand by for further instructions Viceroy Graperon." he said.

"Aye Sir, standing by." confirmed Viceroy Graperon.

"FO Cornelius." said FO Marrowlar attracting his attention. "These are the last transmissions from a Mechanoid probe in the Arctolimba region before we lost contact with it. What do you make of it?" he enquired.

FO Cornelius tapped into the Computron and stood shaking his head, the look on his face one of a bamboozled state.

"It would appear the region has somehow undergone a terrainial change." said a confused FO Cornelius. "Look here, this is the reading from the probe scan thirty starhectoids ago. Now look at this. It would appear that sometime between then and two Startechtoids ago that has appeared." he continued pointing at the screen

"A mountain?" said FO Marrowlar in shocked surprise.

"Of sorts yes Sir, but, not in its usual context." exclaimed FO Cornelius. "No mountain as we know it, FO Marrowlar." he continued. "This mountain is made of raw silicone; sand! It could be the start of a dune formation caused by the sporadic storms in the region?" he concluded finally.

"Thank you FO Cornelius that will be all." FO Marrowlar dismissed him deep in thought.

"Aye Sir." said FO Cornelius, walking back to the main party.

"Viceroy Graperon." said FO Marrowlar engaging his personal channel. "Ensign Strawballis had prepared a Roboprobe on standby. Is it still on active standby?" he enquired.

"Yes Sir." confirmed Viceroy Graperon.

"Have it re-directed to the Arctolimba region and see if we can't find that Mechanoid probe." ordered FO Marrowlar.

"Aye, aye Sir." agreed Viceroy Graperon.

"FO Marrowlar over and out."

"Viceroy Graperon out."

"FO Marrowlar," said Captain Peabazzare. "I wonder if you could have somebody scan the crew of the O.S.S Satsumuroo for anything strange. Before we departed Earthanon surface we were allocated some thirty new crew members. Their papers are in order, but I just want to eliminate the possibilities." said Captain Peabazzare. "Ensign Broccleman told me of the infiltration possibility, this has set me thinking," he continued. "what better way to smuggle out Vegimatter than under our noses and on our own ship's."

"You think they were plotting to overthrow the ship's crew and use it to transport the Vegimatter?" asked FO Marrowlar.

"It's a long shot, but it is possible." admitted Captain Peabazzare. "Then Ensign Broccleman said something that I believe Confirmed my suspicion." he continued. "So I gave orders that all the O.S.S Satsumuroo crew are confined to quarters until after the de-briefing. FO Marrowlar," he whispered quietly. "all the new crew are red skinned. Ten Apploneons and twenty Tomaldons." "Well done Captain Peabazzare, leave it with me. The Captain will be very pleased to hear this new development. Maybe the tide is turning and good fortune is beginning to come our way! FO Marrowlar to Ensign Strawballis, come in please."

"Ensign Strawballis here Sir." she replied.

"Ensign Strawballis, will you activate a priority secure channel to all Sun-Fleet ships I want you to speak direct to all Captains? Also have them scan all of their ships again. We believe that all ships that have docked in the Earthanon districts have been compromised by the infiltrators. They must apprehend all infiltrators immediately and hold them under close arrest." insisted FO Marrowlar.

"Yes Sir," she confirmed. "I presume you would like me to interrupt your meeting if your suspicions are correct?" she enquired.

"Indeed Ensign Strawballis, you presume correctly! FO Marrowlar out."

"Ensign Strawballis over and out."

Whilst they stood chatting, the main doors to the strategy room de-energised and in came Professor Goosegorgon with his usual bouncing energy.

Boing.. Boing.. Boing.. Boink.. Splatt! "Organigirls, Organiboys. I amma sorry I amma late. Work, work, work and well, you know how it is'a no? Is'a all a big rush these 'a days. Ahh. FO Potatree, I do wonder if 'a you could have somebody check the air ducting channels. See if something is present in the air supply that shall we say, shouldn't be there?" added Professor Goosegorgon.

"What on Earthanon are you talking about Organiman?" asked FO Potatree. "The air ducting channels are fine. I checked them all before I departed for the Earthanon surface."

"You did?" interrupted Professor Goosegorgon.

"Aye Professor, I have had to re-configurate the air supply mixture for when we switch to minimised stature." confirmed FO Potatree.

"Well if you are sure, I must be wrong, but Dr Kiwitranus just came back to the lab singing, What'a on Earthanon could hav'a got into him? Most unlike the good Doctor. Maybe I amma just pushing him to hard and he is'a finally cracking up under the strain." said the Professor.

"If it's any help Professor, I think anyone working under you for any considerable length of time, would crack up eventually." said FO Potatree as the rest of the room broke into raucous laughter.

"Yes may be you are 'a right, but, hang on one 'a minute this is'a insult, no?"

"No, more like a fact Professor." quipped FO Cornelius.

"We will soon see who is'a the first to crack on this ship, huh! You imbeciles." shrugged Professor Goosegorgon.

"Come now Organipeep's." FO Marrowlar took his place at the table. "The time for jokes is over. I am sure the Captain would not appreciate bringing the Admiral Ducarrotain into a room with a full blown brawl under way!" said FO Potatree.

"As'a usual you are quite right FO Marrowlar." said Professor Goosegorgon sharply. "Please forgive these 'a heathens. They only have 'a limited understanding." chortled Professor Goosegorgon.

The doors de-energised to the strategy room as Captain Carrot accompanied Admiral Ducarrotain to the a chair at the end of the table while the others stood with respect. When both he and the Captain, who sat at the other end, were seated, the rest took their places and the two security guards stood at the outer entrance of the strategy room. Then, as the doors re-energised, Captain Carrot, opened the meeting.

"Admiral Ducarrotain, Commodore Cu-Cumbala, Organigirls and Organiboys." he said addressing the group. "You will observe the time is thirty starsecs short of Fourteen hundred thirty starhectoids." Activating his personal channel, he contacted Ensign Strawballis.

"Captain Carrot to Ensign Strawballis come in, over."

"Ensign Strawballis here Captain, yes Sir?" she replied.

"Put me on the ship's communicator please Ensign Strawballis, and have Ensign Melonture signal the piper respect at fourteen thirty starhectoids and again at fourteen thirty two starhectoids."

"Aye Sir, you have open channel."

"This is Captain Gillespie Jethro Carrot addressing all crew and civilian members of the O.S.S.S Earthanon. When you hear the piper respect, we will undertake a two minute silence to honour those who lost their lives in the brave struggle to control the O.S.S Satsumuroo in the Sodium Star belt. In the face of adversity they stood by their posts in order to preserve the lives of their fellow crew members. We, the entire United Foliage of Organitron, salute your bravery and remember the souls of those who lost their lives. Though your bodies are now part of the Solar System you're souls are in our hearts and your memory will always live strong." said the Captain bowing his head.

Then the piper respect was played and silence fell on the inhabitants of O.S.S.S Earthanon. All areas of the ship stood silent with heads bowed low and hands clasped tight. Even the children stood in silence as the emotion could be felt throughout the ship like a cluster cloud of piercing electricity; invisible but present without a doubt. Then the piper respect resonated again and gradually the ship returned to normality.

"Thank you everyone." said Captain Carrot. "You're silence is their strength and comfort on their long last journey to peace. Captain Carrot out."

Captain Carrot turned his attention to the meeting at hand.

"Now, let's get this meeting under way," he said. "I fear we do not have much time! FO Potatree. I have digested your report from the Earthanon surface. Did you run full diagnostics on the ultra ray reflection shields?" he noted.

"Aye Sir, I did." confirmed FO Potatree. "You can rest assured Captain the Blimit level deficiency does not emanate from that section. All systems were Ay'Ok."

"What is the Blimit situation now Chief?" enquired Captain Carrot.

Chief Potatree scratched his head. It was obvious he was confused and worried. There was a problem and he couldn't beat it. Problems that he could not beat were rare and unwelcome visitors to his little grey cells.

"Well Sir, the readings that we are getting from around the Earthanon surface are variable," explained FO Potatree. "but at best, the average rate of descent has increased from four point seven to five point one Blimits per Starhectoid. We are now operating at thirty-four point four Blimits below usual operational levels. That gives us a little over one starhectoids before our energy cycle is compromised. I took the liberty, Captain; after consultation with FO Marrowlar of course." he clarified. "I took the liberty of closing down all remaining mining operations when, as we agreed, the thirty blimit minus level was exceeded." reasoned FO Potatree.

"A wise move under the circumstances Chief Potatree." agreed Captain Carrot. "FO Cornelius," he continued. "still no indication of atmospheric degeneration to explain the increased drop in the Blimit levels?" he said.

"All particle scans show nothing unusual in the atmosphere Sir;" confirmed FO Cornelius. "apart from, of course, the increased sodium content as the Sodium Star belt nears the Earthanon Solar System. Captain

Peabazzare is also correct in his assumption. The storm is indeed gathering momentum and velocity as it approaches Earthanons gravitational pull." FO Cornelius punched in some data at his Computron then connected his hand set on to the side and it started to churn out reams of information.

"Sir, with the aid of Captain Peabazzare's on the spot data." said FO Cornelius after studying the data. "My indications are that the winds inside the Sodium Star belt have increased to seven hundred starmillo's a Starhectoid. However, the Sodium Star belt itself is travelling at some twenty thousand starmillo's per starhectoids. This means that at the current rate of approach; taking into account an overall speed increase of eighteen percent, the Sodium Star belt will be within Earthanons atmosphere in approximately twenty starhectoids. I would like to try and limit the Blimit losses by creating what we refer to as an "Ozone layer" that myself and Professor have been working on for some time. I have two thousand Robopods loaded with the mixture of gases ready to launch. They can complete the task in one point five starhectoids Captain. All I need is your go ahead." asked FO Cornelius.

"Very well," said Captain Carrot as he perused the data from FO Cornelius. "launch the Robopods immediately." he ordered deep in thought. "Anything that can buy us time is most welcome." FO Cornelius activated his personal channel.

"FO Cornelius to SO Tulipina, come in please."

"SO Tulipina here Sir." she replied.

"SO Tulipina." said FO Cornelius. "Captain Carrot has given permission to go ahead and launch the Ozone Robopods. Could you please have Ensign Broccleman escort Dr Kiwitranus to the launch pad in the starboard pod bay. He will need help supervising the operation. Ensign Broccleman is on standby with the launch clearance codes," he added. "You had better detail him Dr Kiwitranus will need his assistance to operate the micro pod launch consul."

"Will do FO Cornelius. Ensign Broccleman is on his way Sir, this is SO Tulipina out."

"FO Cornelius over and out. It is done Captain Carrot."

Captain Carrot turned to FO Marrowlar and placed the landing party reports in front of him.

"I take it you have read the reports FO Marrowlar?" he enquired.

"Yes Captain." he confirmed. "As you requested I have been working very closely with FO Melonicord on the security front, concentrating in particular with the emergency evacuation plans." he stated, acknowledging

FO Melonicord. "All the civilian freighters have been loaded with the Mineral deposits and Vegimatter stockpiles." he continued. "Convoy formations have been agreed with the Star Fighter squadrons. Fighter command Commodore Auberoal is briefing his pilots as we speak. They are on standby and awaiting take-off clearance."

Captain Carrot stood slowly, the anxiousness in his movement becoming very apparent. His mind, running wild with the massive task in front of them. This had been the home of many generations of Organitron; exiled by a situation, over which they had absolutely no control. Earthanon had become a home for which they had become most grateful. They had owed their lives to this safe haven; this retreat. Here was yet another change that the Organitron could ill afford just as they had come to feel secure. Roots would have to now be ripped from the very heart of their being, the uncertainty, the change, the new direction of the unknown. It would indeed be a turbulent time. The order for evacuation would have to be met with the strength to bolster the moral of every Organitron. There may even be those that would not want to leave; a mutiny in affect. One that would be understandable by way of insecurities, however, one that must be avoided at all cost. Captain Carrot knew that at no other time in the history of the Organitron's had it been so necessary for the Organitron to effectively run; turn their backs on this place that had delivered to them the means to re-establish their home world colonies. Now that the evacuation plans were in place, Captain Carrot and every Organitron alive knew that they had reached the point of no return. They were committed and a change of heart and mind was not a luxury that remained an option. As the Captain came to terms with the massive responsibilities placed upon his shoulders, FO Marrowlar coughed to attract the attention of the deeply burdened Captain.

"Ahh.. Hum.. Captain Carrot," said FO Marrowlar constructively, "may I be permitted to offer some good news in this whole situation?"

Captain Carrot relieved himself momentarily of the torment that played on his mind so.

"Good news would be very gratifying FO Marrowlar, please, enlighten me."

"Captain Carrot," said FO Marrowlar as he smiled confidently. "We have uncovered we believe-that is, Captain Peabazzare and myself-the true nature of the infiltration plot against the Earthanon Organitron settlements. Let us ask ourselves three prominent questions. One; what are they after? Two; how much have they gained access to so far? And finally but most importantly; how were they to escape after plundering our stocks undetected." said FO Marrowlar with an air of satisfaction running through his bones.

Captain Carrot seemed to sit up straight, his ears pricking with eager anticipation of the news that seemed to bring a lighter side of the predicament that they found themselves in.

"Go on FO Marrowlar, you have my complete attention." he said in a jovial manner.

"Well Sir," continued FO Marrowlar. "point one; we know that the Fasterfoids were after our Vegimatter stockpiles. We now believe they were also after something more intrinsic to their survival; technology. Technology that they have scoffed and belittled since time immemorial. Point two. We know that the stockpiles are at full capacity. In order to Vegitamise the stockpiles into the freighter holds we had to run full stock checks to estimate the mass Vegitamisation calculations. I can assure you that all stocks are still in place and accounted for. Therefore we can safely assume that the Fasterfoids plundering to date is the sum total of nil; or not a Sausagia if you will excuse the pun." he said laughing. "Point three. We now know that they were to achieve their dual aim of gaining the technology and Vegimatter by way of Sun-Fleet infiltration. They would board our ships, overrun them, then using the security clearance matrix, they would fill the ships with the stockpiles and then disappear. This is just a guess Captain, but I think they were confident that they would not be fired upon if discovered prematurely. Firstly, because of the fact that the ships were Sun-Fleet property, and secondly, because the ships would contain all of the Vegimatter stockpiles." he reasoned as his personal channel came on line.

"Ensign Strawballis to FO Marrowlar. Come in please."

FO Marrowlar activated his personal channel in response.

"Excuse me Captain, may I?" he asked politely

"As you will FO Marrowlar." said the Captain

"Thank you Sir. FO Marrowlar here Ensign Strawballis." he said.

"You were right Sir," continued Ensign Strawballis. "all ships have completed security scans. We now have five hundred and seventy Fasterfoids held prisoner. Ship's Captain's request further instructions how to proceed." she enquired.

"Captain Carrot?" asked FO Marrowlar, awaiting directions.

Captain Carrot sat quietly and pondered the fate of the enemy within.

"Have them beamed aboard the O.S.S.S. Earthanon." he confirmed. "I want to know once and for all what it is they are playing at. Have them placed under full house arrest, then have SO Okralate see if he can't wheedle out the ring- leaders." he continued.

"Aye Sir," said FO Marrowlar. "Ensign Strawballis did you get that?"

"Yes Sir." Came her reply. "I am on it as we speak FO Marrowlar."

"FO Marrowlar over and out."

"Ensign Strawballis out."

"Well done FO Marrowlar, not to forget you Captain Peabazzare. I shudder to think what would have happened if we had not had this crisis on our hands to scupper the plans of the Fasterfoids?" noted Captain Carrot breathing an ironic sigh of relief.

"I am sure that we would have spotted their evil plan Sir!" said FO Marrowlar.

"I am afraid that my intuition disagrees with your theory FO Marrowlar." said Captain Carrot. "It would appear that Sun-Fleet would have been caught with their proverbial trousers around their ankles. FO Marrowlar." he continued. "I want a complete and detailed report on the apparent lack of security on the Earthanon surface."

"Aye Sir!" said FO Marrowlar smugly.

"Then, FO Marrowlar, you may begin your report on the less than proficient performance of the ship's security aspects. Starting may I suggest, where Sun-Fleet uniforms and Earthanon passes were obtained, also, the source of the written orders to the various ships." suggested Captain Carrot.

"Aye Sir." shrugged FO Marrowlar, knowing that the Captain was right. What they had effectively done was bolted the door after the Dindivar had run from the stable.

"FO Melonicord what is the status of the evacuation plan timetable?" asked the Captain, moving on rapidly.

"Well Sir, all Earthanon personnel have completed the Minimisation programme. Seventy five percent of the personnel have undergone double regeneration periods. We estimate that this will be achieved within the next Starhectoid, then we have to get started on the civilian inhabitants As you are already aware, the Mineral and Vegimatter stockpiles are safe and sound in the freighter holds under full security protection. We have now rounded up four hundred and seventy infiltrators on the Earthanon surface. It was unfortunate for them at least, that this crises coincided with their plans to make off with the Vegimatter stockpiles. You see Captain," explained FO Melonicord. "the cloaking device does many things except allow for the possibility of the Vegitamisation, Minimisation and the Organitron regeneration processes."

Captain Carrot sat in his chair and looked at ground station Commodore Cu-Cumbala.

"Might I suggest Commodore Cu-Cumbala," suggested Captain Carrot. "that we transfer all prisoners to the O.S.S.S Earthanon."

"As you wish Captain. It would make sense to have all the little blighters together where we can keep an eye on them."

"I agree Commodore." said the Captain sharply. "FO Melonicord," he continued. "Grow with the flow."

"Aye Sir," she agreed. "Ensign Strawballis, come in please." said FO Melonicord activating her personal channel.

"Ensign Strawballis here Sir." she replied.

"Ensign Strawballis," continued FO Melonicord. "would you organise the Vegitamisation of all Fasterfoid prisoners held on the Earthanon surface to join the rest of the prisoners on board the O.S.S.S Earthanon. You will need to increase the security respectively to allow for the extended numbers." advised FO Melonicord.

"Aye Sir," replied the Ensign.

"That will be all Ensign Strawballis. FO Melonicord, over and out."

"Ensign Strawballis out."

"Vegitamisation is underway Captain." confirmed FO Melonicord.

"Excellent FO Melonicord." replied Captain Carrot. "Admiral Ducarrotain, is there anything that you wish to add or suggest perhaps?" asked Captain Carrot.

Admiral Ducarrotain had sat quietly throughout the whole debriefing, this was an obvious source of worry to all concerned. Admiral Ducarrotain was an Organibeing renowned for his principles and his leadership qualities, but was never known to be a man of few words. Admiral Ducarrotain stood slowly and walked across the strategy room, viewing Earthanon from the observation window with a heavy heart. You could cut the atmosphere with a knife, the longer the silence went on the more became the concerns of Admiral Ducarrotain's possible displeasure.

"Captain Carrot, Commodore Cu-Cumbala, Organigirls and Organiboys." said Admiral Ducarrotain. "Technology." he said with thrust in his voice. "Technology is ever changing, ever extending the boundaries of our understanding for the good of the Organitron cause. It is true is it not?" said the Admiral. "That today's technology is merely the product of theories born of yesterday's successes and mistakes?" Turning to address the silent group assembled around the table, he smiled softly, then opening his arms and outstretching his hands whilst looking around the room, he continued. "I, as you are no doubt aware, am getting on considerably in Startechtoids. There is no wish on my part to go back and re-live my life. It has been eventful to say the least but Organigirls and Organiboys it was achieved without most of the technology which you have at your disposal today. Do not get me wrong, I am in no way trying to say that because of this my generation was better than yours. After seeing the intensity and complexity of the operation in hand; the potential catastrophe that could possibly be awaiting the Earthanon Sun-Fleet Organisation, I Organigirls and Organiboys, commend you. Even if my generation had this starlectoids technology at their disposal, it is very possible that we would neither have had the capacity of understanding it, nor the flexibility to deal with it rationally. What you see before you is a reputed warrior of great bravery." continued Admiral Ducarrotain. "I have to tell you that every action I took at the height of my career was taken because frankly, our backs were against the wall. It was simply a case of try to defeat or die in defeat. There is no shame in either. What I have seen in the last five starhectoids or so has made me both proud and frightened. It is a different universe we see today, and if honesty were to run its full and natural course I wouldn't change places with you for love or credits. However, I may be past my sell-by date, but, whatever I have left to offer is yours. Now, is there anything left of this meeting, or may a bag of old bones retire to his quarters and have a triple dose of regeneration?" asked the Admiral.

Captain Carrot stood and took Admiral Ducarrotain by his arm. "Admiral Ducarrotain." said Captain Carrot with a genuine sense of feeling and admiration for the infamous Admiral. "I think I can speak for everyone when I say," he continued. "that in a time of trouble I couldn't think of a stronger more reliable and resilient wiser head than that which your shoulders carry. In a time of crisis there is no more stabilising agent on this ship than the presence of your being. Organigirls and Organiboys that concludes the debriefing. You may all return to your stations. FO Marrowlar, have the crew of the O.S.S Satsumuroo allocated to their posts.

Captain Peabazzare you and your bridge crew will join me on the bridge, but first, will you escort Admiral Ducarrotain to his quarters?" he asked.

"It would be an honour Captain Carrot," he said holding out his arm toward Admiral Ducarrotain. "Allow me, Admiral Ducarrotain?"

"Thank you Captain Peabazzare. Oh Professor Goosegorgon, will you spare me some time later please? I would like to hear more on this Ozone layer you have perfected?" asked Admiral Ducarrotain.

"When 'a you are ready Admiral Ducarrotain. I will be 'a willing and able." confirmed Professor Goosegorgon.

"Thank you. Well if you will excuse me, I feel you have much to do. Until later then." said Admiral Ducarrotain as the doors to the strategy room de-energised. All stood to attention as Admiral Ducarrotain made his way out of the strategy room.

"Commodore Cu-Cumbala do you wish to stay on board the O.S.S.S Earthanon and supervise the evacuation from here?" asked Captain Carrot.

"If you don't mind Captain Carrot." said Commodore Cu-Cumbala. "I would like to tie up some paperwork on the surface. If it meets with your agreement I would like to Vegitamise back up to the ship when all personnel have completed their regeneration periods. There are also plans to finalise with regard to the automatic destruct sequence for all Earthanon regions. We will dismantle what we can, but time is of a premium and we must not leave anything tangible that can be used after our departure. Although judging by the information on the Sodium Star belt. When that baby hits, the chances of anything surviving look very slim." said Commodore Cu-Cumbala.

"Very good Commodore Cu-Cumbala." agreed Captain Carrot. "FO Melonicord," he continued. "will Vegitamise down with you; her services are at your disposal. FO Melonicord I want you to let me know as soon as all personnel have been Vegitamised off of the Earthanon surface."

"Aye, aye Sir." replied FO Melonicord. "It will take approximately fifteen starhectoids Captain."

"Very well, go to it FO Melonicord, FO Marrowlar, will you accompany me to the bridge please?"

"Yes Sir,"

"Organigirls, Organiboys, you are dismissed." said Captain Carrot, as he went out of the Strategy room.

Part three

If the mountain won't come to Marrachinello!

Time 15.30 starhectoids

On the bridge, Ensign Strawballis turned to SO Tulipina as she signed the log reports from Viceroy Graperon.

"Excuse me SO Tulipina," she said. "but I am receiving reports from the Robopod sent to investigate the probe disappearance in the Arctolimba region. The Silicone mountain that has appeared was constructed by an intelligent life form. The storms are in fact wiping it away as opposed to creating it, as you can see from the weather patterns forming the wind cycles. On screen now Sir." said Ensign Strawballis initiating the visual screen.

"You will notice Sir that the pulsating beacon that is showing up in the area is coming from the inside of the mountain."

"Yes I see it Ensign Strawballis, tell me what is it?"

"That Sir, is the probe that was lost. It is the emergency transmitter wave that is set in motion whenever it's security is compromised."

"Surely if it's security is compromised then it would invoke it's self destruct mechanism?" asked SO Tulipina.

"Unless it felt it more beneficial to alert us to the presence of its captors Sir." explained Ensign Strawballis. "If indeed it has been captured," she continued. "it may have sneaked in to wherever or whatever unnoticed and found a safe place to hide."

"Surely if it were sending distress transmissions they would detect it on the ship in question?" reasoned SO Tulipina.

"Not necessarily Sir!" said Ensign Strawballis. "The Mechanoid probe in this case is the "Probonoid five thousand Qt." It has an in-built back up probe, a sort of pre-programmed scrambler. It transmits in an untraceable language that jumps across all frequencies. They will have detected it all right, but it will be almost impossible for them to triabulate its source of origin. You see it jumps from frequency to frequency in milli-starsecs. They simply would not have time to run a trace." confirmed Ensign Strawballis.

"I see, keep monitoring it Ensign Strawballis. I will bring it to the attention of the Captain when he returns to the bridge." said SO Tulipina.

"Aye, aye Sir." agreed Ensign Strawballis turning towards the Communications com.

"Viceroy Rhubarblatt, run the Grid Finder particle scanner on those co-ordinates. Let's see if there is some kind of ship in the centre of our mysterious mountain." ordered SO Tulipina determined to get to the bottom of the Mechanoid probe's disappearance.

"Running particle scan now Sir." confirmed Viceroy Rhubarblatt.

Just then the doors to Elevation chamber de-energised and out walked Captain Carrot and FO Marrowlar. The bridge crew stood to attention as Viceroy Graperon approached SO Tulipina with the log book which she signed again in order to hand over the Command com.

"Captain on the bridge." shouted Ensign Rasperillo.

"Pheweeeeee... Phewoooooh." whistled Ensign Melonture as he piped them on the bridge.

SO Tulipina handed Captain Carrot the log book which he scanned and signed then handed back to her.

"You have Command com Sir." she confirmed standing down.

"Thank you SO Tulipina," he said as he took his seat at the helm. "Stand easy on the bridge. Status report SO Tulipina." said Captain Carrot as he looked at the screen.

"Certainly Captain. This is the information transmission from the Robopod sent to investigate the probe disappearance in the Arctolimba region Sir. The beacon pulse that you can see on the screen pinpoints the exact position of the lost probe."

"Right in the middle of our magic mountain." said the bemused Captain. "Have you run a particle scan on the Grid Finder SO Tulipina?" he asked.

"Aye Sir, Viceroy Rhubarblatt is running it now." she confirmed.

"Is there anything inside our strange mountain Viceroy Rhubarblatt?" said the Captain directing his attention towards him.

"The information is coming through now Sir." said Viceroy Rhubarblatt as he viewed the gyroscope. "Yes Sir," he confirmed. "we have definite traces of olio plasma Captain. The storms have removed such a huge amount of silicone that we can now pick up on the unidentified ship's reactor emissions. She is definitely a Fasterfoid vessel Captain!"

Captain Carrot activated his personal channel. "Captain Carrot to Chief Potatree come in please." he called hurriedly.

"Chief Potatree here Sir." replied a flustered chief Potatree.

"Chief Potatree," continued Captain Carrot. "is it possible to use the blazer beam on an enemy vessel without drawing power capacity from the Vegitamisation and Regeneration processes?" he asked.

"Oooh now, that's a negative, Captain Carrot. All spare power is being directed to the Earthanon surface in order for them to complete the evacuation in time. We are at full stretch down here Captain! I can give you the power if you want it Sir, but it will be thirty Starmins before she's ready to go at full strength!" confirmed FO Potatree.

Captain Carrot paused as he considered the alternatives.

"Do we have any indications as to the type of ship in there. Viceroy Rhubarblatt?" enquired Captain Carrot.

"Judging by the amount of emissions emanating from the mountain Sir, no. Their reactors will be barely idling. However, the fact that we can detect olio plasma would indicate a flash cruiser or possibly a Mayo class star station. Other than that Sir, I'm afraid that is as specific as I can be." replied Viceroy Rhubarblatt.

"Very well, one would have assumed that they would have attacked by now, they must realise we have their men and foiled their plot." said Captain Carrot. "Ensign Strawballis." he continued. "Get me Ground station Earthanon fighter command," he said spurring into action. "If the mountain won't come to Marrachinello, then Marrachinello must go to the mountain."

"Aye, aye Sir." she said activating the Communications com. "This is Ensign Strawballis of the O.S.S.S Earthanon to Red Sector Leader Commander Marrachinello, come in please."

"Commander Marrachinello here O.S.S.S Earthanon. What can I do for you?" came the response after a brief interval.

"Put him on visual Ensign Strawballis. Secure the channel." requested the Captain.

"Aye Sir," she said. "Commander Marrachinello I have Captain Carrot on the line. He wishes to speak to you. I am putting you on visual now Sir. On line now Captain." she said.

"Thank you Ensign Strawballis," said Captain Carrot as Commander Marrachinello appeared on the screen. His familiar small frame typical of an Organitron born of the space race Cherrykeyko from the Planet Cherrynova which was situated in the pip minor system of the Fruitalia Quadrant. His skin was its usual shiny, velvety complexion in the deepest possible maroon red. As he greeted Captain Carrot he snapped his heels to attention and gave the Organitron salute, twanging his handlebar moustache in the process; almost taking his eye out as it slapped back into place.

"It is good to see you again my friend. How are you?" asked Captain Carrot, smiling at the Commander fighting to control his moustache.

"Very well Captain, all except that is for this infernal moustache. When I got up this morning, I just couldn't do a thing with it. Ow..." shrilled Commander Marrachinello as he fought again to straighten his unruly growth. "Imagine," he continued. "in years to come, dining out with the chaps at fighter command re-unions and having to explain the loss of my eye to the great battle of the moustache's revolt. Helios sakes Sir. I'll be the laughing stock of all Organitron. umm hay what, umm?"

"Indeed commander," guffawed Captain Carrot. "That would not be good for one's image, I can quite imagine. Unfortunately Commander Marrachinello, it would appear that we have an infiltrator ship hiding out in a silicone mountain in the Arctolimba region." said the Captain.

As Captain Carrot informed Commander Marrachinello of the Fasterfoid presence. His moustache stiffened immediately, his eyes, one of which was as bulbous as a small weather balloon while the other; retreated into his head almost closing completely, whilst the hairs on his neck stood on end.

"Gadzukes Sir, You just point the way and we'll get together a bit of a gravy bash for the blighters, hay what! umm? So Captain Carrot, what kind of a ship are we up against? No doubt some kind of Fasterfoid rust bucket Hey what, huh ha." he laughed.

"We think that it could be a Mayo Class Star station Commander." confirmed Captain Carrot.

"Exactly Captain Carrot, a rust bucket of the highest order. What do you want me to do with them? Blast them with gravy till their puny little carcass's go all limp, or maybe drop sprout gas on them and giggle them into submission, yes, hay-what umm?" continued Commander Marrachinello

Captain Carrot thought for a second as he contemplated his actions carefully. The Planet Earthanon was facing certain doom. This provided, in some way, an opportunity to strengthen relations between the Organitron's and the Fasterfoids. As it was, they already had a thousand of them in the brig houses. "No!" he thought. "now perhaps, more than ever, was a time when bridges could be built. It was time to show that the Organitron could respect the enemy when all were in danger. In the hope of one day peace breaking out between the feuding Nations. It was all very well to defeat the enemy in battle, but there was no glory in slaying a sitting target."

Clearing his throat, ready for the shock reaction of the notorious warrior of the skies, Captain Carrot took his seat at the helm and presented his case.

"Commander Marrachinello." he said. "Follow my train of thought if you will." he continued. "In approximately twelve starhectoids thirty Starmins, it is my intention to start the evacuation of the Earthanon Civilian freighters. It is essential that the main fighting force remain with the convoy for protection purposes. Quite apart from the threat of Fasterfoid's attack out in the Solar System, there is also the possibility that you and your Organitroops will have to stave off stray Aqua Asteroids. As you are aware most of the Civilian Freighters are prevented from carrying any form of laser protection by the UFO-Fasterfoid treaty. This treaty obviously prevents them from protecting themselves against any sizeable Asteroid bombardment. I think the size of this problem is an exception, therefore we are fitting the larger ships with auxiliary laser capability but even so, they are unskilled with such equipment and will need all the help they can get. Now, you have five squadrons at your disposal. That is five hundred Star Fighter units to cover a total of two hundred and forty ships in all." said the Captain. "We must, whatever happens, maintain a protection ratio of two to one. This leaves us with twenty ships that will escort the three O.S.S.S Mother ships. All Star Fighters that are based on the Mother ships. Eighty eight in all will remain on standby in the launch bays. What I want you to do my friend is this, take six Star Fighters and one Vege-cruiser which will contain a ground force of twenty thousand Organitron."

Commander Marrachinello was obviously unnerved by the Captain's most recent brain wave.

"Now, I want you to make sure your approach is under the three hundred Staryards particle scanner viewfinder range. Any higher and they may just pick you up. Hopefully this will get you close enough to the ship in order to off load the ground force should the need arise." Commander Marrachinello scratched his head unsure of the Captain's motives.

"This is where you come in Commander Marrachinello. We are all aware of your track record as a Star Fighter and as leader of fearless Organitron into and home from battle, but I want you, and you alone, armed with nothing more than a white flag,..." said the Captain as a furious Commander Marrachinello interrupted him.

"A white flag Captain Carrot? D... d, d, D... Did you say a white flag? March into the clutches of the Fasterfoids armed only with a white flag? What pray tell, am I to do if the blighters turn nasty umm? No.. no.. let me guess; blow my nose and then threaten to modge them to submission with my mucus clad flag of surrender. Captain Carrot, Sir, I must protest. I'm afraid to say that I think you have lost your head. And what's more Captain, you want me to lose mine! Holy Helios man, I'm Star Fighter Command! Not a wet nurse diplomat! I have never been so insulted; not in my long but if you have your way, soon to be cut short, life. Sir." said the Commander huffing and puffing.

Captain Carrot raised himself out of his chair and leaned on the hand-rail in front of the screen.

"Have you quite finished Commander Marrachinello?" said Captain Carrot calmly.

"Captain, Sir." continued the Commander. "I will say just one more thing. I have never refused an order and I do not intend to start now, but as part of my job I feel it necessary to point out elements of a plan that are to say the least, suicidal; Sir." Commander Marrachinello laughed at the screen nervously.

"As I was about to say, Commander Marrachinello." continued Captain Carrot. "It is precisely who you are that makes it imperative that you are the messenger of peace. There is no glory in defeating the enemy through the back door." reasoned Captain Carrot. "What we have here is the opportunity to forge the foundations of peace with the Fasterfoids. It is my guess that the silicone is blocking their capability to scan the Solar System. I don't think they are aware of the Sodium Star belt; let alone the Aqua Asteroids. They may even be beached there with no capability of taking off. Whatever the case, we must remember that first and foremost we are a collective Nations' of peace, and it is they that are the perpetrators of war. It is only fair that we offer them the opportunity of peaceful transportation out of the Solar System."

Commander Marrachinello Pondered the scenario placed at his feet by his good friend Captain Carrot, and lulled into a feeling of self realisation, pity and disparity. As the words of common sense flowed from the lips of Captain Carrot. Commander Marrachinello found himself asking some fundamental questions. A fighter he was, for as long as he could remember he had done exactly what was asked of him. Had he lost the real meaning of the UFO organisation? Was he so inflexible that he could not contemplate the prospect of helping to carry the olive branch of peace to its once fiercest enemy? Deep down he knew the answer and suddenly he was overcome with guilt. Captain Carrot was right. As usual the level head that sat on the shoulders of his much respected friend and leading Organitron diplomat, steered the course of change for the better of the universe. As of yet it had not been shaped, but was being moulded by the very hands of people like Captain Carrot. A visionary of peace and architect of the future. Captain Carrot knew that Commander Marrachinello would be re-evaluating his position in the UFO Organisation. He felt sure that he would see clarity in the intentions of his request and after jumping in the air with shock, land firmly on the side of common sense.

"Commander Marrachinello," said Captain Carrot. "You know me of old my friend, there is no question that I would order you to go. I am in torment with my request, I will go myself if you cannot find it in your heart to try for a peaceful solution." reasoned Captain Carrot. "Yes, I realise the dangers of entering the heart of the enemy unarmed, but I also see the dangers of benign complacency. It is true there is a strange security in the state of war but we must push forward the ideal of peace..."

Commander Marrachinello held up his hand, interrupting Captain Carrot.

"Captain Carrot." he said quickly. "If you can understand my scepticism of your plan, then you must know that I would no more let you march into that situation than ask you to forget your ideals. Besides my friend," continued the now calm Commander. "you will be needed in the near starhectoids to undergo the smooth transition of the evacuation. No my friend, I will go. We may want our heads examining, but as usual I will bow to your visions of a better and safer place. Tell me your plan quickly now before I change my mind, hey what?" he said shaking his head. Captain Carrot turned his attentions to the plan he had formulated in his mind, happy with the knowledge that the most respected fighter of the UFO organisation will be on side. Especially as even the enemy had more than a sneaking respect for Commander Marrachinello.

"Thank you Commander Marrachinello," said Captain Carrot smiling. "I can't tell you how much this could mean to our cause. Firstly we will not send you in there without any protection whatsoever. You will be fitted with an automatic particle scanner homing device hidden in your utility belt. If there is any problem at all, then you would simply activate the Vegitamisation sequence using a pre-set phrase and the Vegimatter computer will have you out of there before you can say UFO. Secondly, we would be offering only one solution to the problem. We cannot allow them to fly in Earthanon airspace unescorted due to the Organitron Fasterfoid treaty. A treaty that they are already in violation of by the fact of their presence. Thirdly, the point that we need to get across is simply this; we will inform them of the imminent arrival of the Sodium Star belt containing Aqua Asteroids. Then, we will offer them safe passage out of the Earthanon Solar System. This will be in the first convoy which was to be leaving in the next half starlectoids. We have some room to manoeuvre so we will hold off departure until they confirm compliance. As soon as we are out of the Solar System and clear of the Sodium Star belt, they will be free to go. The only proviso is, that we place a minimal skeleton crew of UFO personnel on the ship, until such time as we feel they are safe to continue the journey. At that point, the skeleton crew will Vegitamise off the ship.."

Commander Marrachinello interrupted the Captain.

"I am considering the plan you have put forward, Captain, but what if they perforate my eardrums with laughter and tell me they don't believe me? If I were to put myself in their position, I would ask why the UFO organisation would want to board my vessel in order to give us safe passage then let us go Scott free. Frankly I would accuse us of a back-door reconnaissance mission?" said the Commander

"I agree with you Commander." smiled Captain Carrot. "On board the ship." he continued. "We believe, we already have a Mechanoid probe in hiding. You can tell them that the reconnaissance mission is complete and has been for some time Commander. The probe will act as a communication satellite in order for them to communicate with me. You can tell them that we have tried to contact them for some time, but the silicone mountain that they have used to shield their presence is also the cause for their ignorance of the Star belt. It is blocking our ability to communicate, therefore we assume it would block or distort their information gathering capability."

Commander Marrachinello looked surprised at the news of the probe. "Have we really had a probe on board the ship for some time?" asked Commander Marrachinello.

"Yes; quite by chance I grant you but we don't have to tell them that. I will then talk to the Captain of the ship and offer him my ultimatum, whilst you my friend, will have your verbal finger on the Vegitamisation button. My senses tell me that this is about the time all Helios could break loose." said the Captain, thinking that at this point honesty was the best policy and only fair to Commander Marrachinello who strolled up and down with his hands firmly grasped behind his back.

"Very well Captain," said Commander Marrachinello. "when do we go?" he asked.

Captain Carrot turned to FO Marrowlar. "FO Marrowlar are the ground force on standby?" he asked.

"Affirmative Captain Carrot, the ground force are on board the Vege-cruiser. They are at fifty percent stature; if things do turn nasty then we will want them to be a harder target to hit, Sir." confirmed FO Marrowlar.

"Very wise FO Marrowlar. Tell me, how long before they can be in the air?"

FO Marrowlar punched in some data at the ship's analyser com. "The Vege-cruisers Calorific reactors will be at full capacity in five Starmins Captain All military ground-force are onboard." acknowledged FO Marrowlar.

Captain Carrot returned to the screen where Commander Marrachinello was standing by. "Five Starmins Commander," he said. "gather your best men and rendezvous with the Vege-cruiser at the Co-ordinates FO Marrowlar will send through to your on board computer. We will monitor your approach and have the ship's Star Fighters on green alert; in case you need back up. The ship's systems analyser is on stand-by for the Mechanoid probes frequency transmissions." said the Captain, again trying to assure Commander Marrachinello of the safety factors built into the plan.

Commander Marrachinello clicked his heels to attention and gave the Organitron salute. "Is that all Captain Carrot? I will have to brief the men on route." Captain Carrot returned the Organitron salute and winked an eye at Commander Marrachinello.

"That is all Commander Marrachinello, I have every confidence that the right man for this job is you. I can't tell you how important the outcome of this mission is to the peace process. Grow with the flow Commander Marrachinello. Captain Carrot out, end transmission."

"Commander Marrachinello UFO and out, end transmission."

The screen cleared and Captain Carrot sat back at the Command com.

"FO Marrowlar." said Captain Carrot firmly. "Have ten Star Fighters on stand-by from each of the Mother ships. Alert them to the plans and the terms we are trying to negotiate."

"Aye, aye, Sir." said FO Marrowlar as he hailed the fighter Command post on board the O.S.S.S Earthanon in the defence sector of the ship. "FO Marrowlar to Fighter command Lematra, come in please."

Captain Carrot turned his attentions to Ensign Viola.

"Ensign Viola," he said. "I have scanned your proposed route for the evacuation procedure. It appears to be in order. Have all the co-ordinates been sent to all ships using scrambled communications?" he asked.

"Aye, aye Sir." she replied.

"And confirm course trajectory to all ships. Alert them to standby for a delay to the time table. We will advise as to when the departure time is fixed." continued Captain Carrot. As he took time out to study all aspects of the operation in his mind, the doors to the elevation chamber de-energised, and out came Captain Peabazzare with the bridge crew of The O.S.S Satsumuroo.

"Captain Peabazzare and the bridge crew reporting for duty Sir." said Captain Peabazzare, offering him the Organitron Salute.

Captain Carrot turned to the group assembled in front of the elevation chamber.

"Captain Peabazzare, Organigirls, Organiboys. I am about to ask you to put your trust in me. You may even consider me completely nuts when you hear what I have to say. I want you to report to Ensign Broccleman in the Vegimatter room. There, you will arm yourselves with Blazer guns. Place yourself on standby to board the infiltration ship in the Arctolimba region on my command. If all goes according to plan you will be required to supervise it's safe passage off the Earthanon surface as part of the main convoy. Once we are free of danger from the Sodium Star belt, we will Vegitamise you back on board one of the mother ships. Are there any questions?" asked Captain Carrot as the bridge crew of the O.S.S Satsumuroo looked at each other in amazement.

"Captain Carrot." said the surprised Captain Peabazzare. "Am I to assume that they have agreed to this plan willingly?" he wondered.

Captain Carrot looked pensively at FO Marrowlar. "Not as yet, but your departure orders will only be given if they do so! You will also requisition utility belts from Ensign Broccleman. These will be pre-set with Vegitamisation instructions. The pre-phrase will be given to you to initiate the particle scanner homing device. Is there anything else?" enquired Captain Carrot.

"No Captain Carrot, everything seems to be covered." said Captain Peabazzare.

"Very good Captain Peabazzare." said Captain Carrot. "Pick twenty of your own crew to accompany you; your best crew, is that understood?"

"Aye, aye Captain, understood." acknowledged Captain Peabazzare.

With that Captain Peabazzare offered the Organitron salute and took his crew off the bridge and headed for the Vegimatter room.

Down on the Earthanon surface the Star Fighters and the Vege-cruiser were making ready for departure. Commander Marrachinello approached his ship and was muttering to himself with fervour.

"Holy Helios man, you must be stark, raving crazy. Years, absolutely years I stared death right in the eyes. Laughed at it even! But never! Never offered myself as a hostage to a bunch of fry by nights. Oh the shame of it. If my Organidaddy could see me now, why he would turn in his compost heap." At this point, he noticed his mechanic and valet, Engineer Oliver, laughing under the fuselage of the Star Fighter.

"Yes Engineer Oliver?" said the commander. "You seem to find something funny my friend?" He grunted as he pulled Engineer Oliver from under the fuselage by his ear.

"Ahh... Ahh... Commander Marrachinello what is'a your problem I swear I am 'a just very happy honestly." he pleaded.

"Well if I find you are laughing at me my little green friend, I will strap you to the wing of my Star Fighter and jump to light speed until your green little skin resembles a prune, Is that clear umm.. hey what?" shrilled Commander Marrachinello.

"A prune," quivered Engineer Oliver. "a wrinkly little prune. Mamma Mia, no! What about 'a the dames? They won't a'like 'a me anymore. Please Commander have a heart." he begged as he ear seemed to twist a full one hundred and eighty Blimits. Suddenly Commander Marrachinello smiled on his friend and gave him a hug.

"My dear friend." said Commander Marrachinello. "You know I wouldn't do that to you!" he said.

"You wouldn't boss? I'mean'a of course you wouldn't boss. We have 'a too much water under the bridge, no? I know 'a that you are joking, I am too valuable an asset to lose no?" said Engineer Lematra.

"Don't push it Oliver old bean. The more I think about it, prunes are said to be a very healthy Organitron. I may start to consider you could do with being a little healthier." laughed Commander Marrachinello.

"Healthier, me boss? No... N... No, look at 'a this." Flexing his muscles he then picked up a fuel can and raised it above his head. "Look boss," he said. "four times my own 'a weight, how healthy do you want ah?"

"Very impressive Engineer Oliver old chap. It would be more impressive however, if there were anything in it." he joked getting into the Star Fighter. "OK Oliver, chocks away!" he shouted as he saluted Engineer Oliver and dropped the canopy while putting on his head set.

Engineer Oliver returned his salute and pulled the chock pins from the vessel launching system. "Good luck my gooda boss. May Helios hold your hand." said Engineer Oliver.

Smiling at Engineer Oliver, he started the take-off procedure.

"This is Red Leader Sector control to all Red Sector units. Confirm rendezvous data receipt!" he asked as he finished his final checks.

"This is Red Sector number two confirmed and ready to go."

Then Red Sector units' three to six confirmed and Commander Marrachinello applied for permission to take off.

"This is Red Leader Sector control. Permission to depart for the Arctolimba region over."

"This is FO Marrowlar, your flight path is configurated and you are cleared for takeoff. May I remind you that you are to observe communication silence within five hundred starmillo's of your target." said FO Marrowlar.

"Thank you FO Marrowlar, this is Red Leader Sector control UFO and out."

"FO Marrowlar UFO and out."

Slowly the bay doors of the launch pad opened revealing Earthanon in its full beauty. It was decided that they would not use the Catapult tubes in case they were monitored by the Fasterfoids. Instead they would use the deck catapults.

"Red Leader Sector control, go-go units one two and three." confirmed Commander Marrachinello.

"UFO Red Leader Sector control." came the response as the ships took off through the catapult expulsion point doors, disappearing against the satin blue of the Earthanon atmosphere, Commander Marrachinello gave the order to launch the rest of the Star Fighter patrol.

"This is Red Leader Sector control units four and five follow my leave."

"Aye, aye Sir," came the reply.

"Three, two and one activate, now."

The remainder of the ships set off to join the other ships in the patrol. Engineer Oliver sighed as his true friend and mentor flew off into the great unknown.

Time 17.30 starhectoids

On the bridge, the Captain of the Vege-cruiser Currantana came through to Ensign Strawballis on the Communications com.

"This is Captain Wilbur Wheatanzra of the Vege-cruiser Currantana calling the O.S.S.S Earthanon, come in over."

"This is Ensign Strawballis, Communications officer of the O.S.S.S Earthanon, come in please."

"This is the Vege-cruiser Currantana confirming the arrival of Red Leader Sector control. We are travelling in arrowhead formation heading for the Arctolimba region. This will be the last transmission before entering the no communication zone. All systems are go and we are beginning silent running in two Starmins thirty Starsecs. Please confirm communication receipt?" asked Captain Wheatanzra. Captain Carrot activated his personal channel and confirmed the transmission.

"Transmission received and understood. We hope that the order to go will not be necessary, but the order to activate ground force will be Red Sector green and mean, please confirm?" said Captain Carrot.

"Red Sector green and mean, received and understood." confirmed Captain Wheatanzra.

"This is Captain Carrot of the O.S.S.S Earthanon, good luck Captain Wheatanzra, UFO and out."

"Thank you Sir, Captain Wheatanzra UFO and out."

FO Marrowlar took the readings of the Earthanon Atmosphere and presented the information to Captain Carrot.

"Excuse me sir. All Robopods have completed the Ozone drop and are returning to the ship. We have seventy percent returns to date. As you can see Sir, it has slowed down the blimits decent to one percent per hour. Current status of the Earthanon surface is minus Thirty seven point two below usual operational levels." confirmed FO Marrowlar. "We believe that the one percent loss is due to the Earthanon storms, therefore making the Ozone layer a complete success Sir."

"It's ironic is it not, FO Marrowlar? That we manage to find a natural solution to the Earthanon weather cycles, combine it with a natural protection against the ultra violet, Gamma and radiation rays, just in time for the evacuation of Earthanon." Captain Carrot gave a small but defeatist laugh and turned to FO Marrowlar. "Nevertheless," he continued. "we must praise the efforts of FO Cornelius and dare I say it Professor Goosegorgon? Not forgetting of course Dr Kiwitranus." said Captain Carrot.

"Yes Sir," replied FO Marrowlar. "It may be a little late for our long term benefit, but I feel sure it has bought us valuable time in the short term."

Captain Carrot smiled, and knocked FO Marrowlar on the arm playfully.

"Besides," said Captain Carrot. "We may be able to come back here sometime in the future and who knows, hopefully find it still in place?" he continued.

"Indeed Captain that may be so." replied FO Marrowlar.

SO Tulipina called the attention of Captain Carrot and FO Marrowlar.

"Captain Carrot, FO Marrowlar." she said "The Vege-cruiser Currantana and Red Leader Sector control have arrived at the drop zone sector. Commander Marrachinello will be splitting off any moment now to make his final singular approach." she confirmed.

"Put the Earthanon map on screen SO Tulipina." ordered Captain Carrot. "Then tie us into Red Leader Sector control Visaid. This is where the ride could start getting a little bumpy!" said Captain Carrot.

"On screen now Sir." said SO Tulipina.

The screen came up with the Arctolimba region mapped out in front of the Captain on the bridge. There were seven beacon blips on the map. The orange blip by far the largest, indicating the position of the Vege-cruiser Currantana. Four purple blips showing the position of the ancillary back-up fighters, with one green blip indicating the secondary pilot command and one red blip indicating the Red Leader Sector control ship of Commander Marrachinello. The red blip moved on alone whilst the others stayed in their fixed positions, as Commander Marrachinello made his final approach toward the infiltration ship co-ordinates, which was situated in the heart of the storm zone. He set his Star Fighter down in a gully, just short of the silicone mountain. He began issuing a cross frequency distress beacon. The remaining Star Fighters set off to encompass the infiltration ship as pre agreed on the five hundred stormily boundary and awaited the command for attack.

On the bridge the Captain and crew were monitoring on the Visaid as soon as Commander Marrachinello embarked on his lonely and dangerous task. Before Commander Marrachinello broke off from the Star Fighter convoy, he signalled to the Red Leader Secondary pilot to break off and hold position and flew into the turmoil of the storm. "Goodness gracious this isn't a storm it's purgatory." He looked down at the control panel and could see the Visaid was operational. "I hope you chaps have taken your air sickness tabs. If not there's going to be one whole load of fainting on the bridge." The ship took a sharp dive as the vast, powerful wind currents took hold of the Star Fighter. Commander Marrachinello fought with the joystick as he struggled to contain the sophisticated piece of technology at his fingertips against the simplistic, yet far more powerful persuasions of the elements. Finally, bringing the ship under control he corrected it's flight path, narrowly missing an earth and rock formation. "Wha.. Woo.. Wwowee that was too close for comfort! The things I do for my race." As he corrected his course, the bridge crew reacted in a sort of a Chilean wave. With Fungola, the Mushroid who was now present on the bridge, covering his eyes.

Suddenly, as Commander Marrachinello could see the sand mountain in the distance, he employed the multi frequency distress beacon. "This is Star Fighter command UFO Red Leader Sector control, calling the unregistered Fasterfoid ship in the Arctolimba region come in please." He paused momentarily, eagerly awaiting their reply. "This is an emergency, I repeat, this is a UFO Star Fighter control emergency, come in please." Commander Marrachinello knew they would not be able to resist the bait of ensnaring a prized Sun-Fleet Star Fighter commander. "Ahh, now let's see the colour of your skin. Is it yellow, or just plain green I wonder? If you answer this call, not only are you greener but also dumber than I gave you credit for." he said chuckling to himself.

Starsecs later came a petulant reply to his distress call.

"This is the Fasterfoid ship FF Francaisfry and I am Principle Officer Gammachip. We have you on our range scanners and are locked on to you with Gunge lasers. If you land and give yourself up we will spare you your miserable life, do you understand Organitron?" said the voice on the line. Commander Marrachinello laughed at the idiocy and arrogance of his enemy.

"Now you listen to me you great glob of starch and saturated fat. This is Commander Marrachinello of Star Fighter command of the United Foliage of Organitron. If, as you say, you had me on your scanner, then you would be aware that my ship had already touched down, therefore you cannot possibly have locked your Gunge laser on me." said the Commander. "So let's cut the junk and get to the point shall we? I come in peace, alone and unarmed. I request consul with the Captain of your ship, or perhaps somebody of more importance if they are available. I don't have much time to waste explaining the purpose of my mission, only to find that they do not have the power to make any decisions." explained Commander Marrachinello

Inside the ship Principle Gammachip handed over to his superior officer, General Satuese. Who more than usual was particularly greasy for a little character of the Crinkleozone ilk, sporting his battle dress eye patch over his left eye, his small black tufts of hair protruding from his ears perfectly stiffened with lard, and a nose of quite sizeable proportions; constantly dripping with sticky thick secreted fat.

"This is General Satuese Commander Marrachinello. I must say, this is a most unexpected pleasure. Tell me, to what do we owe the honour of your surrender?" he chuckled.

"In your dreams grease ball," quipped Commander Marrachinello. "This is not a social call or one of surrender but one of much importance. If you and your comrades are to make it off of the Earthanon surface alive that is. In short my Calorific misfit, this is a flag of truce and unless you grant me consul I fear, though I must admit with some relish, that your ship and crews starhectoids are numbered! Under the Organitron-Fasterfoid treaty, of which might I add, your very presence here is in violation, may I suggest that you grasp the olive branch of peace and see me without delay, or this little attempt at being reasonable may just run out of serious momentum. From thereafter my deep fried little dimwit, your unexpected pleasure will become a sure fired guaranteed displeasure, capiche?" Commander Marrachinello knew that he would have to bully them into seeing him. The Fasterfoids were many things, but thick skinned and beings of substance they were not! Awaiting their reply, he scanned the mountain for a possible entrance to the Silicone mountain but the storm was too intense to gain any firm readings. Meanwhile on the bridge of the FF Francaisfry, Principle Officer Gammachip was spoiling for a fight. Seething for retaliation he begged General Satuese for permission to go out and deal with him.

"Let me at him General. No one is going to call you grease ball and get away with it, no Sir. Why I'll bog him down in ketchup then I'll make vegetable oil of him, I swear I will!"

General Satuese laughed loudly and pointed at him as the rest of the Fasterfoids laughed too. Principle officer Gammachip shrugged off the jibes and turned to his station ignoring the mimic torments of his fellow shipmates.

"You mean like the way you dealt with Legionnaire Chickonplaza from Chickonaldirs? What was it you were going to do again? Oh yes I remember, turn him inside out and make Ghi from his gizzards. Now enlighten me again, was that before or after he threw you head first into the dripping estuary?" laughed General Satuese.

Principle officer Gammachip turned to General Satuese and protested the indignity of being laughed at by his own comrades. "That's not fair you shouldn't poke fun at me in front of the crew. Besides, it is bad for ships discipline." Principle officer Gammachip stopped and thought briefly. "Anyway," he continued. "How was I to know that he was the Chickonaldirs weight lifting champion seven years running?" For some reason this only seemed to increase the laughter of the crew, much to the annoyance of Principle Officer Gammachip.

"Well, what is so funny now eh?" he said confronting several members of the crew. "Actually," stirred General Satuese fighting to contain his stomach cramps. "I'm afraid I think I can help you there. You see he, he, Ahh, ha, ha, ha, he wasn't." spluttered the General unable to hold himself together any longer. "We told you that so that you wouldn't get too embarrassed." Principle Officer Gammachip started to go red in the face though not with fury, more with an embarrassed shame.

"Then who was he?" he asked slowly, un-eager for the reply.

"He, he, he, he, he, he was a garbage handler from the Chickenora City depot before he enlisted. You, you weren't beaten by the famous Chickonplaza smash."

"I wasn't?" enquired Principle Officer Gammachip.

"No, you were beaten by the trash thrash bash. Ahhh. Hahaa." Announced General Satuese, who was now laughing uncontrollably as he rolled off his chair at the helm, eventually crumpling up in a lump on the ground, waving his arms in the air as his feet beat a rhythm on the floor.

Commander Marrachinello, who was becoming more irritable as time passed and no response came forward, hailed the ship again.

"This is Commander Marrachinello requesting an immediate response to my last transmission, please respond over."

Then suddenly the voice of General Satuese was back on line. "Very well Commander Marrachinello, you may come aboard. However, there are certain conditions." said the General

"How did I know you were going to say that, scus ball." he muttered under his breath.

"Very well what are they?" he acknowledged.

"That you come alone, unarmed, and swear to a dialogue aimed towards surrender, or I may be forced to set my Principle Officer on you as he has requested, do you understand?" bluffed General Satuese.

"Understood General Satuese. You have my word." promised Commander Marrachinello with his fingers crossed. "But I didn't say whose surrender." chuckled Commander Marrachinello again under his breath.

"Very well, we are opening the port hull door now." confirmed the General.

Commander Marrachinello activated his utility belt and left the ship. As he was battered by the winds fighting to keep the sand from his eyes, he could just make out a dim light in the distance. "That must be the entrance," he thought. As he entered the ship, the doors closed behind him and he was surrounded by Fasterfoids. FasterFritters and Crinkleozones both encircled him. Commander Marrachinello placed his hands in the air and was ushered to the bridge of the ship. Standing on the elevation steps, they moved upwards and onto the command centre level where he was met by General Satuese. Still with his hands in the air he stepped off the platform and on to the dreary bridge, very grey and stiflingly hot. With the command panels flashing all around him, he thought to himself this was not a ship they had seen before. Not massive by comparison to the Mayo-class star station, yet larger than the traditional flash cruiser.

"Fasterfriends, Fasterfriends, you can see that the Commander is unarmed." said the General. "Let us not be the ones to point weapons first. Welcome Commander Marrachinello, I am General Satuese of the FF Francaisfry. Please, step this way won't you." he said, showing him to the main bridge which was much brighter by comparison, with bright red electro rings hung from the ceiling emitting a loud, fluorescent, scarlet glow, considerably warmer than before. He could feel himself wilting where he stood. One thing was for sure, he would not be able to withstand this environment for too long. As he entered the bridge the crew were lined up to receive their distinguished guest. General Satuese offered Commander Marrachinello the hand of friendship.

"Please put your hands down Commander." he said with his arm stretched out. Commander Marrachinello looked down at his hands which were dripping with a fatty secretion; another unusual trait of the FasterFritters and Crinkleozones. He closed his eyes as their hands grasped together squelching on contact, sending a shot of the secretion in the face of Principle Officer Gammachip.

"May I introduce you to my Principle Officer Gammachip," Who again offered a hand in friendship.

"No offence," he said. "But I think this will just make things a little too messy for my liking." smiled Commander Marrachinello, looking at the fatty substance dribbling off the head of the Principle Officer Gammachip. "Of course, none taken Commander. It is quite, shall we say, understandable." said General Satuese looking at Principle Officer Gammachip in disgust. "Go and redress yourself at once Gammachip. You're a disgrace to the uniform!" said the General his eyes rolling with disappointment. Then moving down the line he continued. "This is Vice Principle Officer Waffleat, Vice Principle Officer Fritz and Vice Principle Officer Roastie. Over here we have Prefect Beefychip, Prefect Crinklet and Prefect Roastard. Last but not least, may I introduce Medical Officer Crispin and his deputy Medical Officer Sautate. Gentlegrills, Gentlefrills that is all. To your posts please. Come Commander Marrachinello, will you take refreshment in my bunker room?" continued General Satuese.

Commander Marrachinello was agog at the state of the ship.

"Helios knows what the personal habitats were going to be like." he thought. "I may not partake, but lead the way General." said the Commander, unsure of what the good General would consider refreshing.

"Very well Commander, follow me please. VPO Fritz have Principle Officer Gammachip meet us in my bunker room when he returns for duty!" he ordered.

"Aye fry Sir!" said VPO Fritz standing to attention.

CHAPTER TWELVE

The olive branch and the brave

Time 18.45 starhectoids

On the bridge of the O.S.S.S Earthanon, Captain Carrot stood in the very place where he had watched his good friend and faithful colleague Commander Marrachinello, disappear into the distance. Within the Commanders brief were instructions not to rush the Fasterfoids to try and let them judge the Organitron by reaching their own conclusions, hopefully the right conclusions. FO Marrowlar stood behind him knowing that Commander Marrachinello and the situation that he had flown into would be playing heavily on the mind of Captain Carrot.

"Well it looks like all we can do is wait Sir?" said FO Marrowlar.

"Indeed FO Marrowlar, it would appear that is the case." agreed Captain Carrot.

"Sir, if I might be so bold? Captain, was Commander Marrachinello really the best man for the job? Personally, if I were the enemy, I would have doubted the sincerity of the Commander's claim of peace, by the very tone he used in his communications with the General and agreeing to talk of surrender well, one can't help but wonder Captain?"

"Exactly FO Marrowlar. They would move Helios and Earthanon to get him on- board that ship, especially if he were as rude as could be. There is a sneaking respect for Commander Marrachinello throughout the whole of the Galaxies and Solar Systems, even from the enemy. No FO

Marrowlar they couldn't resist it. He is the only man for the job, after all he is going in, isn't he? In fact by now he should be well and truly in…or on it. One might say." said Captain Carrot softly

FO Marrowlar bowed to the opinion of Captain Carrot and returned to his station at the security section of the ship's analyser.

"Yes Sir, of course Captain," he said knowing that yet again the Captain's actions were as a result of deep lateral thinking. "SO Tulipina," he continued. "the port protective energy shield is detecting a fluctuating imbalance in the primary subspace energiser. Can you run a full circuit test along the proton chamber conduits? Just to make sure we are not experiencing any static reflux in the traversed polarity field?"

"Aye, aye Sir, running the test sequence now."

"Thank you SO Tulipina."

"SO Okralate to FO Marrowlar come in please." FO Marrowlar activated his personal channel.

"FO Marrowlar here. Come in SO Okralate." Captain Carrot turned in his chair to hear the report of the SO in charge of the prisoners on board the O.S.S.S Earthanon.

"Sir," said a very irritated SO Okralate. "we have managed to establish the identities of the most senior Officers held within prisoners, and put them in isolation from the rest of the prisoners. Frankly Sir, that's about all they want to talk about. Name, Rank and number, strictly by the book. The most senior Officers would appear to be, one Ground-force General and five Principle officers."

"Has the Ground-force General made any requests for, or on behalf of his men?" asked FO Marrowlar.

"Just one Sir, but I am not comfortable with using that kind of language Sir. However, you can read it in my report." remarked SO Okralate in a most indignant tone.

"How do you wish me to proceed FO Marrowlar? Shall I blast them with sprout gas? Give them something to chew on, like a full Vegimatter banquet, or just bath them in gravy? That will sort the blighters out."

"Please hold SO Okralate." said FO Marrowlar, as he indicated to Captain Carrot for his direction in the matter.

"Will do Sir." acknowledged SO Okralate

Captain Carrot thought long and hard. It was no good feeding them Vegimatter banquets. The rumour was, that even the Fasterfoids had started to consume Vegimatter as part of their natural diet. Some reports suggest that they are even preferring it to their own Fatty matters, or at least as a balanced part of their diet. It had been suspected for startechtoids but, as was ever in negotiations with the Fasterfoids, they were too proud to admit, that the Organitron ethos was right all along. As if the fact that the Organitron's live twice as long, and are three times more advanced in terms of technology, isn't proof enough.

"This ground General, what is his name?" enquired Captain Carrot.

"SO Okralate, what is the ground General's name?" asked FO Marrowlar.

"General Crinkleark Sir."

"Have General Crinkleark and the Principle Officers brought to the strategy room in four starhectoids, under full security, FO Marrowlar. I think it's time we turned the tide in our favour."

"Aye Sir, said SO Okralate." Captain Carrot returned his attentions to the events on Earthanon surrounding the infiltrators' ship.

"Ensign Strawballis. Make ready a channel for the infiltration ship to contact us, intensify several frequencies to ensure a link. After all, Commander Marrachinello will be relying on us to get him out of there safely. We must do everything in our power to honour our commitment!"

Time 21.30 starhectoids.

In the bunker room of General Satuese, Commander Marrachinello, was fast feeling the effects of the heat, sweat caressing his temples with increasing speed. General Satuese offered Commander Marrachinello a drink.

"Will you partake in some chilled olive fat Commander? You will forgive my rudeness, but since you have come aboard you have refused all sustenance, you look like you can use it!"

To Commander Marrachinello, it rather resembled a murky green play-dough that the children would use in the education suite on board the O.S.S.S Earthanon.

"Thank you no." he said holding a handkerchief over his face. "I don't suppose you have any water on board?" enquired Commander Marrachinello.

"Alas no Commander, but I can offer you a glass of potato wine. We are not strictly supposed to have it on board but, well, we all have our little weaknesses, wouldn't you agree?"

Commander Marrachinello waved a hand in denial, the stench from the olive fat becoming quite nauseating.

"We find a perfectly balanced diet, leaves us no need for little weaknesses General." he said, wondering how anyone could stomach the delights of the Fasterfoid diet, let alone any of their weaknesses

"Just then Principle Officer Gammachip entered the bunker room."

"I am sorry I am late Gentlemen, work cannot stop for anyone, even a supposed Organitron hero." Commander Marrachinello stared at him, his face not even showing the signs of anger. "I may be an un-proven hero, but you my friend are a proven idiot." observed Commander Marrachinello.

General Satuese asked his second in command if he would like some refreshments.

"Principle Gammachip, a nice cold refreshment, to cool your temper perhaps?"

"Thank you General that would be most welcome." he agreed smirking wildly.

General Satuese walked around the table and poured the Olive fat over the head of Principle Gammachip. Slowly it was dripping down his face and into his lap. He sat silently as the General scorned his attitude.

"For the last time Principle Gammachip, you will hold your tongue, or I will see to it that you lose it, once and for all, is that understood?"

"Yes Sir, fully." he said clearing his face of the gooey gunk.

"Please Commander Marrachinello forgive my comrade, he is young and hot headed." pleaded General Satuese.

Trying to contain his laughter, Commander Marrachinello released the handkerchief from his face.

"He may be young General," said the Commander. "but I think his head has cooled somewhat recently." Commander Marrachinello smirked, making Principle Gammachip feel even more belittled.

"That is enough frivolity Commander. We have discussed the ship, our mission, your conquests, ours, now we must get down to the serious business of your visit." said the General.

"Indeed," agreed Commander Marrachinello. "General Satuese," he continued. "We believe that the Silicone cover that you have used for the purpose of your mission, which I might add, has already been noticed and scuppered, is blocking your capability to read the atmospheric changes in the Solar System surrounding Earthanon."

"Nonsense Sir, our equipment is registering perfectly!" interrupted Principle Gammachip, scorning the very notion of Commander Marrachinello's suggestion.

"Really Principle, you could not even pinpoint the whereabouts of my ship. How do you explain that?" retorted Commander Marrachinello.

"That, is simple Commander Marrachinello. Surely even you noticed the storm that has been raging in this Helios forsaken place." answered the Principle firmly.

"And how long has the storm been raging as you so eloquently put it?"

continued the Commander, becoming more and more ratty with the Principle.

"Some thirty two starhectoids Commander." he said smugly.

"Well, at least you can tell the time with some accuracy!" slammed the Commander, wiping the grin from the principle's face.

"General," continued Commander Marrachinello ignoring the buffoon opposite him. "I have come here to inform you, that within approximately thirteen to fourteen starhectoids, there will be a Sodium Star belt pelting the surface of Earthanon."

"This ship is amply constructed to deal with salt storms Commander Marrachinello. Really, I don't think you need concern yourself." said the General obviously unnerved by the ship's lack of information. The glare towards Principle Gammachip on the other hand, told a very transparent story.

"There is no doubt about that General!" continued Commander Marrachinello. "However, contained within the Sodium Star belt, is an Aqua Asteroid field some of which we believe, are the size of a small Planet." assured Commander Marrachinello.

"Really Commander? Our particle scanner shows nothing of the sort." reasoned Principle Gammachip interrupting again.

This time, it was the turn of General Satuese to silence the second in command.

"Commander Marrachinello has already proved that you can't see a ship approaching within four hundred Staryards. This would be the same particle scanner would it not?" General Satuese sat in silence awaiting his reply which was not forthcoming.

"Carry on Commander, I'm all ears." said the General quietly.

"Thank you General. We already have your men from the Earthanon surface, on board the O.S.S.S Earthanon. Just over a thousand at the last count. They are there for your protection. We are evacuating the Planet Earthanon. By now certain stages are almost complete. All Vegimatter and mineral substances, have been Vegitamised aboard a mass convoy of Sun-Fleet and civilian Freighters. Earthanon personnel are miniaturised in stature awaiting transferral, and the equipment Vegitamisation process is underway as we speak. We the Organitron's, wish to escort you out of the Earthanon Solar System with a skeleton crew of UFO personnel on board of course, as is laid down in the Fasterfoid-Organitron treaty. After all, you are in violation of that treaty, General. Your presence here is of, no doubt, a volatile nature. However, as soon as we are free of the Sodium Star belt and clear of the Earthanon Solar System, you will be free to proceed on your way, after the Fasterfoid personnel on-board the O.S.S.S Earthanon have been Vegitamised back to your ship, and the UFO personnel are safely back on board the O.S.S.S Earthanon."

General Satuese sat in silence as he sized up his options. The doors to the bunker room opened and a strange little fellow, oozing with grease and in the form of a deep fried jacket wedge, sloped across the room. Leaning across the table, he muttered something to the General and Principle Officer Gammachip. Commander Marrachinello was pleased with the way the meeting was progressing. With his energy levels flagging, he had to get out of there soon or this would be his last mission. Apart from the heat, the stench of greasy fat was becoming more than over-powering. General Satuese dismissed the Officer who sloped out of the room with all the speed and finesse of a slug.

"Well Commander it would appear that we have indeed lost contact with our ground forces, but this could be due to the storm. We will need proof of the prisoners being held aboard your ship!" said the General.

"We like to think under this situation, that they arc our guests." Standing up, Commander Marrachinello activated his utility belt, initialising the communications homing transmitter with the probe in hiding on the ship.

"Gentlemen, we have had on board this ship, a Mechanoid probe for some time." Suddenly, a huge commotion could be heard from the ship's crew, as they tried to launch themselves on the probe in order to catch it, but to no avail.

Entering the bunker room with several Fasterfoid passengers on board the little probe, it floated in and started to spin gradually disposing of the unwanted foreign bodies. One by one, they flew off in different directions splattering against the walls, leaving a trail of gloupy substances all around the room. General Satuese leered at the crew for their idiotic inefficiency, angry at the lack of security displayed by the ship's crew in general, especially for allowing a probe to stow away on board; but his anger was aimed in the main at Principle Officer Gammachip.

"Will you all stand up and take a look at yourselves," said the General. "Is this the sterling results of the training this, this moron is placing on you?" He said pointing a finger at Principle Officer Gammachip. "If it is, there is no future for the Fasterfoid race. I have never been so embarrassed in my life and believe me, working alongside this utter dipstick, I have had more than my fair share of embarrassing situations. Forgive me. No, no, forgive us Commander Marrachinello, I am sure you are sickened with the sight set before you, and I would understand if you were to break down in uncontrollable fits of laughter"

Commander Marrachinello chuckled as he viewed the chaos around him.

"Thank you but no, really General, time is running out and I feel it is necessary to use the probe, to make contact with the O.S.S.S Earthanon, as soon as possible."

"Yes of course Commander, please go ahead."

Commander Marrachinello tapped in some data to his utility belt, then he made some adjustments to the Mechanoid probe.

"There we go. It will take some time to establish a link but I am confident that it will find a strong enough frequency and proton boost its wave band."

Time 21.45 starhectoids

Back on the O.S.S.S Earthanon, Captain Carrot was making his way to the strategy room with FO Marrowlar, when FO Marrowlar's personal channel activated.

"Are all the Fasterfoid officers gathered in the strategy room FO Marrowlar?" asked Captain Carrot.

"Yes Captain, though I am afraid their attitude will be, to say the least, frosty."

"Frankly it can be frozen solid; that way we can fire them at the Aqua Asteroids. That will show them what cold really is."

"SO Tulipina to FO Marrowlar. Come in please."

"FO Marrowlar here." he acknowledged.

"Sir, we have run the circuit tests on the ship's energy shield. We have had to increase the reflux, to account for the increased moisture in the air, due to the approaching Sodium Star belt and Aqua Asteroids."

"Are we back up to full output SO Tulipina?" enquired FO Marrowlar.

"Aye Sir, one hundred percent shield output." she confirmed.

"Good work SO Tulipina, keep an eye on it. We don't want to get caught with weakened defences in a freak advanced Star belt?"

"Aye, aye Sir. We have received confirmation from Earthanon surface, that all strategic and technical equipment have been Vegitamised aboard the allotted ships in the civilian fleet. All Sun-fleet personnel have been Vegitamised on board their allocated ships. The O.S.S.S Milkymarrow way has reached full active crew capacity, the Junipitaris has completed its transfers and the only personnel left are the five hundred thousand Organitron allocated to the O.S.S.S Earthanon. After they are on board all that remains is the Earthanon inhabitants. Ground Commodore Cu-Cumbala is requesting permission to start clearing the Earthanon surface so that he can set the self-destruct sequence." enquired SO Tulipina.

"Is Ensign Broccleman ready to start the Vegitamisation programme?" asked FO Marrowlar.

"Yes Sir, and the City Vegitamisation modules are prepared to receive them for transfer."

FO Marrowlar looked at Captain Carrot awaiting permission. Captain Carrot nodded as they approached the strategy room doors, the passage-way lined with twenty security guards standing to attention on his approach.

"Bring them aboard FO Marrowlar. If the moisture levels are increasing already, then I feel we are in more danger than our original estimates forecast. Ask Commodore Cu-Cumbala to set the charges for twelve starhectoids, that's 09.45 next Starlectoid. Then Vegitamise him on board immediately." said the Captain thoughtfully.

FO Marrowlar passed on the Captain's instructions then brushed down his tunic anxious that the Fasterfoids saw the Organitron at their finest.

"Please confirm time-table with ground commodore Cu-Cumbala as follows, set destruct sequence for twelve starhectoids, that's **09.45 next Starlectoid**, begin last phase Earthanon inhabitants' transferral immediately. FO Marrowlar out."

"Aye, aye Sir, SO Tulipina out."

"Stand easy Organigirls and boys." said Captain Carrot." How are our guests behaving Ensign Chickoria?" he asked peering through the secret mirror.

"They are as quiet as mice Captain. Maybe the cat has got their tongues." stated Ensign Chickoria.

"SO Tulipina to FO Marrowlar. come in please."

"FO Marrowlar here. Yes SO Tulipina?"

"Sir. Ground Commodore Cu-Cumbala agrees with the proposed time-table. Do you want him to proceed?" she asked.

FO Marrowlar looked at Captain Carrot awaiting the order clarification.

"Once the Sequence is set, there's no going back. The Sodium Star belt was estimated to arrive in," Captain Carrot checked his time piece. "a little under fourteen starhectoids. Ask SO Tulipina to get a revised ETA. If we are still on target for fourteen starhectoids, let's give ourselves a little more time. Knowing the Fasterfoids as we do, we might just need it. Have Ground Commodore Cu-Cumbala set the self- destruct sequence for thirteen and a half starhectoids then proceed as agreed." said Captain Carrot.

"Proceed SO Tulipina," confirmed FO Marrowlar. "but make some alterations to the time-table, get an update on the sodium Star belt ETA and issue countdown orders to Commodore Cu-Cumbala. Ask him to set the timers for the self-destruct sequence for thirteen and a half starhectoids, provided the Sodium Star belts arrival is on course for fourteen starhectoids. Alert him to advise us as soon as he has completed the sequence initiation programme, then proceed as agreed. FO Marrowlar out."

"Aye, aye Sir, SO Tulipina over and out."

The doors to the Strategy room de-energised and Captain Carrot entered the room with FO Marrowlar, dismissing all but two of the guards from inside the strategy suite, he then sat at the table, where all of his guests were already seated in silence.

"Thank you for your co-operation Ladies, Gentlemen. Before we start, allow me to introduce myself. I am Captain Gillespie J. Carrot of the O.S.S.S Earthanon. This is my second in command, First Officer Benzo Marrowlar. Firstly, is there anything that you wish to point out about the conditions in which you are being housed?" There was nothing but silence from the assembled Fasterfoids.

"This silence is almost deafening, don't you think FO Marrowlar?" said Captain Carrot smiling at the sullen fry-babies, who refused to even acknowledge his gaze.

"Indeed Captain, one is finding it difficult to hear one-self think."

One of the Fasterfoids yawned and threw his arms in the air, then shivered.

"Suddenly I feel a cold chill in the air don't you?" he said to his fellow captive Officers.

"Yes, much more of this and one's bones could crumble." replied the smallest of the team.

"Me thinks Captain, that certain bones are already weak; the spine for instance. No back bone, do you know what I mean?" commented FO Marrowlar.

"Absolutely FO Marrowlar, children can be such a menace don't you agree?" chuckled Captain Carrot.

"Personally speaking Captain, my children tend to be rather more intelligent, certainly they have better manners." reasoned FO Marrowlar.

"Okay my fat filled Fasterfoid friends," said the Captain, raising his voice. "You want to act like children, then we will treat you like children. Now listen very carefully, because I am going to say this only once. Take my advice I beg of you, and listen very carefully indeed. Your ship is in great danger." he said returning to his usual calm disposition.

"What ship?" said the ring leader, grinning nervously.

"The ship hidden inside the newly acquired silicone mountain in the Arctolimba region. Did you really think we would overlook the small matter of a mountain appearing over night?" stated Captain Carrot.

"I don't know what you are talking about we are a medical ship that had to ditch in a storm. Lightning took out our communications module. It was a crash landing and we had no time to get clearance."

"I see General Crinkleark, so this is the sum total of your crew; a little over a thousand Fasterfoids." observed Captain Carrot.

"Yes, that is correct." confirmed General Crinkleark.

"What would a thousand lowly medics be doing with cloaking devices in the form of Organitron's I wonder?" questioned Captain Carrot.

"Protection for just such an event. We are technologically far more advanced than you, you.. "Organitron's" Captain!" sniped General Crinkleark.

"Very well General, then you will know all about and be totally un-concerned by the Sodium Star belt and Aqua Asteroids heading for Earthanon. I must admit we are very concerned. In fact, we are mass evacuating the Earthanon surface as we speak. It is almost complete and no joke General." said Captain Carrot.

General Crinkleark sparked as the Captain finished speaking.

"You can't frighten us by telling lies, Captain Carrot! We Fasterfoids are made of stronger stuff than that."

"For once, I agree with something you have said." laughed FO Marrowlar holding his nose."

Captain Carrot thumped the table and shouted at the top of his voice.

"This has gone on for long enough! Now hear this you ungrateful, poor excuse for a high ranking Officer. The first rule of an Officer is to make sure, that no matter what the conditions of war, their men, must at all times be the first and most important element of account. Now you may believe that it lies within your brief to stay silent, but let me tell you something General Crinkleark. You have comrades down there. They are certain to die if you do not co-operate with us. I implore you, convince them to allow us to escort them from the Earthanon Solar System. Once we are clear of the Sodium Star belt and the Earthanon Solar System, you will be free to go on your way!" General Crinkleark looked out of the plasma steel observation plate towards Earthanon. "Could he trust these Organipeople? Why would they try to help and what would they have to gain by helping?" He turned and strolled back towards his chair, the look on his face telling a story of confusion and at the same time despair.

"Let us suppose that we did have a ship on the Earthanon surface. Which of course we haven't..."

"Of course not, no!" interrupted FO Marrowlar.

"As I was saying," continued General Crinkleark, leering at FO Marrowlar. "If we did have a ship there, would we not be able to see for ourselves this, mythical Sodium Star belt?" joked General Crinkleark, as if he had scored some major victory.

"Yes, we do posses such things as radar and electron particle scanners." quipped one of the other Officers, with an indignant force.

"Oh, indeed you do my fair weathered friends," observed Captain Carrot. "but the Silicone mountain that you are using as a cover for your vessel; hypothetically speaking you understand, well, we believe that this Silicone mountain will block your scanning capabilities, or at least render it unreliable." The group of Officers looked at each other passing comments between themselves. Some nodded and others shook their heads in disagreement. However the most important head, that of General Crinkleark, remained static.

"Then Captain Carrot," said General Crinkleark, "we are having to ask ourselves, why, would the enemy with whom we are at war, as have we been for many generations past. Why would they go out of their way to help us?"

Captain Carrot leant forward. "Why?" retorted Captain Carrot. "I'll tell you why? For once we have here, the opportunity to forge peace between our nations. Don't get me wrong, we know it won't happen overnight. But the foundations, the building blocks will be set for the future generations of both nations to build on. It is as painful for me to do so, but do so I must! UFO is an Organisation dedicated to peace. Our mission is and always has been, to seek out and return to the bosom of our Nations, lost Organitron's and their homelands that were separated from the old Bubbleonion Squeak Solar System, as a result of the great star cluster explosion in which you too lost the Sausagia Fasterfoid Nation. We cannot be sure that they survived, but until we can be sure they did not, we will search for them. This brings me to my last and, perhaps the most important point. We are a peaceful organisation. It is you, the Fasterfoids that choose to wage war. Yes, we are enemies. Yes, we do have different cultures and beliefs, and yes, we have no pretence in the fact that your culture, whilst it can be respected, cannot be forced on anyone. That my friend works visa-versa. Let us not forget that we are your enemies because you make us your enemies. You rule your lands by totalitarian means. That is bad enough, but then you try to take the homelands of my people, to use for your own selfish reasons, forcing them from the heart of their ancestors' past.

That, General Crinkleark is the warring faction between us, but there is no glory in slaying a helpless enemy. With one slash of the sword of peace, we can achieve more than a thousand victories of war."

Captain Carrot stood in silence, his eyes speaking to each individual; pleading to the decent being inside, surely even a Fasterfoid had a decent being inside. he reasoned.

"We do not propose to be your best friends, but even our worst enemy deserves a fighting chance! The choice is yours. The destiny of your colleagues is in your hands." Captain Carrot handed them the weather chart surveys of the Earthanon atmosphere, and the spectral data on the sodium Star belt. "I think you might find this is proof enough of our intentions. The reasons for my proposed actions, I believe have been explained. FO Marrowlar will be here if you wish to ask him any questions about the data you see before you. You will notice we estimate the arrival of the Sodium Star belt in twelve starhectoids and forty Starmins. I will return in two starhectoids for your answer to this, this, shall we say hypothetical scenario?" Captain Carrot turned and left the Strategy room, his temper in a shallow and fragile state. After the doors had re-energised, the Captain called Ensign Strawballis on his personal channel.

"Captain Carrot to Ensign Strawballis, come in, over."

"Any news on Commander Marrachinello or the Mechanoid probe?"

"No Sir, we are scanning all frequencies and we think that we may be linked, But the storm is interrupting our capabilities. We are trying to run a proton boost on the wave band to enhance the reception." said Ensign Strawballis.

"Keep trying Ensign Strawballis. It is imperative that we forge a strong link. Captain Carrot over and out." said the Captain mopping his brow. "Aye Sir, Ensign Strawballis over and out."

FO Marrowlar was seated as the Fasterfoids digested the information. He could not believe that he was sitting in the same room, let alone trying to forge peace with this group of smelly fat-dripping inconsequentials. But the Captain had an aim, and like it or not, the Fasterfoids were in his sights. The question in FO Marrowlar's mind had to be this. One might be strong enough to offer the olive branch of peace, and the other, strong enough to grasp it, but, could both be brave enough to hold on to it? Yes indeed this was a long and bumpy road, only co-operation with each other could ease the perilous journey.

CHAPTER THIRTEEN

Coupe de Gra`ce
The finishing strokes!

Time 23.45 starhectoids

Back in the bunker room of General Satuese, Commander Marrachinello was now feeling the incredible limitations of the FF Francaisfry humidity on his body and state of mind, his train of thought becoming impossible to hold for any significant length of time. Suddenly the probe after starhectoids of trying had initiated contact with the O.S.S.S Earthanon inside he felt that the end of his mission was nearing. That was of course provided that the Fasterfoids could analyse the situation objectively, and overcome their delusions of grandeur and paranoia.

"Here we go chaps. I knew this little beauty would get through," said a relieved Commander Marrachinello his finger becoming poised on the utility belt escape activator. "Just a couple of starmins now for the de-scrambler modulator to clear the wave band and chocks away we are in business, hey what?" He smiled.

Principle Gammachip and General Satuese had been in conference privately in the corner of the bunker room. Huddled up like two naughty school children sent to face the wall for much of the time, taking time occasionally to look over their shoulders and monitor Commander Marrachinello and the probe which would occasionally make a strange whirring noise, the sort of noise that would normally be found at a

Fasterfoid dinner table after much celebration. Returning to the table to be seated, General Satuese addressed Commander Marrachinello with a fervent passion.

"Commander Marrachinello," he said striking the table. "For the moment you are here as a willing participant in what is, for all we know, a well staged bluff of incredible proportion. But remember this! Should you fail to convince us of this so called threat to Earthanon, you will become an unwilling participant in our jail cage. You are a brave and respected warrior, but, rest assured we have no compassion for rank or privilege. You will be made to work like any other prisoner that is unfortunate enough to fall into our grasp. The only difference where you are concerned is that you will possibly last a little longer than your other unfortunates who have found their way into our custody, due to your stubborn tenacity and stamina. Then we have ways of breaking the heartiest of Organitron; Pirate Milnedew rings a bell." Said the General gathering Commander Marrachinello's full attention.

"Oh really and what did you do to him? We haven't seen or heard of him in startechtoids." Said the Commander feigning ignorance.

"We caught your exiled friend trying to smuggle Vegimatters to one of our outpost observation stations in the F2 sector. We boarded his ship, took him prisoner then destroyed both his vessel and the cargo within. Oh you should have seen how he cried like a gibbering baby as his ill-gotten gains disappeared in a flash before his very eyes. We transported him back to the mines of Chickonaldir where he perished under his own steam. Sent crazy by the constant contact with acidulated gastric acid in the cutting shafts. But fear not, we showed him mercy. We allowed him to bath daily to wash away the irritant but unfortunately the bathing solution of Ketchup and vinegar was somehow worse." Then General Satuese laughed violently with Principle Gammachip in the hope of raising some kind of reaction from Commander Marrachinello.

"Well done chaps, we've been after the blighter for ages but he always seemed to elude us. Oh don't look so surprised, he was an exile after all and let's face it, there's only one good pirate and that's a perished one don't you know? Hey what."

"Well, regardless of your feelings towards pirates," said a surprised Principle Gammachip, "you will find us treating you with the same callous contempt. But then we too have a saying along the same lines. The only good Organitron is a perished one!" He sneered. Just then the probe activated a visaid screen projection unit and a camera popped out from its stomach.

"Contact established. Repeat. Contact established." Confirmed the probe in an electronic voice simulation.

"Commander Marrachinello of Sun-Fleet, please place your hand on the identi-plate for final connection, thank you." Said the probe.

Commander Marrachinello placed his hand on the plate and the probe began scanning the commander's security prints.

"Voice comparison. Please speak clearly." Asked the probe.

"This is Commander Marrachinello, Star Fighter Command. Red Sector Leader."

"Identi-print and voice clarification acknowledged. Prepare to receive priority transmission, stand by for connection. Ensign Strawballis is on the line. Activating visaid now, you are through to the O.S.S.S Earthanon."

General Satuese and Principle Gammachip sat back and awaited the communication from the O.S.S.S Earthanon with some trepidation. The further along this path of communication they went, the deeper the dialogue became between the two parties, the more General Satuese felt that their mission had failed.

"This is Commander Marrachinello calling the O.S.S.S Earthanon, come in Ensign Strawballis." Said the Commander awaiting a reply.

"This is Ensign Strawballis of the O.S.S.S Earthanon. You are through to Captain Gillespie J. Carrot." Confirmed Ensign Strawballis.

"Switching to visaid Captain." said the commander activating the probes visual projection unit. Suddenly, Captain Carrot appeared in the centre of the room in a three dimensional form. Slightly fuzzy and transparent in appearance due to the partially hampered connection caused by the silicone mountain surrounding the FF Francaisfry.

"Commander Marrachinello," said the Captain turning towards the Commander. "I am pleased to see the Fasterfoids are looking after you sufficiently. Well if it is not my old adversary of the space frontiers General Faturno Satuese." Said the Captain turning his attention towards the Fasterfoid ranks sitting at the top of the table. "Greetings General." General Satuese nodded as the Captain could be seen standing in front of the doors that led into the strategy room on board the O.S.S.S. Earthanon. "General Satuese," continued the Captain. "I trust that Commander Marrachinello has briefed you on the situation with regard to your personnel held on board the O.S.S.S Earthanon, and as to the situation of the Sodium

Star belt and the Aqua Asteroids contained within that is approaching Earthanon as we speak?"

"Indeed Captain. Commander Marrachinello has talked much but I am afraid he has proved nothing. If my personnel are, as you say, aboard the O.S.S.S Earthanon then show us them. If you can!" Jeered General Satuese convinced that this was one large bluff, and that this would prove an impossible task for the Captain to achieve.

"General Satuese you know me to be many things, but a liar, I feel sure, is not one of them. After all, in the battles of the past when we have met, I have frequently promised to tan your backside, and, I think you will admit that tan your backside is exactly what I have done every time. But this is not about scoring points this is about reaching out the hand of friendship for the good of all. Overcoming our differences to help each other in a time of crisis..." continued the Captain who was halted yet again, only this time by the smug and egotistical Principle Gammachip.

"A crisis that yet again you cannot prove Captain. You tell a good yarn Captain but you offer no evidence or facts." Laughed the Principle Officer.

"Indeed, in a few moments General, you will receive through the probes data- bank print-out the most recent spectral analysis of the Earthanon Solar System, along with the last twenty starhectoids of Earthanon weather chart surveillance. I believe that this will lie to rest any doubt of our integrity. I just ask you to observe the information with open minds and reach no definite decisions until you are in receipt of all the facts. I know that the most puzzling question in all this is, why? Why would we bother to show mercy or to help the survival of a warring faction with whom we have little or no peace? To pre-empt this question I can say only this. The Fasterfoids I know are as honourable in death due to battle as the Organitron are, but by treaty we are both dedicated and sworn to non-life endangering battle encounters. For millions of stardectoids, we have fought with honour up until the attack on the O.S.S.S Milkymarrow way most recently which nearly ended in tragedy for nearly a half a million Organitron and countless loved ones. It was a callous and unreasonable attack, one for which we should blow you out of the sand without compassion. So you see, this really is an olive branch, all that I... we ask, is that you grasp it firmly for what it is worth." Said the Captain with as much sincerity as he could muster under these trying times.

The Probe started to process the information coming through from the O.S.S.S Earthanon, while Commander Marrachinello collected it together and handed it to General Satuese and Principle Officer Gammachip. As they perused the information, General Satuese sank back into his chair and stroked his chin pensively. Principle Officer Gammachip leaned across and whispered into his ear while Commander Marrachinello kept his finger firmly on the utility belt button to signal his emergency exit should he require it. Then General Satuese nodded in agreement and turned back to the Captain who waited with his hand's firm behind his back.

"This is a very interesting Captain Carrot, and I must say you make a very touching speech. This information however can be composed to play the tune of any scenario. It proves nothing and frankly unless I see my personnel you say you have on board the ship, and then I will assume that you are holding them un-accessible prisoners. That my friend is against the Organitron treaty and may push us into battle." He said, still convinced that Captain Carrot was bluffing. Captain Carrot hung his head low, realising that time was running out and that even when presenting the enemy with all the facts, they still could not see through their own hatred and the propaganda machine that was rife in the Bapmacdo Aurora.

"Very well General Satuese, you are determined to play this game to the full and place all our lives at risk. I will take you to see your men but remember this, from the moment you have laid eyes on them you may converse with them. You will have ten starmins to discuss their housing conditions and validate what Commander Marrachinello has already briefed you on. The time is now ten starmins to the mid-night cycle. We wish to be reasonable in all aspects so I am proposing this. After you have conferred with your colleagues aboard the O.S.S.S Earthanon, you will be extended the privilege of two starhectoids in which you must make up your minds whether to co-operate, or, to face the task force that as we speak is surrounding your ship. I will speak to you in ten starmins, oh, and should we spot one grain of sand moving from your hideous and pathetic disguise through your trying to escape, then we will fire regardless and without mercy. I, for one, pray to Helios that you see sense and it does not become necessary." Captain Carrot turned and de-energised the strategy room doors to reveal Ground-force General Crinkleark and his five top ranking Officers. As General Satuese sat with Principle Gammachip their mouths wide open in disbelief, General Crinkleark and the others spotted General Satuese on the Computron placed next to FO Marrowlar. Standing to attention immediately they saluted General Satuese nervously. This was the proof both parties needed to confirm that there may be some truth in the mutterings of the Organitron Evacuation. Particularly as the convoy of ships in the surrounding airspace became huge and more powerful as every second passed, also FO Marrowlar had scanned the Planet Earthanon for life signs revealing that it was indeed evacuated. The only signs of life remaining were in the Arcticus region in the main City where the Vegitamisation modules were situated, and small life signs surrounding the silicone mountain in Arctolimba where the FF Francaisfry was situated. The life signs being confirmed as a strike force ready to take the FF Francaisfry by force.

"General Crinkleark, what is the meaning of this?" Shouted the frustrated General Satuese. "You are supposed to be the pride and joy of our ground-force that is why you were picked. And what do I find? Snug as a bug in a rug with nothing to report but capture. Gadzukes man! This is the sort of result I would expect from the likes of a mission led by the notorious nincompoop, Principle Gammachip. I do hope, General Crinkleark that your mouth has remained firmly closed at all times?" Asked the General secretly referring to the ship's cloaking capabilities.

"Absolutely General, I haven't given anything away about the purpose of our visit." He said quietly.

"What a mess this is, Crinkleark. The top brass is going to be mighty peeved by this situation when they get wind of it." Blustered General Satuese.

"I would have thought that all Fasterfoids would have been used to a touch of wind by now General Satuese." Laughed FO Marrowlar, unable to resist a quip at the expense of the Fasterfoid hierarchy.

"Very funny Benz-Baby, but if it is wind that you are analysing try a halitosis test. That should give you some indication as to the real problem in the wind stakes. Anything we can produce is sweet and aromatic by comparison, believe me I can even whiff it through my visaid."

"Please can we get back to business? The Sodium Star belt is due to strike in a little under twelve starhectoids and you, General, now have only five starmins to conclude your discussions." Interrupted the Captain checking his time piece.

General Satuese gritted his teeth and diverted his attention towards the Ground- force General who sat in silence.

"Putting aside the fact that you have failed dismally in your mission, Crinkleark, and that you have placed the Fasterfoid's reputation as incredulous and superior tacticians in the sludge bucket. What is your honest assessment of the Earthanon situation? Are they telling the truth?" He asked.

"Well Sir, there would appear to be little life forms left on Earthanon, Apart from the Main City itself, and it would appear to be large enough to comprise of the whole of Earthanons inhabitants, they most certainly have cleared the globe. That is..." he paused.

"Well don't just stop there. That is what you blithering bucket of starch dropping? Carry on." Shouted the now impatient General Satuese.

"Well, the only two life form clusters that appear on the whole of the planetary surface, are situated in Arcticus at the transferral stations, and the rest... the rest are surrounding the FF Francaisfry. I would estimate twenty to twenty five thousand ground troops in all, six Star Fighters and proton armed Vege-cruiser. I think they are telling the truth General. As painful as it is to admit it, they appear to be trying to do the right thing by us." He said cowering under the table his eyes barely above its surface.

"Are you mad!" shouted the Principle Gammachip. The only honourable Organitron is one submerged in ketchup! Have you taken leave of your senses? Trust... trust an Organitron? I haven't heard anything so ridiculous in all my given starlectoids."

"Slap!" Landed the full force of a fist full of condensed fat, as it flew in the face of Principle Gammachip from the direction of General Satuese.

"Your given days will be numbered if you don't shut up you... You great pile of mashed "Doo doo" brain. It is brains like yours that have helped us into this mess, now cease! Before I drag you outside personally and make you eat the entire sand mountain that we are under, is that clear?" Said the irate General.

"Glug... err... glug... em... Ur... Glugerglug." dribbled Principle Gammachip, fat oozing into his lap from his mouth.

"You have two minutes," said the Captain as he de-energised the doors and stepped outside. "I will be back, please excuse me but I have to make sure that my transferral team will make it in time for our departure." He continued. As the doors re-energised behind him he called Ensign Broccleman on his personal channel.

"Captain Carrot to Ensign Broccleman." He said tapping the communicator relay.

"Ensign Broccleman here Sir," came the reply, the noise in the back ground defining.

"How is our schedule going Ensign Broccleman? What percentage of the Vegitamisation programme is on board, and how long will it take to complete the process?" Asked the concerned Captain. They were indeed cutting it fine and he would soon have to give orders for the main convoy evacuation to disembark from Earthanon air space to ensure their safety.

"Well Sir, the Junipitaris and the Milky Marrow Way are fully loaded. We are approximately one third there. We have successfully Vegitamised on board three-hundred and thirty-thousand Organitron at fifty percent minimised stature, this leaves us one-million, one-hundred and seventy-thousand inhabitants to transfer to the mother ships, the remainder have all been placed on the allocated civilian and Sun-Fleet ship's. I estimate that the transferral of personnel will be complete in approximately seven starhectoids fifty-five starmins, that's 07.00 hundred starhectoids Captain. Commodore Cu-Cumbala has just Vegitamised aboard and the self destruct sequence has nine starhectoids forty-five starmins to run, Sir. We are cutting it very fine!"

"I know Ensign Broccleman, but if you can name me a crisis of this magnitude that wasn't cut fine, I will give you a thousand credits." Retorted the Captain.

"I know Sir, I just thought that you ought to be told, there was no disrespect intended. After all we are working on the forecast arrival of the Sodium Star belt and there is every possibility that as it hits Earthanon airspace, it will accelerate beyond our wildest imagination."

"Of course Ensign Broccleman you are right to air your concerns, Captain Carrot out. Captain Carrot to Ensign Strawballis."

"Ensign Strawballis here Captain. Yes Sir?" Came the reply as he switched channels.

"Ensign Strawballis. Have the O.S.S.S Junipitaris and the O.S.S.S Milkymarrow Way convoy's log on to the pre-set course of the escape route and have them depart at 24.00 hundred starhectoids. There is not much time to waste. Tell me, has Envoy Milnedew reported on board the O.S.S.S Earthanon for duty yet?" He enquired.

"Well Sir, his Mother, Father and family have, but he chose to stay on Earthanon and is organising the departure of the remaining Organitron Personnel with FO Melonicord." She replied.

"Very good, have him report to me as soon as he arrives on board!" Said the Captain, his gut instinct was beginning to tell him that the evacuation process was nothing short of a very tall order. "And Admiral Ducarrotain, has he logged on to the personnel file with his siblings?" He asked flustered, as the pressure of the Fasterfoid situation began to mount.

"Yes Sir, Admiral Ducarrotain said that he would stick by us through thick and thin and it would appear that he meant every word. He and his family Vegitamised on-board from the Junipitaris ten starmins ago." She replied.

"Thank you Ensign Strawballis. Captain Carrot out." With that he turned and entered the strategy room straight faced and determined for an answer.

"Gentlegrills, Gentlefrills." he said addressing General Satuese and the Officers present. "The time has come for discussions to end and serious thoughts to be pondered upon. I can afford you no more courtesy to do so will place the lives of one point five million Organitron in jeopardy." He said stone faced and unwilling to barter.

"Captain Carrot." Said the anxious General Satuese. "May I have thirty starsecs with my second?" He asked.

"Of course you may but that is all." he replied looking at his time piece as both he and Principle Gammachip scuttled out of the bunker room. Outside the earshot of the probe and Commander Marrachinello the two officers began to reach their decision. General Satuese and Principle Officer Gammachip returned and delivered the outcome of their brief deliberations.

"Captain Carrot." said the General, "We believe you are trying to do the right thing by the Fasterfoids and I thank you for your honesty. However, I have heard your case, but, my men have not. I would like the opportunity for them to know the facts and join in the decision process. We believe that the two starhectoids you offered should be sufficient in which to bring them around to your way of thinking?" He confirmed.

"Very well General Satuese the time is now **24.00 starhectoids** precisely we will speak again at **02.00 starhectoids**. Captain Carrot out."

Time 24.05 starhectoids

General Satuese gathered the Gentlegrills and Gentlefrills of his crew for an extraordinary meeting. Eventually, after much soul searching, they all agreed to join General Satuese in the convoy with the Organitron for safe passage through the Sodium Star belt. They only one left fighting the decision was Principle Gammachip. Right up until they approached the bunker room doors Principle Gammachip, pleaded for his case to be heard.

"Free vote or not General! I cannot justify your proposed course of action." sighed Principle Gammachip.

"Principle Gammachip," squirmed the General. "You don't know this but my orders are to not let the Organitron into the secrets of the Cloaking device. If they place a skeleton crew aboard the ship then they may ask questions, they will be making notes of its capabilities at least." He said desperately trying to find a way around the problem.

"General," replied Principle Gammachip. "that being the case then surely it is our duty to fight to the bitter end and die with honour." he replied.

"Normally Principle Gammachip I would agree with you, but in this instance it would take some considerable time for the reactors to reach a level in which we could take off at full power, let alone fight. No I think it is time to establish a pattern and self destruct the ship, or phase four to be precise."

Principle Gammachip stood back in amazement. "You are talking surrender here General. I had you down as a bigger warrior than that." he shouted.

"It is a big Warrior who lives to fight another day and enters into battle from an equal footing. Sometimes it is the right thing to do to save yourself for the better cause and while we are on-board the O.S.S.S Earthanon we can evaluate their capabilities since her re-fit." He said slyly. A gleam came to the eye of Principle Gammachip and he smiled. General Satuese took this as an action of agreement, but he could not have been further from the truth if he had tried.

"Then General, let me be the one to stay behind and set the self destruct sequence. Otherwise, if you are not on board they will not believe your intentions are serious." He said with an uncanny honesty. "But how do you intend to avoid an Organitron boarding party?" He continued.

General Satuese thought of Principle Gammachip's reasoning and could find no fault in his argument or logic.

"Just watch and you will see, agree to everything I say. Nod by all means, but on no account speak or the plan will be scuppered without a doubt." Then he turned and entered the bunker room poised to deliver his plan.

Time 02.00 starhectoids

"Captain Carrot." Said General Satuese running to the visaid as the Captain awaited their arrival in the bunker room. "Time is short and we have little time to waste as you say, but first I must tell you that we have not been entirely honest with you. We are a medical ship that has been converted for recognisance purposes but as I am sure that you are aware, our new method of infiltration is not fool proof. That was one of our tasks. Obviously it failed. But upon our entry into Earthanon airspace we experienced a breach in our frontal hull which caused an overheating in our crystalline reactor. I'm afraid that it would be impossible for this ship to go anywhere, it is all we can do to take rough scanner readings. What I propose is this. We would be grateful for transportation out of here on-board your ship, we have a compliment of one thousand two hundred and twelve left on board, your Commander here can verify this. I will vaporise aboard after the rest of my crew within the half starhectoid, after collecting my various log books and ships papers. However, in accordance with the Fasterfoid battle tactica resolution, Principle Gammachip, will stay on-board and initiate the self destruct ship computer mechanism. Then he will Vaporise aboard the O.S.S.S Earthanon immediately afterwards, the whole process should take Principle Gammachip one starhectoid. Do you agree?" Said the General.

"This is Captain Beetrouly to Captain Carrot."

"This is Captain Sunfleur to Captain Carrot."

Came the voices over the Captain's personal channel.

"Captain Carrot to Beetrouly and Sunfleur. Yes Captains.

"We are ready for departure Captain Carrot, is there anything we can do for you before we set off, Captain Carrot?" Said Captain Beetrouly as silence fell on the line. "Captain Carrot do you read Me." he repeated.

"Just make it home safe and well my friends, if you could spare a prayer to Helios it would be much appreciated."

"You don't have to wait for the Fasterfoids you know you can leave them there to perish!" Chuckled Captain Sunfleur.

"Stop it Organiman," yelled Captain Beetrouly. "I think that what you are doing is admirable Captain Carrot, and we all salute you. When this is all over you will possibly have achieved the impossible. Made the Organitron and Fasterfoid's, who knows, maybe friends?"

"Of course Captain, it is very brave and noble of you." uttered a more sincere Captain Sunfleur.

"Thank you Organimen but it is not bravery, merely the right thing to do. I bid you farewell, until we see you on the other side, may Helios travel with you a see you safe. This is Captain Carrot UFO and out, end transmission."

"Captain Beetrouly, Captain Sunfleur UFO and out, end transmission."

Captain Carrot turned to the observation window and watched as the cascading ships led by the Milkymarrow way and the Junipitaris left the Earthanon Atmosphere. It was a spectacular sight but they had to go the long way, because they could no longer guarantee safe passage in the Slithervoid, the Sodium Star belt was that close. Silicone Sphere had already evacuated and could provide no definite guidance as to the progress of the Sodium Star belt and without Volcadis they could not judge her distance and passage in time. Yet Captain Carrot thought to himself there was one unanswered question.

How did the FF Francaisfry manage to evade detection whilst entering Earthanon airspace? The answer he felt could be found on closer inspection of the ship but time was short. And for once in his life, he felt it necessary to extend the hand of friendship to a Fasterfoid, in the hope of its long term affects coming good.

"Very well General Satuese, prepare to have your crew Vaporise aboard. We will send fixed co-ordinates for you to lock onto. There is one condition, however, Captain Peabazzare will Vegitamise down to your ship and ensure that the destruction sequence is followed. Upon his arrival Commander Marrachinello will be free to leave, agreed?" Asked the Captain.

"Agreed." Replied General Satuese.

"Prepare to receive Captain Peabazzare in thirty starmins, this is Captain Carrot out." Captain Carrot paced up and down the strategy room frantically, the thought of having twelve hundred Fat dripping, saturated smelly personnel extra in the brig area, on top of the thousand or so they already had in detention was a little off putting. All things considered however, in the interest of Organikind it had to be done. Turning to the two security guards, he de-energised the doors and approached the Ground-force General and his Officers, who were feeling quite humbled by the amount of compassion being shown by Captain Carrot, and if the truth be known all of the Organitron crew that they had come into contact with.

"SO Auberiniol, please escort our guests back to their temporary quarters. Inform SO Okralate that she will need to make provision for a further twelve hundred Fasterfoid personnel within the half starhectoid." Said the Captain showing the Fasterfoid delegation to the door. When they were gone, FO Marrowlar sat in silence while Captain Carrot stared into oblivion as the last remnant of the Organitron Convoy could be seen jumping into Califoric K speed. All that was left was Commander Marrachinello's Star Fighter squadron patrolling the surrounding airspace, awaiting the departure orders for the O.S.S.S Earthanon to move under way.

"Captain Sir." Said FO Marrowlar in a slow drawl.

"Yes FO Marrowlar what is the problem?" Asked the Captain.

"Aren't you the tiniest bit suspicious that they are giving in so easily?" He said slowly, something niggling in the back of his mind.

"Yes Benzo I am! But we have no time to lose in chasing our tails. We need action and clear direction. I'll admit the situation is far from perfect and I am sure that there is much that General Satuese is not telling, but if we build our security around all eventualities, then to be honest I care very little for the reasoning behind their quick submission. Just so long as they come peacefully and without trouble, that is all I pray for."

"I agree Captain, I think all things considered the avoidance of a confrontation is a major achievement in your diary." Observed FO Marrowlar.

"Not quite all my doing old chum, a lot of the credit must fall at the feet of Commander Marrachinello on this one. It is he that has taken the risks, I... I was just the catalyst in the affair.

"Ensign Broccleman," said the Captain, activating his personal channel. "Prepare to Vegitamise twelve hundred Fasterfoids aboard the O.S.S.S Earthanon inside the half starhectoid. Take your co-ordinates from the frequency transmissions from the Mechanoid probe on board the FF Francaisfry. Transportation of the Fasterfoids will require a change in the Vegitamisation configuration, you must remember to allow for the saturation transferral." Said the Captain trying to cover all the possible areas that could go wrong.

"Aye, aye Sir, I am working on it now. We are nearly two thirds complete on the Organitron Vegitamisation programme, we will be complete within five starhectoids and twenty starmins Captain." Confirmed Ensign Broccleman.

"Very good Ensign Broccleman, you are making excellent time. Let me know when they are all aboard. Oh, as soon as Captain Peabazzare is with you, Vegitamise him onto the FF Francaisfry and bring Commander Marrachinello out of there. He must be fit to drop after being cooped up with those roasted renegades." He laughed

"Aye, aye Sir."

"Ensign Strawballis," continued Captain Carrot. "Communications line open to the O.S.S.S Milkymarrow way immediately. Inform Captain Beetrouly that we are intending to rescue the Fasterfoid crew from the Earthanon surface and we expect to depart Earthanon airspace in approximately five starhectoids and thirty starmins. We may have to skirt pretty close to the Sodium Star belt if we are to get out of here in one piece so have them track us for as long as they can." Ordered Captain Carrot.

"Aye, aye Sir. Is that all?" She asked wandering whether Captain Carrot may choose to send another back-up proton probe pilot.

"Me thinks, Ensign Strawballis, you know me too well. Prepare two back-up proton pilots. Release one immediately with all the relative details that I have given you loaded into its memory banks, place our co-ordinates relative to the Earthanons surface in case something unforeseen happens. Set course for Carridionaries via the escape route ready for initiation. Have the other on emergency stand-by, connect it to the main computer terminal and voice transcript box, we may need to launch it in a hurry." he said, not wishing to spread panic to the bridge crew.

"Aye, aye Sir, as you wish. Ensign Strawballis out."

"Captain Carrot to Dr Kiwitranus, come in please."

"Dr Kiwitranus here. Yes Captain." Came the reply.

"Dr Kiwitranus. We are bringing aboard another twelve-hundred Fasterfoids. Will you and FO Cornelius see to it that they have adequate atmosphere chambers set for their comfort, and see to it that we intensify the power output to enable them to regenerate on a more regular basis." asked the Captain. Remembering the terms and conditions of the Organitron-Fasterfoids prisoner of war treaty declaration.

"Aye, aye Captain leave it with us. How long before they arrive?" enquired the doctor.

"Within the half starhectoid." Replied the Captain aware that it was short notice for such a tall order.

"It'll be close Captain, but we will do our best." Said the doctor signing off.

"That's all I or anyone can ask. Captain Carrot out. Captain Carrot to Professor Goosegorgon, come in please."

"Yes Capatano, Professor Goosegorgon at your service. What' a can I do's for you." He asked.

"Professor. I want you to go to the Vegitamisation room and await the arrival of Commander Marrachinello. He has been in the Fasterfoid vessel for some time now and I worry that the Vegitamisation process will affect him in some way, the sheer heat inside those ships can create adverse affect both during and after the process. Also can you take an emergency Medilab team and standby to receive some Fasterfoid patients, they may not take well to the adjustment from Vaporisation to Vegitamisation. If you could assist Ensign Broccleman to man the transferral consul and supervise the medical clearance bay." Said the Captain.

"You 'a hav'a got it Capatano." Answered the little professor.

"Thank you Carrot out. Captain Carrot to FO Potatree, come in please."

"Aye Captain, I am the one and only." Said the jolly voice on the return.

"FO Potatree, I want you to wire up the blazer guns to the phaser modules. Increase power output to full intensity, we are cutting our departure fine so we want to be able to shoot our way clear if we must!" Ordered the Captain.

"As usual I am one step ahead of you, I have got FO Milnedew who has just Vegitamised aboard, and my new Deputy Chief Engineer Marrowmilne on it right now." Chirped FO Potatree.

"I didn't doubt it for one moment." said the Captain in reply. "Captain Carrot out." he said closing down his personal channel.

"FO Potatree over and out."

"FO Marrowlar. I want you to take Captain Peabazzare and de-brief him on the way down to the Vegitamisation Room. Tell him to inform Ensign Broccleman as soon as he is ready to come out of there, also ask him to take Commander Marrachinello's utility belt from him in case of an emergency."

"Aye, aye Captain. I'm on my way." With that FO Marrowlar had left and Captain Carrot was left alone to prepare himself for the task that lay ahead on the bridge. Namely, steering a ship approximately five starmillo's long by one and a half starmillo's wide by one starmillo deep through a Sodium Star belt filled with Aqua asteroids.

Time 02.40 starhectoids

Captain Carrot stepped out of the elevation chamber onto the bridge as Ensign Rasperillo announced his arrival and Ensign Melonture piped him aboard. The crew stood to attention and FO Marrowlar handed over the running of the ship to the Captain, taking his place at the secondary command com.

"You have Command Com Captain." He said moving aside as SO Tulipina handed him the bridge log.

"Thank you FO Marrowlar." Said the Captain. "SO Tulipina, ship's status if you will?" He enquired.

"All systems are on line clean and clear. Power output is at the maximum, shields running at one hundred percent. Blazer guns and Proton phasers are at full displacement, Sir." She confirmed.

"Excellent, FO Marrowlar Earthanon status." He ordered scanning the gyroscope Grid Finder.

"FO Melonicord will Vegitamise aboard Captain in an estimated, one starhectoid thirty starmins. We have nearly completed the Fasterfoid transferral and Captain Peabazzare is awaiting Vegitamisation to the FF Francaisfry. Commodore Cu-Cumbala has Vegitamised along with Admiral Ducarrotain and their families, I have placed them in quarters fitting to their position and they will report to the bridge thirty starmins prior to departure. The self destruct sequence is set and verified, self destruct in.." FO Marrowlar looked at the bridge timepiece. "Approximately seven starhectoid and five starmins Captain." Said FO Marrowlar.

"Thank you FO Marrowlar. Viceroy Rhubarblatt have you fed the course co-ordinates for our departure into the Vegimatter room computer?" Asked the Captain feeling the tension on the bridge and eager to displace any unnecessary nerves.

"Yes Captain, Computer fixed and logged, calorific reactors are on-line clean and clear, auxiliary engines are primed and standing by, all systems are Ay'Ok, Sir." Answered Viceroy Rhubarblatt at the steering column.

"Ensign Viola, ETA Sodium Star belt?" ordered the Captain.

"Seven starhectoids fifty starmins Captain, Sir. Atmospheric pressure is already at optimum level. We should start to feel the affect of increased electro activity any time now. Energy recoil shields are in place as a protection against a direct hit and Anti-magnetic dampers are in place on the main engine bulkheads." Confirmed Ensign Viola at the ship's scanner.

"Captain Carrot to Ensign Broccleman." Said the Captain activating his com channel.

"Aye, aye Captain. Ensign Broccleman here." He replied swiftly.

"How close are we to the Fasterfoid transferral completion?"

"Almost complete Captain, It is just Commander Marrachinello, the Mechanoid probe, General Satuese and Principle Gammachip to come. Captain Peabazzare is on the platform now, Captain I estimate Earthanon clear with the starhectoid Sir." Confirmed Ensign Broccleman activating the Vegitamisation cycle.

"Have Commander Marrachinello take an immediate regeneration period upon his return and ask General Satuese if he would like to come up to the bridge when he comes aboard." Said the Captain.

"Aye, aye Captain. Sir Captain Peabazzare is on his way." confirmed Ensign Broccleman.

Down on the Earthanon surface in the belly of the FF Francaisfry, General Satuese was huddled in the corner with Principle Gammachip. Commander Marrachinello thought their actions strange, but then they were Fasterfoids. Presumably General Satuese was handing over details of the self-destruct sequence to Principle Gammachip.

"General Satuese, I implore you, please do not do this!" Begged Principle Gammachip. "This is the Prototype Cloaking vessel. If we destroy it, we will be in big trouble back home and there's no mistake. I'm sorry General but I feel a traitor when I hear such talk as self destruct." He continued mopping his brow.

"Principle Gammachip, we were here to carry out a mission, that mission has been aborted due to unforeseen events. Now it is our duty to see to it that we protect the Fasterfoid technology advances by destroying the evidence. You have volunteered to do this and this I trust you to do. I realise that it will come as something of a shock to relinquish the second command in such a prestigious craft, but relinquish it you must. Believe me it is for the good of all concerned, besides they already had a thousand of our troops as prisoners. No, I will carry out the deed if you feel you cannot do so?" Asked the General turning towards Commander Marrachinello.

"Oh no General, I will do it Sir." He said with his eyes developing a cunning smile all of their own, as if somehow the mouth was no longer necessary. Then Captain Peabazzare appeared and shook hands with Commander Marrachinello.

"Commander are you OK?" he said seeing the Commander's complexion had seen better days.

"Yes thank you Captain Peabazzare. At least I will be once disembarked from the hot house of a ship," he said handing him the utility belt. "I'll stay with you if you wish Captain?"

No, Commander, my orders are to relieve you immediately and ask you to report for immediate regeneration upon your return to the O.S.S.S Earthanon. You are to return with General Satuese and the Mechanoid probe at once." Said Captain Peabazzare.

"Very well, General Satuese, I'm afraid it is time that we left, time is short so if you wouldn't mind?" Said the Commander grabbing the General's arm. "Commander Marrachinello to Ensign Broccleman, Vegitamise two personnel One Organitron, One Fasterfoid and a Mechanoid probe in the immediate vicinity." he said.

"Aye, aye Commander, Vegitamising now, Sir." Replied Ensign Broccleman. Suddenly they disappeared leaving only Captain Peabazzare and Principle Gammachip to finish the dastardly deed. But as it turned out unbeknown to anyone including General Satuese, Principle Gammachip was not ready to give in quite so easily.

Captain Peabazzare turned to view the bridge as Principle Gammachip activated what appeared to be the command com. For the next thirty starmins or so Principle Gammachip was a role model of surrender, or so it would seem. Captain Peabazzare was unaware that the good Gammachip had realigned the engines ready for a dastardly deed. After a while, Captain Peabazzare, stepped up to the flight deck platform and could not envisage working in the surrounding environment for any length of time.

"Not exactly very homely is it Principle Gammachip? A little sterile for my taste, but then," he said turning back to face the principle Gammachip, "taste is, something that you acquire with cultural learning...Ahh!" he shouted as principle Gammachip struck him on the side of the head with one swooping blow knocking Captain Peabazzare unconscious. As the Captain fell to the floor gripping his head, Ensign Strawballis, who was monitoring his life signs from the bridge of the O.S.S.S Earthanon called to Captain Carrot. As she did so, the elevation chamber opened and out of it walked FO Potatree with General Satuese held under close guard.

"Captain Carrot, Sir." shouted Ensign Strawballis. "Something is wrong on board the FF Francaisfry. Captain Peabazzare's vital readings are down to forty-seven percent on the grey matter activator. Those are the sort of readings we would expect from an Organitron in a sleep cycle, or.. Or if..." She muttered as Captain Carrot pre-empted her evaluation.

"Or if he had been knocked unconscious." Swiftly he turned and faced General Satuese on the bridge upper deck and pointed a finger at him. "If I find this is anything to do with you General Satuese, your life will be filled with misery, turmoil and plentiful helpings of humiliation."

"Captain." Said the General in a genuinely confused state of mind. "I know nothing of what you are inferring. Are you sure your readings are correct?" He asked.

"Ensign Strawballis," continued the Captain staring General Satuese straight in the eyes, not altering his gaze for one moment. "What are the life signs of our friend Principle Officer Gammachip?"

Ensign Strawballis punched in the necessary diagnostic changes to evaluate a Fasterfoid subject.

"Captain, the Organitron on board is running at above normal levels, as if he were exerting himself, Sir."

"Captain Carrot to Ensign Broccleman." Said Captain Carrot almost snarling at General Satuese. "Are you satisfied that our readings are correct now General?"

"Ensign Broccleman here. Captain?"

"Ensign Broccleman fix and log co-ordinates on Captain Peabazzare and the Fasterfoid situated on the enemy vessel then stand by for my mark to activate."

"Aye, aye Captain."

"Ensign Strawballis. Open channel communications with the FF Francaisfry, merge all frequencies if you have to but do it! Captain Carrot to Red Sector Leader secondary control." said the Captain.

"Red sector leader secondary control standing by." came the response.

"Lock on task force phasers and prime the blazer guns. Do not! Repeat, do not dispatch ground troops. Red sector green, lean and mean on my mark. Confirm acknowledge and comply."

"This is secondary red sector leader. Green, lean and mean on your mark. Standing by acknowledge and compliance." confirmed the Secondary pilot.

On the FF Francaisfry, Principle Officer Gammachip had tied the Captain to the Command Com chair, initiated the main crystalline chamber and turned on the force shield. Then with the force shield initiated he activated the cloaking device and powered up the main reactors.

"Call yourself a General do you Satuese?" said Principle Gammachip. "You are nothing more than a yellow bellied traitor. I spit on your rank and laugh at your title." Then the communication channel activated.

"This is Ensign Strawballis to the FF Francaisfry, come in please. You are in violation of the Fasterfoid-Organitron agreement supplemental to the Organitron- Fasterfoid treaty. We are standing by with our task force, please respond."

Back on the bridge of the O.S.S.S Earthanon, General Satuese approached the Communications Com and asked if he could try to establish contact. Captain Carrot looked at him slowly and nodded agreeing to at least give it a try.

"Very well General Satuese you are welcome to try. FO Marrowlar monitor the transmission. If he does anything wrong, anything at all, then douse him in gravy." he said taking to the Command Com seat.

"Aye, aye, but Sir." said FO Marrowlar adjusting the ship's Security Com, then rushing towards the Grid Finder. "The Francaisfry she has gone, vanished without a trace." he confirmed.

On the bridge of the FF Francaisfry, a frenzied Principle Gammachip stood at the ship's systems terminal and slowly the ship left the ground. Then the voice of his so called superior Officer could be heard over the communications channel.

"This is General Satuese to Principle Officer Gammachip, I don't know what you're playing at but this course of action must cease immediately, respond please. That is an order Principle Gammachip."

With the cloaking device operational and Principle Gammachip managing to take off single handed, he felt as if he were invincible. It was time to answer the General.

"Orders?" came his reply on the bridge of the O.S.S.S Earthanon. "What right have you to issue orders? You leave your ship to run under the wings of the enemy for protection, and then you try and throw your weight around by giving me orders. You are a traitor, an Organitron confident, an Organitron aide and trustee. If that is the way you want it to be Faturno then you can die like an Organitron. This is the Commanding officer of the FF Francaisfry, Fasterfoid flagship and pride of the fleet signing off. Oh, and prepare to meet your doom." Then the line went dead and there was a feeling of great unease on the bridge of the O.S.S.S Earthanon.

"Ensign Broccleman to Captain Carrot."

"Captain Carrot here Ensign." he replied.

"Captain. Sir, I have lost the tracking beacon of the FF Francaisfry. I couldn't Vegitamise them back unless I had a fixed position." he confirmed.

"I understand Ensign Broccleman. Keep sweeping the area, there may be a chance that Captain Peabazzare can activate his emergency utility belt. Let me know if and when you find anything, Captain Carrot out." Captain Carrot looked round at General Satuese with a certain amount of compassion in his eyes. He could at least understand what must be going through his mind.

"General Satuese," said the Captain slowly. "I apologise. I was wrong and I want you to know that what you did was.. is the right thing to do.

You could however be of further use to us! What has the FF Francaisfry got that enables it to disappear into thin air. If he is serious, and I believe that to be the case, then he will come after us in a matter of minutes. We need to know what to look for if we are to stand any chance of survival!" said the Captain. General Satuese looked around him and saw the good in the faces of the Sun-Fleet crew, but that was not as important as the Fasterfoid crew on board the O.S.S.S Earthanon. They were his first priority. If saving them meant also saving the enemy then so be it. Save them all he would.

"Captain Carrot." smiled the General. "The FF Francaisfry comes with a cloaking devise on a much larger scale than that with which the infiltrators managed to elude detection on the Earthanon surface."

"Does it have the same chemical breakdown?" asked the Captain hoping that they could seek out Cochinello gas pockets as an aid to detection.

"No! It is formed with a different mixture of elements of which not even I know. I'm afraid trying to track her will be futile. The only way you may find her, is to lock on your Grid Finder to the ships weapons expulsion point; and fire at those co-ordinates in the hope that she is still there, but her shields remain down for the firing duration only, if they are up then I feel sure you cannot harm her to a sufficient degree." said the General.

"Nevertheless General, we now know that we are looking for something that we cannot see. And only our sixth sense can locate. It is better that we have at least our intuition to fall back on than nothing at all. FO Marrowlar, scan the Solar System for any energy expulsions and fire up the proton reactors. Set blazer phasers to maximum output and tie them into the Vegimatter room computer. Viceroy Rhubarblatt, maintain position and switch co-ordinates at five starmin intervals, make distance alterations at five hundred starmillo's at each manoeuvre. Ensign Viola, keep on that Grid Finder and plot any spatial distortions that appear. SO Tulipina, full power output to the defence shields. Increase Grid Finder sweeping distance to one thousand starmillo's and place all crew divisions on green alert. FO Potatree, see if you can get the Califoric propulsion system diverted to the blazer phasers for a little extra kick."

"Aye Captain, but once it is off the main momentum drive it will take five starmins or so to realign and initiate for K Factor jump speed. This means that if we have a surprise visit from a freak Sodium Star belt pocket we could be left high and dry without sufficient power to outrun it!" said a concerned FO Potatree.

"That is a risk we will have to take FO Potatree, besides if we don't do it the Sodium Star belt may be of no concern to us." he reasoned.

"Well, you do have a point there Captain. I'm on my way. Ensign Rasperillo keep your eyes on this one will you?"

"You bet FO Potatree!" said the Ensign staring at General Satuese keenly.

"Ensign Strawballis, contact Admiral Ducarrotain and Commodore Cu-Cumbala's quarters. Have them stay there for their own protection and ask them if they need to leave them inform the bridge of their destination."

"Aye, aye Captain." she said.

Time 4.10 starhectoids.

Down on the surface of the Earthanon, FO Melonicord, who was unaware of the recent events up above, was just sending the last of the Organitron personnel through the Vegitamisation process when Ensign Broccleman called her on the open channel.

"Ensign Broccleman to FO Melonicord. Come in please." she heard as the Vegitamisation platform completed its last cycle.

"FO Melonicord to Ensign Broccleman. Yes Ensign Broccleman, what appears to be the problem?" she asked as her only company was her sceptical mind. She looked around the once bustling, vibrant, humming City of Arcticus now in a deserted state the wind howling around the chambers of the Citadel. Apart from Commander Marrachinello she would be the last Organitron to see, touch or feel the Earthanon surface in Helios knows how long; for all she knew maybe forever.

"That's it FO Melonicord you're all done and dusted, you are the only one left. Are you ready to Vegitamise on board?" he asked.

"I will just check the self destruct sequence modulator and I will be right with you, stand by for my mark!" she didn't need to check it, but she was at pains to leave this place without laying her eyes once more on Earthanons moonlit lush and fertile landscape. As she stepped outside thunder rumblings could be heard in the distance. It had suddenly lost all its charm without the hustle and bustle of everyday life and yet, the air was filled with the beautiful fragrances of Earthanon spring that filled her body and soul with relaxation and thus, freedom.

"Oh if I could put it in a bottle and take it with me!" she said picking flowers from the borders of the garden beds and pulling them close to her face, breathing in deeply as if it were her last chance for a tender moment alone. Although she was alone and a flash of lightning reminded her that this world, the world that they had come to love and cherish would soon be fighting a battle against the elements. She had the opportunity to leave, but Earthanon did not, it would have to face the elements alone, without any defences. A tear rolled down her cheek as the defenceless Planet sent a calling to her sub-conscious. At least that's what she thought but it was more likely the echo's of the wind swirling in her head. Slowly she turned and walked into the main module, the timer was set with one starhectoid ten starmins to go.

"FO Melonicord to Ensign Broccleman. I'm ready Ensign Broccleman, Vegitamise." she said wiping her eyes and looking around for one last time. Within seconds she was gone and back aboard the O.S.S.S Earthanon. As she appeared on the ship's platform she stood silently as if she had lost a loved one.

"Are you all right FO Melonicord?" he asked taking the flowers from her and helping her off the platform.

"Ask me in five starhectoids and thirty five starmins time." she replied quietly.

Time 4.20 starhectoids

Back on the bridge of the FF Francaisfry, Principle Gammachip had shot off into space to practise manoeuvring the ship single handed. Captain Peabazzare started to stir from his unconscious state and slowly focused on the back of Principle Gammachip. While Principle Gammachip's hands were full trying to run all of the ship's systems at once, Captain Peabazzare struggled with his bound hands to reach the utility belt activation switch.

"That's it," whispered Principle Gammachip. "come around. Where shall we hit them? Wait a minute, if I fire at them they will fix my position and fire. That's how they found the attack force last time. It looks like the General was right I will have to destroy the ship, so why don't I destroy them both. Ahh... Ha... Ha... Ha! I'm a genius, setting course for the O.S.S.S Earthanon." he said punching in the terminal instructions. "Let us ram them head on. That should finish the battle once and for all." Quickly he turned around to see if Captain Peabazzare was conscious, but the Captain had managed to play dead just in time.

"Oh what a pity." laughed Principle Gammachip. "I was rather hoping to share this little development with you, but alas, it is not to be." Then he turned back towards his station. "ETA O.S.S.S Earthanon collision one starmin seven starsecs. He.. He.. He.. He." he laughed again this time licking his lips. Captain Peabazzare managed to free one hand but still could not reach the activation switch which was on the other side of the belt.

"Collision in fifty starsecs and counting." said Principle Gammachip increasing to full speed.

"On the bridge at the Nav Com. Ensign Viola watched for any unusual movements in the spatial surrounds of the ship and its immediate area. General Satuese suddenly jumped onto the lower bridge floor. "Captain Carrot he is here. I feel it in my bones."

"Then why hasn't he fired, or do you think he is trying to psyche you out before he goes in for the kill?" asked the Captain.

"I don't know Captain. Unless..?"

"Unless he is going to ram us instead!" they shouted together.

"Collision in ten starsecs," screamed an elated Principle Officer Gammachip. "goodbye universe, it was nice knowing you." he shouted unaware that Captain Peabazzare was not free but was loose enough to be able to shift his position enabling him to grip Principle Gammachip between his legs.

"Captain Carrot, Spatial distortion dead ahead seven starsecs." shouted Ensign Viola.

"Viceroy Rhubarblatt evasive action. Pull her up, now! Sound general alarm." shouted the Captain.

"Aye, aye Sir." confirmed Viceroy Rhubarblatt

"Shall I fire at the displacement Captain?" asked FO Marrowlar.

"Negative FO Marrowlar not while Captain Peabazzare is still on-board." he said opening the ship's channel.

"Captain Carrot to all ship's company, brace yourselves for a collision." he shouted.

On board the FF Francaisfry the O.S.S.S Earthanon could be seen on the visaid changing course heading and Principle Gammachip altered his course to match. "So you want to take it in the belly do you? Well that's just fine by me. ETA Five starsecs." Then Captain Peabazzare grabbed Principle Gammachip around the waist and pulled him away from the Command com. As the steering column was released the ship changed direction to a less direct angle, and skimmed the underside of the O.S.S.S Earthanon. As Principle Gammachip fought with Captain Peabazzare, the ship shuddered as it struck the underside and headed straight down towards Earthanon in a frantic spin. Captain Peabazzare managed at last to free both hands and pushed Principle Gammachip away. Principle Gammachip pulled himself onto his feet and corrected the course of the ship except for one small problem. The collision of the two ships had taken out the FF Francaisfry's cloaking capability by dislodging the electro fusion housing, while its level propulsion equaliser had bent on impact, meaning, that the ship was only manoeuvrable backwards and forwards, and was losing height rapidly. Principle Gammachip hurled abuse at Captain Peabazzare. "We didn't bring her down thanks to you. You great Organitron misfit. What is it with the Organitron eh? Doesn't anyone practise the art of dying with honour in your outfits? Cowards the lot of you, why I bet when you bleed its yellow! You do know we are going to crash? Our only hope is to increase full gravity buffer shields to maximum output, and put her down in the water reservoir estuary four blimits from Arcticus." Setting the co-ordinates he turned towards the dazed Captain Peabazzare.

"Thank you very much for stealing my hour of glory!" he shouted like a child. "We'll be lucky if we survive this one." he continued.

"But I thought you wanted to die?" said Captain Peabazzare. "Grow up or let the big boys take over. Your ship is finished but we can still make it aboard the O.S.S.S Earthanon." shouted the Captain.

On the bridge of the O.S.S.S Earthanon, Captain Carrot and the crew were also suffering problems with the stabilisation of their ship. The collision had buckled their Pivotal thrusters and forced them into an irreversible down position. The Port side thrusters were non-functional and the starboard thrusters were under a tremendous strain.

"Captain Carrot, Ensign Broccleman here." Came a voice over the personal channel.

"Yes Ensign Broccleman what is it?" he asked as he regained his balance.

"I have managed to fix positions on both Captain Peabazzare and the Fasterfoid Officer. Do you want me to Vegitamise them aboard Captain? Their ship is out of control and free falling towards the Earthanon surface!" said Ensign Broccleman.

"Grow with the flow Ensign Broccleman, bring them aboard. Have Principle Gammachip placed in the brig house upon his arrival." said the Captain. "Ensign Viola, Nav Com status?" enquired the Captain

"The good news Captain, is that we can still steer the ship, the bad news is we can only steer it downwards in a controlled landing." confirmed Ensign Viola.

"So we are stuck on Earthanon whether we like it or not!" sneered FO Marrowlar at General Satuese.

"Ensign Strawballis," continued the Captain. "I want FO Potatree, FO Cornelius, FO Melonicord, FO Milnedew, Professor Goosegorgon, Dr Kiwitranus and Mushroid Funguy in the strategy room at the double. When Captain Peabazzare gets aboard have him meet us there, also contact Viceroy Councillor Au Paw-Paw to see if she is available for consultation. FO Marrowlar, General Satuese, you will join me so that we may all suffer the consequences of your second in commands actions together. Viceroy Rhubarblatt, you know the old Arcticus spring mines?" said the Captain.

"Yes Captain."

"Bring use to rest, if you can, in the old estuary mouth. As close to under the continental shelf as you can. When the Aqua Asteroids hit we are going to need all the protection we can get. SO Tulipina you have Command Com. Let me know the full geographical status when we have set down on the surface. Gentleman if you will follow me, we have an estimated six starhectoids before the Sodium Star belt hits. Ensign Strawballis, have the ground attack force Vege-cruiser leave Earthanon atmosphere along the agreed escape root, but first contact Admiral Ducarrotain and Commodore Cu-Cumbala, ask them if they would like to transfer to the Vege-cruiser for safe passage home. I am afraid I have not the time to inform them myself so send them the communication transcripts between the O.S.S.S Earthanon and the FF Francaisfry. If they wish to transfer I will bid them farewell from the Vegitamisation room before they go. Plot our final calculated landing co-ordinates and transfer the information to the Vege-cruiser, at least when the Sodium Star belt has past they will know where to find us, and have the Star Fighters re-join the ship, we may need them."

"Aye, aye Captain." she replied opening the communications com.

As they stepped into the elevation chamber, General Satuese was quiet and deep in thought.

"Worry not General, none of this is your fault but how we will fair in our battle for survival is uncertain; one thing is for sure, it is not without danger." Then the doors closed and they were gone.

"Captain Carrot off the bridge." shouted Ensign Rasperillo.

"Pheweeeeee.. Phewoooooh." piped Ensign Melonture.

SO Tulipina sat at the Command Com preparing herself for the job ahead, to land the O.S.S.S Earthanon safely and to ensure as much protection from the Sodium Star belt as possible.

"Viceroy Rhubarblatt, reduce engines to one quarter pulse speed steady as she goes and make this landing count, because, believe me. All our lives depend on your skill and judgement." she said with a cold and calculated air of calmness.

"Aye, aye SO Tulipina. One quarter pulse speed, activating Graviton proton force field." confirmed Viceroy Rhubarblatt, breaking into an incredible sweat under the pressure but anxious to appear completely under control. Ensign Viola looked across and mouthed the words. "Good luck." Offering the thumbs up sign. And so the scene was set to reach Earthanon in one piece, hopefully not to reach the final resting place, but a place in which they could ride out the storm.

The emergency meeting to be held in the strategy room, would soon be in session. The requested delegates were gathered in a quiet and sombre mood the realisation that they would not be going home weighed heavily on all minds. As Captain Carrot entered the room with FO Marrowlar and General Satuese, a chilling quietness fell and the looks glared toward the disgraced Fasterfoid Commander told a simple and not surprising story. They had under the guidance of Captain Carrot, agreed to offer the hand of friendship and a position of trust towards the Fasterfoids in their hour of need. They felt betrayed and angry at the actions of the one and judged the whole accordingly.

"Ensign Strawballis to Captain Carrot. Come in please." came the voice over his personal channel.

"Captain Carrot here, go ahead Strawballis." said the Captain aware of the building resentment in the direction of General Satuese.

"Captain. Admiral Ducarrotain and Commodore Cu-Cumbala are here for the duration, they said they have every confidence in your ability. The Vege-cruiser is awaiting your permission for departure. SO Tulipina estimates arrival on Earthanon surface in exactly five starmins, it could be rough so buckle up." she said awaiting the Captains directive.

"Tell the Vege-cruiser to proceed. When we have landed have Admiral Ducarrotain and Commodore Cu-Cumbala meet me in the Medilab." Captain Carrot paused as he continued to fathom the complexity of the situation they found themselves in. "Have Ensign Broccleman bring Principle Officer Gammachip to the strategy room immediately. That will be all Ensign Strawballis, Captain Carrot out."

"Aye, aye Sir, Ensign Strawballis out." she said signing off.

"Organigirls, Organiboys, Gentlegrills. Time is short and there is I fear much to be done. I have in the last few minutes, noted a strong resentment towards General Satuese. Nobody has said anything but nevertheless it is there. I want it to stop and stop now! General Satuese did try to do the honourable thing by his crew, although I for one, would like to know how the ship managed to take off when it was supposedly severely damaged. I suspect, however, he was trying to protect the ship's cloaking capability from falling into the wrong hands. As a Captain in Sun-Fleet I can understand his actions.

All that I ask is that you try and do the same. If you want to vent your anger then you may do so at the right time with Principle Officer Gammachip. This is neither the right time nor place for such actions. I want Principle Gammachip to view firsthand the consequences of his actions, and to learn that above all, we can be a forgiving force, even when his actions have placed all of our lives on the line. For now all I will say is this, I don't believe that we came through the Voidwell Blottmeager and the Garlicazure experience to meet our doom on Earthanon."

General Satuese looked around the room and spotted a familiar face in FO Milnedew, at least the face was familiar then the name struck him like a bell tower in his head. "No, surely not Pirate Milnedew." he thought with deep reservation. Pirates are exiled never to be bought back into the fold, it must be a striking coincidence. General Satuese snapped out of his trance as his worst nightmare walked through the strategy room doors. Principle Gammachip, accompanied by Captain Peabazzare and Ensign Broccleman. As if that wasn't bad enough, strolling behind them was Commander Marrachinello. If that was Pirate Milnedew, he was going to look a complete and utter fool after telling the commander that they practically worked him to death. The only upside in this whole event, was the pitiful face of Principle Gammachip as they entered and the change from one of sorrow to one of fright when he spotted Pirate Milnedew in the room.

"Ahh," said Captain Carrot. "Good to see you safe and sound Captain Peabazzare. I trust the Idiot Gammachip has been no further trouble Ensign Broccleman?"

"Apart from the obvious waste of good oxygen, and the odd outburst of blubbering tears, no Captain, none at all." replied Ensign Broccleman. General Satuese could not look at Principle Gammachip, he was disgusted by his actions and could only look at the floor because of the shame the

Principle Officer had brought upon himself, his crew and the Fasterfoid Nations.

"I am glad to see you are back to full flow Commander Marrachinello. Now if you wouldn't mind strapping yourselves into your seats? We are due to land in approximately three starmins, it may get a little bumpy."

As they sat down, Captain Peabazzare addressed the assembly with a heavy heart.

"Before the meeting gets under way, I would like to offer my apologies for getting us into this impossible predicament, I feel that I have let you down, all of you, so very badly. I should have been more alert." he reasoned.

"No Captain Peabazzare, if anyone is to blame it is I." said Captain Carrot. "I took the word of a Fasterfoid General who could not control his men. And I should have had the foresight not to have sent you alone. Your conscience, my friend, is clear!" he said with force.

"Thank you Captain, but all the same. I am very sorry." repeated Captain Peabazzare.

Captain Carrot stood up and activated the three dimensional hologram sequence. Then he lowered the lights in the strategy room just as Viceroy Councillor Au Paw-Paw entered the room.

"I'm sorry I am late Captain, but as you can imagine hysteria is running very high on the ship." reasoned Viceroy Councillor Au Paw-Paw.

"I understand Councillor." said the Captain. "I would have been knocking at your door myself only the queue was too long." he smiled trying to lighten the heavy atmosphere. Then he continued to deliver their situation analysis and his plan to survive the Sodium Star belt.

"As you can see the Sodium Star belt has a little under Five starhectoids fifty starmins before it reaches us in the Arcticus region. I see by FO Potatree's report that we have lost the capability of upward mobilisation, and side by side manoeuvrability thanks to the actions of the Fasterfoid Officer Gammachip. What I propose is this, we head for the redundant spring water mines and try to manoeuvre as best we can under the continental shelf. This should provide us with some protection from the falling Aqua Asteroids. Then I propose that we activate at full power, the energy proton defence shields and convert them to heat emulating buffers. My idea is that this will soften, if not melt, the Aqua Asteroids before impact. To guarantee a half starmillo radius completely surrounding the ship, I propose mobile vitiminal reactors hooked up to an electromagnetic network dragnet, exactly the same way as we used to fool Blottmeager except placing the Robopods ten staryards apart. Then I propose we utilise the Land crab mobile phaser blasters to help shoot the Aqua Asteroids out of the sky, melt them before they reach us, or, if we are talking the very biggest of them, we may be able to redirect their course heading with controlled simultaneous directional shots. Now, obviously we will not be able to work on the O.S.S.S Earthanon to undergo any kind of repairs for any significant length of time. One can only assume that with this much moisture falling from the sky, the O.S.S.S Earthanon will be submerged in no time at all. Therefore, I suggest that as soon as we have touched down on the surface of Earthanon, and the work schedule has been completed within the half starhectoid, we reduce power output to auxiliary back-up only and conserve our oxygen until Sun Fleet can come and rescue us." said the Captain taking his seat.

"Excuse me Captain. But how exactly, will Sun-Fleet know where to find us?" asked FO Marrowlar. "The co-ordinates supplied to the Vege-cruiser were planned assuming the ship was clear to land there, besides, there are many reasons why even if we did land at those co-ordinates, the ship may move, and with us unable to control it." he continued.

"FO Marrowlar is right Captain." interrupted FO Potatree. "To start with the water movements created by the falling Aqua Asteroids may result in some fierce undercurrents. They may even smash us against the continental shelf breaking us up completely, regardless of any damage created by the actions of Principle Gammachip. Until I have a closer inspection of the craft when we have landed! I can't give you any more positive vibes than that Captain." said FO Potatree.

"Haaatchoo... Hatchooo... Thud!" came a loud sound as FO Cornelius thumped the table. "Captain, may be allowed to offer an opinion?"

asked the nervous FO Cornelius.

"Gladly FO Cornelius." responded the Captain.

"Well Sir, It is my experience with Sodium Star belts mixed with Aqua asteroids, that once the Earthanons crust is covered the temperatures will drop well below freezing for hundreds, thousands, even millions of startechtoids. Assuming we land at the right co-ordinates and that we manage to avoid a direct hit from an Aqua Asteroid creating no further damage to our hull. The water surrounding our ship will freeze very rapidly, as it expands it will firstly shift our position and then crush us forcing the O.S.S.S Earthanon to implode. Of course I cannot be sure, but that is the way my feelings are Captain." said FO Cornelius. "Even if after landing the structure of the ship is breach free, we simply cannot survive." Then FO Cornelius stopped and mulled over the options for a split second. "Of course if the hull is breached in anyway, there is every chance that we will drown regardless. I'm sorry I cannot be more optimistic Captain, but that is the way I see it." continued FO Cornelius.

"I know the plan is not perfect FO Cornelius." said Captain Carrot. "And I am grateful for your honest and realistic observations, with all these worries and scenarios submitted we can at least have the chance to overcome them, perhaps give ourselves a fighting chance of survival, but whatever happens don't write us off yet. We have come through worse, and I refuse to let us simply lie down and die."

Out of the observation window in the strategy room, Captain Carrot and the others could see that the ship was beginning to be shadowed by the spring water mines entrance, and the rock formation seemed to surround them as they lowered as close to the perimeter wall as they could.

"Viceroy Rhubarblatt to Captain Carrot," came the voice over the personal channel.

"Captain Carrot here, go ahead Viceroy Rhubarblatt."

"Captain. We are now making our descent into the spring water mines. I'm afraid with a ship this size it is difficult to find a secure resting place. Do I have your permission to use the Phasers to establish a flat landing bed?" asked Viceroy Rhubarblatt.

"Indeed Viceroy, whatever you consider is necessary is fine by me. Just remember, once we have touched down that is where we are set to stay!" said the Captain.

"Acknowledged Captain, the spot that I have found will take us some two point seven starmillo's deep into the mine. This will give us a clearance below the Earthanon surface of one point two starmillo's. But sneaking in under the continental shelf is going to be tight Captain. My geographical echo soundings show, in some places, our clearance is less than twenty staryards. Because of our sheer size the shelf will only give us a third of the cover that we would require, and it could hamper the Sun-Fleet rescue attempt at a later date, particularly if the shelf falls on the ship. That could be the thing that finishes us off, the Grid Finder does show signs of sub-terrainial fractures running into the bedrock. I think under the circumstances Captain, it would be best to consider these factors before finalising our resting place co-ordinates." noted Viceroy Rhubarblatt

"Absolutely Viceroy Rhubarblatt, hold your position and stand by for further instructions." said the Captain.

"Aye, aye Captain, Viceroy Rhubarblatt standing by."

Captain Carrot turned to those present and threw the problem open to the forum.

"Any suggestions?" he asked racking his brains for the best options possible.

FO Milnedew raised a hand and coughed to gain the Captains attention.

"Aahum... Captain, may I say something?"

"Indeed FO Milnedew." he replied taking to his seat again.

"In my first few days here on the O.S.S.S Earthanon, whilst familiarising myself with the ship and her stocks, I came across the dangerous chemicals strong room, in there I noticed we have over a thousand dry ice capsules, each one able to freeze a thousand stargalls instantly. May I suggest we situate the ship free of cover from the continental shelf, magnetise the capsules to the hull at equal spacing and place small incendiary devices to them to go off when they become submerged, instantly freezing the water surrounding us. At the same time placing alternately with the capsules, empty fuel pods. As the water surrounds and expands upon freezing, these pods will create ample space for the expansion to take place as the pods will crumple under the pressure, alleviating the problem of pressure on the hull." FO Milnedew sat in silence as Captain Carrot thought over the plan. while FO Melonicord busily tapped into the Computron.

"Captain, if I may interject?" asked FO Melonicord quickly.

"As you will FO Melonicord." replied the Captain.

"A thousand Capsules will barely be enough Sir. The immediate surface area of the vessel well exceeds one million stargalls. However, we do carry two million stargalls of liquid nitrogen in the forehead fuel tanks for the on-board Eco-Farming Programme. We could load another thousand fuel pods as well and magnetise those to the hull with incendiaries of course we will need to increase the empty pods to match the expansion increase. Unfortunately the expansion will be immediate and even this may not give us sufficient expansion protection..." she said as she was interrupted by Professor Goosegorgon.

"FO Melonicord, Capatano. The fuel pods that are filled 'a with 'a liquid nitrogen, if 'a we, as you say, were to release 'a the liquid nitrogen by injection rather than explosion, that would leave those 'a pods a 'free to double up as'a crumple pods to make safe the expansion margin, no?

All we need to do is use the sea feeder nozzles from the kelp farms' management system. However I do spot 'a one small but significant flaw in'a the plan. Well, two actually. Number one; what if the bombardment of Aqua Asteroids knocks off the pods and or the capsules and sea feeder pods? It would only need to remove a third to eliminate our safety margin. Then there is'a my second concern, if the capsules and 'a the sea feeder pods are linked to submersion incendiaries, then as soon they are completely covered in'a, say, a downpour of Aqua Asteroid vapour from above, this will trigger the device prematurely and set them off, wasting valuable freezing capability. Do you see my point?" he asked.

All heads around the table nodded in agreement, even General Satuese and Principle Gammachip were nodding.

"That is a very good point Professor. One that we will have to overcome. Captain Carrot to Viceroy Rhubarblatt. Set us down in line but not under the continental shelf. Then have ground teams scour the external hull for breaches while SO Tulipina examines the internal hull through the ships systems analyser. That way we double check for all we are worth and stand a better chance of eliminating any problem areas swiftly and without delay. Once we have set down, I want you to secure the ship to the mine bed using the hydro-calorific suction tentacles. Oh and Viceroy Rhubarblatt, I want it all completed in twenty starmins is that clear?" he asked.

"Aye, aye Captain, Viceroy Rhubarblatt out."

Outside the ship, the phasers were fast at work levelling the old mine floor to fit the ship's vast bulk as precisely as possible. As the phasers struck their designated areas the open cast mine became alive with a glorious array of Technicolor, but from the inside of the ship in the heart of the mine, the beautiful colour spectrum was almost blinding. Captain Carrot activated the shutters then re-directed his attentions to the situation at hand.

"FO Potatree, FO Milnedew, FO Cornelius, Professor Goosegorgon." began Captain Carrot. "I want you to go and prepare the dry ice capsules, fitted with incendiary devices, the fuel pods and then the sea feeder pods with the injection systems. I want all devices activated by a manual electrode coding transmission, we can't risk premature explosions being the cause of our demise. I don't want to go into detail of how it will work exactly, we do not have much time. All that I ask is that you trust me. FO Melonicord will go with you along with Ensign Broccleman. I want you two to programme the Robopods to position the capsules, pods and sea feeders at regular intervals. Then I want them to go and form a half starmillo protection network as soon as that is completed. Now go, and let me know when this is accomplished." said the Captain looking at his timepiece. "Which by the way I expect to be in no more than thirty starmins, the time now is **05.10** starhectoids**.** For the safety of all personnel minimal time outside the ship is essential. I want everyone back on board by **05.40 starhectoids,** it's going to be tight but that's the way it has to be. Good luck." As the party left and the strategy doors closed, there was just Captain Carrot, Dr Kiwitranus, Viceroy Councillor Au Paw-Paw, FO Marrowlar, Commander Marrachinello, Captain Peabazzare and Mushroid Funguy along with the two Fasterfoid Officers present in the room. Suddenly the ship shuddered to a halt as she came to rest in the relative darkness of the spring water mine.

Captain Carrot walked towards the observation window opened the shutters and looked up towards the sky. His heart felt heavy with the knowledge that, no matter what he did, the beloved homelands of the Organitron were not to be graced with the presence of the population on board the O.S.S.S Earthanon. Not for the foreseeable future at least. As he watched the crew milling around the ship like a family of ants a shuttle craft began emerging from the expulsion catapults and started the search for damage. As some crew whizzed past the window by way of mobile space packs his immediate thoughts went back to his quarters where his family were waiting for him to join them. No matter what happened when the Sodium Star belt hit, he felt that at all Organitron should be with their loved ones. After all it may be the last time they ever saw each other. The question was how to achieve this without having to be present on the bridge to make good any damage to the ship during, and who knows, even after the storm. Deep down even he did not rate their chances of survival too highly, but for now this doubt must not manifest itself in any way, he thought, returning to the table.

"Commander Marrachinello, I would like you and your Star fighter pilots to remain with the ship, it is my opinion that the firepower of our entire squadron will be minimal against a Sodium Star belt of this magnitude. Instead, I want you to take your best Engineers and take a look at the Pivotal thrusters housing. If we can get minimal lift, then come the time of the rescue we will, indeed, be in better shape to cope with it. Go now, you and your teams have thirty starmins." Captain Carrot paused and held his head in his hands. Without lifting his head he spoke softly as Commander Marrachinello rose from the table. "Commander!" I can't tell you how important it is that we have manoeuvrability for when the Sodium Star belt has passed." he continued.

"Don't worry Captain you don't need to explain. If you say it is vital, old chap, then vital it jolly well is. I'm not promising anything my friend, it is a rather tall order, but if it can be done then you can rely on us to make it happen. Captain, FO Marrowlar, team, tootle pip, what ho, aye.. Umm." he gave the Organitron salute and left, re-energising the doors behind him.

"SO Tulipina to Captain Carrot, come in please." came the call from the bridge over the Captain's personal channel."

"Captain Carrot here. Go ahead SO Tulipina." he replied.

"Captain, we have landed in a secure spot and we are fixing ourselves to the mine bed as we speak, but we do have a problem Captain." SO Tulipina stopped suddenly as if she were frozen in time, she found herself unable to communicate.

"SO Tulipina, what is the problem? SO Tulipina come in!" shrilled the Captain.

"I…I…I'm sorry Sir. I have just received confirmation from the ship's analyser.

It has confirmed only one breach in the hull in the lower forequarter section. The external ground crews are just confirming the information." she said.

"Can the breach be repaired?" he asked quickly.

"Yes Sir, the breach itself is rather small but it was caused by an internal explosion. When the pivotal thrusters were knocked out of operation, the momentum shafts went into overload and created a recoil power aneurysm in the power feeder conduits. This became trapped in the engine housing facility and blew the bulkhead into the next compartment. The component of plasma steel that flew into the next compartment, embedded itself into the oxygenation rejuvenation converter. In short Captain, the oxygen that is in the ship is all the oxygen that we have. Apart from the emergency mobile units which will supply six starhectoids of oxygen per Organitron, but that will not be enough to carry us through this little problem." she said slowly.

"How long will the oxygen in the ship last SO Tulipina?" he asked clasping his hands.

"At the current rate of energy output I estimate oxygen depletion inside of six starlectoids, If however we restrain our activities then possibly as much as nine starlectoids." she confirmed.

"Can we repair the Oxygenation rejuvenation converter?" he asked.

"Yes Sir, but we would need at least one starwektoid. If we were air born though, Captain, we could rely on external intake to fill the conversion tanks." she confirmed.

"I'm afraid that is not a possibility SO Tulipina." Captain Carrot whispered under his breath as he thought of a way around this quite sizeable problem, but, only one option repeatedly came forward for consideration.

"SO Tulipina." said the Captain. "As soon as all the external preparations have been accomplished, I want you to close down all but the auxiliary power and the phaser reactor at the forehead section; and keep the back-up proton calorific reactors on line for the Robopod protection network. I want all the bridge crew to assemble in the Eco Farming Plantation Chamber. When all systems are set and all personnel are accounted for, hook up the Robopod network above the mine and clear the bridge. I want you to hand over the ship's control to Mushroid Fungola, is that clear?" he asked awaiting acknowledgement. As he checked his time piece the Sodium Star belt would be with them inside **five starhectoids fifteen starmins.**

"Yes Captain. I understand." she confirmed.

"Thank you SO Tulipina. When you have handed over to Mushroid Fungola, I want him to place the open ships communication Channel on standby I will need to address the ship's compliment in full. Captain Carrot out."

"Aye, aye Sir, SO Tulipina out." she confirmed signing off.

The rest of the party in the strategy room were party to the information and the stark concern was obvious in their faces.

"As I see it," said FO Marrowlar looking up slowly. "with the Vegitalis Bubbleonion Squeak system at a minimum of forty starlectoids away, we are doomed. We could not possibly survive that long!" he reasoned. Captain Carrot got up and paced the room he had an idea but it was too risky to contemplate under any other circumstances.

"Dr Kiwitranus, do we have any of that sleeping draught left?" asked the Captain.

"Sleeping draught Captain, our world is about to effectively end and you want to take a nap?" chuckled Dr Kiwitranus nervously.

"No Dr Kiwitranus, this is serious. The sleeping draught that you gave the Garlicallians when we liberated Garlicazure from Blottmeager, do you have any left?" he asked.

"Yes Captain, about two hundred thousand capsules. Not nearly enough to rest the entire ship's compliment, and it would take at least two starlectoids to make sufficient quantities." he answered.

"Then answer me this." said the Captain. "Do you have sufficient raw materials to make a bulk batch of sleeping draught, which could be fed through the entire ship's air ducting system in the form of a gas?"

Dr Kiwitranus looked surprised at the request but nodded in agreement. Then he wiped his brow with his handkerchief.

"Yes Captain, I have enough raw materials to make at the very most one batch of sleeping draught that will give us I would say six to eight starhectoids low respiratory status. But Captain, I fail to see what good that could possibly do us now?" he remarked warily.

"Never mind the rationale Dr Kiwitranus, just tell me how long it will take you to make the solution and then load it into the air ducting pump housing?" reasoned Captain Carrot.

"That is easy Captain Carrot, I could use the centrifugal astronaut training chamber as a large mixing vat. That is linked directly to the air ducting system as it is also the weightless training module. With some help I could have it mixed and in the air in twenty starmins." confirmed Dr Kiwitranus.

"Set to it Dr Kiwitranus, have it mixed and ready to circulate in five starhectoids. Rig up some kind of mobile activator and carry it with you at all times. Whatever happens don't let it out of your sight is that clear?" Dr Kiwitranus stood and acknowledged Captain Carrots request. "Captain Peabazzare," continued the Captain. "will you go with Dr Kiwitranus, give him all the support he needs, whatever happens this is one phase of the plan that must be absolutely right." he said. Captain Peabazzare stood and accompanied Dr Kiwitranus to the doors which were de-energised as Captain Carrot caught their attention.

"Organimen." he shouted running towards them and began to whisper quietly. "You must be in the Eco System Farming Chamber if you want the full details in fifteen starmins, so make haste and no mistakes." he said smiling.

"Aye, aye Captain Carrot." said the saluting Captain Peabazzare.

"You can count on us Captain. We'll be there." confirmed Dr Kiwitranus, and so Dr Kiwitranus and Captain Peabazzare left as the doors re-energised.

"Captain Carrot to Ensign Strawballis." said the Captain facing Mushroid Funguy, who frankly was beginning to wonder why he was called to the extra-ordinary meeting, as, to date, he had served no real purpose but to watch and listen and to record the meeting transcripts.

"Ensign Strawballis here. Yes Captain." she replied.

"Ensign Strawballis please locate SO Okralate and have her load the secondary back-up proton pilot into a Mushroid Trans Vege-cruiser. I want to give it the best chance possible of getting through the Sodium Star belt. An on-board oscillator and manual pilot are the best options we can put forward. Have it ready for departure from pod bay four in seventeen starmins. Cancel the deployment of the Land crab phaser housings there has been a change of plan due to a new development." said the Captain with a heavy heart.

"Aye, aye Captain Carrot. This is Ensign Strawballis out." It was then that Mushroid Funguy knew his fate. It was he who was to pilot the probe through the Sodium Star belt. The realisation was obvious in his little metallic face. Then he realised the incredible trust and responsibility that Captain Carrot was about to place in him. Quickly he wheeled his way to the strategy room doors and asked permission to leave. Captain Carrot knew that Mushroid Funguy knew the task that was set before him.

"If I may be excused Captain, there are a few final preparations that I will have to make prior to my departure." he said slowly. Among other things he needed to say goodbye to the Captain's children and Carrelda for whom he had devoted startechtoids of service.

"Of course Mushroid Funguy," whispered Captain Carrot, walking over to him and rubbing Mushroid Funguy's head. "It is the best way forward that I can see; you my dear friend are my number one trustee. I will meet you in my quarters in two starmins, run along now." he said waving Mushroid Funguy through the doors. When he was gone Captain Carrot looked at Viceroy Councillor Au Paw-Paw. She sat in silence as she tried to work out exactly what Captain Carrot was planning.

"Councillor, will you do me the honour of attending the meeting of the highest order of the seed consul in the Medilab meeting rooms in five starmins. I think then you will understand your purpose in this whole affair!" he said knowing that she struggled to find where exactly she did fit in. "If you go there now you will find Commodore Cu-Cumbala and Admiral Ducarrotain. It would save some time if you would brief them as to the situation to date. I will be with you very soon, please convey my regrets and apologies for keeping them waiting but I am sure they will understand." continued the Captain.

"Yes Captain, I will do my best." she said as she left the room. Captain Carrot re-energised the doors and returned to the table.

"FO Marrowlar. You may be asking yourself what can be achieved in such a little time that can save our skins from what is apparently a hopeless situation. I know I was." said Captain Carrot. "General Satuese," he continued. "I hope now you can fully understand the enormity of the resulting chaos that your actions, or rather, the actions of your crew have caused. What should have been a matter of simple navigation around a Sodium Star belt and a sure passage to safety has become a head on collision with the unthinkable. We don't know what to expect when it gets here, what to do when it gets here, even what will become of us when it finally arrives." At that moment from the skies above came an awesome clap of thunder followed by fork lightning the likes of which Earthanon had never been graced with before. Captain Carrot stood his ground as hail, rain and wind beat at the plasma steel observation windows of the strategy room. Principle Gammachip on the other hand could be found nestling under the table sucking his thumb and whimpering like a frightened puppy. Captain Carrot walked around the table and picked him up throwing him into the chair.

"Look at you…you wimp. Call yourself a warrior of the skies, do you? This is your doing, and by hook or by crook you are going to make amends if it is the last thing that you do. If we are to save the lives of all our crews, there are things to be done and they must be done quickly. You are central to my plans whether you like it or not. Helios knows that I don't like it, but believe me when I tell you this. There is a price for your safety and you are going to pay it or so help me I will vaporise you into oblivion here and now." shouted the Captain trying to shock some sense of responsibility into Principle Gammachip.

"Yes, yes, I am sorry Captain, FO Marrowlar. I don't know what came over me; it was madness I know. A fit of pique for which there is no real excuse, but believe me if there is any way that I can help to rectify the wrong that I have done, then I will do so gladly." Principle Gammachip cried into his hands as General Satuese hugged him briefly.

"Captain Carrot, what Principle Gammachip did was wrong in your eyes and mine, but that is only because we are older and wise enough to know that there are times when discretion plays the better part of valour. Even now the hierarchy of the Fasterfoid senate will view him as the hero. It will be I who is the failure, not he. What he did, he did because it was expected of him and has been drummed into us for billions of startechtoids.

Whatever we can do to improve the odds we will do Captain, you have my word and the word of a much changed Principle Gammachip. I cannot speak for him but the way you are dealing with this frightening situation is, to my mind, incredible. I hate to say it but the average Fasterfoid would have fallen to pieces by now. So whatever you require from us just ask and it will be done!" said General Satuese looking in the eyes of Principle Gammachip.

"Yes, Captain Carrot we are here for you, we will die for you!" said Principle Gammachip.

"It is better late than never Principle Gammachip, but I hope that it will not come to death for any of us. Here is what I want you to do. Dead ahead is the perimeter wall of the spring mine. It is some thirty staryards deep at most points but here," said the Captain rolling out a map of the area. "just to our right is the weakest point of the wall. It is only twelve staryards wide. I want you to lead a team of twenty Fasterfoids and place Calorific plasma protonic bombs at the base of the wall. If we blow the whole wall the tidal wave will pick up the O.S.S.S Earthanon and throw her around as if she were a balloon in a running river. However, if we place, I would say, ten charges in an arch of forty staryards high at intervals of twenty staryards apart and blow them all at once, that should create a hole big enough to allow the water through at such a speed that it will not move the ship, cover us well before the Sodium Star belt hits Earthanon air space and leave enough of the structure above to maintain its strength and hold together. If we issue you with space flotation back packs you can be out of the ship, attach the bombs in place and back inside the ship within ten starmins. FO Marrowlar will accompany you to make sure all goes as well as planned!" said the Captain awaiting their response. General Satuese and Principle Gammachip looked at each other and nodded in agreement.

"We'll do it Captain, you can trust us this time and that is the truth!" said General Satuese jumping to his feet. Captain Carrot looked at Principle Gammachip and smiled.

"Yes, this time I think I can. FO Marrowlar you had better get a move on. I will see you and the Fasterfoid Officers and crew in the Eco Farm Chamber in fifteen starmins. Don't be late."

"Aye, aye Captain. Come along Gentlegrills, there is much to be done and not much time in which to do it." said FO Marrowlar as they left the strategy room and Captain Carrot made his way to his quarters.

When he got there Mushroid Funguy was standing in front of the children and Carrelda telling them of the exciting adventure that he was going on, and assuring them that he would be back soon so they were not worry. The children started to cry as they could not remember a day when Mushroid Funguy wasn't there when they woke up. The family spent a few brief moments in reminiscent talks and things that would come of the future. They danced and they sang and when it was time for Funguy to depart they cried with much sorrow. Mushroid Funguy kissed the hands of the children and Carrelda. As he whizzed towards the doors with Captain Carrot at his side he turned to face them for the last time in Helios knows how long.

"I will always be with you, children, I have always been with you and will continue to be so. If you need me just close your eyes and picture me and in your mind you will see me, happy I will be. Never far away, always will I stay." Mushroid Funguy fought back his oily tears as he turned and left. When the doors shut behind him they made for the elevation chamber and Captain Carrot accompanied him to the launch pod where SO Okralate was waiting. They had said their fond farewells in the elevation chamber and Mushroid Funguy was loaded on board the Mushroid Trans Vege-cruiser.

"I have finished the transcript of my final proposed actions, I would appreciate it if you did not read it until you were well into space and safe from the clutches of the Sodium Star belt! Believe me you will have enough on your plate without worrying about us. Our final co-ordinates are also in there, the previously sent back up proton pilot had slightly different co-ordinates as does the Vege-cruiser, from those of our final resting place, but still in the same zone area of the Region. Until we meet again Mushroid Funguy our hearts go with you and our lives are in your hands." Captain Carrot stood back and gave Mushroid Funguy the Organitron salute.

"Whatever it takes Captain, I will return with help, you have my word." said Mushroid Funguy as the canopy closed around him.

"This is SO Okralate to Mushroid Funguy, final check confirm all systems are clean and clear?" she said manoeuvring the small ship into the expulsion catapult.

"Clean as a whistle and ready to roll, take me high and let's fly!" he confirmed.

"Launching in five, four, three, two and one launch M.T.V.C now!" said SO Okralate as the Mushroid Trans Vege-cruiser shot off and disappeared down the expulsion tunnel.

"Maintain Radio contact and tracking for as long as you can SO Okralate. Please be in the Eco-Farm Chamber in eight starmins." said the Captain heading for the pod bay exit.

"Aye, aye Captain." confirmed SO Okralate as Captain Carrot left for his rendezvous in the Medilab.

"Captain Carrot to Ensign Strawballis, come in please."

"Ensign Strawballis here Captain Carrot."

"How goes FO Marrowlar and the Fasterfoid delegation, Ensign Strawballis?"

"They have just reached the perimeter wall and are laying the protonic charges Captain."

"Let me know as soon as they are on their way back to the ship."

"Aye, aye Sir, Captain Carrot." she said light heatedly. "When this is all over you will wonder what all the fuss was about!" she chuckled.

"I hope you're right Ensign Strawballis. Captain Carrot out. I certainly hope you're right." he said stepping into the elevation chamber. "Deck 10 section k. Medilab meeting rooms." The doors closed and he was on his way.

Outside the ship, FO Marrowlar and the Fasterfoid Officers struggled against the elements to stay with the perimeter wall. The wind thrashed them about like the branches of a tree, indiscriminate and without warning, sometimes smashing them against the rock face. The wind pelted them with rain the likes of which they had never seen before. Every time they opened their mouths to communicate they seemed to fill and empty like a small tidal river. The thunder and lightning sounded around their ears and blinded their eyes with a frightening velocity. Every crack and flash seemed to ring in their heads for an eternity.

"General Satuese, you start at that end and place the charges, when we meet at the top of the arch we will set the charges. Place the charges in parties of two, as soon as you have placed the charges make your way back to the ship. Principle Gammachip you come with me. You and I, General Satuese and Ground-Force General Crinkleark will be the last ones to leave the perimeter wall. We want to be finished in less than four starmins. Right, let's go and whatever you do, don't drop the protonic bombs or we will all be puréed matters." he shouted as gradually each team of two placed the charges in its respective position. Suddenly, as FO Marrowlar and Principle Gammachip placed the last protonic bomb in line with General Satuese's bomb, a bolt of lightning struck the wall next to Principle

Gammachip and a rock fall fell on top of him knocking him to the ground. FO Marrowlar set the bombs and went down to check on Principle Gammachip with General Satuese and Ground General Crinkleark. As they approached they could see Principle Gammachip's foot was caught under a rock while FO Marrowlar struggled to move it. They all joined in but It was impossible, the rock was just too heavy for them to cope with. Principle Gammachip cried out in pain as the slightest movement of the rock sent what seemed like bolts of lightning down his body.

"It's no use, leave it. This is a fitting end for me. You must go now before it is too late. Please, waste no time on me. This is my punishment, my destiny." he said as more loose rubble fell from the perimeter wall loosening one of the bomb placements.

"General Satuese go back up there and secure that placement I will free Gammachip I promise!" shouted FO Marrowlar struggling to remain on his feet. General Satuese went back up the perimeter wall and secured the bomb while FO Marrowlar, and Ground General Crinkleark looked around for some kind of instrument to provide some leverage under the rock, but there was nothing. Then in the distance he saw two lights approaching. It was FO Potatree and FO Milnedew coming to the rescue.

"Thank Helios you came!" shouted FO Marrowlar. "I thought I was going to spend the rest of my life with Principle Gammachip on my conscience." he laughed.

"It's no use!" shouted Principle Gammachip. "Get back to the ship I am not worthy of this. Please, my conscience is plagued enough… Ahhh.. Go" he pleaded.

"You tried to make a mends didn't you?" asked FO Potatree.

"You know that what you did was wrong, don't you?" shouted FO Milnedew.

"Yes but this is…." shouted Principle Gammachip as the three Organitron interrupted him.

"But nothing!" they shouted together.

"When we lift, you pull your leg out, no matter how much it hurts, then get back to the ship." yelled FO Marrowlar above the howling wind. "One, two, three and lift."

Together they began to apply every last ounce of strength they could muster. Slowly the rock began to move and gradually Principle Gammachip pulled his leg free. When his leg was clear he activated the back pack and looked around for General Satuese, but he was nowhere to be seen.

"The General." shouted Principle Gammachip. "I must find the General. I'll meet you all back at the ship."

"Negative soldier!" screamed FO Marrowlar. "You are in no fit state to rescue anyone. Now go, we will find the General. That is an order Principle Gammachip! General Crinkleark take this Gentlegrill back to the ship" he continued.

"Aye, aye, Sir." said General Crinkleark and Principle Gammachip turning and making their way to the ship and the safety of the Medilab sick bay.

FO Milnedew shouted down from the ridge in the wall that had been caused by the lightning strike.

"He's down this gully, the wind must have swept him in and knocked him unconscious."

"Can you reach him?" shouted FO Potatree on his way up.

"Negative, he is too far down." came FO Milnedew's reply.

"General Satuese. Can you hear me? wake up General Satuese, wake up please." bellowed FO Marrowlar.

"I've got an idea!" said FO Potatree, pulling a grappling hook from his tool pouch. "I'll tie this to the end of this guide rope, lower it down and hook it onto his safety harness. Then it will take all three of our backpacks to lift him out of there to safety OK." he said. They nodded as FO Potatree lowered the rope down the gully. He just caught the harness and pulled but the hook slipped away. Again he tried to hook the harness, but instead caught the General's uniform, through the shoulder pad of his jacket. "It will have to do and let's hope it holds." Slowly all three of them pulled upwards as General Satuese's limp body inched its way up the gully. Suddenly the hook tore the seams of his jacket partially but seemed to still bear the weight of the General. As they pulled him to the mouth of the gully, the hook gave way completely and just as the General began to slip back into the small ravine Principle Gammachip who had returned, grabbed his superior officer and held him until the others could join him and they pulled him to the safety of the ship together. When they were back on board the ship they lay on the launch pad floor breathless for a moment their clothes saturated.

"FO Marrowlar t... T... To Captain Carrot. Charges are placed and set Captain. R... R... Ready to blow on your Command Captain." he said struggling to maintain audible speech.

"Understood FO Marrowlar, well done. Report to the Eco-Farm Chamber and await my arrival. Have all ship's ranker Officers converge there, I think it's time I spilled the beans on what exactly is going through my mind. Organise for an escort for the Fasterfoid delegation to the chamber under full security if you will. Is FO Milnedew with you?" he asked.

"Aye Sir." confirmed FO Marrowlar.

"And I have no doubt that where I find him, I will also find FO Potatree!" said the Captain.

"That is correct Captain." laughed FO Marrowlar.

"FO Potatree." asked the Captain."

"Aye, aye Captain. FO Potatree hearing you loud and clear." he replied.

"Take FO Milnedew and empty the leisure Complex hydro-pools. Then I want you to fill them with our best quality Olive oil, is that clear?"

"What, all of them Captain?" asked the surprised FO Milnedew.

"Every last one of them. Don't worry I will explain when I arrive at the Eco-Farm. Might I suggest that you Vegitamise the contents of the pools straight into the spring mines. Then Vegitamise the olive oil straight into the hydro-pools." said the Captain concerned about the time element.

"Aye, aye Sir, whatever you say. FO's Potatree and Milnedew UFO and out"

"This is Captain Carrot out."

On his approach to the Medilab meeting room doors, Captain Carrot prepared himself for the meeting ahead. He felt sure that, given that the O.S.S.S Earthanon was stranded on the Planetary surface without aid of cover, the highest ranking Officers who were attached to the seed consul, albeit distantly, would have resigned themselves to certain doom. Little did they know what was running through Captain Carrot's mind. It was so off the wall it could actually work. It had to work, there was no other option. He had to make them see that if they were to survive then their full trust had to be placed in him and his ability to dodge death at every opportunity. That, if ever there was a time for the Organitrons finest hour, this was it.

"Ensign Strawballis to Captain Carrot. Come in please." came the voice over the com channel.

"Captain Carrot here, yes Ensign Strawballis." replied the Captain.

"Update on the Sodium Star belt ETA Captain. It will reach Earthanon airspace in exactly five starhectoids and three starmins. SO Tulipina has ratified the figures with the Grid Finder and the Vegimatter computer. Dr Kiwitranus has confirmed completion of the chemical substance that you asked for and is awaiting further instructions. All the Dry Ice Cylinders,

Fuel Pods and Sea Feeder Pods are in place and the Robopod Electro Proton Network is established and running. The ship's open channel is standing by and ready for implementation Captain." confirmed Ensign Strawballis.

"Are all personnel aboard the O.S.S.S Earthanon Ensign Strawballis?" "Affirmative Captain, all personnel are present and accounted for including the Fasterfoid delegation." confirmed Ensign Strawballis.

"Is Mushroid Fungola on the bridge?" asked the Captain.

"Yes Sir. He is connecting himself up to the ships command com as instructed."

"Are we still tracking Mushroid Funguy?" enquired the Captain. His hands trembling with the thought of his faithful valet facing that Sodium Star belt alone. "Affirmative Captain. We lost vocal contact two starmins ago but we can still barely pick him up on the Grid Finder. The signal is getting weaker, we estimate he should be entering the Star belt in a little under ten starmins. Captain?" said the Ensign quietly

"Yes Ensign Strawballis?"

"Before we lost contact we received a message from Mushroid Funguy. I have stored it on the vocal transcript box. He specifically asked that I play it to you when you were alone. Would now be a good time Captain?" she awaited his response.

"Yes Ensign Strawballis. We appear to have gained a little time on the Sodium Star belt arrival. Now would be a very good time." he replied wiping a tear from his eye.

"Here goes Captain." confirmed Ensign Strawballis.

"Hi Cappo! This is your old metallic nut case friend Funguy. Gees it's cold up here but once you get used to it.. It.. It's kind of OK. It's quiet though, boy is it quiet. You should be travelling with the protocol back up pilot, wowee what a sad case he is. Listen though, seriously. Don't worry about us, somehow we will make it and get the information to Carridionaries. I miss you guys already, I guess there is more human in me than they thought. Listen, I know what you're planning on doing and if you want my honest opinion it's one Helios of an Idea. Hey, maybe you should patent it, this little gem holds all sorts of applications you'll see if I am not right. I don't know why you chose me for this job, but choose me you did and I hope I can serve as you expect. Tell the children I love them, and give your Organiwife a squeeze from me. It's because of them I know I will make it. Together we make too good 'a team to bust up, even if I do, do all of the work. I'd say wrap up warm but under the circumstances that would seem a little idiotic. So take care now I'll see you on the other side, wherever that is? I can see…it, in front of me it's vast. From this distance it is almost beautiful. By the time I get a little closer, I guess my opinion would have changed somewhat dramatically. It's getting a little choppy now I had better sign off. PS, the Sodium Star belt will be with you in about five starhectoids and ten starmins, so batten down the hatches and be prepared me matey's. Helios be with you and guard you well. This is Mechanoid Funguy 5000 series UFO and out."

Captain Carrot took time out to compose himself before entering the meeting room. He had become attached to the little Mechanoid probe known as Funguy. It was almost as though he were part of the family unit.

"Captain Carrot to SO Tulipina. Come in please." he said.

"SO Tulipina here Captain."

"Close all external hatches, seal all lower level bulkheads as they become vacant, move all personnel to the Living and leisure levels. As each level is sealed, close down the power supply to those areas and re-direct the oxygen supply to the hibernation decks. Did Commander Marrachinello manage to rectify the Pivotal thruster housing in any way?" he asked.

"We think so, Captain, but until it is time to manoeuvre again it is impossible to tell for sure!" she replied.

"Very well SO Tulipina. Once all of the personnel are confined to those three levels and the above and below decks are sealed off, hand over the command Com to Mushroid Fungola. He will know what to do from then on in. Have all bridge crew report to the Eco-Farm as soon as they come off assignment. Is that clear?"

"Acknowledge and compliance, this is SO Tulipina over and out." she said signing off. Captain Carrot turned and de-energised the doors. In front of him were the worried faces of the top ranks and Viceroy Councillor Au Paw-Paw. The doors re-energised and the meeting was under way.

Far, far away in outer space, Mushroid Funguy and the Trans Vege-cruiser dodged and weaved its way through the Sodium Star belt.

"Ahh.. Ahh.. No! Move it you great lump of frozen dishwater. Wow.. Wowee that was a close one. So you thought you could take me on and win did you?" he said looking behind him. As he turned back to face the onslaught of Aqua Asteroids, his mouth hung open like a trap door in the municipal waste outlets below deck on the O.S.S.S Earthanon. Before him, encased in what was possibly the largest Aqua Asteroid he had ever seen, was a meteorite of the strangest coloration he had ever come across. It was a bright rustic yellow. In fact the only rock that he had ever heard of that was coloured in this fashion was,

"Templevegarial." he shouted. "I have found Templevegarial." Once the initial excitement died down, he realised that Templevegarial had found him. What's more if he didn't alter course immediately, he was going to run right into it. For some reason the oscillator had not activated and shifted their course accordingly.

"It must be emitting its force field even through all that ice!" he shouted as he hurriedly tried to skirt around it. But every time he seemed to turn a corner, there seemed to be another wall of ice in front of him. "Holey vegmoley, there is no way out; I'm going to crash. Wait a minute, head for Earthanon, yes that's it, outrun it. That's what I'll do. Then when all this blows over, I'll head for Carridionaries when it is safe." And so Mushroid Funguy turned the Trans Vege-cruiser towards Earthanon and slowly but surely pulled away from his vast Captor. "That is what must have happened to the Satellite Volcadis." He thought fighting with the controls. "I must contact the ship and warn them." But the interference was too much for him to do so. Mushroid Funguy had lost his bearings and pre-loaded the O.S.S.S Earthanon's last Co-ordinates into the on-board computer. However, he was hampered by Aqua Asteroids in front of him this time, which he must try to beat on the journey home. While the ship ducked and dived Mushroid Funguy shouted out to the back-up Protocol Proton Pilot. "I don't think we are going to find the O.S.S.S Earthanon at this rate! So if you have any good ideas or suggestions now would be a good time to part with them." Mushroid Funguy awaited with eagerness some sign of camaraderie, or flash of brilliance to come forth from his silent and uneventful pinion passenger. "Come on now don't be shy." yelled Mushroid Funguy as the back-up Pilot remained silent. "Well, it sure is good to know who your friends are and who you can rely on. I guess we're just going to have to wing it then, umm?"

Back on-board the O.S.S.S Earthanon Captain Carrot emerged from the Medilab Meeting room with Admiral Ducarrotain, Commodore Cu-Cumbala and Viceroy Au Paw-Paw. The mood was silent but a certain ease seemed to be present as if all was possibly not lost.

"Do you really think it will work Admiral Ducarrotain?" asked Commodore Cu-Cumbala, with a rather sceptical tone harbouring in his voice.

"To be honest Commodore, I haven't a clue! But if anyone can pull it off, that Organiman Carrot can."

They all stepped into the elevation chamber and Captain Carrot closed the doors behind them.

"Computer." "Eco System Farming Programme Chamber." said the Captain not relishing the next phase in his vital plan for the survival of the entire ship's company. Telling them, in detail, his proposals to enable them to survive long enough for the rescue mission from Carridionaries. All except for the last detail that is. Admiral Ducarrotain had taken it upon himself to reject Captain Carrot's decision to tell them the whole truth, for fear that it would create a condition on board the O.S.S.S Earthanon that did not bear thinking about; mutiny at the very least, Or a frenzied self destruction at the very worst. Captain Carrot was only allowed to brief the top ranking officers after the general meeting that would be held in the Eco-Farm Chamber.

When the doors opened it gave sight to the vision of thousands upon thousands of miniaturised Organibeings and the Fasterfoid delegation. In the elevation chamber on the other side of the main platform, the entire bridge crew appeared. Captain Carrot stepped onto the platform and the multiple hushes came to an end as Admiral Ducarrotain and Ground Commodore Cu-Cumbala joined him alongside FO Marrowlar, FO Potatree, FO Cornelius, FO Melonicord, FO Milnedew, Viceroy Councillor Au Paw-Paw, Viceroy Rhubarblatt, Professor Goosegorgon, Dr Kiwitranus, SO Tulipina, SO Okralate, and SO Brocclebreeze. These were the immediate ranking crew of the O.S.S.S Earthanon. Across from them stood Commander Marrachinello, FO Onionack, and Security Chief Lemaron from the Earthanon Ground station. Captain Peabazzare, FO Pepperat, FO Fusailliot, SO Appledope, and SO Almondino from the ill fated O.S.S Satsumuroo Standing in the side lines were also Ensign Strawballis, Ensign Viola, Ensign Melonture, Ensign Rasperillo and Ensign Broccleman. Part of the honour of bridge and Vegimatter duties was the trustee status placed on them, this meant they were honoured with the privilege of standing with the top brass at occasions such as these. Though today Ensign Strawballis whispered.

"Today is a day not for rejoice I fear."

Immediately behind each member stood their families and loved ones. They too were not privy to the news that Captain Carrot had come to deliver, but by the shear style and magnitude of its hasty delivery, they knew it was to be news of the worst possible kind.

"Captain Carrot to Mushroid Fungola. Come in please." said the Captain.

"This is Cap.. I... Err. I.. I mean this is Mushroid Fungola. Yes Captain Carrot." he replied.

"Status report Mushroid Fungola." asked the Captain calmly.

"All sections are sealed and power outputs eliminated except for decks me, J and K. All the oxygen has been re-directed into the aft oxygenation storage tanks. All air ducts have been sealed and linked to the centrifugal astronaut training suite. We have lost tracking capability on Mushroid Funguy and the Trans Vege-cruiser as of two starmins ago. The Robopod network is fully set and operational. All the charges are in place at the perimeter wall. As soon as you give the command I will blow them. All dry ice capsules, fuel pods and sea Feeder pods are activated and awaiting initiation. The ship's systems analyser indicates all systems are clean and clear. Ship's scanner shows all breaches contained and under control. Wait a minute…" said Mushroid Fungola searching the communications waveband frequencies. "No... No Captain, it's all right I thought I was picking up a signal on a May-day Channel, but it would appear that it is some kind of acoustic rebound of our own transmissions from the surrounding stratosphere." reasoned Mushroid Fungola little knowing that it was in fact Mushroid Funguy trying to establish contact. "The Sodium Star belt will be with us in approximately fifty three point five starmins Captain." confirmed Mushroid Fungola.

"Thank you Mushroid Fungola, open ships communication channel. That will be all for now stand by for further commands." said the Captain as he cleared his throat in preparation for addressing the ships company and guests. As he did so he held out his hands behind him for his wife Carrelda and his two children to join him at the platform's edge. If ever Captain Gillespie J. Carrot felt that he needed the strength of a third party, it was now. As they joined him he began to speak while Carrelda squeezed his hand affectionately.

"Admiral Ducarrotain, Commodore Cu-Cumbala, Organigirls, Organiboys, and Fasterfoid friends." he began as the general company gathered together, wondered whether Captain Carrot had taken leave of his senses.

"Fasterfoid friends indeed." shouted a voice from the back. "With friends like those who needs enemies... Eh?"

The crowd began to stir in half-hearted agreement. Gradually the noise increased as Captain Carrot looked around him to see the despondent faces looking upon him, turn to faces of disbelief. Slowly Captain Carrot raised his hands and shouted abruptly.

"Please, please hear me out. Time is not a commodity with which we can barter. My friends, my colleagues and my enemies of old. We have been through much and survived through all. All except, that is, for now; now we are faced with the ultimate problem the likes of which we have never faced before, and I prey we may survive never to face such like again. Such is the danger that we find ourselves in, we have to for the first time admit that the odds are against us..." Captain Carrot halted as he was sharply interrupted

"Such is the danger that the Fasterfoids placed us in with their stupid attempt at sabotage." "Here here, that's right, sabotage." echoed a growing number of hecklers around the great chamber.

"That may be the case," shouted Captain Carrot. "but ultimately I am the one who has let you down! If you must pass judgement then do so at my expense. Let us not now, at the hour of our need, tear each other to shreds with needless retributions, slanderous remarks, or defamatory statements. It will not help us now and if we are honest with ourselves it has never served to help us in the past. I know that many of you are doubtful of my actions towards the Fasterfoids. Helios knows you may yet be right; but I have to tell you this. The Fasterfoids have on the whole behaved with courage and bravery in boarding the O.S.S.S Earthanon when they did." Captain Carrot looked at principle Gammachip and General Satuese. "The reason we are here in this position is because of the actions of two people. One was of the Fasterfoid Space Race, whom in his heart of hearts believed he was doing the right thing by his actions. As taught in the Fasterfoid Military academy. The other; the other was I. Captain Gillespie J. Carrot legend of the skies, defender of the Organitron culture.

I made a mistake. Not in trying to help the Fasterfoids, but in underestimating the powerful indoctrination of generations of Fasterfoids with the use of propaganda to harness their hatred for the aims on war with the Organitron. It was I who let the guard down for a split second and got a bloody nose; correction, we have all got a bloody nose. Now it is time to lay the cards on the table and explain exactly how I propose to beat this Sodium Star belt predicament. We have sent a back-up Proton Pilot with our original estimated surface alignment co-ordinates. Unfortunately due to steering restrictions we have landed some distance from those co-ordinates. To rectify this I have sent a Secondary back-up Proton Pilot with our new co-ordinates, accompanied by a one Organiman Trans Vege-cruiser piloted by a Mushroid as a secondary safety measure, should the ships guidance oscillator fail to kick in. Those of you, who are aware of the Satellite Volcadis incident and its failure to negotiate the Sodium Star belt, will understand the reasoning behind this precaution. Those back-up probes will be heading for Carridionaries as we speak." Captain Carrot took a deep breath and prepared to deliver the exact plan and its implications.

"We have three main problems to overcome and this is how I propose that we do it. Firstly when the Sodium Star belt hits Earthanons surface, we are in severe danger of being crushed by Aqua Asteroids. To solve this I propose breaching the perimeter wall between us and the estuary reservoir beyond and flooding the spring mines in which we are situated…." Captain Carrot stopped again as he was interrupted.

"A great lump of frozen water isn't going to hit the surface of a lake and just stop. We will still be crushed!" shouted the voice.

"You are right, we would. We have taken this into account and we have decided to do the opposite of fighting fire with fire. We will fight ice with ice!"

"With ice?" came the confused mumbles.

"When the spring mine has filled to its optimum level," continued Captain Carrot. "we will freeze the surrounding waters using liquid nitrogen, dry ice capsules and a series of safety crumple pods to bear the load of the expansion. The second problem we face is the Pivotal thrusters housing that sustained damage in the collision with the FF Francaisfry. Commander Marrachinello and the best engineers available have made sufficient repairs to manoeuvre us out of this mine when the rescue team gets here, we think. Unfortunately, we will not know for sure how successful the repairs are until it is time to leave. And this brings us to the third and most critical problem. The Sodium Star belt, once it has arrived, could last for a duration of up to twelve starlectoids. That is twelve starlectoids of constant bombardment. Why, I can hear you ask, do we not just sit it out and when it is all over just melt the surrounding water and take off? The answer my friends is simple. When the Pivotal thruster housing was hit, it caused a chain reaction that breached the external and internal hulls of the ship. These breaches have since been shored up and made safe. However, the explosion caused a chain reaction that carried on to the next compartment where the oxygenation regeneration tanks are stored, and fractured the storage tanks of oxygen. Leaving us only with the aft tanks of oxygen used to service the Eco Farm and the emergency mobile tanks to rely on for survival, plus what is circulating in the ship itself. We estimate that this will give us if we remain as we are at the moment, relatively inactive, six to nine starlectoids of oxygen supply. I propose that we go one step forward and enter into a state of near hibernation by putting the entire ship in sleeping mode for the duration of our stay here. That should give us ample oxygen to last the twelve days and some to spare. The bridge will be operated by Mushroid Fungola and he will man the ship's systems analyser as well as all security features aboard the ship. He will de-activate the sleeping mode when the Sodium Star belt is over." Captain Carrot had said all that he had to say, the rest was up to the ships company. It was the longest and the most uncomfortable silence that he had ever had to endure, then FO Potatree stepped forward to address the crowd.

"Well Captain Carrot. I for one think that the plan is brilliant. I wish to announce now that you have my every confidence in your ability to see us through this crisis, as you have done on many occasions. I am with you!" shouted FO Potatree. Slowly all the Sun-Fleet personnel stepped forward and raised their hands and shouted at the top of their voices. "Me too, hip; hip for Captain Carrot." Before long, everyone had accepted Captain Carrots apology for what it was worth-its weight in gold and the ship resounded with echoes of "hooray" and "we are with you all the way." Captain Carrot fought back the tears and raised his hands to stop the noise; which took some time.

"Very soon my dear friends and colleagues." Yelled the Captain desperately trying to be heard. "Very soon I want all personnel to return to their loved ones and spend ten starmins with each other. Then it is straight to your allocated Vegewells for the sleeping cycle. All will go to sleep, there will be no exception. Frankly I am looking forward to the rest... General Satuese, Principle Gammachip, we have done all in our power to extend every comfort to you and your troops. If you follow Ensign Broccleman in a few moments he will take you to the hydro pool complex where you will find ample oil reserves to store yourselves in while you are in sleeping mode. You will notice that all of your team have been issued with facial breathing apparatus. We do understand that you require total submergence during this period, therefore we will feed the breathing apparatus directly from the bridge systems controller."

"Thank you Captain Carrot." said General Satuese propping up the Principle Officer who was weary of his crutches.

"Yes, thank you Captain!" smiled Principle Gammachip. "May I just say a few words Captain? I would appreciate it." he continued. Captain Carrot looked around and nodded with a certain amount of worry running through his mind.

"Organigirls, Organiboys, Fasterfoids," began the Principle Officer. "Admiral Ducarrotain, Ground Commodore Cu-Cumbala, Captain

Carrot, Friends, colleagues. What we as Fasterfoids have seen here in the last few starhectoids is totally different from what we have been taught by our elders. In our culture we have an ethos that above all, honesty among our own is the basis of a true and good existence. As Captain Carrot has rightly pointed out that we are all in this together I feel compelled to admit something to you all. Don't get me wrong, you may feel nothing like us, look nothing like us, and even share a different culture. But we are all in our own way crusaders of the spatial plains. The more I see the inside of the Organitron ethos, the more I wonder whether the Fasterfoid existence is justified or logical. As Captain Carrot so eloquently put it. "The stupid attempt at sabotage." was my doing and my doing alone. I do not want my colleagues tarred with the same brush as a direct result of my despicable actions. I offer you all my most humble and sincere apologies and throw myself at your mercy. If anyone in this ship cannot accept my apology, or has no room in their heart for forgiveness then I pray that you speak now. I assure you that I will not hold it against you and I will gladly leave the safety of this vessel to meet my fate with the elements in the great outdoors. That is all that I have to say, except for this. Should I have to leave I shall and do wish you all well and pray that your paths of destiny guide you to safety in this time of extreme danger and uncertainty." Principle Officer Gammachip took a seat and held his head in his hands while he waited for the uprising objection to his presence on-board the O.S.S.S Earthanon. The air however was filled with a deafening silence. Suddenly Leisurelando Pinnelexo hovered above the thousands of Organitron gathered in the Echo Farm. "What you have just heard and seen before your very eyes is what Sun-Fleet is all about. Yes, our main aim is to find the lost Planets of the Organitron. Our secondary aim, however, is to reach out to other life forms and secure a peaceful existence for all while we search for the lost Asteroid Plato of Templevegarial. I say let him stay, let us welcome him with open arms for we cannot fairly serve as judge, jury and executioner. We can, though, act as good Samaritans for a right and just full cause." Leisurelando passed his gaze over the thousands of faces and seemed to touch them all individually, until his warmth and sincerity could be felt throughout the ship. Then slowly chants of "Let him stay." Filled the chamber and Principle Gammachip fell to his knees in thanks. Tears streamed down his face as he looked up at Captain Carrot and the upper ranker on the platform. Suddenly Captain Carrot gave him the Organitron salute to officially welcome him aboard the ship as did the other members of the crew.

"As I look upon your faces and see the mighty steps forward that we have taken to-day," said Admiral Ducarrotain. "I feel that if this moment could be set in silver it would be the finest jewel in any ones crown. It is nearly time to return to the safety of our Vegewells." Admiral Ducarrotain turned and whispered in Captain Carrot's ear.

"Captain Carrot." he said gripping the Captain's shoulder. "I realise that Oxygen is not a commodity which we should freely waste. But there is a chance that we may not survive your plan! I have a request."

"What is it Admiral?" Asked the Captain.

"I would like us to join together and sing for our dreams and aspirations, our achievements and our shared glories. Helios knows that we may not be alive tomorrow, so I say that we should live a little today. It will use up some of our precious oxygen but wouldn't it be good to go to sleep with the vision of their smiling, happy faces nestling in your mind. Eh?" he smiled. Captain Carrot nodded and stepped forward to the very front of the platform with the Admiral.

"First, with Captain Carrot's permission we will part with a song in our hearts. Perhaps something that we can all join in." smiled the Admiral. "So let's all hit it together with the Constellation rock."

(Constellation Rock)
(Organitron)
Let's sing about a story we all find absurd,
The way we fly through the skies like a free spirited bird,
Nothing could be done or said,
That could make us clip our wings,
Simply because of these many wonderful things.

Take Alde baron, Altair, and the Andromeda, with Pegasus that lies there too,
Then take An tares, throw in Auriga and mix the Capella glare it's true.
Look to Aquila and soon you will find,
That we live in a galaxy of a Constellation kind.

These all form parts of the Intergalactic map,
A map that keeps all space races flying on track.
Admit it was charted with Organitron precision,
And you'll have to admit we had the ultimate vision.

Join in with us and free this block,
Let's all pull together with the Constellation Rock.
(Organitron Chorus)
Rock and roll a boogie woogey woogey,
Cha-cha-cha come on and swings those hips.
Let's all hear the Constellation Rock,
And free our minds of the spatial block.

From Betelgeuse to Canis Major, Centaurus to the Corvix Crux,
If you get lost look for the Southern Cross, The star system we call the big boss,
And soon you'll be back on track without any hassle or fuss.

So swing your space packs over your shoulder,
March with us and you'll see you can't knock.
Letting your hair down and grooving to; the Constellation Rock.

Boogie-woogey-woogey, rock-rock-rock,
Boogie-woogey-woogey, sock it to that rock.
Cha-cha-cha, come on and swing those hips,
Strut your stuff and swing with us on the scene,
To the boogie woogey; Constellation Rock routine.

(Fasterfoids)
We too have a boogie tune, of the Constellation Rock.
It has such a hip hop swing your mind block will unlock with a ping.
So join us now, and you'll see,
That the Constellation Rock was a Fasterfoid dream.

Spot Delphinus and Equuleus foogey-hoogey-hoogey,
Hercules to Hydra wha-wha-wha,
Libra to Lyra the Fasterfoids fly her; there is no distance too far.
Yes Orphicus and Bernards Star, Orion; Pavo, Persues and Pleiades,
Look to the skies you will find, the Fasterfoids have mapped it all through
no if's buts' maybe's it's true.
From Pisces, Pollux, Castor and Gemini too.

Head for procyon, speed to the Canis Minor.
And there you will find, the Fasterfoid Constellation Rock,
That will truly blow your mind.
Strut your stuff and swing with the beat of the Constellation rock routine.

(Fasterfoid chorus)
Rock and roll foogey-hoogey-hoogey,
We're heading for Mizar.
Wha-wha-wha with us, and you will truly see,
The benefits, of swinging those hips, to the Fasterfoid beat.

C'mon now let's all hear the Constellation Rock,
Free our minds of the mental block.
Urser Minor-Polaris, Urser Major-Big Dipper or Plough,
No matter where we go, no matter where we roam now.

In our minds to the music we'll sock,
To the one and only Constellation Rock.
Foogey-foogey-hoogey, rock-rock-rock,
Foogey-foogey-hoogey, rock till you drop.
Strut your stuff in time to the swing,
To the foogey-hoogey Constellation Rock routine.

(Organitrons and Fasterfoids together)

Lets both boogie-foogey-woogey and hoogey, cha-cha, wha-wha to the tune,
Swing it and sing it, under the light of the silicone moon.
Let's travel to Rigel, Scoralus or Sirus with a vroom,
Head for Tucana, Triangulum Australe we will zoom.
Fly-fly-high, zoom-zoom-vroom,
And hit the Constellation rock with this catchy tune.

Navigate the Vega-Lyra-Ring-Nebular, cruise to Vela, Virgo or Spica,
We think that anyone will agree they are spe-tac-u-lar.
From Alde baron to Volans the Constellations they gleam from the A's to the Z's,
And so we find the Constellation rock a real scream.

(Organitrons and Fasterfoids chorus)

Rock-rock and roll, boogie-foogey-woogey-hoogey,
Cha-cha-wha-wha c'mon and swing those hips.
Strut our stuff, into the groove we can slip,
The Constellation rock is universally hip.
Yeh-yeh-yeh let's put a smile on our face,
Cha-cha-wha-wha let's pick up the pace.

The Constellation Rock is the tune that guides us safely through space,
No matter what creed or colour, no matter what race.
Let's get it together and swing to a real groovy scene,
Let's strut our stuff, let's shake it up, till we are falling apart at the seams.
(Organitrons) For the one and only, for the holy vegemoley.
(Fasterfoids) For the one and only, for the fat filled controlee.
Let's sing and let's dance and let's dream,
To the hip swinging beat, of the constellation rock routine!
Zip-babalubally-ba-ba-ba, oh yeh, yeh, yeh, yeeeeh-yeh.

As the laughter filled the air and normality returned to the chamber, Captain Carrot sent everyone to their Vegewell stations, promising them that he would take whatever actions necessary to see them through this troubled chapter in the log book of the O.S.S.S Earthanon. The Sodium Star belt was four starhectoids forty-two starmins away. The time was **05.53 starhectoids**. Prior to their departures he informed everyone that they must be in their hibernation places at exactly **09.30 starhectoids**. As everyone left he asked all of the bridge crew to meet him in the strategy room. As they left, Captain Carrot kissed Carrelda and the children giving them all a group hug.

"Go now my precious ones I will be along in a few starmins."

"But Dadski you said…" cried Caroon as Carrelda picked her up.

"Hush now my babies. I mean it, I will be along very shortly." said the Captain comforting Carab. They turned and left as Captain Carrot made his way to the strategy room via the Officer's elevation chamber.

Mushroid Funguy had started to enter the Earthanon re-entry zone with Templevegarial still hot on his tail but far enough away not to be in any real danger. On his visaid at full enhancement. He could see that the Aqua Asteroid around Templevegarial had begun to vaporise, revealing the rich coloured rock in all its natural splendour. As they passed through the re-entry zone it became apparent that the Templevegarial was slowing considerably and had started to alter its course. This was presumably because of the large amount of area that was hitting the re-entry zone, and the fact that Templevegarial as history would have was a complex natural structure of many facets and mountainous properties. Mushroid Funguy tried desperately to reach the O.S.S.S Earthanon on the communications com but still to no avail. As the Trans Vege-cruiser came out into the Earthanon air space he was a matter of four starhectoids twenty starmins ahead of the Sodium Star belt. On his Grid Finder he could just about pick up the co-ordinates of what he considered to be the O.S.S.S Earthanon and punched the co-ordinates through to the ships on-board computer. Once they were in Mushroid Funguy could relax a little. In two starmins he would be over the Arctolimba Region and close to the Mother Ship Sun-Fleet Space Star Station, at least he thought.

Back on board the O.S.S.S Earthanon, Captain Carrot entered the strategy room with haste and went directly to the observation window.

"Captain Carrot to Mushroid Fungola. Come in please." said the Captain staring down the length of the ship towards the mined perimeter wall.

"Mushroid Fungola here Sir." replied the Mushroid.

"Mushroid Fungola, employ ship's defence shields, close protective vision plates and activate the strategy room visaid if you will. Focus on the perimeter wall full enhancement." asked the Captain as the shields dropped over the window in front of him. On the screen at the head of the table the visaid came on line and Captain Carrot took to his seat, then turned to face the visaid.

"Mushroid Fungola, open ship's communication channel." he ordered looking up at the blank wall before them.

"Ship's open channel operative Captain." confirmed Mushroid Fungola.

"Now hear this, now hear this. This is Captain Carrot to ship's company. We are about to blow the perimeter wall. Brace yourselves. I repeat brace yourselves assume crash positions, this is Captain Carrot may Helios be with us. UFO and out." All around the ship, the inhabitants huddled together as they waited for the possibility of the ship losing its anchor advantage under the pressure of the tidal flow that was to follow.

"Mushroid Fungola. Blow the Perimeter wall, activate all protonic bomb devices now." ordered Captain Carrot.

"Aye, aye, Sir, blowing protonic devices now." confirmed Mushroid Fungola.

Suddenly, on screen, the massive explosion could be visibly seen. The ship shuddered slightly but with no real momentum. As the dust began to clear it was evident that the wall had not breached although a very large hole was present.

"Captain Carrot." shouted FO Potatree. "What now? We will have to re-activate the phaser banks."

"Mushroid Fungola." said Captain Carrot raising his hand. "Give me maximum volume enhancement on that area. Let's see what she is up to!" he said. Silence fell in the strategy room as the sounds of crumbling masonry and land shifting mixed with a strange gurgling noise.

"She is breaking up people, look at the bottom of the wall. Water is trickling through." observed Captain Carrot. As he said that, great chunks of rock began to crumble before their very eyes and soon the wall exploded. Just the way that Captain Carrot had intended, leaving behind it a great archway with a flowing river gushing through it. Great echoes could be heard as the outside of the ship was struck by rapid water flows and immense chunks of rock beat at the hull. It seemed that the water would not rock the ship from its anchor after all. Captain Carrot breathed a sigh of relief as he faced the party behind him.

"Captain Carrot to Mushroid Fungola." said the Captain.

"Mushroid Fungola here, Captain." came the reply.

"Open ships communication channel please. I want you to monitor the water level and let me know when it has reached its optimum capacity."

"Aye, aye Sir, O.S.C.C operative Captain."

"This is Captain Carrot. Stand easy, stand easy. This is Captain Carrot out. Well it would appear that part one of phase one is a success." said

Captain Carrot slowly. "Now for part two that is the more difficult part of this whole operation. I'm afraid you are all here under false pretences." FO Marrowlar looked around the room to see if anyone looked as if they knew what Captain Carrot was referring too. General Satuese and Principle Gammachip appeared to be doing the same. To FO Potatree's professional eye the only two heads hung low was the giveaway. They were the heads of the highest ranking Officers aboard the O.S.S.S Earthanon; members of the Earthanon Seed Consul, Admiral Ducarrotain and Ground Commodore Cu-Cumbala.

"The Plan that I put forward in the Eco-Farm Chamber, is exact and true. However, I must plead guilty to omitting one small detail. The fact is that the six to nine starlectoids of oxygen supply was assuming a total state of occupancy in a sleeping cycle. In short, we will not survive the Sodium Star belt under any circumstances, let alone the duration that will fall between now and the arrival of the rescue party from Carridionaries…"

"Then, this is it. We are doomed." said General Satuese quietly, speaking out loud what the others were thinking.

"No! I gave my word that I will get us through this and get us through this I will." he said adamantly.

"But how Captain? As I see it all is lost, there is no upside!" said FO Cornelius.

"Come now, FO Cornelius you are an Organiman of science. I bet you if you were in my position you would reach the same conclusion as I have. And here is how I propose to beat this little predicament we find ourselves in. I am not saying it is without risk, I am not even entirely sure that it will be successful. But, as Captain of this ship, it is my sworn duty to search for the answers to enable us to survive and prosper. You see, when the ship is encased in frozen water, the temperature inside the ship will drop substantially below freezing. None of us can survive for very long in those conditions that is why we evacuated Earthanon in the first place; among other reasons…"

"Can't we artificially maintain the temperatures inside the ship?" asked FO Melonicord.

"Alas no," continued the Captain. "in order to achieve that we would have to maintain the ship's energy shields and that would prevent the ice from forming on the hull. We can't risk an Aqua Asteroid making a direct hit above and forcing the ice on top of us. This could de-stabilise the whole ship's structure and force us into an implode situation. This I cannot allow to happen, given that we are grounded with no choice but to stay, this is how I intend to overcome the problem."

Up in the skies over the Arctolimba Region, Mushroid Funguy could see the Roboprobe protective network in the distance. If they were to come into contact with that, then both he and the back-up pilot were history.

"Oh my goodness we are going to be frying tonight if that net catches us in its sights. But surely the ship's computer would have spotted the network? I know that must be what is blocking our Communications transmissions. They must have spotted us in on the Grid Finder by now and are waiting to deactivate the network to let us in as we speak. Wouldn't you say that is what they are up to Pilot?" he asked turning towards his silent passenger, from whom there was still no response.

"Remind me never to invite you to a Mechanoid soirée! You would bore the pants off of a waste disposal unit. They certainly encompassed your personality when they named you "Back-up" because frankly that is all you seem to have done since we left. Got my back up!" he shouted as the ship approached the Mines opening. Mushroid Funguy looked down just in time to see the O.S.S.S Earthanon covered by water, yet the ship carried on flying over the network and beyond into the reservoir estuary.

"Oh my giddy aunt, where in Helios are we going now?" he shouted as the ship took a dive into the water. When he opened his eyes again, he could see the FF Francaisfry in front of him, or rather above him as the Trans Vege-cruiser was stuck in the estuary bed nose first. As the silt settled, the news got worse. The FF Francaisfry was on the move and heading straight towards them. "Oh my! Oh my! This wasn't part of the deal. We must be near the hole that the Captain blew to flood the spring mine, the tidal currents are dragging that blasted ship towards the sea wall. Well, I'm jiggered if I am going to hang around here to be crushed like a Graperon. No Siree, not me!" he said fumbling for the ejector seat activation switch. "I'll see if I can make the Mother-ship under the dragnet through the hole in the wall." With his hand held tight on the activator switch he turned to the back-up Proton Pilot. "Listen, if you do manage to survive this and you get out alive and in one piece do me a favour will you? If you should find yourself in the same Solar System as me, don't bother to look me up! You have been nothing but trouble since we met." Mushroid Funguy pulled the switch and shot out of the Trans Vege-cruiser into the great lake. Quickly he halted himself before becoming pinned under the slow moving hulk of the Fasterfoid ship's hull. "Ahh.. Get back, gotta get out of here wow-wow-wow. Boy that was close." he shouted whizzing away from its path. He scanned in front of him and found the hole using his echo sounder.

"Aha, dead ahead. It will take a whole lot of trouble to beat me." shouted Mushroid Funguy speeding up his fan propulsion drivers. Entering into the hole the tidal flow grabbed him and spun him out of control banging him against the wall indiscriminately.

"Ow.. Oooh.. Ahh. No not there no, ow, oooh, weeks." "Bang, crash, thud!" went Mushroid Funguy as he came through the other side. He saw the ship in the distance and felt a sharp pain in his side. His solenoid calorific battery was pierced and he was losing calories fast. Without sunshine he couldn't use his solar back-up motors. His speed began to drop as he approached the ship.

"It's no good I'm just gonna have to sit here and try to communicate; hope that they can send help." Mushroid Funguy settled on the mine bed and closed down all but the communication power output. He lay in silence with only his Mayday message bleeping away. What he hadn't noticed as he closed down, was that because of the air trapped in his electronics housing. He slowly began to rise up through the current and was being drifted away from his resting place

Just entering the final stages of the re-entry zone, inside Templevegarial a very wobbly Widdup the wise sat at his throne viewing the outside through his mind's eye.

"Burning, burning we are." he said with his eyes closed tight. "First ice then fire. Confused am I, what place this be, this cold and hot? Cold can hibernate, protect oneself! Hot cannot. Sorry is me. If I do not think of a way out of this little stink. Phew stink! Burning sulphur me thinks. Cold then hot Planetary re-entry perhaps? Yes that is what it be, Planetary re-entry. Must seal the entrance to the archive tomb or burn to cinder I will soon. Send crystal of lost soul, cry for help to fetch me home. Home." sighed Widdup. It had been billions of starlectoids since he had come into contact with another life form. "Home, if so still does exist. Widdup struggled to the archive column and withdrew a crystal. Kissing it he placed it into a chute and closed the door behind it.

"Crystal, crystal fly away. Seek some help for Widdup today, fly like the wind, like a bird of prey. Find home, Widdup must, one day." At the back of Widdup's mind was the thought that the Planet Templevegarial was entering could be one of the home Planets of the Vegitalis Bubbleonion Squeak Solar System. Widdup was weakening with every second. He had no opportunity to take sustenance, he had to seal the entrance. Again, as he began closing his eyes, the throne and the alter began to levitate. The floor of the great Widdup chamber began to open from the centre like a big camera lens opening to catch the light. Up from the centre of the floor rose a third alter, an alter never before seen or heard of by any Organitron except for Widdup's past and present. Widdup's mind carried it to the inner entrance where it upturned and placed itself snugly in the gap. Great shafts of stone moved across from inside the massive alter in all directions, like huge bolts sealing a door.

The floor began to close and gradually the alter and throne came down to rest. Widdup, however, kept his eyes closed and floated towards a large crystal embedded in the temple wall. Once inside the Crystal, Widdup opened his eyes and fed on a Vegimatter substance.

"Widdup, oh Widdup, wise you be maybe? But will wisdom see you through, for wisdom alone is no reason to go on when the wisest thing to do is to pass on and be strong. I am the guardian of all I survey, but, lonely am I for such a long time that my strength has subsided to a pulse. Tired is Widdup of all he surveys for that is all he sees every day. Someone must come and rescue the temple and a host be found for me to rest. Now I must go to sleep, for the Organitron my survival is best." Widdup closed his eyes and entered again the world of hibernation that had sustained his frail body for so long. The intense heat built up on the surface and surrounds of the Templevegarial Asteroid Plato. Then it cleared the re-entry point and began its long skimming fall to Earthanon as its Magnetic force field made its entry and flight rather similar to a stone being thrown across the surface of a river.

Time 06.15 starhectoids

Unaware of the strange happenings above, the strategy room doors of the O.S.S.S Earthanon opened and the bridge crew members followed by the hierarchy members of the Earthanon Seed Consul, accompanied by the Organitron Ground-force security and the Fasterfoid Officers. Filed out to their loved ones in silence. Only FO Benzo Marrowlar, FO Potatree, Professor Goosegorgon and Captain Gillespie J. Carrot. remained to say their goodbyes to each other.

"FO Marrowlar, FO Potatree, FO Milnedew, Professor Goosegorgon. It has, is and always will be an honour to serve with you. We will meet at the great thaw. I feel in my heart and my mind that our time is not yet to pass. I only hope that the general populous will forgive my deception, but there are times when the many must be protected from the burden of knowledge contained by the few. That is the burden of superiority in rank, but not in stature."

"Mushroid Fungola to Captain Carrot. Come in please." came the voice over the personal channel.

"Captain Carrot here Mushroid Fungola."

"Captain. The mine has reached its optimum water level, we have a protection layer of point seven five starmillo's. Sir, I have also received a distress call from the Mushroid Funguy."

Silence reigned as Captain Carrot looked upon the last officers to be privy to the worst possible news to come forward at the last stages of the operation.

"Are you still receiving the distress call Mushroid Fungola?" asked the Captain biting his lip.

"Yes Sir, it is very strong. I believe Mushroid Funguy is on the mine bed situated twenty staryards off our starboard bow. All systems appear non- functional." confirmed Mushroid Fungola.

"Fix log and compute the co-ordinates we will pick him up when the rescue party arrives here. We still have the primary back-up Protocol Pilot to fall back on and that left in plenty of time to avoid the Sodium Star belt. I will be on the bridge in two starmins. Prepare the Compulog to receive my final instructions. Mushroid Fungola, de-energise the defensive force field, activate the dry ice capsules and the sea feeder pods. This is Captain Carrot out." Captain Carrot looked at the assembled party with heavy eyes.

"Affirmative Captain, activation complete. Mushroid Fungola out."

"Well you heard it here first Professor, but Widdup is the word. Sun-Fleet will just have to look a little harder. Besides, there is every chance that they will pick up Mushroid Funguy's distress call as well as ours and find our exact position. With two beacons it must surely increase our chances of being picked up." As Captain Carrot hugged the Professor the ship began to creak and groan as the dry ice capsules and liquid nitrogen quick froze the water to ice. It was like a dying whale's call they all thought, but nobody had the wish to say out loud. Next FO Milnedew stepped forward and hugged the Captain.

"Let us hope FO Milnedew that your service with Sun-Fleet will not go down in the history books as the shortest ever recorded." laughed Captain Carrot.

"Don't you worry Captain, I have a feeling I'm going to be around for a few good startechtoids yet, besides no History book would be complete without a volume of the adventures of Admiral Gillespie J. Carrot." he chuckled.

"I look forward to reading that one my friend." Said the Captain grinning. "FO Potatree! Step forward and receive my full admiration and thanks for your continued friendship and service. You always said I was a cold hearted, hot head, but did you really need to go to such lengths to prove it." he said shivering as the ship's temperature started to fall rapidly.

"Ahh Captain, well now let me tell you this, for an Organiman who lives life with fire in his belly and fireworks in his soul, there will always be a flame of friendship burning for us, no matter where we are or what we are doing; nothing could ever douse that spirit that burns wild inside." A tear trickled down FO Potatree's face and turned to frost. He snapped it off his cheek and put it in the pocket of his friend Captain Carrot. "And who said there wouldn't be a dry ice in the house eh?" he giggled hugging him and stepping back. FO Marrowlar stepped forward and saluted Captain Carrot in true regimental style.

"FO Marrowlar. Benzo, fear not, for one day you will be a Captain of your own Sun-Fleet ship; and a fine Captain you will make too. If your instinct is up to its usual razor sharp self then you will know that it is true." said the Captain.

"Oh come now Captain, I look upon this stalemate in the promotion stakes not as one of a delaying process, merely as put on ice until the time is right." FO Marrowlar had found a sense of humour at last and could not resist a guffaw from the belly. The others all joined in and silence resumed as Captain Carrot ordered them to their quarters, And made his way to the bridge carrying a mobile oxygenation unit.

"Captain Carrot to Mushroid Fungola." he said activating his com badge.

"Mushroid Fungola here Captain."

"I will arrive on the bridge in one point-five starhectoids Mushroid Fungola. Keep an eye on all ship's Vegewells and the Fasterfoid guest bay. I want to know when all accounted for personnel and guests are in their respective hibernation positions. Contact my Organiwife in my quarters and have her stand by with mobile oxygen activators. Sound a general ship's announcement that all personnel must store a mobile oxygen unit next to their Vegewells, Carrot out." Entering the Elevation Chamber, Mushroid Fungola issued Captain Carrot's last directive over the ship's communication system. The doors re-energised and Captain Carrot was on his way to his quarters to spend some quality time with Carrelda and the children. All around the ship, the families, could be heard laughing and joking, playing games and singing their favourite lullabies to calm the nervous young ones as the temperatures dropped. Soon they would have to take up positions in the hibernation cycle. This was a very precious time for all concerned.

Time 08.00 starhectoids

Captain Carrot blew kisses on his way out of his family's quarters and made his way to the bridge via the elevation chamber. When he reached there he sat at the command com and played his final log entry and left procedural instructions for the boarding rescue party to follow. Such was the oddity of Captain Carrot's plan. It was imperative that the instructions must be followed to the letter if they were to survive. It took him the best part of one and a half starhectoids to log all the information and close down the Captains log. Throughout the ship, its inhabitants were bedding themselves down for the final stages of Captain Carrots plan.

Time 09.28 starhectoids.

Captain Carrot stood in a moment of quite thought as Mushroid Fungola caught his attention.

"Captain Carrot," he said. "Captain Carrot, Sir." he repeated.

"Yes Mum.. Mum. Mushroid F.. F.. F. Fungola." replied the Captain shivering.

"Earthanons citadels are one starmin and thirty starsecs from self destruct." confirmed Mushroid Fungola activating the Visaid. On the screen Arcticus citadel stood lonely and deserted. It was a sorry state of comparison from that of its usual glory, but destroy it they must, it was Sun-fleets' belief that all precautions must be taken to prevent technology from falling into the wrong hands at some later date. Suddenly the whole screen lit up with explosions, it must have been only seconds, but it seemed like hours as the disintegration occurred before his very eyes. Even four starmillo's away the muffled explosion could be heard, the vibrations felt. As the dust settled the citadels of Earthanon were flattened into obscurity, gone without a trace. Captain Carrot turned to Mushroid Fungola with a lump in his throat.

"It's your show now Mushroid Fungola, I must make for the Vegewells of my loved ones." he said disappearing in the elevation chamber

As he did so small advance Aqua Asteroids began to bombard the Earthanon surface; the noise was stunted yet quite apparent. It seemed that the protective ice layer was doing the trick and protecting them from being crushed while they were in hibernation. But of course, it was early days and the bombardment had only just begun.

Templevegarial was approaching the Earthanon surface at an alarming rate. Still hot from re-entry, the water vapour from the melted Aqua Asteroids set it in motion like a hot sponge fly through a cold room, steam oozing from every nook and cranny. Its shape and colour had changed significantly, obviously the temperatures reached at re-entry combined with the lapping flames whipping around its entirety, had rounded the Plato except for the flat lands of the Plato surface. No longer did it resemble the descriptions of the history books with its rough and rugged underside and its superb orange glow. Now it was a bright rusty red and it had crashed upside down preventing Widdup from leaving the Temple Archive. Upon realisation of his captivity he once more stepped into the crystal and resigned himself to further unspecified and possibly infinite hibernation. He did however hope that the Plato would be spotted in its resting place. Widdup was too weak to activate his mind's eye to know that its colour and shape had been transformed forever. And what of the crystal of lost souls that Widdup sent before re-entry? It remains above Earthanon orbiting the Planet waiting to be picked up rather like a message in a bottle.

Time 09.40 starhectoids

Back on board the O.S.S.S Earthanon. Captain Carrot was seated at the Vegewells in which his family lay, they hugged and kissed and he told them one of their favourite short stories as the resounding hail of Aqua Asteroids continued to pound the surface above.

"Dadski," said Caroon. "I wuv you! Mumski I wuv you too. Will you be here when we wake up in the morning?" she asked shivering with the cold.

"Yes darling, Mumski and Dadski will be with you all the time from now on." said Captain Carrot as he kissed them both goodnight. Then he kissed Carrelda and whispered in her ear. "If I had my time again I wouldn't change a thing. You always were and you always will be the better part of me, all of you." he said jumping into his Vegewell. Carrelda turned and said slowly.

"Gillespie J. Carrot, what will be will be, you, me and them. I love you too." she said snuggling into her Vegewell.

"Mushroid Fungola to Captain Carrot. Captain Carrot. come in please." Captain Carrot's cold hand, feeling numb, stretched across to activate his personal channel.

"C.. Ca.. Captain Carrot here, yes Mushroid Fungola?"

"Captain, all personnel and occupants are in place for hibernation, Sir."

"Very well Mushroid Funguy, drop the Vegewell tubes and administer the sleeping draughts. When all life signs are minimal, activate the nitrogen vapour and place the thermo controls set at a constant t.. t.. temp.. temperature of freezing. Place all Vegimatter compartments at the same temperature, no.. n.. no point in us waking up with nothing to eat now is there? S.. se.. set the distress beacon to half starhectoid intervals and get yourself into the Mechanoid rejuvenation Com. Once you are there, close down all but the atmospheric and the distress systems programmes and tie them into the Calorific reactor."

"Is that all Captain?" asked Mushroid Fungola.

"N.. N.. No, place visaid on automatic activation. I do not want to take any chances. Oh, and Mushroid Fungola, Thank you for what you are doing! I..I..I am relying on you to hold the fort. May Helios be with us, this is Captain Carrot UFO and out."

The tubes came down from the ceiling and filled gradually with the sleeping draught. All around the ship was the sound of silence. All that could be heard was the buffeting the Earthanon surface was taking. Mushroid Fungola activated the liquid Nitrogen Vapour and placed himself in the rejuvenation Com and awaited the rescue party that was never to come.

The Sundate was officially logged as.

"Sundate 3,000,000,000/ 61 Biltechtoids."

Carridionaries sent vessel after vessel to locate the O.S.S.S Earthanon, or any signs of wreckage. The primary back-up pilot did make it but they could not find the ship. Finally, after ten starwektoids of searching, Earthanon, which was now a Planet completely covered in white ice and snow, not one square inch of greenery had survived the onslaught of the sodium Star belt with its deadly Aqua Asteroid contents. Admiralette Xion Ru Roser finally called off the search, officially closing the book on Captain Carrot and the brave crew of the ill-fated O.S.S.S Earthanon.

Admiral Ducarrotain, was awarded the Premier Seed Council Covenant cup.

Ground Commodore Cu-Cumbala, was awarded the Premier Seed Consul Medal.

Captain Gillespie J. Carrot, was made an Admiral of the Realm.

FO Marrowlar, was made a Captain of the Realm.

FO Potatree, was awarded an Honorary Engineer of the Spaceark Academy.

FO Cornelius, was awarded an Honorary science Doctorate of the Realm.

FO Melonicord, was made an Honorary Captain of the Transport Division at the Spaceark Academy.

Professor Goosegorgon, was made a Life Peer of the Premier Seed Consul.

Dr Kiwitranus, was awarded an Honorary Patronage at the Organitron Institute of Medical Science.

Squadron Leader Commander Marrachinello, was awarded the Premier Seed Consul Medal.

Viceroy Councillor Au Paw-Paw, was awarded an Honorary Doctorate of the Realm.

SO Tulipina, SO Okralate, SO Lemaron and Viceroy Rhubarblatt, were awarded Honorary FO Status.

Ensigns, Strawballis, Broccleman, Rasperillo and Melonture received Honorary SO Status.

Sun-Fleet gave the ultimate honour to all the bridge crew under the insistence of the Planet of Garlicazure whom Captain Carrot and his crew liberated. It was to be that all of the newly Commissioned ships were named after them. These awards were of course given posthumously, but then the Premier Seed Consul and all Organitrons never expected to see them, ever again. But to quote a favourite saying of the legend of the space lanes, Captain Gillespie J. Carrot of the O.S.S.S Earthanon. "Never! Say never! because you can't ever be sure that the impossible at some time, will not become the probable. And where you find a probability, you can then find a solution to make it grow into the realms of possibility?"

Upon the news of the Fasterfoid losses on board the O.S.S.S Earthanon. The Fasterfoid Space Races made much noise in the pursuance of revenge. Swearing a lifelong Vengeance of retaliation towards the Organitron. They struck General Satuese off the Fasterfoid register of warriors, with a dishonourable discharge. Charged as a traitor, a turn coat Principle Gammachip on the other hand, was posthumously elevated to almost angel status, accredited for single handed bringing the O.S.S.S Earthanon and its entire ship's complement to its knees, and ultimately to its demise.

CHAPTER FOURTEEN

Ugh?

Sundate 4,280,999,995/ 126 Biltechtoids.

Earth date 5 may 1995.

Location The Space Satellite Silicone Sphere.

Some 1,280,999,995/ 065 Biltechtoids later.

The Organitron have now taken it upon themselves to control, repair and maintain the Ozone layer and protect the relatively new inhabitants who call themselves the "Human Race." Above the Planet Earthanon, now known as Earth, from the location of the Silicone Sphere, now known as the Moon, the Organitrons were running standard sweeps of the old Arctolimba district looking for atmospheric changes and signs of the weakening spots in the Ozone layer. On the dark side of the moon, a large ship approached as the vast bay door in the moon, disguised as a crater, opened to allow the ship in. Slowly it edged its way through the entry point and came to rest on the landing deck as the entry doors closed behind it. After a few minutes an elevation chamber arrived at the docking deck level and emerging from it came Ground Captain Kirick T. Carrot, Silicone Sphere's Sector Controller, following him were thirteen Organitron personnel. As they stood in the docking bay awaiting the final docking procedures to be completed, Captain K.T. Carrot paced up and down somewhat relieved that the arrival of his brother's Sun-Fleet ship the

O.S.F.S Vegsurprise was secure. It was on the first stretch of its maiden voyage from the space dock peninsular in the heart of the new Spaceark Academy Sector. The O.S.F.S Vegsurprise was the newest of the Super-nova class of Sun ship to be unveiled by the Organitron Space Race. Kirick had not seen his brother for some three startechtoids or three Earth years and was tense as the reunion approached. His brother, Captain Calvin C Carrot, had received his commission from the head of the Premier Seed consul, the Bright Honourable Admiral Paxesbarre De`la Scallion, who was travelling with the O.S.F.S Vegsurprise in the final stages of her space trials, to officially commission the vessel into the fleet and launch her Inaugural flight on official Sun-Fleet duty.

"Docking sequence complete." announced the computer over the Computron loud hailer system. "All systems are clean and clear, initiating atmospheric equalisation." Air hissed out of the large bulky dock doors as the ship and the station made their pressurisation ratios' compatible. An orange light at the top started to flash as Ground Captain Kirick T. Carrot brushed himself down and formed the platoon guard of honour ready to welcome them aboard.

"Platoon, Platoon guard. Upright stance!" He shouted. The platoon came to attention as he walked along and inspected their uniforms. As he reached the end of the second column he met with his second in command, FOC Celerike.

"FOC Celerike. You have Platoon detail." said Captain K. T. Carrot taking his place at the front of the two columns with FOC Celerike at his side. Gradually the great big oval shaped door began to release its complex locking mechanism.

"Pressurisation complete, prepare to receive boarding party." confirmed the ship's computer.

The door began to lift upwards. Great shafts of light appeared at the bottom of the opening revealing shadows on the deck floor in front of Captain K.T. Carrot, caused by several pairs of legs standing on the other side of the door. Finally their faces were revealed as those of Captain Calvin C. Carrot and Admiral Paxesbarre De`la Scallion. They in turn were flanked by FOC Brocktopz and Chief Engineer Pottymash on one side and the ships Medical Officer Dr Savoy and SO Courgietta stood on the other.

As they stepped out of the ship, Captain K.T. Carrot stamped to attention and gave the Organitron salute as Vegsign Fleetrapau piped them on-board. "Pheweeeeee... Phewoooooh." "Admiral on board." announced Vegsign Banannury. "Platoon...Platoon, salute arms!" ordered FOC Celerike. "Admiral De`la Scallion, Captain Carrot. Ground Captain K.T. Carrot of the Satellite Station Silicone sphere at your service. Welcome aboard."

Admiral De`la Scallion returned the salute and accompanied Captain K.T. Carrot to inspect the Platoon. "Admiral De`la Scallion. May I present my second in command, FOC Celerike?"

"Of course, FOC Celerike how are you?" he asked politely. "At this precise moment Admiral, I am honoured. Sir!" he said saluting with a bow. Captain Calvin C. Carrot stepped forward and introduced himself and his crew. "Captain K.T. Carrot, FOC Celerike. May I present my second in command FOC Brocktopz, my Chief Engineer, Chief Pottymash, the ship's Chief Medical Officer, Dr Savoy, and our chief of Security, SO Courgietta?" he said formerly.

Admiral De`la Scallion walked ahead and inspected the Platoon and returned to the group.

"They look fine Captain, just fine. Stand them down and get them back to work. We don't want them gathering dust now do we?" he said jokingly. "No Sir, of course not." said Captain K.T. Carrot. "FOC Celerike, dismiss the Platoon if you will." "Aye, aye, Sir." Platoon... Platoon, back to your normal duties, dismissed!" he shouted as the Platoon quickly dispersed in all directions. "Well." said the Admiral. "I have no doubt you two rascals have a lot of catching up to do. So, if you could show me to my quarters I have an agenda to set for this afternoons meeting."

"Certainly Admiral. FOC Celerike, could you show Admiral De`la Scallion and Captain Carrot's crew to their respective quarters? Admiral De`la Scallion, the meeting is to be held in my tactical suite in three starhectoids." confirmed Captain K.T. Carrot. "That will be fine, I will see you then and please, can we converse using days, hours, minutes and seconds. They save an awful lot of tongue twisting don't you think? Who knows, we may have to converse with the humans at some point. We don't want them to think we are a bunch of weirdoes, so let's try and get to grips with their language shall we?" "Of course Admiral, I couldn't agree more. FOC Celerike will tend your every need. Please don't hesitate to ask if you require anything, anything at all!" continued the Captain. "This way if you will please." said FOC Celerike pointing towards the elevation chamber.

When they had gone, Calvin, the elder of the two brothers gave Kirick a hug.

"How are you Kirick? You young bounder you." "Fine Calvin. It is good to see you, though, I must admit, as soon as you were commissioned on this great beauty I didn't think you would mix with the likes of us anymore." he laughed. "She is a beauty isn't she? But, my dear Kirick, she is made of metallic properties that can be replaced, you, brother, are a one-off. Family, look after them and cherish them while you can, for who knows what tomorrow might bring." laughed Calvin, as they made their way to Kirick's quarters for a brief reunion with Kirick's Organiwife, Carrilia, and their three children, Carrick and Carratio the two Organiboys and Carriba an Organigirl, the youngest of the family unit seedlings.

The Sodium Star belt that caused the evacuation of Earthanon all those years ago, a little over one billion, two hundred million years to be more accurate, caused an ice age that lasted for nearly four hundred and twenty million years. By the time it had begun to thaw, the sun had lost much of its intensity and the thawing process in turn was much slower. Even today there remain parts of Earth completely covered with snow and Ice. The Organitron began to re-establish the Eco Farming Programmes on Earth's surface some five hundred and eighty million years ago. The famous Cornelius belt, or the Ozone layer, was still in operation and self replenishing. The Organitrons worked the new lands of Earth full time right up until seven thousand years ago, when early mankind began to form a sizeable population on Earth. And whilst this population continues to grow the Organitrons missions still remain the same. There are still eleven Planets out there somewhere, whose rightful place belongs in the Bubbleonion Squeak Vegitalis Solar System.

Templevegarial had still managed to elude detection, and the Organitrons had found in their extended space travels new life forms. The Fasterfoids were still in existence and, though they were not the greatest of friends, they had learned to live with each other in the same universe without a war for nearly two hundred thousand of your Earth years. Now the universe is inhabited by many intelligent life forms.

The Organitrons, who are by far the most populated race, the Fasterfoids, the Dindivar, the Rugerplotts, and the Splutterbuns. These, the original known life forms, now share the special plains with the, Rhutari, the Prah, the Nazarka, the Jouranx, the Camenkion, the Synakeers, the Zulan and the Lizegion Space Races. And of course the Humans, but whilst all the aforementioned know of each other's existence the Humans remain blissfully unaware.

Location, The old Arctolimba region, now known as the Arctic Region.

Time 08.00 hours

The wind was blustering with a fierce intensity as four sleds set off from the pre-fabricated base camp of the Arctic exploratory unit. The purpose of the expert scientific team was to evaluate the affects of global warming in the ice cap region. The expedition leaders, Dr Andrew Cartell and Dr Vivian Heart, led the four sleds to the test site where they were to bore holes in order to establish whether the density and thickness of the ice was decreasing. The expedition team had been based there for three years, already a pattern was emerging that the ice was indeed destabilising by approximately two centimetres a year.

Dr Cartell's theory was that the Earth's lakes, rivers, seas and oceans were rising in temperature, thawing the ice under the surface off the seabed and the immediate surrounding regions. If this was true, it was drastic news for the simple reason that as the worlds ice caps melt the water levels of Its lakes, rivers, seas and oceans would increase to an extent that some islands, even whole countries, could be lost under the tidal system, reclaiming inhabited flatlands around the world back into the domain of the sea's kingdom which had been re-populated with all forms of sea life by the Organitron. After several hours travelling by sled to the drilling site in the bleak and severely blistering, bitter, cold wilderness of white.

Dr Cartell and Dr Heart arrived with their team of scientists, meteorologists and a news team from London in Great Britain, who were reporting on the findings of the exploration ready for a TV documentary.

Tired but eager to carry out the test bores, gather the samples and co-ordinate the information into logical and accurate statistics, they set about rigging up a temporary camp as they were to be there for a period of three days. Within a couple of hours the camp was formed and radio contact had been established with the permanent base camp. Dr Cartell and Dr Heart sat in the large tent with Dr Abigail Schiller and Dr Yukarma Hio, who were the co-ordinators for an American-Chinese scientific joint venture. Dr Nathaniel Quest and Dr Bertram Weinburger, who were the co-ordinators for an Anglo-American meteorology joint venture. And Harvey Slater the TV Reporter and journalist, sat with Niles Miller, the chief camera man for the expedition, and Susan Parnell his editing technician.

"Right." said Dr Cartell. "Now that we have arrived we can get to the serious business of work." he said rolling out the map for all to see. "I propose ladies and gentleman that we proceed along this mapped out boundary here and bore new holes where you can see the markings. Dr Heart and myself will take this three kilometre section here, Dr Schiller and Dr Hio this section here, Dr Quest and Dr Weinburger this section here. Mr Slater, you and your team will be led by guide Ngnkumo. You will start at our section and be able to follow the full bore boundary and the spectrum of analysis that each team will be working on. Then you can ask any questions you have about the reasoning and purpose of any particular experiment that you observe, agreed?" asked Dr Cartell.

"Excellent old Chap, that would suit us down to the ground do you agree Niles? Susan.?" he asked.

"Dr Cartell," asked Neville. "Would it be possible to have a dummy-run some time? Just so I can set up the cameras for the right light settings and focus." he concluded.

"And I would like to get the feel for the terrain, the atmosphere and the back drop." reasoned Susan. "We have several few hours of strong light left," Interrupted Dr Heart. "If you will notice this bore line is ten Kilometres long. I suggest that we split this first Kilometre into three section and each team work that area. Will that give you ample provision for preparation?" she asked.

"Absolutely, thank you very much." said Neville while Susan nodded in agreement. "Right then, let's get moving, there is a lot to be done. The bore holes are fifty metres apart, you can pick up your bore sights from the last markings." said Dr Cartell. As they all stood on their feet Dr Heart gave all the teams a detailed map of the area. "Remember its minus forty two out there so keep well covered, or you might gain rather more feeling of the atmosphere than is good for you!" she said as they laughed.

"We are expecting a snow storm in approximately four hours coming in from the north, so we had better make sure that we are back here within three hours to make certain the camp is secure." confirmed Dr Quest.

"Then hopefully, once we are secure we can have a hearty meal and bed down and get some solid sleep. Eh?" joked Dr Schiller. "Sleep oh yeah sure? Like you can sleep in the daytime already. Twenty four hours a day. Light, light and guess what? More light. I don't know about you guys and gals, but boy, what would I give just to see a bit of black, soothing darkness. Hey, we could solve the global warming if we could just find where God left the light switch and turn it off. And while I'm thinking about it with all this juice he's burning, am I glad I'm not a fly on his wall when his electricity bill falls through the door."

Up Above the planet approaching the Arctolimba Region, The Organitrons based in the Silicone Sphere, were preparing to carry out its test programme. On the bridge, Captain K.T. Carrot and Captain Calvin C. Carrot, were monitoring the Earth from the observation window accompanied by FOC Brocktopz and Chief Pottymash.

"Arctolimba," whispered Calvin. "somewhere down there lies the remains of our long lost ancestor Captain Gillespie J. Carrot and his ship the O.S.S.S Earthanon. He fought and died for this Planet. He would be proud of the Organitron achievements if he were alive today." he continued.

"I didn't realise you were descended from such prime stock, Captains." uttered a surprised Chief Pottymash. "Well, well, so the legend lives on in some form at least. I heard that the wreckage was never found. Crushed in action, what a way to go." continued the Chief.

"That's right Chief!" Interrupted Captain K.T Carrot. "but the goodness of his body and soul and that of the gallant crew that were lost at his side, we believe serves to enrich the soil of Earthanon. The Captain's last visit to Earthanon may have been a sorry one but it was a noble cause that they died for." answered Kirick thoughtfully.

"How goes the Earth visitation programme, Kirick?" asked Calvin changing the subject.

"Very well, Calvin. We can't do as much as we would like. The humans are increasing at such an alarming rate that the risk of being spotted is ever increasing with it." he replied.

"They seem to be bent on destroying their environment without giving a thought to their future generations. It is quite maddening, brother!" he said as he viewed the beauty set before him.

"Yes, but we are their guardians, not their parents. They must run the Planet to suit their own needs and culture. Sure, they are going to make mistakes along the way, and we will be here to help clear up the mess. You only have to look at the history books to see that we made our fair share of mistakes along the way. Eventually we realised them and changed our ways accordingly. The humans too, in the passing of time, will I hope, do the same."

"The trouble is Calvin, if they keep pumping pollution into the atmosphere, ripping down the rain forests, destabilising the lakes, rivers, seas and oceans, pumping their bodies with this.. this so called processed food ignoring the goodness of natural ingredients to promote strong and healthy minds and bodies, then I fear the worst for our human friends. I fear that time will, very quickly and very suddenly, run out!"

"If you don't mind me saying so, Captain Carrots." smiled Chief Pottymash as FOC Brocktopz now joined by MO Doctor Savoy giggled behind them. "Our information is, and has been for some time, that these processed foods can be rather, shall we say scrummy? They wouldn't eat them if they weren't surely?" he reasoned.

"Chief," said Kirick thoughtfully. "it is part of our mission to protect these people. I'm not saying that these so called fast or junk food fads should be wiped from the face of the Earth. No, freedom of choice is imperative in a democratic, free thinking and upstanding society. But we must get the message across somehow that to strike the right balance of diet is vital for a good and proper growing cycle. We know that consuming fresh fruit and vegetables at least once a day, increases the brains capability of learning and retention. The Human's body, is like our body! A vehicle and our brains and hearts are our engines, engines that require fuel. Feed that engine with the wrong formula of fuel and it will splutter and eventually stall, maybe even seize up for good. But feed it the right formula of fuel then that engine will run smoothly, get stronger and eventually out-perform the more ill-maintained models. No Chief, choice is good and in itself a healthy thing. All I am saying is too much of a bad thing can only lead down the wrong road." said Kirick turning to face FOC Celerike at the bridge's main systems Command Column.

"You must admit, Chief!" whispered FOC Brocktopz. "That Captain Carrot's arguments are indeed strong, forceful, and reasonable. We are living proof that proper consumption of the right diet leads to a longer, healthier more fulfilling existence. Conserving or not conserving the environment is the difference between. A longer, healthier and more fulfilling existence or no existence at all." he noted.

"FOC Celerike, ETA Arctolimba Region?" he asked.

"Forty starm.. M... M... Minutes; Forty Minutes Captain." he responded, correcting himself remembering the Admiral's request.

"Captain K.T. Carrot to Professor Pinellover," said the Captain, activating his Computron ring.

"Professor Pinellover here. Yes Captain?" came the reply.

"Professor. Are you ready with the sample statistical hydrometic equipment?"

"Yes Captain, we are ready to roll as soon as we hit the Arctolimba space window.

"Very good Professor. Captain Carrot UFO and out."

Captain Carrot turned to address those on the bridge.

"Organimen, we have a meeting to attend please follow me to the tactical suite. FO Celerike you will attend the meeting."

"Aye, aye, Sir."

"SO Mangolee. you have command Com." ordered the Captain, electro scanning the log book.

"As you wish, thank you Captain.".

While the Captain and his guests entered the tactical suite in a side annex of the main bridge mezzanine deck, something more amazing was occurring down on the Earth's surface that was to change the lives of all who would bear witness to the events, all those who suspected an unknown presence and all Organitrons throughout the universe would be forced to review and extend the realms of possibility.

Location, The old Arctolimba region, now known as the Arctic Region.

Time 10.30 hours

The wind was getting up as the last of the bore holes was sunk into the ice. Dr Cartell and Dr Heart were hand cranking the drill at the erect platform, when it stopped and refused to budge.

"How odd, maybe the drill bit is blunt?" said Dr Heart.

"Maybe." agreed Dr Cartell. "Dr Hio, Dr Schiller get over here and give us a hand will you?" he shouted as they came running.

"What is the problem Dr Cartell?" asked Dr Hio.

"I don't know. The drill won't go down any further!" he replied. Each of them took a turn in trying to budge it further but with no success. The film crew were shooting as they fought to push the drill lower into the surface.

"It would appear that you have struck a problem Dr Cartell. Is this a common occurrence when drilling into ice?" asked Mr Slater addressing the camera.

"Well, yes it does happen, although not usually this close to the surface. You see we are at forty metres below the surface and we know that this particular section is some two miles deep. These initial bore holes are to establish temperature deviations at various levels of depth. Sometimes we come across bed rock at the very bottom, occasionally a little higher but it is most unusual to come across it so close to the surface." he answered with a puzzled look on his face.

"So what is the next step Dr Cartell." asked Mr Slater.

Looking at his watch he started to pull the drill out of the bore hole.

"Well, it's getting very windy and the storm will soon be with us so we will pack up for today and come back tomorrow. Dr Hio assures me that the storm will have passed by the early hours of tomorrow morning. We may have to move the bore sight to get to a lower part of the ice. This next bore hole is supposed to reach one hundred and twenty metres as you can see for yourselves, we have fallen well short of our target." Then his face dropped as Dr Heart pulled the drill bit from the ice crust. The tungsten had been worn away till it was practically smooth. Though he said nothing they all knew, except for the TV crew, that bedrock would and could not do that to the drill tip with hand turning alone! They packed away their things and loaded up the sleds ready to make their way back to the temporary camp.

Meanwhile the light from the sun, which by now was directly over head, made its way down the three inch wide shaft. It barely reached the bottom of the shaft but enough to make the world of difference to the Mushroid that lain there for the over a billion years. Mushroid Funguy lay dormant as the fractional rays of light, radiation and ultra violet that come with it hit his tiny patch of solar converter body casing and sparked an ounce of awakening in the little fellow. "Brrrrrr... It's cold in here. Wait a minute-I'm awake-the rescue party-they are here." he thought then tried to move. "Ahhh... Ahhh. It's no good, I am jammed solid. They can't even hear my voice through this little lot, got to make some room-just got to." Mushroid Funguy activated his laser razor and started to melt the snow around him. To vaporise the water that then surrounded him, he set off the Fusion chamber power outlay to bring it to boiling instantly.

On the surface Dr Heart pulled off last as the four sleds pulled away and started the journey back. If only one of them had looked back then they would have seen the steam rising from hole. Mushroid Funguy had created himself a little cabin in the ice and soon could move about freely.

"Hello. Hello rescue crew, where are you?" Why aren't you digging me out? After twelve days in this fridge I could sure use some heat." he said looking down at his damaged batteries. "Oh dear, I'm injured." he said making immediate emergency repairs with his solenoid soldering activator. As the steam dissipated in the skies above her. Suddenly she stopped thinking that she heard a voice. She turned around, but as the steam had disappeared and whatever it was that she thought she had heard, if anything, was gone. She assumed naturally that she must have been imagining things, however, with a sense of doubt niggling in the back of her mind she turned and carried on oblivious to what she had missed.

"Mush... Mush... Ya... Ya... Mush." she shouted commanding the huskies to move on.

Mushroid Funguy sat patiently for all of two minutes wondering where the rescue party were. Then decided to take matters into his own hands while there was still light to power his solar converters. He began firing his vitamin Phaser gradually widening the whole.

"You had better stand back because here I come, ready or not." he shouted to warn the surface crews. steaming away the water with his fusion out lay he began to feel weary from the power drain. He needed direct sunlight and he needed it now. By his reckoning he was approximately five staryards from the opening which was too small for him to get through by about three starinches. He floated back down to the floor of the cabin and aimed at the roof with his telescopic cannon and fired a small charge protonic explosive device. It lodged in the roof and would explode in ten starsecs. As it did so great a crack sounded around the surrounding landscape. Great clouds of powdered ice flew into the sky and Mushroid Funguy shot out into the great sky like a geyser springing from the ground.

"Wheee, I am free, free my friends... Ugh?" he said shocked at the sight set before him, as he looked around he could see nothing. No crews, no ship, no land, nothing. Nothing except white upon white upon white. And four strange transportation units that did not have the life readings of an Organitron. All along the bore border, great rumblings occurred and cracks appeared which then subsided into a quite state of unrest.

Again, as the cracking sound reached Dr Heart and the team of sleds, she stopped and turned around and for one moment, she thought she saw something hovering in the skies, but the sunlight seemed to play tricks with her vision. "Is something wrong, Dr Heart?" asked Dr Cartell, "It's just the early rumblings of the storm. Don't worry, she's quite away from us yet." he remarked burying his head back in his notes.

"But it seemed so close, I thought I saw something in the sky. I can't explain it?" she said confused.

"Oh I can!" said Dr Cartell. "It seems close because the land is so flat we have nothing to give our eyes the depth perception. The brain therefore naturally assumes that because our ears heard it, it must be close!" he smiled to himself.

"And what about what I saw?" she enquired.

"What you think you saw Dr Heart!" snapped a surprised Dr Cartell. "A moment ago you thought you saw something, now you appear to know you saw something. The sunlight and the snow can play terrible tricks with one's vision. Combine that with a confused brain and you have the answer to your question!"

"You think it was just an illusion, my whole body's organs ganging up on me to play a practical joke huh?" she said insulted at the patronising, know-it-all stance he seemed to be adopting.

"Dr Heart, if you travel that way we are forty miles from the ocean, if you travel in any other direction we are at least twelve hundred miles from any civilisation, excluding our colleagues at the permanent base camp of course, so I hardly think it likely that you saw anything out here, eh." he laughed as she pulled a face behind him.

"Of course you are right, Dr Cartell. After all, what would I know? I am only a woman!" she sneered.

"Exactly, that's the spirit." he replied not really listening to her.

"Well you have it your way if you like, but I'm telling you this, something around here just isn't right. I can feel it in my bones." she whispered then spurred the huskies on with a lash of her whip on the ground in front of them.

On the bridge of the Silicone Sphere, Vegsign Tomaldo threw off her headset her face turning an awkward shade of pink.

"SO Mangolee, I.. I.. I think you ought to come and listen to this." she said shaking.

"What is it Vegsign Tomaldo?" asked SO Mangolee in her most Captain like voice.

"It's a distress call Sir, from a Mushroid Funguy o… O… Of the O.S.S.S Earthanon." she looked bleakly at SO Mangolee.

"Ugh? whimpered SO Mangolee taking hurriedly to the Command Com chair.

"SO Mangolee to C.. C.. Captain K.T. Carrot." she said nervously activating her personal channel.

"Captain K.T. Carrot here. I hope this is important SO Mangolee?" he asked.

"Oh, I.. I.. I am sorry to interrupt your meeting Sir, but, I think you will find it important Captain." she said slowly.

"Well don't just stop there Mangolee, spit it out!" he laughed.

"Captain, Sir. Vegsign Tomaldo has received a distress call on the Communications Com." she replied.

"From what ship SO Mangolee?" asked the Captain.

"Not a ship Captain, but from Earth. F.. F.. F.. from a Mushroid Funguy of the O.S.S.S Earthanon."

"Ugh?" Came the shocked reply of everyone gathered in the tactical suite.

The beginning of the end of the beginning for now!

EPILOGUE

Sundate 4,280,999,995/ 126 Biltechtoids.

Earth date 5 may 1995.

Location: The Space Satellite Silicone Sphere.

Time 11.30 hours

As Captain C. Carrot entered his quarters, back on-board the O.S.F.S Vegsurprise he rushed around the rooms checking that he was alone he was in a flustered and almost panicked state of array! Finally, content that he was alone he went over to the drinks cabinet and poured himself a shot of apple and pear high energy cordial. Knocking it back in one, he seemed to instantly relax and his frame loosened under the weight of information on his mind about recent events! He walked over to his wardrobe and disappeared into it starting to reason with himself and evaluate the recent situation out loud! "Unbelievable an S.O.S from a Mushroid that disappeared along with the O.S.S.S Earthanon Biltechtoids ago? Could it be true? Highly unlikely! Maybe it is a test Set by Admiral Paxesbarre De`la Scallion to see how my dear Brother will deal with it?"

He emerged from the wardrobe in full Officers ceremonial dress uniform. Ready for the O.S.F.S Vegsurprise's official inauguration! Then he gulped! Maybe it is to test me? Perhaps it's a dastardly trap set by the break-away Fasterfoid rebellion forces to take our eye off the ball, a diversion, but from what? He poured another shot of high energy cordial and as he put it to his lips FOC Brocktopz's voice came over the Computron!

"This is FOC Brocktopz to Captain C. Carrot!" Activating his wrist com he replied. "Captain C. Carrot here! He said adjusting his tunic in the mirror. "Captain Sir, we have managed to triabulate the position of the of the SOS satellite claiming to be Mushroid Funguy of the O.S.S.S Earthanon!" Captain C. Carrot smiled. "Very good FOC Brocktopz, Send a proton shuttle to the co-ordinates and let us see what a mockery we are dealing with?" "Captain Sir, I have run both a signature and security code protocol check! They are old codes but they are still active. We don't need to go find it! It's on its way here to us! ETA sixty- starhectoids and thirty starmins! Sorry sixty hours and thirty minutes Sir." Captain C. Carrot turned on his heels.

"What!" said Captain Carrot alarmingly. "FOC Brocktopz that Mushroid must not breach our outer marker! Open a communications channel and order it to stand down and stop when it reaches the outer marker or we will shoot to destroy! If it's a trap it could be loaded with explosives or harbouring deadly unknown toxins or diseases! No FOC Brocktopz, if it is legit then at the outer marker it will sit! Take a Proton shuttle our best pilot and MO Savoy! Place the Mushroid in a quarantine capsule and make ready a containment area on the main cargo deck until we can run sufficient tests to clear it for board and passage! You and the crew will have to remain in quarantine with it until we can be sure and keep guard!

"Yes Captain Carrot! So, we either get vaporised into gas, die a horrible pain riddled death or spend an eternity in quarantine? He huffed in distain. "That's about the size of it FOC Brocktopz! You catch on quick I knew I promoted you for good reason, and with it came responsibility my friend." smiled Captain C. Carrot.

"Hum... Will that be all Captain Carrot?" asked FOC Brocktopz.

"No, make ready our fastest vegi-battle cruiser! After the inauguration Admiral Paxesbarre De`la Scallion will be escorted off this ship for safety and transported to the Space-Ark Academy! Choose our best fighter pilot and six Organimen to accompany them on an armed security detail! It is important that he returns to deliver my holographic report to the High Admiralty and the Premier Consul Seed Council. I don't want to send this message through the usual channels with risk of interception!" said Captain C. Carrot.

"As you wish Captain Carrot! FOC Brocktopz out" "Captain C. Carrot out!" he said de-activating his wrist com. He took his glass and drank his cordial then calmly stepped forward onto his holographic platform. "Computron! Activate and enhance holographic programme."

Suddenly Captain C. Carrot was surrounded by a vertical tube of bright green shimmering iridescent light."Holographic programme activated and enhanced Captain C. Carrot!" said the Computron. Captain C. Carrot stood to attention and gave the Organitron Salute! "Run Programme!"

To be continued.

In the next adventures of;

The Space Tracers Organitron U.F.O

"The Veggie-Voyage of Discovery!"

Lightning Source UK Ltd.
Milton Keynes UK
UKOW02f0906031114

240972UK00004B/129/P